GUARDIAN'S MATE

JENNIFER ASHLEY

BERKLEY SENSATION
New York

BERKLEY SENSATION
Published by Berkley
An imprint of Penguin Random House LLC
375 Hudson Street, New York, New York 10014

Copyright © 2016 by Jennifer Ashley
Excerpt from *Red Wolf* by Jennifer Ashley copyright © 2016 by Jennifer Ashley
Penguin Random House supports copyright. Copyright fuels creativity, encourages
diverse voices, promotes free speech, and creates a vibrant culture. Thank you for buying
an authorized edition of this book and for complying with copyright laws by not
reproducing, scanning, or distributing any part of it in any form without permission.
You are supporting writers and allowing Penguin Random House to continue to
publish books for every reader.

BERKLEY and BERKLEY SENSATION are registered trademarks and the B colophon
is a trademark of Penguin Random House LLC.

ISBN: 9780425281369

First Edition: September 2016

Printed in the United States of America
1   3   5   7   9   10   8   6   4   2

Cover art by Tony Mauro
Cover design by Katie Anderson

3 6018 05476449 3

CHAPTER ONE

Rae's job on the day of the Choosing was to stand behind her foster father and hold the absent Guardian's sword. Absent, because the Guardian was dead, had been for months.

The woods were quiet, dark, and cold. Any sane Shifter would still be in bed, snuggled under a few blankets, looking forward to a warm shower and a hot cup of coffee.

But no, the Shifters of the Western Montana Shiftertown had crept out just before dawn, following Eoin, Rae's adoptive father and leader of this Shiftertown, to see whether the Goddess was in a good mood.

Four times in the last six months they'd trudged out here in the gloom and cold, waiting for the Goddess to pick a new Guardian. They'd come at a full moon, a new moon, a waxing moon, a blue moon. They'd turn toward wherever the moon happened to be and wait.

All the young men of the Montana Shiftertown who were past their Transition were required to attend, including Rae's foster brothers. They formed the now-familiar circle, some excited, some fearful, some simply wanting to go back to bed.

Eoin, a Feline Shifter who was mostly mountain lion, sent

Rae an encouraging look. Rae was a Lupine, black wolf, but she conceded that her foster dad was handsome—for a Feline. He was currently mateless, which made him a target for every female Shifter near and far. What some of them would do to try to sneak into his bed was beyond ridiculous. Rae sometimes felt like his bodyguard rather than his daughter.

"Not long now," Eoin said to her. Even speaking softly, his voice was a full rumble.

"Then we can go out for breakfast?" Rae asked. "I could use a stack of waffles. With bacon."

"Sure, sweetie," Eoin answered with a smile, then turned to the circle. Beyond the young males, the rest of the Shifters waited, anxious and impatient.

Months ago, their Guardian, Daragh, had been killed by humans, his sword stolen. Rae still fumed over that terrible deed. The humans had been found, punished, the sword returned by an unlikely messenger and Daragh sent to dust, but no new Guardian had been chosen. The Goddess had not answered their call.

The faintest light came through the stand of trees, turning the mist that had gathered ghostly white. The Shifters dropped into silence as Eoin raised his arms.

"Goddess, mother of us all, lady of the moon," he began in a loud voice, "we beseech thee. Send us your light to touch the Guardian, that most holy of men, so that he may do thy work."

Rae loved listening to her father speak. Her earliest memories were of Eoin reading her books, soothing her to sleep, wrapping her in comfort, letting her know she was protected when he was near. The sword, which she held point down by the hilt, vibrated in time with his words.

The sword gave her the creeps, but no one else would touch it—it had burned those who'd tried, as though it were red-hot. Even Eoin's trackers, the bravest of the brave, refused to put their hands on it. For some reason the sword didn't burn Rae, so she'd had to step up. She didn't mind so much when it was sheathed, but for the ritual the sword had to be naked, the runes on the silver blade catching the dawn light.

They'd done this four times. Rae prayed to the Goddess that the fifth time was the charm, so she could hand the sword to the new Guardian and never hold it again.

Eoin went on chanting. He repeated his plea to the Goddess, his arms high.

In the old days, Shifters had worn robes and crowns of leaves and crap like that for these rituals. Eoin wore jeans, a sweatshirt, and thick-soled boots, sensible attire in the Rocky Mountain woods. Rae, and every Shifter here, wore something similar.

Maybe they should have donned robes and painted themselves with moon goddess symbols, she decided. Or danced naked at midnight. It would make the same difference. The Goddess wasn't coming. She never did.

"We beseech thee!" Eoin shouted.

His words echoed through the woods as the sun climbed higher, brushing the treetops with golden light. The mists thickened and the air became colder.

The sun kept climbing. The mist turned to fog. The Shifters shivered and rubbed their arms, wanting to shift, cuddle up to something furry, or at least go the hell home.

Eoin finally lowered his arms, letting out a sigh, defeated. A whisper of breeze echoed his sigh, then died.

The Shifters didn't look happy. Eoin, as Shiftertown leader, was supposed to solve problems like this. He should ask the human government to bring in a Guardian from another Shiftertown or figure out a way to use the sword himself—*something*.

If the more dominant Shifters got too impatient, they'd start challenging, and then things would really hit the fan. The human government didn't allow Shifters to change leaders without their approval but that wouldn't matter if Eoin were dead.

Rae picked up the sword's sheath from the grass, her braid of black hair falling over her shoulder. A thin finger of light made it through the fog to dance on the blade as she lifted it to slide it into the sheath. The runes glittered and seemed to move.

They did that sometimes. The sword was one creep-toid piece of metal.

The tip of the blade jerked out of the leather sheath. Rae's eyes widened in surprise, then she let out a cry as the sword shot upward, dragging her arm with it.

Rae tried to drop the sword but her hand was fixed to the hilt, her fingers not obeying her command to let go. The sword jerked again, nearly pulling her arm out of its socket.

Rae grabbed the hilt with her other hand, holding on while her heels came off the ground.

"Dad!" she yelled. "Help!"

Eoin, who'd moved off to speak to his trackers, spun back to her. At the same time, the sword yanked itself upward and Rae was pulled all the way off her feet.

She yelped in terror, but she couldn't pry her hand free. She had no idea what the damned sword was trying to do—return to the Goddess? Fly to the next Guardian?

Eoin ran for her, his trackers behind him, but before they could reach her, a brilliant shaft of light shot down from the treetops and enclosed Rae, the sword, and the sheath that lay on the ground.

Pain seared through her, as though every cell in her skin, every bit of iron in her blood, suddenly burned hot. Her Collar went off, arcs of electricity driving into her throat.

Rae screamed. The sound echoed up through the trees, crescendoed into a piercing shriek, and swooped back down again. The Shifters clapped hands over ears, some falling to their knees.

The sword lifted Rae a few more feet in the air, then it suddenly went slack, and Rae fell hard to the ground. She lost hold of the sword, and the blade plummeted toward her, point downward.

Eoin dove for it, but he couldn't reach it in time. The sword plunged straight into the earth between Rae's outstretched arms, quivered, and went still. The light died and Rae's pain faded.

"What the hell?" one of the trackers growled.

Rae slowly climbed to her feet, groaning all the way, having to use the hilt of the stupid sword to brace herself.

Eoin had halted a few feet away, his face drawn, his eyes wet. "The Goddess has Chosen," he said in a hushed voice.

"What?" Rae tore her hands from the sword. "What are you talking about? It was a lightning strike, or something . . ."

Eoin seized Rae's hands and turned them upward. Burned into each palm was the symbol of the Celtic knot, the sign of the Goddess. Though Rae's hands were clearly branded, she felt no pain, not even itching.

Her heart hammered. "No way. Dad—*no*!"

Tears rolled down Eoin's cheeks. "The Goddess has Chosen," he repeated, his voice breaking. "We have our new Guardian."

The Shifters, Rae's brothers most of all, stared at Rae in shock. Dead silence filled the clearing, broken only by the morning breeze that sprang up to clear away the mists.

An elderly Feline male stepped forward, giving voice to the thought in the head of every Shifter present.

"But she's a *woman*!"

*Z*ander's cell phone rang. "Aw, son of a . . ."

Zander vented to every deity, familiar and obscure, as he hoisted himself from the chair at the stern of his boat. His fishing pole, secured to the deck, went on enjoying itself dangling bait in the water, while Zander trudged down the swaying boat, shading his eyes against the setting sun, to where he'd left the damn phone this time.

He should just throw the bloody thing overboard. The point of being in a fishing boat all alone off the coast of Alaska was being *alone*.

Zander knew why he didn't toss the phone even as the thought formed. If someone had dire need and they couldn't reach him, he'd never forgive himself.

Zander's two braids swung against his cheeks as he reached for the phone he'd left on top of the cooler. He figured he might as well grab another beer at the same time, and came up with a phone in one hand, a can in the other.

"Go for Zander," he growled.

He stilled as a voice from far away rumbled in his ear. Kendrick, a white tiger Guardian and leader of a band of rogue Shifters, wouldn't call for no good reason. Zander's reflection in the window of the wheelhouse showed his dark eyes growing wider and wider as he glued the phone to his ear and listened.

"You want me to *what*?" he yelled when Kendrick finished. "Seriously, what the fuck? How am I supposed to teach her to be a Guardian? Hello? *I'm not a Guardian*."

"I know." Kendrick's voice wavered with the bad connection. "But she needs—"

At the end of the boat, the fishing pole started to buzz.

"Kendrick, I'm *busy*. I don't have time to babysit a woman who thinks she's been chosen by the Goddess to be a Guardian, for crap's sake. There are no female Guardians! *I'm* supposed to be the crazy one. When you regain your sanity, call me back."

Zander moved the phone but Kendrick's stern voice had him listening again. "Oh, you've got to be kidding me," Zander snarled. "You're going to play *that* card?"

Over the whirring of the fishing pole came the drone of a motor, a boat rushing toward him across the deep waters.

Zander yelled into the phone. "Do you know how much shit you're in right now?"

Kendrick rumbled something Zander couldn't make out, but he heard the amused bite in Kendrick's voice. The man and his cute little mate must be laughing their asses off.

Zander clicked off the phone and tossed it down. The boat moved closer. Three figures stood on its deck—the man piloting it, a tall stern-looking Feline Shifter, and a smaller woman—a Lupine—with a Sword of the Guardian strapped to her back. The sword's hilt gleamed in the light of the sinking sun.

"Perfect," Zander said. "Just effing perfect."

He squeezed the can of beer until the pop-top burst open, then he poured the cold liquid down his throat, wiped his mouth, and strode to meet the intruders.

CHAPTER TWO

Rae looked across the tossing water at Zander Moncrieff and couldn't decide whether she should jump overboard or leap onto his boat and smack him.

He was huge, a bear Shifter, with muscles bulging out of a black sweatshirt with a Harley logo and hard legs stretching out blue jeans. He wore a long black duster coat that whirled in the unceasing wind and thick-soled boots for walking around a wet deck. Zander's white blond hair was cut short against his head, except for two dreadlocks that hung on either side of his face, swinging down to his shoulders. He'd braided blue beads into the dreads, stark against the white. His trim goatee beard was, in contrast, jet black.

His eyes were the same black, burning with anger and glaring at Rae. Rae read a boatload of other emotions behind those eyes—pain and a loneliness that ran deep.

Goddess-touched, Eoin had called him. Brimming with power but never quite fitting in.

Like me, Rae thought with a jolt.

Zander's fury reached Rae across the narrowing space

between the boats. He was not at all happy Eoin wanted to bring Rae aboard.

Well, tough shit. Rae didn't want to be out here either. One day she'd been an innocuous Lupine Shifter, hanging out with her friends and comfortable with her family, the next she was a Guardian, sent away to the middle of the northern Pacific to be trained by a polar bear everyone claimed was insane. *Doesn't play well with others,* they'd said.

The boats bobbed up and down out of sync, the waves becoming more pronounced the closer the boats slid to each other. Rae was getting seasick. She'd been fine riding on the boat from the island where the small plane had landed, but now that both boats were rocking in the calm, rising and falling at different rates, she grew dizzy.

Eoin sprang to the deck of Zander's boat with the grace of a Feline and faced him, one Shifter entering another's territory.

Now it was Rae's turn. She paused with her feet on the edge of the speedboat, where a gate in the rail had been opened for her. Rae was wolf, okay with water but not with boats. And by *water*, she meant streams, lakes, and ponds, not the vast expanse of cold ocean she found herself in now. If she fell into the drink, she'd freeze to death before she could be fished out.

Zander was a polar bear. Super-cold water and ice off the Alaska coast must be paradise to him. Rae liked beaches in Baja or Hawaii, long stretches of warm, empty sand, breezes, and cabana boys bringing her fruity cocktails. In theory—Rae had never actually been in any of these places.

Zander glanced behind Eoin to watch her impatiently, every inch a bear. *Arrogant shit.*

Rae drew a deep breath and willed her feet to make the jump, but her boat heaved upward while the other dropped. She lost her balance, dancing as she tried desperately not to fall between the undulating decks.

Zander reached Rae before Eoin could. He leaned across the stretch of blue water, grabbed Rae by both hands, and hauled her aboard.

His grip was immensely strong, pulling Rae right off her feet. She floated a few inches above the deck before she landed on the boards with a *whump*. The Sword of the Guardian banged against her back.

Zander dropped Rae's hands and kicked aside an empty beer can, the liquid remnants trickling out. Eoin only steadied Rae, making sure she was all right. He said nothing about her clumsy entrance or Zander's assist.

"Kendrick called me," Zander said to Eoin. His voice was big and deep, matching his size. "I don't get why you all expect *me* to train her. I'm not a Guardian."

"You can show her how to fight with the sword," Eoin countered. "And keep her safe at the same time." His dark brows drew down and his voice filled with anger. "I didn't have a choice. Shifters across the country are furious with me. They suspect me of rigging the sword, of cheating to bring a Guardian into my family. I can't risk sending Rae to a Guardian in another Shiftertown—he might not be able to protect her from hostile Shifters. And no Shiftertown will let their Guardian leave long enough to travel to Montana to train her. I'm out of options."

Zander listened to the barrage of words then held up his hands. "I understand. You need to hide her. You picked me because I'm allergic to happy, dancing-naked-in-circles love-fest Shifters. You also picked me because Kendrick has me by the balls. Doesn't matter that I saved his frigging life. I save everyone's lives. So, what happens if I out-and-out refuse to train her?"

He burned with frustration, while Eoin burned with sorrow. The two men stared at each other, each trying to make the other back down or at least come to some agreement. The forgotten factor in this equation was Rae.

She raised her voice. "Excuse me!"

Neither of them looked at her. Zander and Eoin were battling it out while remaining absolutely still, two Shifter alphas trying to out-dominate the other without lifting a paw. Zander didn't want Eoin there—Eoin was shoving Rae onto him as a last resort.

Males.

Rae swung away on her booted feet and marched to the

stern—at least she thought it was the stern. She knew crap-all about boats.

The speedboat that had brought them here was temptingly near. If she could leap back onto it, maybe she could convince the pilot to take her the hell out of there. Could the speedboat reach Hawaii? It was due south of here, however many hundreds of miles—not that Rae had ever been there. The bad thing about being Collared and stuffed into a Shiftertown was that Shifters didn't get many tropical vacations.

The pilot wouldn't obey her; she already knew that. The guy was human, paid by Eoin and intimidated by him too. Rae glanced down at the hefty man in stained sweatshirt and loose jacket, hands resting competently on the speedboat's wheel. The guy had given her interested looks—many human males did, wondering what it would be like to have a quick shag with a Shifter—but he'd tried to hide his curiosity around her father. Rae supposed she could always promise him a taste if he'd take her out of there, and then overpower him and steal the boat once they'd gone far enough.

Rae shuddered immediately and turned away. Even if she could convince the man to disobey Eoin, he'd probably drive her over the horizon and then demand his price. He might throw her overboard if she refused. If Rae went wolf and subdued him, what did she know about navigating a boat through trackless sea? Plus, the guy might have a tranq rifle lying around, being a human used to dealing with Shifters. Rae didn't want to think about what he'd do once he had her tranqued.

Besides, Eoin really was in a bind about Rae. He couldn't keep her home and he couldn't send her to another Shiftertown. A fishing boat with a crazy Shifter healer in the middle of Alaskan waters was the best he could do.

Rae reached the stern. Two fishing poles had been fixed here and one of them was whirring, the line playing a long way out.

"Hey, you have a bite!" Rae called down the deck.

Neither man paid attention. They'd started debating again, words carried out of Rae's hearing by the wind.

Rae might not know about boats, but she knew about fishing. Montana's lakes were full of fish, and she and her dad and foster brothers went out on lazy summer days and crisp fall mornings to fish. Big cats might hate water, but they loved fish.

Rae caught up the quivering pole and started reeling in the line. Steadily, not too slowly, not too rapidly.

Whatever had grabbed the bait was heavy, strong, and feisty. The fish jumped and pulled, trying to get free of the hook, but Rae kept on reeling, unrelenting.

When it came to the surface, she sucked in a breath. The fish was a giant of a thing; what it was, she didn't know. It flashed silver, its belly white, as it leapt from the water.

"Woo-hoo!" Rae cried as she fought it toward the boat. "Fish steaks tonight."

"Hey, don't touch that!" Zander's big voice rolled down the deck, followed by his stomping footsteps. A rush of air, fresh like a mountain breeze, brushed by as Zander reached her. His duster coat slapped her legs as he snatched the pole from her. "What the hell are you doing?"

"Landing your fish for you," Rae said impatiently.

Zander snarled, his beaded braids swinging. "First rule on this boat—don't touch *anything*."

The fish made a final, amazing leap, and as it came down, the hook somehow worked itself from its mouth, the line snapping at the same time. Bleeding but free, the fish dove hard into the water, streaking away under the foam, and was gone.

"Shit!" Zander threw down the pole, line all over the place.

"I *had* it," Rae growled at him. "I know how to fish—I was bringing him in."

Zander glared at the empty waves, at the pole, at Rae, and then at Eoin, who'd come up behind her.

"Tell her . . ." Zander trailed off. He pointed at Rae, then at Eoin, then Rae again, words failing him. "Just—"

He made an exasperated noise, waved his hands, then spun and strode from them down the deck, his duster swirling.

"Seriously, Dad," Rae said. "You want *him* to train me? He's an idiot."

"Rae, sweetie." Eoin was in front of her, all his focus now on her. His large body blocked out the sea and sky as he cupped his hands around her face.

"There's no choice, honey," Eoin said sadly. "If you won't do it for me or yourself, do it for Daragh."

Oh, so unfair. Rae's thoughts flashed to the first time she'd seen

Daragh, their Guardian, who was now dead and dust. Rae had been a tiny cub, newly orphaned, lost and howling, horribly alone.

She'd been terrified when two Shifters had crashed through the brush to find her, both of them Feline—Eoin, with tawny hair, hard face, and dark eyes, and Daragh, with his intense green gaze, sword drawn. Rae remembered being surrounded by booted feet and stained denim, and then Daragh had crouched down to look at her. "It's all right, sweetie," he'd said. "We'll take care of you now."

Daragh had picked up Rae and tucked her inside his coat, carrying her all the way home. Eoin, leader of his clan, had adopted Rae and taken her into his house, already populated by two Feline cubs who were fascinated by the wolf who'd be their little sister.

Daragh, no relation to Eoin, had stopped by often. He'd looked out for Rae as she'd grown up as Eoin's foster daughter, and Daragh was often her champion against her rough and tumble brothers. He'd been especially protective of Rae when the humans came to round them up into Shiftertowns, interfering when humans wanted to break Rae from her family because she was Lupine. Daragh had helped make sure that Rae, whose parentage was still undetermined, was able to stay with the only true family she'd ever known.

Now Daragh was gone, murdered, and Rae was expected to take his place.

Grief bit her but she stuffed it down and gave her father a shaky smile. "You fight dirty, Dad."

Eoin's hands moved to her shoulders. "We will always honor him. He was brave even in death."

Daragh had sacrificed himself to save others, typical of him. The sword that weighed heavily on Rae's back had been carried by Daragh most of his life.

"Daragh would be proud you were chosen to succeed him," Eoin said. "I will do absolutely everything in my power to make sure you can carry out the Goddess's choice. If it means leaving you with the eccentric Zander Moncrieff, then so be it. He can keep you safe, Rae, better than I can. Better than anyone."

Rae doubted that. Her dad, she was sure, could never be defeated.

She knew though that Shifters in her town were giving him hell about the Choosing. They were calling to have him investigated, and Shifters in other towns were backing that investigation. Even Shifter leaders who believed and supported Eoin had expressed great surprise that the Goddess had chosen Rae. In the thirteen hundred years since the swords had been forged, a Guardian had never been female.

Rae drew a breath, the cold Alaska air filling her lungs. The abandoned cub inside her cried out—*No, don't leave me. Have another Choosing, don't make me do this!*

The adult Shifter she'd become knew that all Shifters' lives were sacrifices. They battled for territory and protected cubs, fought and died to keep their families, clans, and communities of Shifters safe. The Choosing had changed Rae in one instant from protected to protector.

"For Daragh," she said, letting out a sigh. "I'll stay for a while."

The relief in Eoin's eyes was so obvious it cut at Rae's heart. She hadn't realized he'd been so worried about what to do with her. She'd always thought Eoin fearless.

Down the deck, Zander was fighting the tangle of line, letting out a string of colorful curses.

"I'll even try not to kill him," Rae promised, keeping her expression neutral.

Eoin's answering smile crinkled his warm eyes and squeezed pain through Rae's chest. Never, in the years she'd lived with this man had she been apart from him or his two sons, not for any length of time. The orphaned cub had been surrounded by love. Now she faced being alone again and she had to be strong about it. Rae had to man up.

No, she had to *woman* up. Why were all the idioms about being strong male-related?

Eoin's smile deserted him. He caught up Rae in a hard embrace that lifted her from her feet.

"Goddess go with you, little one," Eoin whispered into her ear.

Rae choked back a sob. "Goddess go with you too, Dad."

Eoin set Rae on her feet. He smoothed back a lock of her hair, unashamed tears wetting his face.

Then he squared his shoulders as though convincing himself this must be done. He pressed a kiss to her forehead, touched her hair one more time, and turned away. Nothing more to be said.

Eoin leapt to the other boat, again not allowing the uneven rock of the vessels to unbalance him. He landed gracefully and nodded at the pilot, who brought the motor to life.

Eoin stood in the stern of the small speedboat as it moved away, lifting his arm in a wave. Rae waved back. Eoin remained in the stern, watching Rae, his hand raised, as the speedboat grew smaller and smaller. Rae kept up her waving as well, until the boat finally became a pinpoint on the endless sea, then was swallowed by the horizon.

I won't cry. Rae wiped her uncooperative eyes, digging her fingers in to stop the tears. *I'm only feeling sorry for myself. I'll get over it.*

Right. Because saying good-bye to the only father she'd ever known and being stranded on a boat with a huge bear who didn't want her there was the easiest thing in the world.

Another curse rang down the deck. Rae swiped hands across her face and made her way to the rear of the boat. A tall wave ran up one side, rocking them hard, and Rae stumbled into the cabin wall beside her.

The man in the stern didn't notice. He sat cross-legged, his coat spread out behind him, the snarl of line in his lap.

Rae put one hand on the wall to steady herself and made her way toward him. The fishing boat was on the small side but it was by no means tiny. The cabin took up a chunk of it in the middle with wide areas of deck fore and aft for fishing and storing fish. The pilot house—Eoin had told her that's what it was called—was small and dark. A door in the stern led under the pilot house, presumably down to sleeping quarters.

Zander kept his head bent over his task, his braids falling to touch the line. He was pulling the snarl every which way, succeeding in tangling it further.

Rae unstrapped the sword from her back. She'd been carrying it all day and it was getting heavy.

Never let it out of your sight, Eoin had told her. *Not for an instant, not when you bathe, not when you sleep.*

Do I have to take it with me to pee? Rae had asked crossly.

Yes. Eoin's look had been stern. *You can drape a towel over it if you don't want it watching.*

Rae had laughed but the thing really did seem to be watching her—always. Made her shudder.

She sat down on the deck across from the tangle and set the sword in its sheath next to her. She reached for the line.

"Here," Rae said, not looking at Zander. "Let me."

CHAPTER THREE

Zander glanced at Rae's bowed head, her black hair twined into a neat, slick braid, her jeans smoothed over her thighs, sweater with a cowl to keep out the chill wind. She drew the line into her lap with capable hands and began competently untangling it.

"I told you not to touch anything," Zander growled.

Rae looked up at him with eyes as gray as dawn clouds. "It's fishing line. Get over it."

Zander clamped his mouth shut. Rae bent over the task again, fingertips loosening and smoothing out the tangles.

What the fuck was Zander supposed to do with her? *Train her,* Eoin and Kendrick had both said. *To fight,* Kendrick had said. *Keep her safe,* Eoin had almost begged him. Almost. Shiftertown leaders didn't beg. But Eoin's meaning had rung loud and clear.

"I know damn all about being a Guardian," Zander said, watching her.

Rae didn't look up. "I don't know anything about it either."

Goddess, why the hell had Eoin left this female alone with him? Zander wasn't celibate. Why would a Shifter leave his cub, even a foster cub, alone with a messed-up healer?

Answer—because Eoin would kill Zander if he so much as touched her. Kendrick would kill Zander as well. And this little angel would stick the Sword of the Guardian into Zander and he'd be dust motes on the wind.

Zander didn't know what the hell to say to her. He wasn't usually this tongue-tied. He found it easy to talk to women in bars, often ending up taking one back to his cabin, boathouse, boat—wherever he happened to be staying at the moment. He knew how to pick up human women, and the occasional Shifter woman, for a night of fun and laughter.

Rae was a different case. She wasn't much more than a cub—some years past her Transition, sure, but still very young. Younger than Zander, anyway, who'd passed his hundred and fiftieth year.

Plus, she wore a Collar. Zander didn't. He'd been elusive enough to evade the humans rounding up Shifters twenty years ago and had kept to himself ever since. He lived alone and associated with other Shifters only when necessary. Most Shifters thought Zander was insane and avoided him until they needed him. And maybe they were right.

He watched Rae's hands pick out the snarl, laying the line straight little by little. She opened the tackle box near her, extracted a reel, and began winding the line around it.

She did it in silence. No chattering like some of the ladies he picked up. One woman Zander had brought to his boat had talked nonstop from the moment he'd met her to the moment he'd put her into a cab to send her home the next morning. She'd even talked all through sex.

Rae said not a word. Unnerving. It wasn't natural for females not to talk.

Zander cleared his throat. "You want something to eat?"

Rae smoothed the line around the reel and lifted her steady gaze to him. "I thought dinner swam away."

"Very funny. I have sandwiches. In the refrigerator."

She shrugged and went back to her task. "Sure."

"And beer," Zander said. "I don't have anything to drink except beer. Well, that and water."

"Either is fine," Rae said.

What was the matter with her? She should be jumping up

and down, howling and crying because she'd been dumped on a crazy man's boat, her daddy vanishing into the blue. Instead, she kept on playing with the damned line, either pinning Zander with those gray eyes or avoiding looking at him.

"We're about two hours from Homer," he said. "That's a couple hundred miles south of Anchorage."

She looked up at him again, the sun's fading light brushing her dark hair. "Where's that?"

Zander waved an arm in the vague direction of northwest, where the land was a smudge on the horizon. "Alaska."

She made an impatient noise. "I know Anchorage is in Alaska. I just don't know *where*. I've never been out of Montana."

"South coast. I have a slip in Homer, down the peninsula from there."

Rae's gaze went over him again—critically, he thought. "Do the people in Homer know you're Shifter?"

"No." Zander clenched one fist. "I keep it to myself."

"How do they not know?" Rae's eyes roved him again then rested on his bare neck. "Everything about you screams *Shifter*."

Zander huffed a laugh. "Have you been to Alaska? It's cold most of the time. Everyone's so bundled up, who knows what anyone looks like?"

"You're obvious." Her eyes held his then she bent her head again. "Seriously obvious."

"Don't you like bears, sweetheart?" Zander's voice dropped to a growl. "We're cuddly."

Her scoffing noise let him know where he stood. "I'm Lupine. I like Lupines." Again she raised her head. "*Only* Lupines."

"Oh, I can see we're going to get along great, Little Wolf." He leaned forward, meeting her stare for stare, which was strangely difficult. "Trust me, sweetie, I'm not interested. I get that you had this Guardian thing forced on you—no one is Goddess-touched on purpose. I'm going to teach you fighting and maybe how to deal with Goddess magic, and that's it. Nothing else between us. *Nothing*. And not only because Eoin and Kendrick would kick my ass."

Rae gave him the once-over again, scorn evident. "Fine by me."

"Good." Zander stuck out his hand. "Truce?"

Rae set aside the line—which was mostly untangled; she *was* good at it—and took his hand.

"Truce."

Her hand held warmth despite the cold wind that had sprung up across the water. The pressure of her handshake told Zander she was no pushover but the softness of her skin reminded him that she was young and vulnerable.

Deep inside him, a protectiveness stirred to life. He tried to tamp it down but the spark wouldn't die.

Hmm, Zander thought as he climbed to his feet and started for the aft cabin. *That might be a problem.*

The truce lasted until Zander led Rae into the cabin under the deck—or as he put it, *below.*

Rae looked around in dismay. "You *live* here?"

"Yeah," Zander said. "What's wrong with it?"

It was a huge mess, that's what was wrong with it. Junk lay everywhere, on the tiny table built into the wall, on the counters and benches, on the floor. Every horizontal surface was piled with fishing tackle, maps, books, a laptop, a tablet, clothes, blankets, pots and pans, plates, silverware, coiled wire, tools . . . Rae gave up trying to identify it all.

"Doesn't everything fly around when you hit rough water?" she asked in amazement.

"Sure." Zander picked up a hammer from the table and tossed it to a bench. "But I'm up top trying to keep the boat afloat. There's no one down here for it to hit."

"There will be if I have to stay here." Rae lifted a bench seat, figuring she'd find storage space in there. It was likewise stuffed with junk. "Seriously?"

Zander shrugged. "I don't stay out here forever. It's never been a problem."

Rae growled in frustration and started pulling things out of the compartment. "You're a slob. Like most bears."

"Excuse me?" Zander was down in a crouch beside her, the largeness of him unnerving. "All bears are *not* slobs. Most of them are painfully neat. Obnoxiously neat. Don't stereotype."

"All right, then *you're* a mess."

His warmth touched her. In spite of the clutter in here, Zander was clean, smelling of wind and the outdoors, his clothes spotless. Unlike the pilot of the speedboat, Zander obviously liked to bathe.

"You don't have to do this," he growled as Rae started organizing junk into piles.

"Yes, I do. Didn't you say something about sandwiches?"

"I might not have enough for both of us. I had no idea I'd have company."

"That's not my fault," Rae said, trying to keep the pain out of her voice. "My dad pretty much grabbed me and hustled me away. First I was on a plane, then on that tiny boat. I'd never flown before. Great first time, strapped to a seat so I wouldn't run like hell."

Rae heard her words breaking but she would not cry. Not in front of Zander the weird-ass, slobby *bear*.

"Peace, Little Wolf." Zander's very large hand landed on her back with gentleness she wouldn't have guessed. "I know this isn't your doing. The Goddess chooses whom she pleases, and Shifters like you and me pay for it."

His touch was soothing, nice. Eoin and Rae's brothers calmed her with hugs or caresses when she was upset but this felt different. Zander's hand was as warm and strong as her brothers' or father's but the tingle in her blood was new.

But then, Zander was a healer. Probably some healing magic or whatever seeped into her when he touched her. It wasn't a bad feeling—not that she'd ever admit it out loud.

Zander lifted his hand and unfolded to his feet, the sudden absence of his warmth making Rae cold. He discarded his duster, tossing it on top of another pile, and moved to the small refrigerator tucked under the table.

"There's no reason to clean the place up," he said. "I know where everything is."

Rae kept on sorting things into categories—tools, fishing gear, books, and . . . miscellaneous. Into the last pile went stuff she had no idea what to do with—old coins, a bunch of sage wrapped with wire, a compass and an astrolabe, unused spiral notebooks, sticks of incense, empty water bottles.

"What is all this for?" she asked, curious.

Zander was clattering around in the refrigerator. Rae didn't want to think about what kind of mess could be in *there*.

"I'm always looking for ways to enhance the healing," he said. "I never know what might help."

Rae drew out a book on the magical properties of crystals and stones. "This stuff is for humans. Has nothing to do with Shifters."

"Some humans are magical," Zander said, his voice muffled as he went through the small refrigerator. "Not the same way as Shifters or Fae—thank the Goddess. But some can do spells and shit. I know a lady from New Orleans who has all kinds of abilities. She even mated with a Shifter. Go figure."

Eoin had told Rae that Zander was an amazing healer, that he'd pulled more than one Shifter back from the brink of death, even healed a Shifter who'd gone completely feral. He did it by closing his eyes, touching them, and saying prayers to the Goddess. No incense or crystals, magic circles, or any other accoutrements.

So why was he hoarding human magic charms, many of which, Rae had heard, didn't work at all?

When he didn't answer, Rae glanced across the cabin to see Zander's jeans cupping a very trim ass as he bent double at the small refrigerator.

He straightened up, arms full of foil-wrapped packets, his two thin braids swinging on either side of his face. Made her wonder why he'd done his hair that way. Because he thought it looked cool? Or believed it another way to enhance his magic? Or to keep up the idea Shifters had that Zander was crazy?

"I've got ham and cheese, roast beef, and salami, I think," Zander was saying. "Or maybe it's pastrami. Which do you want?"

Rae gaped at the shining foil pile, counting a dozen packets. "Why did you say you didn't have enough sandwiches?"

"For two Shifters? For who knows how long?" He shook his head. "We're going to have to stock up."

"I'll have the ham and cheese," Rae said.

Zander plucked a foil lump off the top and tossed it to her. "I think that's it."

It was roast beef. Rae shrugged and bit down after she'd inspected the sandwich. It looked fine, no mold on the bread, nothing that smelled like it shouldn't. At least he kept his food clean.

Zander had bought these sandwiches; he hadn't made them. A deli somewhere had put together the chewy bread, whole-grain mustard, pile of meat. Rae found a label inside one of the folds that read *Marny's Fine Sandwiches.*

The sun finally disappeared as they ate, but the light lingered, the June sky through the small windows showing a dusky twilight. Not a sound came from outside except the creaking of the boat and the soft slap of water against the hull.

"Is it always this quiet out here?" Rae asked, unnerved by the immensity of the stillness.

"Yep," Zander answered. "Isn't it great?" He chewed his third sandwich, clearing off a space on the bench on the opposite wall to sit down.

"It's noisy in Shiftertown." Rae heard the wistfulness in her voice. "My brothers are always banging around, yelling at each other, then my dad yelling at them. Shifters are out in the neighborhood every night, prowling or playing with their cubs or just talking. Even in the deep cold, we're out in Shifter form, enjoying the snow."

She broke off. Zander had stopped eating and was staring at her as though *she* were the crazy one. He grunted. "Sounds peachy."

"Why do you want to be alone?" Rae asked. "With no one? If Eoin and Daragh—our Guardian—hadn't found me when I was a cub, I'd have died. Being alone isn't a good thing."

Zander's dark eyes fixed on her, a spark in them she couldn't decipher. "It's different for us. The Guardians, the healers, the empaths. Being with Shifters is more than just noisy; it's noisy in here." He tapped the side of his head. "I can't shut out the pain, the fear, the grief when all my fucking Goddess powers can't save someone. I need the solitude to recover."

He spoke in a hard voice but matter-of-fact. Rae heard the frustration in him, anguish he tried to keep under control.

"Is that why you're out here right now?" Rae asked.

"Yeah. And I don't want to talk about it, don't want to open up and discuss my feelings. I just want to fish and drink and get on with my life."

"That's all I want—to get on with my life," Rae said, swallowing her last bite of roast beef. The sandwich had been tasty. "Instead, the stupid sword picked me up off my feet and waved *me* around. Now everyone either thinks I'm a Guardian or a fraud and I'm stuck out here eating sandwiches in a sty of a boat with a crazy man."

Zander frowned at her a few seconds longer, then a grin split his face and deep laughter filled the cabin. The laughter rattled the windows and wrapped around Rae, warming her in spite of herself.

"Yeah, you are screwed, Little Wolf." Zander's eyes crinkled, his whole body shaking. He didn't look as scary when he laughed.

"Not if you call my dad and tell him to come back here and get me."

"Love to." Zander got to his feet, wadding up his sandwich wrapper. He popped open the lid of a plastic garbage can and tossed it inside.

He actually had a garbage can. Rae had to admit that while the cabin was cluttered and in disarray, it wasn't dirty. She saw no dust, grease, or grime. Her Shifter nose would have detected any foul scents but nothing here made her hackles rise. There was just a lot of . . . stuff.

"I go to bed when I feel like it," Zander was saying. "Get up when I want to. I don't pay attention to what time it is."

No clocks were around, that was for sure. Rae had her cell phone but for some reason she didn't want to fish it out and check the time.

"Where do I sleep?" she asked, looking around. There wasn't a spare surface except the bed in the bow, the door in front of it half closed.

Zander stepped across to what Rae had assumed were cabinets set above the bench on one wall. He slid a door open to reveal a futon stretched inside of it, about Rae's length. "I have sheets around here somewhere. Maybe."

Rae stared at the narrow cabinet, then at him. "You want me to sleep in *there*? You've got to be kidding me."

"I'd give you my bed but I'm way too big for the bunk. And if we sleep together, your dad will come back and cut off my balls." Zander waved his hand at the cabinet. "You're a wolf. Pretend it's your den."

Rae growled. "Seriously, you are . . . Never mind. I'll sleep outside."

She grabbed at the futon, intending to pull it out of the cabinet and drag it up on deck, but it got stuck in the narrow opening. Rae wrestled with it, more and more frustrated, until she was screaming through her teeth.

"Let it go, Little Wolf."

Zander's growl flowed around her and his strong hands stilled hers. His bulk was at her back, the warmth of it seeping into her and calming what roiled inside her.

"You take the bed." His words vibrated through her as he tucked the futon back into the cabinet. "I'll sleep up top." He opened a cabinet next to the bunk and extracted a blanket. "If you want clean sheets . . . hunt around. They're here somewhere."

"It's cold outside," Rae said quickly. "I'm sure we can fix something up. I could put the futon on the floor . . ."

He was giving her the you're-insane-and-don't-know-it look again. "I'm a polar bear." Zander tapped his chest. "I *like* the cold."

He snatched up his coat, flung the blanket around his shoulders, and ducked out into the twilit night.

Rae heard his heavy tread as he climbed up to the pilot house, where he'd no doubt hunker in one of the chairs. She imagined him, wrapped in coat and blanket, staring out across the ocean with his enigmatic eyes.

Rae did find sheets in the cupboard under the bed, which was a cushioned platform in the narrowing front of the boat that could be closed off by a sliding door. She shook the sheets out over the mattress that was mercifully free of junk, neatly tucking them in. She added a blanket then pulled off her boots and climbed onto the bed.

A hum filled the cabin behind her. Rae swung back on her knees to see the Sword of the Guardian lying across the bench where she'd left it. The hilt sparkled in the dim lamplight, the runes etched on it shining with their own light. The music of it filled Rae's ears, its pitch rising as the hum increased.

The sound would never shatter glass, she knew, because it wasn't really making noise. No one could hear it but her.

Thump. Thump. Zander pounded from above. "Can you shut that thing up?" he yelled down. "I'm trying to sleep."

Rae's eyes widened. *No one* could hear the sword, not her father, brothers, or any Shifter she knew. Another Guardian might, but she'd never met any Guardians but Daragh, so she wasn't even certain of that.

Rae scrambled out of the bed and closed her hand around the sword's hilt. It made a happy, jingling sound, then settled down and went quiet.

"*Thank* you," came the growl from above.

Rae climbed back onto the bed, the sword firmly in her grasp. She laid it beside her and crawled beneath the sheets, which smelled of lemon.

A switch on the wall beside Rae shut off all the lights in the cabin. The cabin went dark, the windows too small to let in the fading twilight.

Rae huddled down in the bed, the silence of the night filling the boat. It pressed at her, that silence, heavy in the darkness. Water lapped at the hull, endless, unceasing, the boat in a constant, rocking motion.

She had never been away from home before. She'd camped out in the woods, of course, but always with Eoin or her brothers or both. This was the first night of her life, since Eoin had rescued her, that she'd been without her family.

Rae knew she was going to feel sorry for herself now. She fought as long as she could, but the grief overwhelmed her in a sudden wave, and the sobs came.

Zander heard her. From his perch on the captain's chair, swiveled away from the controls, he heard Rae's broken crying.

The poor thing was terrified. He'd seen it and sensed it. Stupid-ass Shifters had dumped a scared young woman on Zander because they couldn't handle that the Goddess was capricious.

Why were all these Shifters so surprised that the Goddess

had chosen a female to represent her? The Goddess was female, after all. The biggest surprise was that she'd waited so long.

The Shifters, even Eoin, alpha that he was, had sent Rae to Zander because they were afraid *of* Rae. Afraid of what she represented, afraid of what she'd become.

Rae with her dark hair and rain-gray eyes had been forced to leave everything she'd ever known in order to eat sandwiches with half-insane Zander on his cluttered boat in the middle of nowhere. He wasn't amazed to hear Rae cry; he was amazed she hadn't become a raving lunatic the moment Eoin had left her.

"Poor Little Wolf," he whispered to the dusk.

Zander gazed across the water, tracing the path of moonlight, which had finally appeared. The roof of the wheelhouse cut off the stars directly above him but he picked the bright ones out on the horizon. No other lights for miles meant the heavens were spangled with stars, the beauty of it tugging his heart.

The northwestern horizon was darkening a little though, clouds filling the space. They'd have rain and more wind by morning.

Below him, Rae's sobs died away. Good, she'd sleep, worn-out, and be fresh and ready to yell at him in the morning.

Zander chuckled. He kind of liked her shouting at him. Her eyes got sparkly and her cheeks flushed, and she forgot her fear.

He closed his eyes, picturing her in the sunshine, scowling at him, and let himself relax. The chair wasn't so uncomfortable, though he'd probably end up stretching full length on the deck . . .

He was just drifting off when Rae's terrified scream cut through the night.

CHAPTER FOUR

Zander was on his feet and plunging down the ladder to the cabin before his sleep-filled brain truly cleared. Rae's screams changed to a wolf's snarls as Zander burst inside to find the lights blazing. Rae's half-human, half-wolf paw came down to strike at what looked like a rope on the floor.

"Stop!" Zander yelled.

He shoved Rae aside and dove for the rope, coming up with his hands full of long, cool reptile.

Rae shifted back down from half beast to her human form faster than Zander had seen anyone shift before. The big shirt she was sleeping in hadn't even had a chance to tear. Her eyes were wide, pale gray, her black eyebrows streaks in all the white. "What the hell is *that*?" she cried.

Zander turned the snake around to face him, looking into its startled reptile eyes. "Hey, buddy, I've been looking for you. I bet you were sleeping in the bed, weren't you?"

"Zander."

Color flooded Rae's face again, her cheeks brilliant scarlet. She was disheveled, hair coming out of her braid, her sweatshirt not too loose to cling to the soft curves of woman beneath.

Zander let his gaze drift over her a moment before he lifted the creature coiling around his arm. "It's just Jake. Jake the Snake. He's harmless."

"He tried to get into bed with me!"

Zander didn't blame him. "Jake likes to be warm. He's not poisonous or anything."

Rae waved her hands. "Why do you have a *snake*? On a *boat*?"

Zander shrugged. "He cuddled up to me one night a couple months ago when I was camping out. He didn't want to leave me. I think he was someone's pet that got lost or dumped. I give him the run of the place and he keeps the vermin under control."

Rae planted both hands on top of her head, her black hair leaking around her fingers. "You couldn't have warned me?"

"I thought I'd lost him when I was last in port. I guess he followed me back on board. Follows me everywhere."

Rae's hands now covered her face until they drifted down, revealing her red-rimmed, tear-dampened eyes. "Well, he can't sleep with me."

Zander carefully lowered Jake into the pocket of his duster. "No problem. He'll sleep with me."

Rae glared at him with her fists on her hips, a storm in her eyes. The shirt covered her to her thighs—below that her bare legs were firm and strong, her cute toes curling on the floor.

What the hell was the Shifters' problem with her being a Guardian? If the last thing Zander saw in his life was the beautiful, fiery Rae coming to send him to the Summerland, that would be fine with him. What a way to go.

Zander didn't like the spark in his blood as he watched her chest move in her agitated breath. He made himself turn from her. "Go to bed. Long day tomorrow."

"It's not that I'm afraid of snakes," she said behind him. "I'm just not used to them in bed with me. Most of the ones we get near our Shiftertown are rattlers. I've learned to be cautious."

"I understand, Little Wolf. Cautious is good." Zander sent her a grin over his shoulder that brought her glare back. He loved that.

"Just go," Rae said tightly.

Zander went out the door. As soon as he closed it, he heard

Rae bang her way across the cabin and slap home the bolt, locking him out.

He laughed softly as he returned to the wheelhouse. As though a lock could keep out a snake. Or a polar bear. Sweet Little Wolf had a lot to learn.

*C*rash!

Rae peeled open her eyes as something slammed against the door of her bedroom. She jumped, then cursed as her head hit a low ceiling.

Where the hell was she? Rae looked around in panic, the only light coming from two minuscule windows at the top of the room. She saw polished wooden walls and ceiling, a bed that was wider at the foot than the head, and a sliding door that rattled as something else banged into it.

Memories zoomed back—the long ride in the speedboat, her dizziness climbing aboard the fishing vessel, her first dismayed glimpse of the Shifter called Zander. Eating sandwiches with him in the cramped cabin, his bulk somehow comforting, crawling into bed and leaping out again when a snake's cold nose touched her arm.

Rae bunched the covers over her chest. What other creatures did Zander have hidden on this tub? Which one was turning over all the crap in the main cabin?

Clatter. Thunk. Thud!

Rae scrambled on hands and knees to the edge of the bed and carefully eased the door open a crack.

Zander's black duster coat swung into her view, followed by a white braid strung with blue beads. He came up with an armful of stuff and dumped it into an open crate.

Rae shoved the door all the way back. "What are you doing?"

Zander looked up without surprise and dropped a couple pots and pans into the box with a loud *clank*. "Cleaning up. What's it look like?"

"Right *now*?"

"It's nine in the morning. Yesterday, you wanted me to clean up."

"You're not cleaning. You're just dumping."

Zander gave her a black stare. "You could get your lazy ass up and help. This isn't a bed-and-breakfast."

Rae yanked the door closed. She'd kept her clothes with her on the bed, along with the small duffel bag she'd hastily packed when Eoin announced they were leaving Shiftertown. She slid into a tank top and jeans, reached for her sweater from yesterday to pull on, then opened the door to climb off the bed and tug on her boots.

Zander had done a good job, she had to admit. The floor was clear all the way to the cabin door, the cabinets shut, the benches and stove empty. Zander dumped the last load into his crate and stowed it in the cupboard beneath the bed Rae had just been sleeping in.

The difference in the place was remarkable. The cabin, as she'd observed, had been clean, just messy. Now she could see gleaming, sealed wood, polished brass, the crisp black of the bench cushions, the flood of light through the open windows.

"Nice," she said admiringly.

"Glad you like it. There's food in the fridge. Fix breakfast and we'll have it up on deck."

Rae's eyes widened. "Excuse me? You expect me to make breakfast for you?"

Zander swung back to her, his eyes holding irritation. "I told you, I'm not running a free hostel. I know you aren't happy to be here, but I wasn't asked if I was okay if they dumped you on me. We both have to suck it up. I cleaned up so you'd stop whining—now you can make me breakfast in return. I'm not your daddy, or even your sugar daddy. I'm your trainer. Got it?"

Rae raised her hands. "All right, all right. Got it."

"Good." Zander swung away and strode for the door. "Go light on the carbs." He slammed himself out and was gone.

Rae listened to his boots clump on the deck above, then she heaved a sigh.

He was right—they were both stuck with each other. She either had to make the best of it or jump overboard.

Although . . . Rae ran through an idea as she brought out eggs and a rasher of bacon, fished a frying pan out of a cupboard, and started cooking.

* * *

Zander, sitting cross-legged in the sunshine on the stern deck, downed the mess of eggs and bacon, seasoned with spices he'd had in his cupboard, and drank the coffee Rae had made. The coffee was seriously good, as was the breakfast, but he decided not to tell Rae that. She needed to be a little edgy. Training to be a Guardian wasn't going to be easy on her—hell, it wasn't going to be easy on *him*.

"Zander, I was thinking."

Rae's tone caught his attention. Zander dropped his fork to his empty plate, set the plate on the deck, and picked up the coffee. Fresh wind blew across the stern to set the wisps of hair around Rae's face dancing, and sun glared off the water. The clouds that had gathered last night had ended in a squall way off to the southeast, while Zander's boat remained in the clear.

Rae sat on the deck, her back to the wall of the pilot house. Her eyes in shadow became the darkest gray, like the sea in a storm. She had a lithe but strong body—he bet she was a formidable wolf.

"Thinking is dangerous," Zander answered when she didn't go on.

Rae flicked her eyes to his. No submission there. In spite of having been orphaned and abandoned then raised by Felines, Rae was not afraid to pin him with her gaze. She should be—Zander was pretty high in dominance. He'd guess she was an alpha, born of alphas, even if she didn't know it.

"You don't actually have to train me, you know," Rae was saying. "You can drop me off somewhere and I can . . . I don't know. Find an apartment. Get a job. Hide my Collar. Live. Who has to know?"

Zander rested his elbows on his knees. He caught the sharpness in her voice, the restlessness, the anger. The same kinds of emotions had flowed through him all his life.

While he agreed with her, he shook his head. "It's not that easy. Anyone looking at you is going to figure out you're Shifter. I've never worn a Collar but it makes no difference. You told me I scream *Shifter*, and so do you. My neighbors have always been cool and didn't turn me in. Alaskans are laid-back. They have enough to deal with fighting the weather to worry about much else."

"So, they'll be cool with me too, then," Rae said. She peered at Zander closely. "*You* don't want to train me. *I* don't want to be here. Why do we have to do what all the Shifters want? They'd be happy if I disappeared. I didn't ask to be a Guardian. You didn't ask to be a healer. I say screw it and let's just live our lives." She finished, her body tight, her chest rising swiftly.

Zander ran his thumb around the bottom of his coffee cup. One of his braids brushed his wrist, the beads cool. "Let me ask you something, Little Wolf. If you came across a Shifter lying dead, or dying, too far gone to be saved, would you step over him and leave him there? Pull out your cell phone and call some-one else to deal with it? Let him wait in pain and fear until another Guardian comes—if one ever does? It's not death Shift-ers fear; it's their souls lingering in this world for the Fae to steal. I heard what happened to your Guardian—Daragh? Wasn't that his name? Heard the whole story from Broderick down in Austin. When Daragh died, there was no new Guardian to dust him right away and the Fae snatched him quick as anything. Knowing shit like that, would you walk away from a dying Shifter? Tell him sorry, you didn't want to be Chosen?"

Rae's eyes flashed. "Don't talk about Daragh."

The sudden flare was interesting. So she'd had a jones for the old Guardian, had she? Huh. And then Daragh had gotten himself murdered. Zander's heart squeezed in sympathy. *Poor Little Wolf.*

"Maybe we *should* talk about Daragh," he said. "Sounds like you knew him pretty well. Would he want you to walk away? Get a job in Anchorage, hide the sword, forget about it?"

Rae deflated a notch but remained defiant. "Probably not."

Zander turned the coffee cup in his hands. "When I figured out I was a healer, I didn't want to be one. I wanted to hide out, to tell people to leave me the hell alone. But it got slammed into me that I couldn't walk away from a Shifter who needed me. Could I really let a woman die bringing in her cubs and leave them motherless? No, I couldn't. I had to heal her and deal with the pain that comes from working my gift. Like I said, we both have to suck it up."

Rae made a show of looking around at the empty water. "You *are* hiding out and telling people to leave you the hell alone."

Zander shook his head. "Appearances are deceiving. Shifters can reach me if they *really* need me. But I learned that I'm not a bottomless pit. I get totally drained and have to recharge or I'm no good to anybody. A Shifter has to seriously need me and make the effort to track me down. If I didn't make it difficult, I'd be healing every paper cut until I was too drained to help a Shifter who truly needed saving. I give my gift freely but I have to protect it as well."

She listened closely, leaning toward him a little bit. "You mean, you pick and choose who you heal?"

"No." The word was sharp. "I didn't say that. I mean they really have to be desperate. Desperate enough to figure out how to find me. There are other Shifters with lesser healing abilities who can help, and Shifters heal up pretty good naturally. You know that. I'm what you'd call the last hope."

More staring, a pucker between her brows. "My dad found you easily enough."

"That's because of Kendrick," Zander said, suppressing a growl. "And Dylan. Kendrick's a white tiger who leads a bunch of un-Collared Shifters down in Texas, and Dylan kind of runs South Texas. I owe them, so they feel free to call on me when they want me."

Rae went silent as though digesting his words. Zander wished he knew what she was thinking, what thoughts were dancing behind her pretty face. But he wasn't a telepath, wasn't really an empath, wasn't even that good at reading body language. Polar bears liked to be alone, so he hadn't had much practice understanding other Shifters.

"You don't need to train me to use the sword," Rae said, returning to her previous argument. "How often do we get into sword fights these days? It's not like we're still battling the Fae or fighting in the Middle Ages."

"You'd be surprised," Zander said. "What you'll be using the sword for mostly is sending Shifters to dust."

"Exactly." Her eyes sparkled in triumph. "The sword is perpetually sharp, I'm told. All I have to do is put the point over the Shifter's heart and press down. Easy."

Rae spoke with confidence but Zander saw the shudder run through her. She was terrified of that part of being Guardian and he fully understood that fear. Zander's job was to heal—when he was successful, the Shifter lived to embrace his or her cubs another day. When Rae was successful, it would mean the Shifter was dead, gone to the Summerland.

Zander set his coffee cup on the deck beside him. "So tell me, Little Wolf. Where is a Shifter's heart?"

Rae blinked, startled. "What?"

"Say I'm a dying Shifter and you need to find my heart. Where is it?"

Zander pulled his duster all the way open and leaned back, exposing the large plane of his chest. "If you miss, all you do is prolong the Shifter's agony. He's dying and you just shoved a big sword between his ribs." He spread his arms. "Where is it, sweetheart? Come here and put your hand over my heart."

CHAPTER FIVE

*S*hit, he was right.

Rae had never thought about it before. What happened if she drove the sword all the way through a Shifter and *missed*? He'd be pinned to the ground with a sword, bleeding, dying, in horrific pain, and it would be her fault.

Rae swallowed. She put aside her empty plate and scrambled to her feet.

Zander leaned back against the gunwale, his long legs in stained jeans crossed at the ankles. He had his arms spread, a thick black sweater stretching across his broad chest.

His dark eyes glittered like the translucent black stones called Apache tears that Eoin had told her was obsidian heated into glass. Those eyes held the look of a man who'd seen it all, experienced pain no one could understand. So much pain that he'd hidden in the middle of the cold Pacific, growling when anyone crossed into his territory.

Zander said nothing as Rae took a few staggering steps to him. His look wasn't arrogant—although *he* was arrogant. He was waiting to see what she'd do.

Rae absently wiped her hand on her jeans, fearing to smear

bacon grease on him. She halted, her foot an inch from his thigh.

Rae didn't have to lean far to him. She moved her hand toward his chest, saw it shaking, and tried to make it stop.

Didn't work. Whether he noticed her trembling or not, Zander's gaze never left her face. Rae gingerly rested her palm on his chest, on the rough wool of his black sweater.

The warmth of him came through the fabric, heating her like a furnace. How a man living in this open, unending cold space could have so much heat in him she didn't know. She felt his breath moving his chest, a vibrancy that sparked through her and made her heart pump.

Rae drew a breath and spread her fingers, pressing her hand more surely to his sweater. The solidness of him threatened to rob her of the breath she'd just sucked in. Zander's chest rose sharply, his warmth increasing.

Rae made herself meet his eyes. This close, his gaze was powerful. Zander was an alpha, she could tell, even though he had no one to be alpha over. He claimed to be under obligation to Kendrick and Dylan, but as she studied him, Rae understood that Zander *chose* to be obligated. No one could coerce this man to do anything.

"There?" Zander rumbled when Rae said nothing.

The deep timbre of his voice vibrated up her arm. Rae resisted the urge to snatch her hand away and made herself keep her fingers still. His heart beat swiftly beneath her palm.

"There," she answered, nodding.

Zander's expression didn't change. He closed strong fingers around her wrist and moved her hand a few inches to her right. "*There.*"

The heartbeat strengthened, his life's blood pumping. Rae's cheeks went scalding hot.

Zander's eyes stayed on her and Rae realized her fingers still rested on his chest, feeling his heartbeat, absorbing his warmth. Her face burning hotter, she yanked her hand away. "All right, so I need a few lessons in anatomy."

"One or two," Zander rumbled. "If you'd stuck the sword into me there, I'd be screaming and flopping around. You need to get it right the first time, Little Wolf."

"Will you stop calling me that?"

"Nope." Zander heaved himself off the deck, rising to his full height. "You're smaller than me and you're a wolf."

He bent to lift his empty plate and mug, giving Rae a terrific view of his backside, and headed for the ladder down to the cabin.

"How about if I call you Big-Ass Bear?"

Zander glanced behind him, amused. "If it makes you feel better. I've been called worse."

"Yeah, I bet you have," was all Rae could think of to say.

Zander shook his head and took himself down the ladder, balancing plate, cup, and himself with an ease Felines would envy.

Stupid comeback, Rae told herself. *Was that the best I could do?* But it was hard to think around the growling, arrogant . . . Big-Ass Bear.

Of course, his ass wasn't big. It was tight and firm under those jeans, just like the rest of him. He was a conceited pain in the butt, though that didn't mean Rae couldn't appreciate a hard-bodied man when she saw one.

Not that she'd ever tell him she watched his broad shoulders and sway of his back as he vanished below. She'd never, ever let him know *that.* Or that his gaze held hers whenever she looked at him as much as she struggled to pull away. Or that she liked the contrast between the very white hair on his head with his trim dark beard.

Never tell him. He'd laugh and call her Little Wolf again, dismissing the interest of a messed-up woman who wasn't much more than a cub.

Rae sighed and followed him below with her cleaned plate, pretending she didn't feel a shiver when he turned around and grinned at her.

Zander helped Rae clean up from breakfast, then he shooed her out of the cabin to the stern deck, the only place there'd be room to train. High time she started learning something. The sooner he had her trained up, the sooner Eoin could come back and fetch her, leaving Zander once more in blissful solitude.

That's what he wanted, wasn't it? He could wave good-bye

to Rae, never again seeing her gray eyes, sweet body, lips he could have kissed when she'd leaned to him and pressed her hand to his chest.

His heart had sped like a rocket. Her dark hair had fallen over her shoulder, a pucker creasing her forehead as she laid her palm on his breastbone. Rae's face had been close to his, her eyes focused, lips parted. Only Zander's hellaciously good self-control had kept him from sliding his hand behind her neck and easing her down to kiss her mouth.

Yep, training couldn't start fast enough. Zander preferred living alone but that didn't mean he was a monk. He had needs and Rae was a beautiful, desirable young woman.

Zander grabbed a few weapons of his own from a cupboard and followed Rae outside. The sun was high, the sky clear blue, and the boat rocked gently on the waves. A perfect day to sit around and fish, contemplate the universe—basically do nothing.

He briefly considered going along with Rae's idea—heading to Anchorage to find some place for her to stay, leaving her there, forgetting about her.

Then he saw Rae. She'd stripped out of her sweater to reveal a tight, ribbed tank top that smoothed over her breasts and left her arms bare. Her dark braid swung against the white top as she struggled to unsheathe the Sword of the Guardian.

Goddess, Zander couldn't leave her alone in the world. She was out of her depth, had no idea what to do with the new magic raging inside her.

Rae wouldn't feel it raging, exactly, but she was different now. One couldn't be Goddess-touched and ever be the same again.

The tip of the sword snagged on the sheath. Rae lost hold of the big hilt and the sword fell forward and clattered to the deck. As she wrung her hand and muttered swear words, Zander stooped over and retrieved the sword.

"No!" Rae cried, lunging for him. "It'll burn you!"

Zander looked at the sword in his hand. The hilt rested easily in his palm, runes shimmering in the sunlight, but nothing happened.

He shrugged, handed the sword to the gaping Rae hilt-first, and slid off his boots and socks, then his coat and sweater. He rolled his shoulders, bared by the gray muscle shirt he wore underneath.

"It doesn't like anyone touching it but me," Rae said, her eyes wide as she gingerly clasped the hilt.

The sword didn't seem heavy for her. Rae held it as though it had almost no weight but Zander had felt its pull. It was a hefty sword but Rae wasn't bowed by it. The thing must truly like her.

"Creepy," Zander said.

"That's what I think. My dad tried to hold it for me after the Choosing and it burned his hand. Everyone's scared of it. And of me."

"Shifters." Zander waved them away. "Bunch of superstitious sticks-up-their-asses."

"Says the man with Goddess powers who lives alone on a boat." Rae set the tip of the sword on the deck and rested her hands on the hilt.

Yep, if she came for him when it was his time to go, Zander didn't think he'd mind. Her ribbed tank top hugged her curves, her hips were soft under her jeans, and sunlight touched her smooth face and the eyes he knew he'd never be able to get out of his mind.

To think, the Shifters in her Shiftertown had driven her away. What total dumb-asses.

"You need to learn to hold it," Zander said, trying to tamp down the thoughts stirring inside him. *Long twilit evenings, Rae next to me in the bed below, the boat rocking as the setting sun trickles through the windows.*

Zander cleared his throat and lifted the sheathed sword he'd brought out for himself, one with no magic at all, as far as he could tell.

Rae watched him. "Explain to me who I'm going to be fighting with a *sword*?"

Zander shrugged. "You never know. The Fae still use them. They charge out of their world from time to time, trying to do whatever shit they take it into their heads to do. They have swords that control the Collars—did you know that?" Zander jerked his finger at the Collar around Rae's neck.

The black and silver of it gleamed against her skin, enhancing her instead of detracting.

"I know," Rae said. "My dad explained it to us."

The Fae had, twenty or so years ago, had a hand in making the Collars that the human government put around the neck of every Shifter they could round up. Since that time, the Fae had been crafting magic swords that worked to activate the Collars when they were near a Shifter, thus rendering whatever Shifter they pleased in horrific pain.

The Fae hadn't yet burst out of Faerie waving their magic swords, but everyone knew they would someday. Shifters with Collars were now working, in secret, to take off the Collars and replace them with fakes so the humans would be none the wiser. The cubs and Shifters far down the hierarchy already had replacements, but it took time. The secret of removing the Collars painlessly was an influx of Fae gold, which was rare and hard to obtain. Their supply, given to Shifters by a Fae who actually wasn't a total bastard, was small.

Zander had never worn a Collar and wasn't about to start now. The Shifters he'd visited in Austin had tried to get him to wear a fake so he could avoid arrest if someone realized he was Shifter, but Zander couldn't bring himself to try even that. The touch of the metal did something to him—sucked out his soul maybe. He didn't know.

As nice as Rae looked in her Collar, Zander would love to see her out of it. The symbol of her captivity bothered him a lot.

"So," he said, balancing himself on his bare feet. "Say a Fae gate opens in the middle of the ocean and I, a crazed Fae, spring through it. What do you do?"

Zander drew his sword with a *whoosh* of steel. Sunlight flashed on the blade that he kept polished in honor of the man who'd bequeathed it to him.

Rae started to lift her sword, holding it all wrong, then her eyes narrowed. "I don't think the Fae carry samurai swords."

Zander moved the sword in front of him, the blade perfectly balanced. "Maybe not."

"Where did you get it?" Rae asked with curiosity, but she also had a teasing light in her eyes. "A souvenir shop?"

"No, from a samurai," Zander said. "He was a friend. He left his swords to me when he died."

"Oh." Rae flushed. "I'm sorry."

"He was a good guy. A Shifter. I saved his life once and then when he was dying of old age, he sent for me and gave me the swords for safekeeping. He didn't have anyone in his pack left alive and he didn't want humans getting hold of them."

Rae lowered the sword, looking interested in his story. "There are Shifters in Japan?"

"Not as many as there were. Harder to hide these days—most have come to the States. But yeah, there are Shifters in Japan. Bears in the north and some wolves in the mountains. This guy was Lupine." Zander raised the sword again, holding it with perfect steadiness. "There are Shifters all over the world. It's called diaspora."

Rae's brows went up. "Ooh, the bear knows the big words."

"Pay attention, smart-ass."

Zander tapped the end of her blade. Rae raised the sword clumsily, but not as clumsily as he would have thought. She'd either been practicing or it was helping her.

"Like this," he said.

He stepped to her and showed her how his sword rested loosely in his grip, his fingers light, his thumb rotated toward the outer part of his arm.

"Keep your wrist flexible but not too loose, straight but not stiff," he said. "It's not like in the movies where they hold the swords like clubs and go *clang, clang, chop, chop.* A good swordsman can do anything with his sword. Peel a grape if he wants to."

Rae tried to copy his hold, his stance. "I don't think I could *hit* a grape with this thing. Or even a cantaloupe."

"It takes practice. Get used to the weight of the blade, the momentum when you swing it. Eventually it will become an extension of your arm—you'll feel what it feels."

Zander took a step to his left, reached out with his blade, and hooked Jake the Snake, who'd slithered out from his box in the wheelhouse, over the blunt side.

Rae took a step back, bringing the sword up in a perfect defensive move.

Zander's amusement rose as he set Jake on his other wrist. "You're a Shifter who grew up in the woods. A *snake* scares you?"

"The snakes in the woods are rattlers, all different kinds of them. I keep a respectful distance."

"Respect." Zander turned away. "Is that what you're calling it these days?" He stepped quickly into the wheelhouse and returned Jake to his box. "Sorry, guy. She'll come around, don't worry."

Zander made sure Jake was comfy and came out to the deck again, shutting the door behind him.

"Let's do some swings," Zander said. "Controlled," he growled as Rae whirled the sword at her side.

Rae scowled in frustration. "I can't help it. I think it wants to play."

"Great. A piece of metal with ADHD."

Zander gave a moment of thanks that the samurai had been a Shifter without any Goddess magic, just a regular guy who happened to be a perfectly trained warrior. The Lupine's entire clan had been samurai over the centuries, the people around them completely unaware they were Shifters. Or at least, if the villagers had guessed, they'd never betrayed them.

"I'll put you through some drills," Zander said. "Maybe that will calm it down."

He showed her some easy moves, a block, a lunge, a parry. Rae learned them quickly. She had the litheness of a Feline even though she was wolf—maybe all those years of living with Felines had rubbed off on her.

"Keep your elbows soft, not stiff," Zander said as they lunged again. "Locked elbows means the sword can be yanked from your grip, like this."

Zander turned around and struck out, the move abrupt. Rae brought her sword up in a clumsy parry, though not an incompetent one. Zander's sword met hers. Rae twisted to take the blow, but as Zander had said, her arms were too stiff.

The sword snapped out of Rae's grip. It flew astonishingly

high into the air, flipping end over end, the blade flashing in the strong sunlight.

As they watched, it came down, down, down, missed the deck, and plunged straight into the ocean off the starboard side. As one, Zander and Rae rushed to the rail, hitting it at the same time.

A few bubbles boiled on the surface of the water as the sword swiftly sank, and then it was gone.

CHAPTER SIX

"*Shit!*" Panic burned Rae's chest. She grabbed the railing, desperately searching the water, then started to climb over, every instinct making her want to heave herself after the sword.

Zander hauled her back with strong arms. He released her with a suddenness that made her stumble and then launched himself over the boat's side in a perfect swan dive.

"Zander—no!" Rae rushed to the railing, clinging to it as she peered over.

Nothing but blue-black water and streaks of foam met her eyes. Empty ocean under empty sky.

Shit, shit, shit!

Zander would die down there—that water was frigid. Even a Shifter couldn't survive it.

Rae frantically tugged at the life preserver lashed to the side of the wheelhouse. She'd throw it onto the water, for all the good it would do, then call 911. She wasn't sure what good that would do either. The boat must have some kind of distress signal mechanism in the pilot house, but how she'd figure out which button did what, she didn't have a clue.

The stupid life preserver wouldn't come free—*damn it*. Rae knew she hadn't dropped the sword—it had jerked itself from her grasp. She'd heard a faint, silvery tone, as though the sword had been *laughing*.

The water where Zander had gone in began to roil. Rae pushed herself from the life preserver and ran to the side again. Below her, foam churned, bubbles hissing.

The head of a giant polar bear abruptly broke the waves, his ears flat, eyes open, the Sword of the Guardian clenched firmly between his big teeth.

The polar bear's body followed. The great beast, its white fur sodden, catapulted from the water, its torso rising above the side of the boat. The sword clattered to the deck as the bear let it go.

Great black paws scrabbled on the railing, the small boat listing heavily, then the bear lost his hold and slipped back down under the water.

Before Rae could run for the life preserver again, Zander in human form broke the surface. He grabbed the railing with hard hands, got one bare foot on the gunwale, and heaved himself over the side, landing on his feet.

He stood dripping on the deck, his chest rising with his heavy breath. His bare, wet body glistened, sunlight picking out a chain tattoo around his biceps, another around his ankle.

Zander was a big man, hard all over, everything in proportion. Including . . . Rae couldn't stop her gaze falling to his cock, which hung thick and long. The rest of him—arms, thighs, shoulders, pecs—were worth looking at too. The water darkened his hair, making his beard black and the hair at his phallus just as black.

Zander shook himself like a dog, showering Rae with freezing water. Rae thrust up her hands and shrieked and Zander started laughing.

She liked his laugh, a deep rumble that vibrated the air. Zander put his hands on his hips, naked to the sky and wind, unashamed and unafraid.

Rae leaned down and retrieved the sword. "Thank you," she said shakily.

"It wasn't going to let you lose it that easy." Zander swiped his hands down his arms, dislodging water that rained to the deck. "It was floating six feet under the surface, waiting for me. Stupid hunk of metal."

The sword flashed, runes dancing, as though it teased them.

"Enough for today," Zander said. "Keep practicing holding it and finding your footing. I'm not going in that water after it again. Brr." He shuddered.

While he stood there, robust and obviously not dead, his skin was rising in gooseflesh and his lips were going blue.

Rae laid the sword on the bench and pointed at the cabin. "Inside. You need to dry off. *Now.*"

Zander's dark eyes widened. "Yeah? You boss around your dad, a Shiftertown leader, like that?"

"Yes." Rae put her hands on her hips. "Go!"

"All right, all right. Pushy."

Zander took his time sauntering to the stairs to the cabin. This let Rae see his tight backside brushed with water, another chain tattoo on the small of his back.

By the time Rae unstuck herself and followed him below, Zander had already opened a cupboard and pulled out a towel. Rae pushed around him and grabbed a fleece blanket off the bed. The towel Zander had produced might be large for humans but it was like a washcloth for a bear-man like Zander.

Rae draped the blanket across his shoulders. Zander caught it and wrapped it around his body and wiped his chest with the towel. "Thanks," he said.

Rae stepped back so she'd break the temptation to touch him—help him dry his back, his shoulders, his chest . . . "Why aren't you dead?" she demanded. "I mean, I'm glad you're not, but I thought I'd be calling my dad and having you fished out to be sent to dust. Or maybe never finding you again."

Her teeth chattered on the last words and she clenched her mouth shut.

Zander's face softened as he lifted one damp hand to touch her cheek. "Don't worry, Little Wolf. I swim out here all the time. If I shift to polar bear, I can take the cold."

"*Real* bears have layers of fat to keep cold out. *You* don't have any fat." Rae poked a finger at his rib cage under the blanket. There was no give anywhere.

"I do when I'm a polar bear," Zander answered in a reasonable tone. "Everything shifts into the best of us in either form. The Goddess knew what she was doing."

"The Fae made us, not the Goddess," Rae pointed out. "The Fae dinked with genetic coding and gave us a hefty dose of magic. Shifters aren't natural."

Any amusement fled Zander's face. "Who the hell told you that? Is that what you start believing, living Collared in Shiftertowns?" He flicked his fingers across the Collar on her throat.

His hands should be cold from his dive into Arctic waters but Zander's touch held heat that tingled across the links of her Collar. Fires ran all the way down inside her, stirring something to life.

"Isn't it true?" Rae asked, trying to pretend she wasn't melting. "The Fae made Shifters to fight battles for them."

"Sure, but Goddess magic runs strong in the Fae. If the Goddess decided to let them 'dink' with genetics, as you call it, she made sure we were made to be the best of her creatures."

Rae backed a step. "Please don't tell me you're a Goddess fanatic. Burning offerings every full moon, chanting over talismans, believing that every single thing you think was planted in your head by the Goddess?"

Zander gave her a look of amazement. "What the hell kind of people do you live with, Little Wolf? First of all, there's nothing wrong with burning offerings every full moon. It's respectful. Second, the talismans are to impress the humans, and third, the Goddess gave us free will to think what we want."

"There's a contingent of Goddess fanatics in our Shiftertown," Rae said darkly. "My father leaves them alone as long as they don't harass others, but they're growing in popularity. Shifters are afraid of the Fae, and the Goddess fanatics are promising they have a solution, even if it's only more chanting in circles."

Zander looked troubled. "Eoin's letting this happen? Hmm. Probably smart of him, I guess—if he suppressed Goddess worship, that would backfire on him." He rubbed the towel over his hair, the beads in it clinking softly. "Understand why I live alone now? What a pain in the ass."

"Shifters aren't meant to be alone." Rae watched him

squeeze water from each braid, liquid dribbling to the clean floor. "I didn't learn that by living in a Shiftertown. It's the truth. We hang on to family and keep near our extended clans. Well, most Shifters do. I don't know what my clan is—no one ever found out who my parents were," she finished wistfully.

"But you were lucky, Little Wolf." Zander sounded sympathetic. "You were welcomed into Eoin's clan. He has a lot of affection for you—I saw that."

Rae nodded, softening at the mention of her father and his kindness. "He's taken good care of me. But no Lupine wants to mate-claim me, in case it turns out I'm from his clan, too closely related. That means if I want to mate, I have to take a Feline. Or a bear." She gave Zander a dubious glance.

Zander burst out laughing. "The look on your face when you said that . . ." He laughed for a while then let it die away. "If you don't have a choice, Little Wolf, better get over it and accept a Feline mate."

"Huh. Felines and bears aren't exactly falling all over themselves to mate-claim me either," Rae said, tasting bitterness. "Shifters don't like people they know nothing about. And now that I'm a Guardian . . ."

"They're avoiding you like the plague. I'm sorry, sweetheart."

Zander did sound sorry for her. Like he understood—the first person to ever since the fateful day of the Choosing.

"Everyone needs the Guardian." Rae folded her arms and leaned against the table. "They go on about how wonderful it is to have one, how sacred is the sword, how the Goddess touches her own. But a Guardian walks near them and they all but run away."

Rae had seen that happen to Daragh, and now it was happening to her. Daragh had taken it in his stride—nothing seemed to faze him. But then, Daragh had been a male and had been Chosen long before they'd been rounded up into Shiftertowns.

Rae had received everything from outright hostility—rants to Eoin that Rae had to be sent out of Shiftertown for everyone's sake—to Shifters crossing the road when they saw her coming.

"They don't want to be reminded of their own mortality,"

Zander said, pulling the blanket closer around him. "We're not vampires—we don't live forever. Hell, even vampires don't live forever—at least not the ones I've met. The same kind of thing happens to me. Shifters want to be healed but whenever a Shifter sees me coming, they know whoever I'm there for is a long way gone and might not make it even with my help. When I can't save them, they blame me and run me off." He let out a breath. "That doesn't bug me so much as not being able to heal the Shifter. But I can't save everyone."

The note of grief in his voice was raw. Zander had an incredible gift, so Eoin had told her. The fact that he'd lost people in spite of that gift obviously hurt him deeply.

Rae wanted to comfort him. She didn't know how Zander would take it if she tried to touch him or hug him, to soothe him in the Shifter way. Her brothers, when they were cubs, hadn't always wanted her touch. Not because they didn't like her, but when they were at their most distressed they wanted their true family, their pride and clan.

It had stung to watch her brothers seek each other and Eoin, not her, but Rae had come to understand. There was magic in family bonds that Rae didn't share. So, she'd learned how to comfort by distracting them.

"Wait," Rae said, deciding to go with distraction. "You've met *vampires*?"

Zander absently rubbed his hair with the towel. "Sure. One was a good guy. The other, kind of a bastard."

"Vampires are real? You mean that seriously."

"Yep. They aren't Fae made, not High-Fae made anyway. They don't have Goddess magic. They're the creations of ancient demons, beings defeated by the High Fae a long time ago. We were made as the Fae's battle beasts—you could say the vampires were the *demons'* battle beasts. Vamps propagate like we do—you know, sex and offspring—so they stuck around even when their masters died off. Except it's much harder for vampires to survive in this world. *They* need to feed on human blood, while Shifters just need burgers and beer."

Rae stared at him in surprise. "Are you making this up?"

"Nope." He gave her a fleeting grin. "I really have met vamps, two of them, each when they tried to take a chomp out of me. I hang out alone, so I'm a good target. I might be big, but to a strong vampire, that's nothing. Surprised the hell out of them when I turned out to be Shifter."

Rae's curiosity flared. "What happened? Did you kill them? Is that why you said they didn't live forever?"

"The one who's the good guy is living in Canada. Toronto, last time I checked. He goes to butchers and drinks cow blood. The other—yeah, I had to kill him. I didn't mind so much that he wanted to suck on *my* blood, but when he got away from me, he went after a human woman and her kiddies, so I offed him."

Zander explained this calmly, as though he'd shrugged, said *oh, well,* and had broken the vampire's neck.

Rae squeezed her eyes shut and opened them again. "How is it that I've only ever heard of vampires in stories but *you* walk around bumping into them?"

Zander moved to towel off his back and the blanket slipped down to hug his hips. "The biggest reason is that vamps avoid Shiftertowns. No vamp is stupid enough to walk into a town full of Fae-bred Shifters who would smell them coming ten miles away. Another reason . . ." He shrugged his large shoulders. "I get around. See the world, meet people."

"I've never been anywhere but Montana." Again the wistfulness. Rae loved her life in Montana, hiking with her brothers, Logan and Colin, arguing with them and making up, hanging out with her friends, sleeping in her own bed knowing she was well protected by her father. Safe. Never alone.

"You're not in Montana anymore," Zander pointed out. "How do you like the world?"

Rae glanced out the open cabin door behind him. "Bigger than I thought it would be."

Zander chuckled. "Tell you what, Little Wolf. While we're training, I'll take you around, show you some of this world you want to see. Give you a taste of life before you bury yourself back in your Shiftertown."

"I *like* my Shiftertown," Rae said quickly.

"I know you do. But you can get tunnel vision if you never go anywhere. You stop thinking."

"You mean you don't have tunnel vision sitting out here

in a boat all by yourself?" Rae returned. "What about your family? Your clan? Where are they? Or are you an orphan like me?"

"Oh, I have a clan." Zander let the blanket drop all the way. "I stay the hell away from them, and we're all happy."

Rae's gaze followed the blanket to the floor, her mouth going dry. Zander took up a large part of the cabin, his muscles playing under wet skin as he calmly dropped the damp towel and caught up another dry one.

He was large but not ungainly, moving with a grace that belied his size. The tats on his biceps and lower back were part of him—the ink had been etched into his skin but didn't look artificial.

Rae realized he was watching her, waiting for her response. She snapped her gaze from his flat abdomen and the arrow of dark hair below it to his face, which held amusement.

"How can you live apart from your clan?" she asked, her voice a croak. "Don't you miss them?"

Zander's eyes flickered and his humor died. "Let's just say I don't fit in. I think they're close-minded pains in the ass and they think I'm effing crazy. They tell me I should find some way to get rid of my healing ability and stay in hiding with them. Do nothing all day but fish—eat, fish—eat. We get along much better when we don't live near each other."

Rae wouldn't have understood that a few weeks ago but she did now. Zander's clan obviously couldn't handle the fact that he had Goddess magic. It tingled through him and made him nuts, like the magic was making her. His people probably regarded him in grave suspicion, not understanding why he couldn't be "normal" like them. Just like the Montana Shifters now did to her.

"I'm sorry," she said.

Zander stilled, the towel around his neck. He looked down at her, really *looked* at her, his dark eyes filled with something she couldn't read.

"You're sweet, Little Wolf."

The growl had left his voice. For the first time, Zander seemed aware that he was alone with her, truly alone. They were Shifters, unmated, not related, their only tie having been chosen by the Goddess while they'd been standing around minding their own business.

Shifters had no taboo against an unmated male and female sharing a bed for comfort and sex. It tainted neither of their reputations nor hurt their chances for a permanent mating down the line. As long as Rae wasn't mate-claimed by another Shifter, both she and Zander were considered fair game.

The only taboo, apart from stealing someone else's mate-claimed mate, was having sex with a member of one's own clan. Shifters had an instinct to not weaken their genetic code by breeding too close to the line, which was why the Lupines in Rae's Shiftertown avoided her.

Zander was a bear, purely so, from what Eoin had said, so there was no chance that he was related to her. He was lonely, as was Rae, and she was a long way out of her comfort zone. It would only be natural for them to turn to each other.

Rae realized in a flash that this was another reason Eoin had sent her out here. If she formed a relationship with Zander, that would solve the problem of finding Rae a mate. Guardians had difficulty as it was—as Zander had said, while Shifters revered Guardians, they didn't want to be reminded of death every second.

If Rae mated with Zander, she'd be under his protection, and Eoin could exhale in relief.

In the moment Rae formed these conclusions, Zander brushed one finger down her cheek.

Knowing she and Zander were being coerced didn't change the fire in his touch, didn't change the heat that ran through Rae.

She looked up into eyes that weren't entirely black, as she'd thought, but a very, very dark brown that blended into his pupils. One of his white-colored braids fell forward and touched her shoulder.

Slowly Rae lifted her hand and placed it on his. A flicker lit Zander's eyes. He understood.

He bent to her, drawing closer, his wet lashes sweeping down as he shifted his gaze to her lips. Rae's heartbeat sped as fire flowed along her spine to fix her in place.

They moved closer. Zander's breath touched her, tangling with hers. A droplet of water from his hair trickled across her shoulder, dampening the strap of her tank top. His face was an inch from hers, mouth so close that Rae would only have to lift the tiniest bit for their lips to meet.

There was strength in his face, in his mouth, and she imagined his kiss would hold as much force, as much deftness, as he'd shown wielding the sword, a weapon that was a work of art.

Zander closed his hand around hers, bringing it to the space between them to press it to his lips. The light kiss seared her fingers and sent Rae's heartbeat into numbing swiftness. She needed his touch, his nearness, and she knew she craved it for more than a basic need for comfort.

A glance into Zander's eyes told her that he needed the closeness too. They'd hold each other and make everything bad go away, if only for a little while.

A shrill, buzzing tinkle split the air. Rae jumped. Zander, unmoving, slowly closed his eyes.

"Fucking cell phones," he muttered.

He opened his eyes again, silver glittering in the black, and carefully released Rae's hand. The chain tatt on the small of his back stretched as he reached to the bench where he'd left his phone.

He swiped it on and lifted it to his ear. "Go for Zander," he growled.

Rae was about to make a quip about lame people who said *Go for* when they answered their phone but it died when she saw his face.

All impatience, interest, or teasing drained from him, leaving Zander's expression absolutely blank. His gaze rested on the wall in front of him, his face unmoving, no warmth in his eyes.

Rae couldn't hear the words on the other end, even with her Shifter hearing, as much as she strained to listen. A man, was all she could tell. He was pitching his voice low, likely deliberately, which meant he knew Zander had a Shifter with him.

One emotion crept back into Zander's eyes—anger. "Why don't you use your own?" he snapped. "What's the point?"

He listened to the answer and then said, "Yeah, yeah, all right. We'll be there."

Zander ended the call and threw the phone to the bench. When he turned to Rae, she took an involuntary step back. The rage in his eyes burned through him in white-hot heat.

Rae saw in that moment that while Zander might play the half-insane recluse who only lived to fish, he was in truth a huge, fearsome polar bear, stronger and more ferocious than any bear Shifter she'd ever met. He could have stopped Eoin and Rae coming on board, if he'd decided, with one swat of his giant paw. He'd let them on because *he'd* chosen to.

Rae watched Zander suppress his fury and the power that went with it. When he spoke, his voice was level though tinged with sorrow.

"A Shifter is asking for a Guardian, Little Wolf. We're the only ones who can get there in time and so that Guardian is going to have to be you."

CHAPTER SEVEN

Zander watched Rae go through a rapid succession of emotions—surprise, disbelief, dismay, anger, terror.

"Why?" she asked, her gray eyes enormous. "I'm not ready. There are plenty of Guardians who know what they're doing. Why do they want *me*?"

Zander kept his voice as gentle as possible, knowing she could spook any second. "It's an elderly Shifter, a wolf, out in the country on the Alaskan peninsula, not far from here. He's un-Collared and doesn't live in a Shiftertown. All members of their clan have either gone to dust or have been taken to a Shiftertown in the lower forty-eight. He wants a Lupine Guardian, and the son was determined to find one even if it has to be a woman. The lesser of two evils, his son says." The son had said many more choice words, expressing his fury that he had little alternative. "His dad's old and highly respected and gets what he wants."

Rae shook her head, wisps of hair moving about her face. "There are other Lupine Guardians. The Guardian in the Las Vegas Shiftertown—Neal, I think his name is—is Lupine."

"Too far away. We're close and can get there in time. The Las Vegas Guardian can't, even if he arranged to fly."

Shifters weren't allowed to fly on commercial airlines—they weren't allowed to even leave their state without special permission. That said, Shifters were excellent at getting around the rules. There were people out there who would fly Shifters where they needed to go, in secret—like the one who'd flown Eoin and Rae to the sparsely populated, cold island where another human who didn't mind helping Shifters kept his boat, but it took time and money to set it up. Plus, it was a huge risk. If Neal was caught, he'd be arrested and probably killed.

"You said we were two hours from Alaska," Rae pointed out.

"Probably a bit closer now." Zander knew she was arguing from fear, willing him to tell her she didn't have to go. He opened a cupboard and pulled out dry jeans and underwear—the clothes he'd worn to train had shredded and drifted away when he'd turned bear underwater. "We can get to the Lupine before he dies."

"Can't you heal him?" Rae asked in rising alarm.

Zander dropped the towel to slide into the clothes. While a few minutes ago, Rae had gazed at him in hunger, now she only watched, frozen.

"I plan to try," Zander said as he zipped and buttoned. "But he's nearly four hundred years old, which is the upper limit for a Shifter. At this point, keeping him alive might not be the kindest thing to do."

"But you'll at least try," Rae pleaded, clamping her arms over her chest.

"I can't know until I walk into the situation. I promise you, Little Wolf, if he can be healed, I'll do it."

Zander pulled on a dark gray sweatshirt and buckled his belt around his jeans. Rae remained in place, every line of her body tight, as though she'd fall to pieces if she unclenched.

Zander held out a hand to her. "I'll be right beside you the whole time. I won't leave you alone, sweetheart. Promise."

Rae regarded his outstretched hand in panic. "Zander, I can't do this. I'm not ready."

"I know you're scared. But you don't have to worry. The sword will do the work." Zander opened the door, still holding out his hand. "Think of it this way—if I can't heal him with my gift, you can ease his pain with yours. This Shifter will either live today or go cleanly into the Summerland."

Rae's eyes never left his hand. Her chest rose and fell under the ribbed tank, then finally she lifted her head and gave him a tight nod.

"All right," she said, without taking his hand. "We'll go."

She snatched up her bulky sweater, not looking at him. Zander curled his fingers to a fist, then led the way out of the cabin and topside.

The boat started to Zander's touch. It didn't always—sometimes he had to coax it, swear at it, even go below to the engine and kick it. Today the engine roared to life and the readouts came up without a problem.

Rae plopped onto a bench as the vessel leapt forward, dropping the sheathed sword next to her.

Zander gave the sword a grim look before he steered the boat north to the coordinates he needed. He knew the sword had been playing with them when it had flown out of Rae's hand and plunged into the sea. He'd felt a tingle when he'd grabbed it, as though the hunk of metal had been laughing at him. It seriously needed to get over itself.

Rae had her arms folded again and had hunched into herself. She looked out across the water but wasn't truly looking at it—her eyes were empty.

Zander's anger surged. What the hell was the Goddess thinking, putting her finger on this young woman who should be laughing with her friends, and chasing male Shifters and making them crazy? Why the hell did the Lupine demand she dust his father—Rae, who was barely more than a cub? The Lupine was as furious as Zander but for different reasons. He didn't want a female Guardian, didn't want Rae, but realized he didn't have a choice.

Fucking Lupines, fucking Shifters. The heat of Rae's breath lingered on his lips—the nearness of her had crackled the air between them. Her touch and the taste of her fingers had fanned the sparks that had ignited in him when she'd first come on board.

Zander pushed the boat faster. He had plenty of fuel—he never went beyond the distance his capacity could take him. The sooner they got this done, the better. Then Rae could go back to being sassy and in his face, and laughter would light up her eyes.

How many times would this happen, though? Rae's entire life would be like this, her heart plummeting every time the phone rang, every call maybe being a Shifter who needed a Guardian. She'd face sadness, grief, Shifters avoiding her because her presence meant death.

Sweet Little Wolf didn't need that. Why the hell hadn't her father simply pretended the Goddess hadn't chosen, sent Rae to the ends of the earth, and tried again?

Wouldn't have worked, and Zander knew it. When the Goddess chose, you either obeyed or you went insane. Zander was trying for both.

The vessel began speeding over the tops of the waves and Rae grabbed hold of the bench. The boat flew into the air and slapped back down on the water, flew and slapped.

"Do you get seasick?" Zander called to Rae over the noise.

"I don't know." She wouldn't let go of the bench. "Not so far."

"Come and sit next to me." Zander pointed to the padded copilot's chair next to his, both seats built large for his bulk. "I'll teach you to navigate. Who knows when I'll be passed out and you'll need to drive?"

Rae gave him a dark look. She squared her shoulders, pushed herself to her feet, grabbed the sword, and lurched the few steps to the second chair. The sword clattered to the deck when she grabbed the back of the swiveling chair to steady herself.

Zander said nothing as she dragged herself around the chair and into it. Her jaw was clenched tight, to keep her teeth from chattering, Zander guessed. Rae gripped the edge of the dashboard, peering out through the windows at the land coming at them.

Zander had told her he was out in the middle of nowhere, but that wasn't exactly the case. The mountains of Kodiak Island rose sharply to their left, the crags of the Kenai stretched in the distance to their right. Zander guided the boat around the headland, making for Homer.

It was a fine early summer day, sun high, clouds inland but not over the sea, and not too much wind. Perfect for boating, fishing, napping—not for rushing to a dire errand.

Zander heaved himself out of the captain's chair. "Take the wheel."

Rae jerked her head around. "What?"

"Take the wheel. I told you I was going to teach you how to pilot this thing."

"You said navigate."

"They go together. Sit."

Rae dragged in a breath then launched herself from one chair and landed in the other. Zander calmly seated himself where she'd vacated and pointed at the readouts.

"This is how fast we're going—about twenty-five knots. My boat will go a little over thirty but that eats up fuel and is hard on the engine. This is where we are; here's depth beneath us and the distance to land around us. Don't hit anything."

Rae shot him a glare. She gripped the wheel tightly at first but in a few minutes, she loosened her hold as she felt the boat under her like a living, breathing thing, as Zander always did. Sailing was as much about surrendering to the boat and its every sensation as it was checking numbers.

The color returned to Rae's face as she concentrated on following his instructions. As Zander hoped, the distraction of running the vessel, of staying away from rocks or other fishing boats out for Alaska's bounty, helped calm her fears.

Boat traffic increased the closer they got to the town, including ships bringing loads of tourists to gawk at how people lived in cold country. But mostly those tourists came for the beauty—high volcanic mountains, blue waters, tall glaciers, and amazing scenery that Zander had only found in this place on earth.

He could see that Rae found it beautiful too. She gazed, enraptured, at the narrow waterway, the blue sea between cliffs and mountains. Zander wished he were showing the wilds to her in better circumstances. But maybe, once they'd finished this task, they could sail leisurely to the fjords, where they could linger in the sapphire blue harbors and contemplate the amazing beauty of land and ice.

He'd take her ashore to explore the wilderness. Not many roads traversed the best places on the Alaskan Peninsula, but as Shifters, they didn't need to worry about roads. A wolf and a polar bear could run where humans could not.

The long spit of land that ran from Homer into the bay came into sight—the longest natural spit in the world, or something like that. Tall mountains, sharp today in the clear air, were its backdrop.

Zander let Rae steer the boat all the way into the marina, showing her how to slow, how to turn. He raised his hand to other boaters as he passed, recognizing most of them. The fishermen acknowledged him—he'd be a dim figure through the window to them at the moment but everyone knew Zander's bulk, not to mention his fifty-eight-foot craft.

Rae was a natural. She made every careful turn as Zander slowed their speed. The marina was active today—on such a beautiful afternoon fishermen, tourists, and locals were out enjoying the water and the weather.

"Time to cover up," Zander said to Rae, as he took the wheel for the final docking. "Find a hoodie or something in my cupboards. We don't need anyone seeing your Collar."

Eoin had broken about ten laws bringing Rae to Zander, and they both knew it. Didn't matter so much out on the water but now they were in a human town, with human police.

Rae's worried look returned as she nodded, but she took up the sword and quickly went below. They'd have to disguise that too.

Zander's engine barely murmured as he pulled into the slip he leased. The advantage of not wearing a Collar was that he could do human things like rent space for his boat—buy a boat at all. Really what had Collars done for Shifters?

Rae came topside again. She'd found one of his flannel shirts and a jacket, both of which were big enough to hide her neck. They'd be too warm for this time of year but Zander would explain to his acquaintances if necessary that she came from the lower forty-eight. They'd laugh. Non-Alaskans had a hard time with even a mild Alaskan summer.

The engine went silent. Zander left the wheelhouse to tie off, and the two fishermen in the next boat spotted him.

"Zander!" one yelled.

"Where you been, man?" the other said almost on top of the first man's word.

"Out." Zander stepped over the rail to the dock to secure the lines. "Fishing."

The two men sitting on their deck, a beer cooler between them, made a show of looking over the stern of his boat. "Where's the fish?" the first man asked.

"Ate 'em," Zander said, not glancing up from his task. "I was hungry."

The men laughed. They were good guys who liked to fish, drink beer, and talk about how hard-ass their wives were, whom they adored in truth.

Rae peered out from the pilot house. Zander beckoned to her—might as well. People had to see her sometime.

The men on the next boat stopped in mid-laugh as Rae walked out to the deck. They took in her curved body, which the lumpy shirt and coat couldn't hide, her dark hair, and her unforgettable eyes. They gaped, and Zander felt a surge of pride. *Eat your hearts out, my friends.*

The second man cleared his throat. "*Fishing*, eh?"

"Yep." Zander let himself grin. "Caught me a beauty. Rae, come and meet the boys."

Rae was shy—how could she help it, having been buried in Shiftertown all her life? Zander had told her he'd show her the world and suddenly he had a great longing to do it. Right now. Take her away from what she had to face and present to her the wonders of life. He wanted to see the wan look gone, the sparkle return to her eyes, the laughter to her voice.

She had grit though. When Zander held out his arm, Rae stepped onto the deck, her head high, and let Zander pull her against him. She looked straight at the men on the other boat and said "Hello" in a friendly voice.

The men's surprise returned and their leers went away. They recognized, in the way humans seemed to, that Rae was a "nice" young woman, not a hook-up.

"Hello," the two men said, less certainly.

"Rae, that's Tanner and that's Johnny. They're losers who hang out here when they have perfectly good homes to go to. This is Rae. A friend."

Johnny and Tanner grinned and waved. "Hi, Rae," they said at the same time.

Zander liked having Rae in the circle of his arm. "Ready to go, sweetheart?"

"Sure," Rae said. She was rigid in his half embrace but she looked up at him and gave him a perfectly believable smile.

Zander drew her back into the pilot house, where she'd left the sword. He'd had an idea how to disguise it, and now he zipped it into a long fishing-rod case. The case was a little bit short but he wrapped a piece of canvas over the top, hiding the hilt. Now if the damn thing would stop *humming*.

Humans couldn't hear it, he was pretty sure. Zander could hear the sword and Rae could, from the scowls she kept shooting it. Humans, though, were usually oblivious to Goddess magic.

Rae reached for the case but Zander turned from her and slung it over his shoulder. If she took it, Johnny and Tanner and other humans would wonder why he was making his woman tote his gear.

Zander led Rae out onto the deck again, closing and locking the cabin and the pilot house, shutting down the power. Johnny and Tanner lifted beer cans in salute as Zander stepped off the boat and helped Rae to the deck. Zander knew they'd make sure anyone who wasn't supposed to come to the boat kept away.

Rae wobbled a little, getting used to unmoving land after a day and night at sea. Zander felt a little rubbery himself but he knew he'd be over it by the time they reached their destination.

They had to drive. The Shifters who'd called lived inland between here and Anchorage. Beautiful country but their place was hard to reach.

Zander kept a pickup at the docks. The one road from the marina would take them into town and from there they'd ride into wild country. On the other side of the mountains that split the peninsula were the fjords, jagged folds of land that were both beautiful and deadly.

Zander had to stop and greet other men and women who were either heading out to fish or heading home. He hadn't realized he knew so many people but they all seemed to be around today.

Finally they were at the truck, a hefty 350. Zander opened the door for Rae to get in, earning a puzzled look, but she went along with it. Shifters weren't supposed to let their females enter a building, vehicle, or wherever first, in case there was danger.

Zander boosted Rae in, giving her a nod that acknowledged he understood her confusion. Then he went around to the driver's side, sliding the sword from his shoulder and laying it across the seat, the hilt resting on Rae's lap.

He climbed in and started up, waved at more acquaintances, then he was driving out of the lot and up the narrow road toward the main town.

Rae looked around, her balled hands easing open as she took in the scene. Sunlight danced on the waves on either side of the narrow isthmus, turning the long sands golden and brushing the black green of the woods in the distance.

"It's beautiful here," Rae said. "I understand why you like it."

"When it's not freezing, wet, drizzly, snowy, or windy as hell, sure," Zander said, concentrating on the road. "Not to mention earthquakes, volcanic eruptions, and huge chunks of ice threatening to fall on you all the time. This is Nature's place. She barely tolerates humans—or Shifters—living here."

"Isn't what humans call Mother Nature our Goddess?"

"Probably." Zander shrugged. They reached the mainland and he navigated through town, then drove out the other side, back to open country. "I'd like to think the Goddess doesn't get as pissed off as Nature seems to," Zander said as he peered down the road. "But yeah, when it's not trying to kill you, Alaska can be the best place on earth."

Rae was studying him with those penetrating gray eyes. Many, many thoughts went on behind them—Zander was pretty sure that the Felines she'd been living with had never understood the depths of the Lupine they'd taken in.

Wolves could be taciturn, giving you their level stare, while behind those eyes they were planning world domination . . . or maybe the best way to hole up and take a nap. You could never be sure. Zander was the largest land predator on earth and still, Rae's wolf gaze unnerved him.

"What?" he asked in irritation.

"You're not from Alaska," Rae said. "Eoin learned all about you from Dylan, in the Austin Shiftertown. You're from the Shetland Islands and you were living in Texas most of this spring."

"So? Doesn't mean I don't like it here." Zander took a tighter grip of the wheel. "I've traveled quite a bit over the years and this is a good place. Besides, if I want to run around as a polar bear and someone sees me, it's not a huge shocker. I just make sure I'm someplace remote so they don't tranq me and drive me back to the ice floes."

"Then why were you in Texas?"

Zander understood that she was asking about him to keep her mind off what was to come. He didn't like to talk about everything he'd done in Texas but she needed the distraction. "A Shifter there truly needed me. I helped him, then Dylan asked me to stick around in case I was needed again. I hung out there for a while, then decided I needed to get away from Shiftertowns and remember what it's like to be on my own. So I came back here."

He left out a lot with this explanation. From her look, Rae picked up that fact but she didn't pursue it. One day, maybe, he'd tell her the whole tale, like why he'd moved to Homer instead of back to his trailer in the woods north of Anchorage.

Zander turned off the highway once they reached Anchor Point and took narrow and winding roads inland.

Rae fell silent as they traveled away from the sea through a flat plain studded with evergreens, open fields rolling away from the road, the stark mountains rising to the east. Rae looked around curiously but they didn't speak, the weight of what they'd find at the end of the road pressing on them.

Zander slowed for the town of Nikolaevsk, a tiny community built by Russians in the 1960s. These Russians were called "Old Believers" who'd resisted changes in the Russian Orthodox services several centuries before, or so Zander's friend

Piotr Ivanov, who lived here and fished out of Homer, had told him. The onion-shaped dome of the church rose over the small cluster of the town's buildings, and residents were walking about on errands on this pleasant day.

A man whose wife wore a long skirt and head scarf in the Russian way, their son in jeans and a light jacket, spied Zander and raised his hand.

"Hey, Moncrieff!" he called.

Zander waved back without slowing. He knew Piotr would ask him when they met up again why he'd simply driven through without stopping for a chat and a drink. For now, Zander drove out of town and into a remoter area, heading for the mountains.

Rae was watching him again. "Do you know *everyone* in Alaska?"

Zander considered. "Well, I know at least one person in every part of it, so, maybe."

"And they know you're Shifter?"

"Some do, some don't. Piotr there does but he doesn't say anything. The people in Nikolaevsk like their privacy—they're not going to call Shifter Bureau to come poking around. Piotr's family ended up here after fleeing Siberia then China, though they lived in Oregon for a while."

Rae looked around at the barren uplands and the rising mountains. "So isolated."

"Right, because western Montana isn't." Zander chuckled. "There are a couple of clumps of Shifters out here, small families only, and they don't show themselves much."

Rae gave him a look that told him nothing and returned to watching the scenery.

Not long later, Zander took a dirt road into the heart of the wild country and pulled to a halt next to a bridgeless river.

He stopped the truck. "Come on," he said when Rae glanced around. "We're here."

CHAPTER EIGHT

Rae never in her wildest dreams thought she'd end up deep in the middle of nowhere in Alaska, outside a town where everyone spoke Russian, following a polar bear to a hidden cluster of Shifters.

She'd never have believed she'd be carrying the Sword of the Guardian on her back in a case designed for a fishing rod, trusting an eccentric Shifter healer to find a house and then get her back to civilization. This had to be a nightmare of unimaginable proportions.

Zander kept a swift pace, unceasing and determined. There was no true path, and trees everywhere. While Rae was used to woods, these seemed to spread out in all directions without pattern. The ground was dry and hard, the undergrowth minimal.

Zander hiked without worry. His broad back filled out his duster coat, which swirled around his boots with his even stride. Rae had to trot to keep up with him.

Just when Rae thought they'd move through these woods forever, Zander stopped. Scrub had been piled up in this cluster of trees, blocking the view of a casual passerby—if any had bothered to walk this far off the road. Zander lifted away enough of the broken branches and brush to reveal a hole in a clearing, within which was a house.

A nice house. Rae gazed in surprise at a snug log abode that was fairly large, with a veranda running the length of the front. A firebreak separated the house from the bulk of the trees and a fence enclosed a garden. While no vehicles stood near the house, an open shed showed her a pair of sleek snowmobiles.

Zander gave Rae a look of faint amusement. "You think we live out here like rats in a hole? Don't think so."

He strode forward, slower this time, his smile fading. He stopped at the porch's bottom step and looked around in growing alertness.

Rae knew he wouldn't simply walk up the stairs to the front door. This was another Shifter's territory—Zander and Rae had to wait to be invited.

Rae scented Lupine, light and blending with the sharp pine smell of the forest. The woodsy odor catapulted Rae back home, to runs in the mountains with her brothers, she a tiny wolf cub trying to keep up with two long-legged felines. Logan and Colin had always waited for her though or stopped to carry her. They never once left Rae behind.

The door opened. The tall man who emerged reminded Rae of Eoin enough to make her breath catch. This man was a Lupine, though, not Feline. His gray eyes and rangy look, not to mention his scent, told her that. He was middle aged, for a Shifter, probably in his two-hundredth year. His dark hair held no touch of gray, his face was unlined, and his body was solid but ropy, as though he liked to run.

The man's gaze connected with hers, recognized her as a fellow Lupine, then shot back to Zander.

"*That's* the Guardian?" he demanded, his thick brows drawing together. "I know you said she was female, but I expected a woman of decent years. *She's* still a cub."

"This is Rae Lyall," Zander said in a hard voice. "Honorary member of the Lyall clan of Montana, foster daughter of the clan leader. Show some respect."

"She's so bloody young," the Lupine continued.

Rae walked forward until she stood next to Zander. She shook all over but she lifted her head and met the man's cold gaze. He wasn't Collared and this was his territory—there was nothing to stop him tearing apart Shifters he considered a threat.

Rae couldn't show fear. The Lupine already knew she was afraid—he'd scent it—but she had to prove to him that she would do her job, no matter how much he tried to intimidate her.

"I passed my Transition five years ago," Rae said in a clear voice. "I'm no cub, and I'm here to help."

Zander rocked ever so slightly on his heels, waiting for the Lupine's reaction. Nothing to stop Zander tearing into the Lupine if he attacked either.

The Lupine pinned Rae with his gaze for a while longer then let out a long sigh, shoulders slumping. "I don't have a choice, do I? But you leave my territory the second it's done."

Zander gave him a nod, not looking offended. "Agreed."

The Lupine moved aside, opening a narrow way through the front door. Zander swarmed up the steps and inside at the tacit invitation, somehow not touching the Lupine as he ducked inside.

Rae followed, her heart pounding. The Lupine's gaze burned her, his eyes white gray, as she turned sideways to get past him.

The Lupine waited until Rae had crossed the threshold, then he slammed the door behind them, shutting out the air. The house was stuffy and dim, the only light a bare bulb in the hall that led to the bedrooms in the back.

The house wasn't primitive though or even a messy bachelor house. The big living room was furnished with a comfortable-looking sofa and chairs, a large dining table, and a big, flat-screened TV on the wall. Rae had noticed a small satellite dish on top of the house, something no Shiftertown Shifter was allowed. Paintings and photos on the walls added a homey touch.

The Lupine faced Zander. The Lupine's hostility didn't drop but both men opened their arms and pulled each other into a Shifter embrace.

The hug was wary but necessary, Rae understood. The Lupine was promising that he wouldn't kill Zander while he was a guest under his roof. Zander, in turn, was promising to behave and respect his territory.

But it was more than that, Rae sensed, as the embrace continued. Zander pressed his closed fist against the man's back, massaging him a little, and the Lupine started to relax, his belligerence fading somewhat.

Zander was soothing him as he'd soothed Rae, no doubt sending a tingle of his healing ability into the Lupine to calm him. Rae had watched Daragh comfort others enough to realize that the Lupine's anger had to do with his grief, his knowledge that when his dad was gone, he'd be alone. The Lupine lowered his head to Zander's shoulder and he hung on to the bigger man.

After a while, Zander put both hands on the man's shoulders and gently eased him away. "All right?" he asked.

The Lupine nodded and wiped his eyes. "Damn it, now I'm going to smell like bear."

"Hey," Zander said softly. "The ladies love that."

The Lupine snorted, straightened up, and turned to Rae. "I'm Ezra Wilcox. My dad is Robert. Welcome, Guardian."

Rae wasn't sure how she was supposed to respond, so she gave him a polite nod. The sword in its case moved on her back.

Ezra's gaze snapped to the case then away, and he turned from her, but not in rudeness. "This way. I warn you, he's not in the best of moods."

Some instinct told Rae to take the sword from her back but not to open the case. Walking in with the sword ready to go might not be the most reassuring thing to do.

Ezra led the way and Zander followed, Rae coming behind. Zander's bulk and presence was comforting, his glance behind him with his dark eyes more comforting still. Rae had resented being dumped on his boat but now she was grateful he'd be with her every step of the way.

As she walked into the bedroom, she recalled Daragh telling her how some Shifters who were dying welcomed him, while others didn't want to see him. The families would sometimes try to pretend he wasn't there, despite his large size and giant sword.

The same sword Daragh had carried now rested on Rae's back. *Daragh, if you can hear me, please don't let me screw this up.*

The bedroom was even stuffier than the front room, the scent of wolf pervasive. Rae saw Zander politely try to hide his flinch.

The old Shifter, Robert, wasn't in bed. He sat in a chair, a blanket covering his lap, leaving his chest and arms bare. He was very old, even for a Shifter—his nearly white hair and his scent told Rae that—but his eyes were as full of fire as his son's.

"Great," Robert said, glaring at Zander as Ezra led them in. "I'm dying and I have to put up with the obnoxious bear. Who let you into my house, Alexander Johansson Bloody Moncrieff? Goddess, what a mouthful. Bears don't have last names, you idiot."

"My mother thought otherwise," Zander said smoothly. "I keep the names to honor her."

"Of course you do," Robert growled. "Let's get this over with. I'm about to expire and I don't want some fecking Fae sucking my soul into Faerie to play with. Where's the Guardian?"

He looked around the room, taking in his son, Zander, and Rae, looking past them for a big Shifter with a sword. Obviously, Ezra hadn't told his father that the Guardian would be Rae.

Zander motioned Rae forward. Somehow knowing it was the right thing to do, Rae laid the case on the bed, opened it, and withdrew the sword. It rang in the silence, filtered sunlight coming through the shaded window to glitter on the silver blade.

Robert's mouth dropped open. "*She's* the Guardian? Are you having a joke, Moncrieff? Who the hell are you, little Lupine?"

Rae quickly spoke before Zander could answer for her. "My name is Rae Lyall. Lyall is my foster name—I don't know my true family or clan. I was made Guardian of the Western Montana Shiftertown at the last Choosing."

Robert continued to stare at her, then he turned an incredulous gaze to Zander. "Holy crap on a crutch, she's serious."

Rae swallowed but moved to Robert, stopping a few feet before his chair. "If you prefer another Guardian, arrangements can be made," she said. "But it might be many hours before they can come."

"I don't have many hours," Robert snapped. "You were pushing it to get here this soon. I swear I can smell the taint of some asshole Fae, just waiting for me to expire. I . . ."

Robert broke off, his sour nature evaporating as his body spasmed. He changed in an instant from crabby old man to a being in fear and pain. He clutched his belly, breath heaving in his chest.

Ezra dove for a bottle on the nightstand but Zander held out his hand, signaling him to stay back. Zander dropped to his knees in front of Robert, and Rae backed away, clutching the sword, her palms sweating.

When Zander spoke, he used a tone of kindness Rae had never heard in him. "I'm going to take away your pain," Zander told him. "Don't fight me. Be at ease."

Robert coughed. "Not like this." His voice rasped. "I came in as a wolf. I'm going out as one."

"Don't shift, Dad," Ezra cried. "You're too weak."

Robert wheezed. "Shut your gob, cub. When I'm gone, you find yourself a mate, ye hear me? Bring in the cubs you would have if you hadn't stayed here to look after me."

"Dad . . ."

"Don't argue with me, son." Robert's words ended in a half growl. "I love you, you know. Thank . . . you . . ."

His bones crackled and he began to shift. The blanket fell and Zander caught Robert as he slid from the chair.

Zander unfolded to his feet, his arms full of shivering gray wolf. He laid the wolf on the bed and stroked his fur, while Ezra folded his arms and leaned on the doorframe, fists clenched.

Zander knelt beside the bed and put his broad hands on the wolf's side. For a moment, all was silent. Then a low sound worked from Zander's mouth, a note so deep Rae was surprised his throat could make it. The note resonated for a long time, filling the room, until there was nothing to hear but that low vibration.

The intonation changed to words, Zander's voice forming the chant to the Goddess in an ancient Celtic language from a time long lost.

Rae whispered along with him. "Goddess, Mother of the Moon, be with us."

A calm stole over her. Zander's chant was mesmerizing, his voice unraveling every knot of tension, every fear inside her. Peace trickled through the room, and warmth, until Rae wanted to bend her knees and slide into the cushion of sound.

Ezra also relaxed, his eyes closing. His grief seemed eased a little bit, Zander taking away all hurts.

Under Zander's hands, the wolf drew a long breath and let out a sigh. His gray eyes cleared of pain and the look he turned to Zander was one of gratitude.

"Ezra," Zander paused the chant long enough to whisper.

Ezra darted forward as Zander continued the prayer. His eyes wet, he laid his hand on his father's head. The wolf sent up a look of love and reassurance, then his eyes slid closed, and a last breath left him.

Ezra moaned. He leaned down and pressed his face to the wolf's, his back shaking with sobs.

Zander lifted away from the wolf but remained on his knees. His face was gray, his eyes full of pain, but he gave Rae a nod.

Rae went cold, her heart banging. Her hands were so sweaty she could barely hold on to the sword.

Zander watched her, not speaking, not reaching out to her. Rae had to do this herself and she knew it. She'd never felt so alone in her life.

But Robert had been correct. He couldn't linger to give the Fae a chance to grab his soul. Daragh's soul had been taken immediately, though his family hadn't realized it. Daragh, it was true, had strong magic in him that the Fae had likely picked up on, but all Shifters carried Goddess magic to one degree or another.

Rae lifted the sword. She moved to Robert's unmoving wolf body and touched the blade to his fur.

Panic suffused her. She hadn't been able to pinpoint Zander's heart—how would she find Robert's? Especially with him as wolf?

Rae was Lupine but picturing herself in her wolf form didn't help. When she was running around on all fours, she wasn't worrying about exactly where her heart was in her chest.

Ezra, fortunately, didn't notice her hesitation. His head was bowed, his hands curled to fists as he waited for the very end.

Rae moved the point of the sword to the wolf's ribs, where she thought Robert's heart would be. Zander, watching her, gave her the slightest shake of his head.

Bloody hell. *Goddess help me,* she prayed.

The Goddess remained silent. Rae slid the tip to the right and Zander shook his head again.

Show me, Rae sent the silent appeal to him.

Zander climbed shakily to his feet, looking ill, and gripped Rae's shoulder to steady himself. He took a ragged breath, closed his hand around Rae's over the hilt, and moved the blade a couple inches to the left.

Rae swallowed hard. She gripped the hilt tighter and gave Zander a faint nod. Strength flowed from him into her as she and Zander together sent the sword into the wolf with one swift push.

The wolf's body jerked, then a breath like a sweet sigh flowed from him. Rae felt a shudder all the way up the blade, and the sword gave a sharp hum.

As the wolf dissolved to dust, Rae lost her balance and tumbled forward. She caught herself on the sword, whose point now rested on the bed.

The dust that had been Robert rose in a soft cloud then gathered itself and streamed toward the window, dissipating in a shimmer in the late afternoon light.

Ezra threw back his head and howled. He half shifted into wolf, his muzzle pointing to the sky, mouth open in a heart-felt cry.

The compulsion to join him overwhelmed Rae's self-control. The howl left her throat, her cry blending with the lonely sound of a wolf deserted by all he loved.

Rae remembered wandering in the woods long, long ago, lost and terrified, her mother gone, her father gone, wandering on her shaking paws. She'd cried until she realized she should remain silent, knowing predators out there stalked her . . .

A vibrating growl jolted Rae back to the present. She was alive, an adult, standing on human feet, and she'd had a good life with a loving family. Her biggest fear about the Shifters not accepting her as Guardian was that she might lose her father and brothers and be as alone as she had been as a cub.

The growl had come from Zander, who was grieving with Ezra. The loss of a Shifter was felt by all.

Zander's voice weakened and he sank back to his knees. "Rae," he whispered. "Get me outside."

CHAPTER NINE

Zander's breath was labored, his face wan. Ezra had crumpled to the floor in grief. Rae realized that at this moment she was the strongest Shifter in the room.

She sheathed the sword. The runes spun as she slid the blade home but the sword seemed calmer now, as though it knew its job was done. Rae returned the sheath to the fishing rod case, slung it over her back, then leaned down and helped Zander to stand.

Zander's strength had gone. Rae had to heave him up, one of his arms across her shoulders. She was much smaller than he was but Rae was Lupine, with wiry strength, and got him to his feet.

Zander sagged against her, sweat beading on his face, as they walked together out of the bedroom, through the big living room, and onto the porch. Rae thought Zander would want to collapse into one of the chairs there but he motioned her to take him down the steps to the yard.

Once in the wide space in front of the house, Zander pushed away from her. To her surprise he peeled off his sweater and shirt beneath it, then pried off his boots. He unbuckled his belt and let his jeans fall, kicking them away. Underwear followed.

Rae found herself gazing at the man who'd leapt bare onto the deck of the boat and stood upright, sunlight gleaming on his wet body.

The body was the same but Zander was now cramped in pain, his tattoos stark black against his skin. He struggled against the shift that came upon him but his body changed as though Zander no longer had any control.

His face went first, his nose elongating to the polar bear's, his head going flat, his hands becoming formidable paws. Within a minute or so, Zander's body fully changed and he landed on all fours. He opened his mouth in a roar, loud and full of anguish.

Zander rose onto his hind legs, his body impossibly big, his fur so white it seemed to glow in the shadowy light. His paws were black with massive claws, his head immense as he roared to the sky high above the trees.

The polar bear came back down, crashing into the ground as though the strength had gone out of him. He took one long, shuddering breath and lay still.

Rae ran to him and dropped to her knees. "Are you all right? What's wrong?"

Zander's eyes opened but they were unfocused and filled with agony.

"What's happening to you?" Rae asked fearfully, her hands furrowing his fur.

Zander growled low in his throat. Rae didn't speak bear, so she had no idea what he said, but she recognized distress when she saw it.

She leaned into his body, resting her head on his side. Zander gave a low grunt, his eyes sliding closed again. Shivers broke in waves across his fur.

Rae became aware that Ezra had come outside. He watched them forlornly a moment then sank to the top step of the porch.

Rae knew she should go to him, comfort him somehow, but she couldn't leave Zander. He needed her.

For a long time, all was silence. Rae remained half lying on the polar bear, stroking his fur, which was warm and wiry, yet soft. Ezra sank his head into his hands but made no sound.

Zander continued to take shallow breaths, shuddering and emitting little moans.

Rae had no idea how to help him. Zander was the healer—there was no other for thousands of miles that anyone knew about. Had his attempt to ease a dying man taken all his strength? Should Rae try to get him back to the boat, call her father and ask him what to do?

She knew in her heart that this was a situation Eoin would have no answer for. For the first time in her life, Rae couldn't turn to him for help.

The best solution seemed to be to remain here, comforting Zander as he lay in quiet torment. Ezra looked up again after a time, wiping his eyes, but he made no move to rise.

"Is he all right?" Ezra called to her, his voice thick with tears.

"I don't know." Rae stroked Zander's fur. "*Are* you all right, Zander? Tell me how to help you."

Zander lifted his head. He heaved his body until he lay on his belly, which dislodged her from him. Rae came to a cross-legged position, her hands moving to his back. Zander swung around and nuzzled her. His nose was cold and very wet.

"Yuck," Rae said softly.

Zander rumbled, sounding very much like he did when he laughed as a human. The pain began to fade from his eyes, the sparkle returning.

Zander gave another growl, then he slowly began to shift back to human while remaining on his stomach. Fur receded under Rae's hands until she rested them on the smooth, warm skin of his human back.

She couldn't avert her gaze this time. The linked tattoo just above his buttocks beckoned her touch and she let her fingers drift across it.

Zander jumped. He rolled over and climbed to his feet in one move, which put his goods right before her eyes.

He was a well-endowed man indeed. Shifters didn't always hide themselves after they shifted, which meant Rae had seen plenty of bare male bodies in her time. However, the Felines and Lupines of the Montana Shiftertown would *wish* they had what Zander had. Zander was bear and, of course, everything about bears was supersized.

A sinewy hand came down to grab Rae's softer one and haul her to his feet. Zander pulled her close for a brief moment, strong arms around her.

"Thank you, Rae," he said softly.

"No problem," Rae answered, her voice shaking.

Zander held her a moment longer, his bare body the length of hers, she against the firm, flat plane of his chest. Though Zander's strength had returned, he breathed a faint sigh into her ear, as though he wouldn't quickly forget his pain.

He at last released Rae, pressed a brief kiss to the top of her head, then bent to retrieve his clothes.

"Ezra, your dad was a brave man," Zander said as he skimmed his sleeveless shirt down his body. Rae, behind him, couldn't look away from the picture he made—loose shirt baring his arms, his firm ass below it, the shirt's hem brushing the links of the tattoo.

"He was in much more pain than we thought," Zander went on as he grabbed his underwear, then his jeans, hiding himself once more. "Your dad had been holding it together until Rae could get here, but he kept his pain from you so he wouldn't upset you."

Ezra frowned but all his belligerence had evaporated. "How do you know that?"

Zander shrugged. "It's a healer thing. Trust me. He needed to go but he didn't want to leave you worrying about him."

Ezra's eyes moistened again. "The old fool."

Zander buckled his belt and sat down on the porch steps to shove his feet into his boots. "We'll honor him with fire to the Goddess," Zander said, patting Ezra's foot next to him. "But right now, I say we all go into town and get pissing drunk."

Zander liked Rae squashed against him in the cab of his truck as he drove back down the long, empty road toward civilization. Ezra sat on Rae's other side, still grieving, but Zander could tell he was relieved that his dad was in the Summerland and that he'd gone free of pain.

The old coot had hidden a lot from his son, Zander had realized as soon as he'd touched Robert's side. He'd understood exactly how strong the dying wolf had been.

Rae had been scared out of her mind but damned if she hadn't stepped up and done her job. She could easily have thrown down the sword and fled, running off through the woods and driving away in Zander's truck, stranding them. He'd left the keys in the ignition—who was going to steal it out here, a moose?

But no, Rae had lifted her chin, hefted the sword that was too big for her, and become the Guardian. *You go, Little Wolf.*

Even afterward, Rae hadn't collapsed into a puddle of goo—she'd gotten Zander out of the house so he could go bear without breaking the furniture. She'd stayed with him as he'd suffered the consequences of his healing gift, soothing him with her touch and her presence.

Rae now stared down the road as they came out of the trees, back to the flattish plain. She said nothing as they slowed to drive through Nikolaevsk and then head into empty country again. Her face was frozen, her pupils pinpricks. Reaction was setting in, and shock. Zander needed to get her somewhere he could pour alcohol into her—after that he'd carry her home and put her to bed.

"Hitchhiker," Ezra grunted. He motioned ahead of them to a bulk of a man walking down the side of the road.

"Piotr," Zander said.

Rae blinked, coming out of her daze. "What?"

"Not a hitchhiker," Zander clarified. "Piotr Ivanov." Zander slowed the truck as he approached the man, now minus wife and son. "Hey, my friend. Need a lift?"

Piotr's blue eyes lit up under his red hair. He was tucked into a light coat against the wind, a bright red thing against the green and brown landscape.

"Be grateful," he said cheerfully. "Off to check the boat, I am. My good-for-nothing brother is not careful with it." Piotr was second-generation of his transplanted Russian community, but while he spoke English perfectly, he would fall back into a thick accent and stilted sentences when it suited him.

"Zander's taxi, at your service." Zander grinned at him and waved his arm to the truck's bed. "Hop in."

Piotr made himself comfortable in the back and Zander drove on through the couple dozen miles to Anchor Point and around into Homer.

After the quiet of the open country, Homer seemed a jumping place. It was nine in the evening but the sun was still high and people were out to enjoy the lingering daylight.

Zander took Piotr to his fishing boat at the head of the marina but he didn't drive away, hopping out to assist Piotr with the boat. Piotr was right to be concerned about his brother-in-law's competence—the man truly didn't know what he was doing sometimes. Ezra and Rae remained in the truck, both of them silent and subdued, not questioning Zander's need to help his friend.

While Zander's boat was for sport fishing, Piotr had the real thing—a trawler with nets and cranes. It smelled like the real thing too, all fish and diesel. Zander helped him make sure the vessel was secure, then they both piled back into the truck and headed into town to Zander's favorite bar.

Not long later, they sat in a row on barstools at Hank's Tavern—Ezra, then Piotr, Zander, and Rae at the end, the sword in the fishing-rod case at her feet. Rae's high-necked shirt hid her Collar, and Collarless Ezra was bright enough to hunker down and keep his Shifter nature to himself.

Zander blessed the Goddess for sending Piotr walking down the road at the moment he did. No one could relax like Piotr when the work was done, and his exuberance was exactly what they needed. Piotr was very devoted to his religion, but he was also very devoted to his vodka.

"Set 'em up," Zander told the bartender. "One shot each—of his favorite." He jerked a thumb at Piotr. "On me."

"Sure thing," the bartender said. Zander and the bartender went way back, and everyone knew Piotr. "And for the lady?" The bartender winked at Rae.

Not so far back Zander would let him become too friendly with Rae. "For her too," Zander said, giving him a scowl.

Rae glanced at Zander in trepidation. "I've never tried vodka."

Piotr leaned around Zander to her, his light blue eyes brightening. "Never? Oh, young lady, you are in for a treat."

The bartender poured it out, clear liquid in four shot glasses.

Zander lifted his. "To Robert Wilcox, a strong man. May he rest in peace."

"To Robert," Rae echoed.

"To Dad," Ezra said.

"I am sorry for your loss," Piotr said. He lifted his glass. "To Robert."

They drank. Zander and Piotr slammed their empty glasses back to the bar and slapped their hands down next to them. Ezra drained his shot but made a face and gently set the glass down again. Rae took a tiny sip, and coughed. And coughed.

Piotr laughed while Zander patted her on the back. "Take it easy, sweetheart," Zander said.

Rae sipped again, this time swallowing more carefully. "It's not so bad," she said, her voice hoarse.

Piotr turned to the bartender, his enthusiasm building. "Again." To the rest of them he said, "I teach you drinking game."

The bartender poured four more shots, his gaze lingering a little too long on Rae. "I'll have to take your keys if you keep this up."

Zander waved that away. "We'll walk. What is this game, Piotr?"

"You drink. You count. The last person who can count to ten without slurring wins."

"Count to ten," Zander repeated. "In what, Russian?"

"No," Piotr said, snorting with laughter. "Chinese!"

"Not fair," Rae said from Zander's other side. "I don't know Chinese."

"In Mandarin," Piotr said, "It's *yi, er, san, si, wu, liu, qi, ba, jiu, shi.*"

"Got it?" Zander asked Rae.

She gave him a steady look, then repeated the syllables back perfectly.

Zander raised his brows. "I thought you didn't speak Chinese."

"I'm good at learning languages. I don't know why."

"Yeah? How many do you speak?"

Rae shrugged. "French, German, Italian, Spanish, Greek, a little Japanese, a little Russian. Some people are good at picking them up."

Zander peered hard at her but Rae only looked back at him,

her gray eyes ingenuous. There was more to the orphaned wolf than she let on, that was for sure.

"Ready?" Piotr asked.

Ezra growled from his other side. "Yeah."

"Then *go*."

Four hands picked up glasses and poured pure vodka down four throats. Rae coughed again, her eyes watering. Four voices called out the numbers in crisp Mandarin and Zander gestured for the bartender to fill them up again.

Piotr had to drop out of the game first. He was laughing too hard at the rest of them trying to wrap their mouths around the syllables to be able to speak. He bowed out manfully. Ezra kept up, determined, as did Rae.

As for Zander, things began to go fuzzy quickly after Piotr surrendered. Zander had dragged them all in here because he'd been hurting, as had Ezra and Rae. Good for Piotr with his level-headed sense of humor. He was the strongest of them at this moment.

Zander made it up to eight on the next round, then he skipped over nine and instead of ending with *shi*, he said, "Aw *shit*."

"You lose!" Piotr cried in delight. "Zander who thinks he can drink the town under the table." He thumped the bar with glee.

Ezra peered around them at Rae. "Give up, little cub."

"Oh, please," Rae slurred. "I'm past my T—" She made a face as she fumbled with the word *Transition*. "Teens," she finished weakly.

Zander grinned at Ezra. "Afraid to lose to a female? I know a few who could kick your ass."

"So do I," Ezra said. His voice was a croak. "All right—you asked for it, Rae. I was trying to be nice."

The bartender poured two more shots. Rae viewed hers in distaste but she grabbed the glass, closed her eyes, and drank.

Ezra downed his shot. He said, "*Yi, er, san . . .*" and fell face-forward onto the bar.

Zander was about to tell Rae not to worry about finishing but she jumped to her feet and yelled all ten numbers in perfect clarity. Then she punched the air. "I win!"

Piotr jumped off his stool and hugged her, lifting Rae from her feet. "You are an amazing young woman."

He set Rae down but Zander snatched her up himself and spun around with her. "That's my girl."

Rae threw her arms up and whooped. Zander decided he'd better stop spinning before he fell over. He set Rae on her feet but stayed next to her.

Ezra lifted his head and looked around, bleary-eyed. "What happened?"

"You lost, my friend," Piotr said patting his back. "But do not worry. We think no less of you."

"Four glasses of water," Zander said to the bartender. "Big ones. I can already feel myself dehydrating."

Rae sat down on her stool again, unsteady but beaming in triumph. She took the glass of water the bartender set before her and drank half of it without stopping.

"You guys are easy marks," she said, dabbing at her wet mouth. "I have two older brothers. I learned to keep up with them a long time ago. I've never had vodka but my brothers have a thing for malt whiskey."

"No, no," Piotr said to her around Zander. "You won fair and square. Do not belittle your skills."

Rae switched her gaze to her glass of water. "I don't think a drinking game requires a lot of skills. Stupidity, maybe."

Piotr laughed his loud, booming laugh. "I like her, Zander. Where did you find her? Out fishing? Is she a mermaid?"

"Better than that." Zander gave Rae a warm look but her gaze was still fixed on her water glass. The mention of her brothers had saddened her.

Zander was suddenly angry. What the hell was wrong with Shifters?—those selfish bastards who'd forced Rae's dad to send her away from everyone she knew? So what if the Guardian was female? Rae had helped Robert without breaking down—she'd put Robert's and Ezra's needs before her own. She'd then helped Zander get through his pain without question.

Now Rae was here, hanging out in a bar with Zander, Piotr, and a grieving Lupine. Rae shouldn't be here at all—she should be home with her father and brothers, surrounded by her loving family.

"Hi there." A burly man in a flannel jacket slid onto the barstool on Rae's other side. A couple of his friends took the stools beyond. "I'm Mike," Mike said to Rae. He paid no attention to Zander, Ezra, or Piotr. "I haven't seen you in here before, sweetheart. You visiting?"

"Yes," Rae said, her shyness wiped away by vodka. "From Montana."

The man gave her a grin. "Cool. Want me to show you around Alaska?"

Rae considered this, then said, "No thanks. I'm with friends."

"Oh, come on." Mike sidled closer, foolishly ignoring Zander, who was leaning back to pin him with his stare. "We can have a lot of fun. Just you and me."

Whatever Rae would have said to that, Zander was never to know. The man, Mike, took hold of Rae's braid and tugged her toward him as though he planned to kiss her.

A human woman might have burned him with sarcasm or become angry and told him to leave her alone. But Rae was Shifter, she was drunk, and she responded in the instinctive Shifter way.

She let out a fierce snarl and slammed a two-handed punch to his face.

Rae hit Mike so hard he fell over backward, his yell of pain cutting off as he landed hard on the floor. His two friends got to their feet and came around him, itching for a fight.

Rae didn't wait. She launched herself at one of the men with a double kick, but when she landed, her Collar went off.

The sizzle of it and her cry of pain made Zander's fury explode. He was next to her, pulling her out of the way before anyone could figure out the cause of her distress.

Then the two defeated men's seven best friends came out of the woodwork and started for Zander. Piotr, big and labor-hardened, slid off his stool with a grin.

"Fellows," he said—and threw himself into them.

Piotr loved to fight. Any time, for any reason. He went at it now, one human against seven. Zander yanked Rae's hood over her head and shoved her down under the bar beside the fishing rod case.

Rae's Collar was still snapping blue sparks but she hunkered down to hide them. Whether or not the other humans noticed,

Zander couldn't tell, because they were cheerfully beating Piotr to a pulp. The rest of the bar shouted encouragement for both sides.

Zander shucked his coat and waded in to Piotr's defense, but before he could engage, one of the men locked his arms around the dozing Ezra and pulled him off the barstool.

Zander lunged for the human, but too late. Ezra, awakened abruptly, his mind clouded, became his half-wolf and tried to rip out the man's throat.

CHAPTER TEN

Rae held her hands over her neck, willing the Collar to stop sparking. If humans saw it she'd be captured and arrested, maybe even terminated, for leaving the state that held her Shiftertown. Eoin and her brothers could be as severely punished for not keeping her home.

Her worry about that took a backseat when Ezra flew by her, wolf paws throwing off his boots, his hands sprouting claws, his face becoming that of a snarling wolf, though he was still upright, his body in human form.

Yells and screams rose. The bartender shouted desperately, "Hey, no Shifters allowed!"

Too late, Rae thought. She tamped down her rage until her Collar finally ceased sparking and then she crawled to her feet.

Ezra was fighting against men who were defending themselves with fists, chairs, bottles. Ezra fought back in instinctive fury, no Collar to slow him down.

Zander got his bulk between Ezra and the men, and Ezra started fighting *him,* trying to get through Zander to the others. Zander's growls filled the room, drowning Ezra's, though Zander wasn't shifting.

The only one not surprised Ezra was Shifter was Piotr. He kept on fighting with glee—kicking, punching, spinning, punching again.

Rae grabbed the case with the sword, holding it to her chest. If she joined the fight, her agitation and inebriation might make her shift to black wolf. Like Ezra, she'd be unable to stop herself.

Over the noise, she heard the distinct metallic *click* that she knew from living in a remote part of the mountains. Rae was pretty sure guns weren't allowed in the bar either but she saw one man raise a shotgun and point it straight at Zander.

Rae had never before heard the noise that left her throat. A cross between a snarl and a scream belted out of her and the sword was out of the case and in her hand before she knew what had happened.

She closed both hands around the hilt, her feet finding balance as Zander had showed her. Rae wasn't certain how she landed in the right stance, because she sure hadn't been able to do it during this morning's lessons. Now she rocked on the balls of her feet and swung the sword in a huge arc, bringing the flat of the blade down on the gun.

The sword's momentum shoved the gun's barrel toward the floor just as the man fired. The shotgun went off with a deafening *boom*, driving shot pellets into the boards beneath them.

The blow and shot ripped the sword from Rae's hands. It tumbled away, landing with a clank before it spun across the floor.

Clank? Not a silvery ring, not a rippling hum, but a metallic thud.

Rae dove for the sword. The human men backed out of its way as it skittered by, until it came to rest in the middle of a cleared space on the floor.

Rae swept it up and saw why it had made the dull sound. The blade, in its middle, was cracked straight across.

"No!" Rae moaned. "Son of a bitch, *no.*"

Men, angry and drunk, closed in on her. Rae looked up at them in anguish, unable to feel her danger. "It's broken."

The guys coming at her didn't appear to care. They were angry, afraid, and not too happy their bar had been invaded by Shifters.

Rae lifted the sword, its blade wobbling. If it snapped all the way in half . . .

The thought died as Zander barreled into her, grabbed her around the waist, and used his momentum to haul her out the front door. Piotr came right behind them, his burly arms around Ezra's half-human, half-wolf form, dragging the man away, or at least trying to.

The night was finally dusky, a smattering of stars peeking out through the velvet blue. Lights were on in the bar's tiny parking lot, though they weren't much needed.

The entire bar poured out behind them, men yelling, shooter guy reloading his gun.

Zander tossed a bundle of cloth to Rae. "Hang on to my coat."

He ripped off his sweater and threw it at Piotr, who'd finally let go of Ezra. Ezra started to run back to the twenty or so men after them but Zander got in his way.

"No," he yelled into the wolf's face. *"Run."*

Zander threw his T-shirt at Piotr, toed off his boots, yanked down his jeans, said, "Get out of the way," and turned bear.

Two thousand pounds of polar bear swung around to the humans in the lot, braced his great feet on the asphalt, and let out a roar.

The collective group halted. Zander roared again, the rage in his eyes glittering in the parking lot lights. His roar showed his very large, very sharp teeth.

The guy with the shotgun raised it and aimed at him.

Rae screamed, "Zander!"

Zander charged. The fighters scattered. The gunman tried to shoot but went down as Zander ran directly into him. Rae heard the gun go off but she could see nothing beyond a flurry of polar bear and men.

Ezra shook himself, shifted fully to wolf, and sprang at the men, knocking aside those trying to surround and bring down Zander.

Rae longed to shift—the wolf in her growled and squirmed, her hands turning to claws and back again. But she couldn't abandon the sword, especially now that she'd broken it. She couldn't let the humans get their hands on it.

But Zander was fighting for his life. He and Ezra, even in

their animal forms, couldn't last against this many, and what if more of the guys were armed? What if the bartender—or worried neighbors—called the cops?

"Rae!" Piotr was shouting to her. He waved at her to follow him before he jumped into Zander's truck and cranked it to life.

Rae's feet didn't move. She couldn't leave Zander to fight on his own. She had to help him.

Protect the sword. Eoin's directive pounded into her head.

This sword had been stolen once from their Shiftertown, when Daragh had been killed, which had nearly led to disaster. Rae couldn't let it be taken from them again.

Her instinct to go to Zander, though, to protect him, warred with her need to protect the sword.

The anguish of it tore at her. Was this what being Guardian meant? Having to choose between protecting those she cared about and always being Guardian first?

Her dilemma was solved by Zander. He sent another human to the ground with the swipe of one big paw, then he bowled over two others and galloped back toward Rae. Ezra sprinted after him, the long-legged wolf overtaking and passing the bear.

Piotr had the truck in motion, pointing it down the road to the marina. Ezra's wolf chased it like a dog after a car, until he leapt and scrambled into the truck's bed. At any other time Rae might have laughed at the sight, but she was too terrified for him and for Zander.

Zander ran straight for Rae. He smacked into her with his shoulder, not knocking her over but using the momentum to send her up onto his back.

Not quite. Rae had to scramble to get on top of him without stabbing him with the sword or dropping his coat. She had the feeling he'd be very upset if she dropped the coat.

Rae clung to Zander's back, feeling the immense power of the bear beneath her. Zander ran with lithe ease, catching up to the moving truck.

Behind them the shotgun went off again, *boom!* Men yelled and sirens sounded.

Zander's white fur rippled beneath Rae's fingers. In one place on his shoulder, the white was tinged with red.

"Zander," she gasped.

Zander growled in response, vibrating Rae's body.

The truck was just ahead of them, tailgate open. Rae stifled a shriek and held on as Zander gathered himself and leapt for the pickup's bed.

Ezra was already there. He squeezed his wolf body into a corner as Zander landed, paws scrabbling on the bottom of the truck's bed until he was solidly on board.

The momentum made the pickup lurch and spin. Piotr cranked the wheel until the truck righted itself, then he stomped on the gas, sending the vehicle screaming down the road toward the marina.

He looked back at the trio in the bed and pumped his fist into the air. "Woo-hoo!" he cried. "Zander, you do know how to party."

Police sirens dogged them all the way to the docks. Zander's shoulder hurt but if he stayed bear it wouldn't be so bad.

Piotr was driving like an insane man, pushing the truck down the narrow spit of land, the flashing lights dropping farther and farther behind them. If he made one mistake and slid the truck off the road, they'd crash into rocks and sand and tumble into the sea.

But Piotr had been driving the back roads of this part of Alaska all his life, in all weathers, in vehicles so broken down it was a surprise they worked at all. Piotr kept the truck going at a speed that would get him arrested and imprisoned, but they made it to the marina in one piece.

Piotr spun the truck to a halt in front of the dock that led to Zander's boat. "Go!" he cried. "I hold them off!"

How he would, Zander had no idea, but he galloped down the dock, still bear, and onto the boat, Rae and Ezra following.

Tanner and Johnny, who hadn't gone home even after all these hours, rose and watched a polar bear, followed by a young woman with a sword, followed by a wolf, run onto Zander's boat. Zander shifted when he reached the deck, his wound ripping pain through his shoulder.

"Zander," Rae's voice came behind him. "He *shot* you."

"Only a little." Zander didn't slow as he made his way into

the pilot house, where he pushed the starter. He checked his fuel—he had enough to get to the port he had in mind, where he'd need to refill. "Go see if Piotr's all right."

Rae gave him an exasperated look, tossed his duster down, and hastened outside, still clutching the sword. Ezra stood on the foredeck, wind in his fur. His feet were planted on the gunwale, watching as Piotr angled the truck to cut off the two police cars and a sheriff's SUV at the end of the dock.

Zander slid on a pair of sweatpants against the cold but didn't bother with a shirt—he'd have to fix his shoulder first. He got the engine going, checked everything he needed to check, and made ready to pull out.

He moved to the doorway to see that Piotr had abandoned the pickup. Piotr was running faster than a bulk-muscled man should be able to, down the dock to Zander's slip. "Go!" he yelled, making shooing gestures.

The police had leapt from vehicles and moved around Zander's truck to chase him. Johnny and Tanner came off their boat and untied Zander's before Zander could move to do it himself.

"Go on, man," Tanner called to him. "We got your back."

Zander lifted his hand in acknowledgment. Tanner and Johnny slipped the boat's ropes free and tossed them on deck. Zander waved his thanks, returned to the wheel, and backed the boat carefully out of its place.

As he picked up speed he heard the thump of Piotr landing on the front deck and Piotr's laughter.

"I have to come with you," he called to Zander through the pilot house window. "If I get arrested, my wife, she *kills* me."

Ezra, still a wolf, sat at the rail, watching the dock recede as Zander took them out into the harbor. The police halted at the slip and simply watched them go.

"Won't they chase us?" Rae asked. She stood in the doorway, her hair and jacket she'd borrowed from Zander stirring in the breeze.

Piotr, who'd made his way around to the stern, answered her. "Nah. It's expensive to take their boats out and we're not drug smugglers, just drunk fishermen. They will think the people at the bar talking about polar bears and wolves were—as Americans put it—drunk off their asses. Pardon me, young lady." He moved past Rae into the pilot house and collapsed onto a bench. "I think I have not had so much fun in a long time. Zander, friend, you have been shot."

"I know." Zander plotted his course, his alcoholic haze gone—Shifters could recover from such things quickly. Adrenaline from the fight and the pain of the wound helped sober him up fast.

The human police maybe wouldn't chase them but if those at the fight reported that they were Shifters, someone might call Shifter Bureau. Shifter Bureau was the coordinator of all regulations and laws regarding Shifters—they didn't have a police force but they had a military attachment and they could alert the local authorities to round up the Shifters causing trouble and bring them in. As soon as the authorities saw that neither Zander nor Ezra wore Collars and that Rae was out of her territory, they'd be in deep shit.

Zander knew how to hide out from Shifter Bureau though. He'd been doing it for a lifetime. He steered the boat toward the coordinates he'd chosen, keeping an eye on his gauges and the readouts on the laptop open next to the wheel.

Piotr was right, however, that Zander's wound needed to be dressed. He opened a cupboard and glanced inside but it didn't contain what he was looking for.

"I have a first aid kit somewhere," he said. "Maybe below."

Rae glared at him. "*First aid?* Seriously?" She left the doorway and stomped her way down into the cabin.

"She's very pretty," Piotr said, his eyes sparkling. "You two . . . ?"

"No," Zander answered quickly. He didn't like the pang of regret the negative answer produced. But Rae was here to learn from him, that was all. She'd return to her Shiftertown when Zander was done teaching her how to fight—though she'd done pretty damn good at the bar—and Zander would go his own way again, solitary, alone . . .

Rae banged her way back inside, her hands full of bandage rolls, alcohol, and a pair of pliers.

Zander swung away from her, putting up his hands. "No you don't. No way am I letting you rummage inside my body with a pair of greasy needle-nose."

"I washed them," Rae said. "Relax. I've pulled bullets out of my brothers more than once. Colin and Logan run in the woods and hunters shoot at them. Taking pellets out of your shoulder will be a piece of cake in comparison."

She dipped the pliers in alcohol and opened and closed them with a few little taps.

Zander flinched and Piotr laughed. "I will hold him down."

Zander growled. "No you won't." He sidestepped Piotr and plunked himself down on a clear space on the bench.

Piotr moved to the wheel without Zander asking and took over the controls. Piotr was one of the best fishermen in the area and he'd guide the boat steadily to open sea. Ezra was still a wolf, watching the wake of the boat as the green and brown shores of Homer receded.

Most humans might suggest Zander go to a hospital. Piotr, however, knew about Shifters, courtesy of Zander, and would know a human hospital might not be able to treat him. Plus the hospital staff would call Shifter Bureau, obligated to report the incident. Rae was obviously used to home medicine and Zander would heal quickly, as Shifters did.

Rae sat right against Zander and put her hand on his shoulder, above the wound. Her touch was warm, already soothing the pain.

She brought alcohol-soaked gauze to the hole in Zander's upper arm and very carefully began to clean it. Zander winced at the sting but tried not to move too much.

Rae wiped the wound then held it open with strong fingers as she very carefully and steadily eased the pliers into his flesh.

Zander snarled, fists balling. He let his head drop back to the wall, his jaw clenched as he fought the pain. He couldn't let it make him shift—if he went bear, he might hurt Rae.

Something like a white-hot pincher tore at his shoulder, then Rae eased the pliers out, a pellet clamped between them. She quickly shoved clean gauze against the wound.

"There we go," she announced.

Zander studied the squashed ball squeezed tight between the pliers. "What the hell did he load in that gun?" he asked, voice a croak. Shot came in several different sizes and this hunter must have used the biggest he could get away with.

Rae didn't move. She kept the gauze against his shoulder, her pressure slowing the bleeding.

"You should be all right," she said. "Can you, you know, help it heal?"

Her eyes held belief in him. Zander wanted to reach up and cup her face, wrap his hand around the warmth of her braid, and pull her down to him.

She'd kicked the ass of the last guy who'd tried that, Zander remembered. "You mean, *Shifter, heal thyself*?" he said, shaking his head. "Doesn't work that way. When I'm beat up and hurt, *I* don't get healed—I just have to live with it."

Rae's dark brows came together. The contrast between her nearly black hair and gray eyes was enchanting. "That doesn't seem fair."

"It's the way it is." Zander started to shrug, then grimaced at the pull of injury. "The way it is sucks sometimes."

Rae set down the blood-soaked pliers and applied both hands to the gauze. She leaned in closer, brushing against him, her warmth working through his body. Rae knew that touch soothed and she was generously offering it.

Her breath was soft on Zander's skin, the scent of her, sweet. Zander leaned closer and ever so lightly pressed his lips to the line of her hair.

Rae started but she didn't pull away. She sat still, her breath lifting her chest, her hands fixing the bandage in place.

Zander moved his kisses along her hairline, breathing her scent, tasting the faint saltiness of her skin. Rae said nothing, did nothing. Zander kissed her temple, the brush of her hair tickling his lips.

He eased back and looked down at her. Rae's cheeks were flushed, her lips parted, her eyes flicking away when he tried to read what was in them.

Anger? Fear? Outrage? Interest? Whatever she felt, Rae concentrated on holding the gauze in place as though that were all-important. At least she didn't spit on him, punch him, go wolf and rake her claws through his already smarting shoulder.

Zander lightly kissed her temple again, then her cheekbone, absorbing her warmth. Her eyelids fluttered, lashes brushing his lips. The sensation made his entire body go hard.

"Hey," Piotr said suddenly, and Rae jumped, scooting back a few inches.

Piotr wasn't looking at them. He had his hand on the wheel but gazed past them to the stern. "Your wolf looks as though he wishes to leap overboard."

Sure enough, Ezra crouched on the gunwale near the fishing poles, peering down into the water as though looking for the best place to dive in.

"Damn it," Zander said. He rose abruptly, the gauze dropping away, and strode out into the cool dimness of the midnight sun.

CHAPTER ELEVEN

Rae sensed Ezra's distress before she reached the deck. His grief and despair came to her in waves—she knew Zander felt them too, because Zander visibly flinched.

Zander put big hands on Ezra's wolf scruff to drag him from the edge. Ezra came alert at his touch, whirling to lunge at Zander with a vicious snarl.

"Stop!" Rae shouted at him.

Ezra paid no attention. He leapt onto Zander, pushing him off balance and landing on top of him, claws raking Zander's chest. Rae dashed to them and locked her arms around Ezra's middle.

Several hundred pounds of squirming wolf easily broke her hold but Rae went after him again. She pulled Ezra off Zander, who rolled out of the way to lay panting and bleeding on the deck.

Ezra then turned on Rae.

He was in fighting frenzy, not knowing or caring who he attacked. When Shifters grieved, they went to a dark place deep inside themselves and sometimes never came out. Rae had nearly gone there as a little cub and only the combined effort of Eoin, Daragh, and her brothers had dragged her back to sanity.

Zander was coming to his feet, the alpha bear in him ready to grab Ezra and slam him to the deck until he calmed down. In the wild, if an alpha couldn't subdue a Shifter endangering another, then the alpha went for the kill. Zander and Ezra weren't Collared—they were as close to wild as Rae had seen in twenty years.

Rae opened her arms to take Ezra's attack. When the wolf leapt on her, she closed herself around him and held on tight.

Ezra's leap sent both of them to the deck. Zander reached down to drag Ezra off Rae but Rae frantically shook her head.

"No. Leave him alone. Let me."

She had to gasp the words, barely able to breathe with a massive wolf crushing her. Zander's growls escalated but he took a step back. He understood what she was trying to do.

Rae warmed despite the situation. No one in her life had read her intentions and understood them as quickly as Zander had just now.

She held tightly to Ezra, keeping her face from his snarling muzzle while she smoothed his fur. Rae stroked firmly, making him feel her touch, attempting with her hands to mimic how a mother or father wolf might lick a frightened cub. At the same time, Rae relaxed her body under him, letting Ezra know she wasn't trying to trap him.

Ezra snarled, his claws digging into the deck, but he shuddered, his frenzy easing. Zander stood by, his strong bare feet next to Rae somehow comforting.

Rae continued to stroke Ezra's fur, feeling him shiver. The man had lost his only family today, the highest member of his pack. Ezra would now have to be alpha; leader, but leader of no one. He was alone, which was a horrible state for a wolf Shifter. Bears had a little easier time in solitude but wolves and Felines needed the presence of others to survive. Even being bottom of the pack, as Rae was considered in her foster family, was better than being alone. Hence Ezra had stared into the waves and decided a watery grave might be a better fate.

"You're not alone, you know," Rae said to him. The engine,

wind, and water made plenty of noise, but Rae could murmur right into his sensitive wolf ears. "Not packless. You have us. We're your pack. We fought together, didn't we? Now we're on the run. Together."

Ezra gave another growl at Rae's announcement that she, Zander, and Piotr were now Ezra's pack, but it was a growl of annoyance. His despair had ebbed.

He wriggled, trying to loosen Rae's hold but Rae, even then, refused to let Ezra go. She ran both hands down his back, continuing to emulate mama wolf. She jerked her chin at Zander, indicating that he should get down here and pet Ezra too.

Zander sent her a look of irritation but he took the hint. He folded down next to Rae, his sweatpants tightening over his thighs as he put his large hand on Ezra's shoulder.

"There, there," Zander rumbled. "Good dog."

Ezra's ears flattened. He turned his head and put his teeth on Zander's arm.

"Not helping," Rae said. "Ignore him, Ezra. He's a shit."

Zander chuckled. "Easy, wolf. I'm teasing you. Rae is right. You're in our pack now. A weird pack, but a pack all the same."

Piotr, who had slowed the boat to let it drift, leaned on the doorframe of the wheelhouse. "We do drinking game together," he said to Ezra. "That means we are family."

Ezra growled again. He'd relaxed a long way though and didn't bite down on Zander. Finally, he withdrew his mouth from Zander's arm and climbed stiffly to his feet.

Rae let him go. Ezra shook himself, moved about six inches away from Rae, and then lay down again, still wolf, right against Rae's side.

Zander's hand on Rae's shoulder was comforting. "You all right?" he asked her.

"Perfectly fine." Rae let him help her sit up. Zander's fingers held strength that warmed Rae all the way through. "He wasn't going to hurt me."

"Didn't look like it from where I was standing." Zander's frown was fierce, made more so by the scratches all over his torso. "Don't ever do that again."

Rae opened her mouth to argue with him, then she closed it.

The look in Zander's eyes was odd, a mixture of fear and anger, of possessiveness and self-deprecation. He looked away when Rae caught his gaze, as though he didn't want her to read him.

Ezra was gazing out to sea again, his wolf face wearing a resigned expression. Sure he needed a pack, the expression said, but look at the one he'd been stuck with.

Rae stroked Ezra's head, resisting scratching behind his ears. There was only so much a wolf would put up with. "Anyway, Ezra, if you'd jumped into the sea, I might not have been able to find you to dust you."

Ezra's scowl returned, wrinkling his brow. He obviously hadn't thought of that. He let out a sad huff and lowered his head between his paws.

Zander cupped Rae's shoulder again and cranked to his feet. "Now that the drama's over, let's eat. I'm starving."

S andwiches again. Zander handed around the last of them as they sat out on deck, enjoying the Alaskan summer night, the sun barely below the horizon. Stars pricked out, only the brightest ones against dusky blue. Zander had stopped the boat, saving the fuel, but there were no other crafts on the horizon. For now, they were alone again.

Rae had never seen the sky like this. They had deep, dark skies in Montana, but they also had trees, hills, and mountains. The entire bowl of the heavens spreading from horizon to horizon was a new experience for her.

Ezra had gone to the bow to shift to human in privacy, and dressed in the clothes Zander had laid there for him. Since Zander was so much bigger than Ezra, the sweatpants and T-shirt were baggy on him, but Ezra didn't complain. Now he sat with his back to the pilot house, his bare feet on the deck as he silently chewed through a roast beef sandwich.

"Marny's," Piotr said, looking at the wrapper. "He does a mean sandwich."

"I'll never be able to go back there," Zander said, mournful. He'd pulled on a black T-shirt, hiding the gouges Ezra had left in his chest, most of which, Rae had seen, had already started to heal. Even in his despair, Ezra had mitigated his attack. "I think I've burned Homer and surrounding towns for me."

Piotr shrugged. "Who knows? When I go home, I put in a good word for you."

Unworried, the human man continued to eat, the fact that he was surrounded by two wolves and a bear not bothering him at all.

Rae watched him. "You don't seem concerned that we're Shifters," she said.

Piotr shrugged. "We are all God's creatures. Not your fault that evil demons decided to make you."

Ezra grunted a laugh but didn't speak.

"We're the *Goddess's* creatures," Rae corrected him, deciding that what Zander had told her as they'd argued about this made sense. "Even if evil people like the Fae made us for evil reasons."

Piotr wiped his mouth with a paper napkin. "You pagans one day will see the error of your ways and return to the fold."

Zander growled. "Rae, do *not* get him started on religion. He can argue all night and on through the next day. Just let him win."

"Speaking of that," Rae said, glancing at Ezra. "We need to send Ezra's dad off."

"I don't have anything to burn," Ezra said. "I got into a bar fight and lost everything in my pockets."

"Not everything," Piotr said. "I saw your wallet fall and I picked it up."

Ezra gave him a stunned look. "You did?"

"Indeed. You might be a pagan creature made by demons, but you need what's important to you. Besides, the police would have traced you if they found your ID." Eyes twinkling, Piotr went back to his sandwich.

"He's not bad," Ezra said to Zander. "For a human."

Piotr snorted behind the wrapper as he took another big bite.

"What we need to do," Zander said, crumpling his empty paper and wiping his mouth, "is find Ezra a mate."

He studied Rae thoughtfully and she looked back at him in alarm. "Hey, don't look at *me*."

Ezra glared at Zander. "She's a *Guardian*," he said, then he looked abashed. "No offense, Rae."

"None taken," Rae said quickly. "Don't worry; I'm not ready for a mate. I'm only a few years past my Transition."

Zander's attention was entirely on Rae, something in his dark eyes she couldn't decipher. "You plan on sowing your wild oats, do you?"

"I don't know. I've never had the chance." Rae met his gaze without worry. "I'd been thinking about starting my wild life when I was picked up and dumped *here*."

"Yeah, well, *I* was perfectly happy fishing on my own before you were dumped on *me*," Zander returned. "I was thinking more of taking Ezra back to your Shiftertown. There are larger numbers of females inside Shiftertowns than out in the wild."

Ezra gave him an incredulous look. "*Collared* females. You want to slap a Collar on me, bear?"

"Don't worry, they'll give you a fake one," Zander said. "Admit it. You need a mate. Someone to look after you."

Ezra huffed. "Speak for yourself. You live like a feral."

Zander rose. The breeze molded his T-shirt to his torso. "I do *not* live like a feral." He pointed to his mouth. "See? No foam."

"Zander isn't wrong," Rae said. The forlorn look in Ezra's eyes tugged at her heart. "We need pack to survive. Even if the pack isn't blood family, we need others. That's why we agreed to live in Shiftertowns."

"Sure," Ezra returned with scorn. "You do know that if Zander lived in a Shiftertown, he wouldn't be allowed to have this boat. He couldn't travel and heal other Shifters—he'd be confined and cut off. Doesn't matter how many 'pack' are around him—he'd die like that."

"Yeah, but I'm a bear." Zander folded his arms and peered off the stern. "We hate the indoors. Lupines, now, like a crowd."

Rae looked up the length of his body, taking her time to enjoy every inch. "You can't hate the indoors—you hibernate in a den all winter."

"With carpets and satellite TV." Zander flashed her a grin. "Actually I hang out in a town all winter and enjoy myself. But I know another place you can go, Ezra, that's not a Shiftertown. Well, it's sort of a Shiftertown. It's a Shifter community for un-Collared Shifters. A secret one."

Rae glanced at Piotr, but he was staring up at the stars, seemingly uncaring. Zander obviously trusted him with Shifter secrets. That must either make Piotr an extraordinary human being or Zander a great fool. Zander acted the fool sometimes, Rae had seen, but he wasn't one. His carelessness hid something thoughtful and watchful. Therefore, she concluded, Piotr must be trustworthy.

Ezra, not so certain, lowered his voice. "If you mean Kendrick's crew, I refused to join him twenty years ago. What makes you think he'd welcome me now?"

"Because he's a good guy, underneath it all," Zander said. "He's got a mate now, and already expecting another cub. We'll head that way. Piotr? You in or out?"

Piotr heaved a regretful sigh. "Out. I would love to go on adventures with you, my friend, but my wife would hunt me down. I have a boat to run, a family to feed . . ."

Zander looked amused. "You can't wait to get home and warm yourself with your pretty wife, and you know it. You can admit it here. Shifters know exactly how wonderful it is to be with a female. We can go on and on about it."

"And on," Rae confided to Piotr. "And on."

Piotr grinned at Rae and nodded. "You say the truth, bear. My wife is like no other. I will radio a friend to rendezvous with us and pick me up."

He went into the pilot house to the radio, as they were out of cell range by now. Zander gathered up the sandwich wrappings and disappeared into the cabin belowdecks. Rae lifted the Sword of the Guardian that had sat next to her and followed him down.

"I need to talk to you," she said.

Zander swung around from where he'd dumped the sandwich trash into the garbage. Under the low ceiling, his bulk seemed larger, filling Rae's personal space. He put his hand on the ceiling, which tightened every sinew on his arm.

"About what?" he asked.

His voice was quiet, unlike the loud rumble he'd used outside. He and Rae had been utterly alone on this boat last night and this morning but for some reason she felt more alone with him now, inside the cabin with Piotr and Ezra on deck.

"Something happened to the sword," Rae said in a rush. Her heart pounded as his gaze sharpened. "I think I broke it."

Zander's frown deepened. "You can't break the Sword of the Guardian."

"I'm pretty sure I did anyway."

Rae gingerly pulled it from its sheath and laid the sword and sheath on the cushioned bench beside her. The crack was visible, a sharp serrated line across the silver blade.

"It's stopped humming too," Rae said, her nervousness growing. "I haven't heard it singing—whatever it does—since it split."

"Hmm." Zander's eyes narrowed as he leaned to study the sword. "Nope, I don't hear it either."

"What am I going to do?" Rae put her hands to her cheeks. "How do I go back and tell my dad that I *broke* the Sword of the Guardian?"

"It isn't broken." Zander reached a broad finger to touch the split. "Just cracked." Slowly he closed his hand around the hilt and lifted the sword.

The sword shuddered, gave a sound like *tink*, and the bottom half of the blade dropped to the bench.

Both of them stared in horror at the silver pieces, the hilt and top half of the blade still in Zander's hand.

"Okay, *now* it's broken," Zander said.

CHAPTER TWELVE

"What do we do?" Rae asked.

She was looking at Zander as though he knew everything about Swords of the Guardians and how to make them magically heal. Maybe she did think that—he was a healer, and the sword was almost alive.

Why had the sword jerked and broken apart when he touched it? Why had it broken at all? The things were supposed to be indestructible.

"Goddess, I hate magic," he growled.

Rae's fetching scowl returned. "You're a healer full of magic *from* the Goddess."

"I know. Don't think that isn't a bitch to live with." Zander studied the sword again. "I might know a guy who can fix it."

Rae's expression turned to perplexity. "What do you mean you *know* a guy? It's a Sword of the Guardian. Eight hundred years old. They don't make them anymore."

"I know that, but he works with metal. A frigging genius with it."

Rae's bafflement continued, then she looked morose. "Daragh would be so pissed off if he knew I broke his sword."

Her unhappiness poured from her. Zander had noticed that whenever she mentioned this dead Guardian, Rae's tone held respect, even a touch of awe. She'd had a high estimation of Daragh . . . maybe even infatuation, as he'd thought when she'd first come aboard.

"Were you in love with Daragh?" Zander asked abruptly.

Rae blinked, then she turned a brilliant red. "No!" she said in a near yell. "What the hell are you asking me that for?"

Zander shrugged, tightening inside. "You really admired the guy and you get mad whenever I bring him up . . ."

Rae's eyes sparkled, her glumness gone. "He was a *friend*. When I was a cub, Daragh was one of the few besides my dad who accepted me. He helped me fit in with the rest of Shiftertown. Of course I get upset when I think about him. He was killed by humans—shot dead. It was horrible . . ." She trailed to a halt, her breath coming fast. "All right, when I was younger, I admit I had a big crush on him. I thought that maybe when I was old enough he'd mate-claim me. It never happened." She shook her head. "But I can't help thinking that maybe if I'd convinced him to mate-claim me, I'd have been with him when the humans caught him. I could have fought beside him. The two of us could have defeated a couple humans, even ones with guns . . ."

She broke off, her throat working. Her pain, guilt, and regret pushed at Zander, stirring the empathic part of his healing gift like static crackling a cat's fur.

"It's not your fault," Zander said quickly. "How can humans shooting him be your fault?"

"I know I'm not to blame. I know that *here*." Rae jammed her fingers to her temple. "But it doesn't help. If I'd been with him . . ." She gave Zander a helpless look. "When the Goddess Chose me, I couldn't help thinking it was a punishment for me not looking after him. Daragh was my best friend." Tears trickled from her eyes and silently down her cheeks.

"Rae. Sweetheart."

Zander put his arms around her and drew her close. Rae resisted at first, her fists on his chest, but gradually she stilled and leaned her cheek on his T-shirt.

Zander recalled how she'd gone into near frenzy when

they'd fought at the bar, how she'd rushed at the guy with the shotgun when common sense should have told her to run the other way. She'd swung the sword at the gun, for the Goddess's sake, trying to keep the man from shooting Zander.

To make up for not saving Daragh? Zander wondered. Or had she simply been reacting to the fight?

Rae had smacked the shotgun in the man's hands and broken the sword doing it. Zander remembered the clanking sound that had vibrated through his body, though he'd been too busy to pay attention to it at the time.

She'd broken the sword trying to save him.

"Little Wolf." Zander gathered her close, his hand coming up under her loose braid. Her hair was warm, nice to caress.

Rae lifted her head, and Zander gazed down into eyes like smoke. She rose to him at the same time he leaned down to her, and their mouths met in a soft kiss.

Her lips were a place of warmth and incredible tenderness. Neither of them moved, their mouths fused in a silent stillness, their bodies flowing together as though they'd been waiting all their lives for this.

Zander's hand tightened on Rae's neck, fingers splaying against her hair. The beads on one of his braids brushed his hand, a cool contrast to the heat of her.

Rae's fist balled on his chest, but not to push him away. She sought strength, comfort.

Her lips at last responded to his, returning pressure. The kiss parted Rae's lips and Zander tasted her heat.

The brush of it ignited him. Mating frenzy stirred deep in his blood, wanting him to run his other hand down to her backside, to lift her against him, turn with her and pull her to the bed. Or to the floor, if they couldn't make it to the bed in time. They would tear at each other's clothes, insane with need, not content until they'd taken each other in a wild storm.

Female Shifters had just as much frenzy as males. The Goddess made them to mate, to keep at it until cubs came.

Who are we to thwart the will of the Goddess?

Rae scooped herself against him, deepening the kiss. He tasted her sadness, her need, and also the bite of Goddess magic that had changed her life.

Every curve of her pressed to every plane of him. Zander learned her with his hands, mouth seeking more.

Rae unclenched her fist, sliding her fingers to his shoulder then his neck, caressing skin unblemished by a Collar. Zander wanted Rae's off her. He'd take her to Dylan Morrissey and stand on that Feline until he got Rae free of her Collar. The chain on Rae's throat, warm from her skin, caught on Zander's fingers.

Her mouth held spice, strength, and Zander wanted her. They'd been thrown together, confined, made to put up with each other, then had drawn together to ease Ezra's father to the Summerland. After that Rae had steadied Zander while he'd gone through his healing hangover, then they'd fought a common enemy. Rae had jumped to Zander's defense, probably saving his life. If that wasn't cause for some mating frenzy, Zander didn't know what was.

Zander lifted Rae from her feet. She more or less climbed him, wrapping her arms around his neck, her legs around his hips. Zander supported her with his hands on her warm, firm ass.

Rae sank fingers into his shoulders as she held on to him, her mouth working under his. Zander felt her tongue sweep in, tasting him, exploring, Rae unafraid of him.

Her breasts were soft against his chest, the points of her nipples hard through his T-shirt. She was feeling the frenzy, which excited the hell out of Zander.

Want you, Little Wolf. Hard and fast, damn who hears us.

Zander slid one hand under the waistband of her jeans, working down behind her underwear to cup her soft backside. Rae drew back. Her eyes held heat and her lips were parted, moisture reddening them.

Fire lurked inside her and Zander wanted to reach in and pull it out. So what if it burned him? Life was meant to be grabbed with both hands and *lived*. He'd never know if he and Rae had anything together if he didn't try.

He pulled her firmly against him, the skin of her sweet ass warm and smooth. Their mouths met again, this kiss deeper and hotter.

The cabin door opened, letting in a draft of cold, dark air, then closed just as swiftly.

Rae jumped, her eyes widening. "Who was that?"

"Well," Zander said. He didn't let go, liking her nestled in his arms. "There are really only two possibilities."

Rae struggled out of his arms, hot with embarrassment. Her body was hot for other reasons—no denying it. Zander kissed like fire and his hands brought forth every need Rae had ever had.

Female in a frenzy, he must be thinking. Females after their Transition were notorious for going out mate hunting. Her close proximity to Zander must have triggered it.

If that's the case, a voice of cool logic inside her whispered, *why don't you want to go after Ezra or Piotr?*

Ezra's grieving and Piotr's already mated. There, that should settle the voices down.

But Rae knew mating frenzy wasn't the entire story. Zander looked at her with dark eyes that held so much, his hands warm as he steadied her.

He wasn't pushing her away, wasn't condemning. Zander caressed her cheek, as though their heated kiss had been natural, something he considered continuing later. She could still feel the imprint of his mouth on hers, his hands on her backside.

"We'd better go see what they want," Rae said, her lips stiff.

"Yeah, probably a good idea." Zander drew a long breath, the beads in his braids winking in the dim light. "I bet it was Piotr who looked in. Ezra would have just stood there until we finished."

Rae hadn't known either man for long but she agreed with Zander's assessment. Shifters weren't embarrassed by mating frenzy—at least, not other people's frenzy. Amused by it, yes; embarrassed, no.

Zander moved around Rae in the small space by resting his hands on her shoulders and turning in a circle with her. He caressed her throat beneath her Collar with his thumbs before he finally lifted away and turned for the door.

Rae's gaze went to his back under the tight T-shirt and the ass his thin sweatpants clung to. Zander the crazy healer kept his body in good shape.

Zander swarmed up the ladder and onto the deck. Rae

quickly went to the sword, slid the pieces into the sheath, then hurried out after Zander.

It was indeed Piotr who waited on the deck right outside the cabin door. "So sorry to disturb, my friends," he said, no amusement in his voice. "But we have a situation."

The situation, Rae saw as she climbed out, took the form of boats, lights blazing through the near-darkness, coming right at them.

Her breath caught. So many. Almost all of them sported flashing lights and all had searchlights. The clear, peaceful night let them come fast.

"Who the hell are they?" Rae asked, shading her eyes.

Ezra answered, "I'd guess every law enforcement agency within a fifty-mile radius. I say we throw the human overboard and let them pick him up."

Rae began a hot answer but Piotr shook his head. "He is not wrong that this is my fault. I radioed my friend to come for me in his fishing boat. Either my friend betrayed me or police heard the call. I said nothing about being with Shifters but someone must have recognized me at the bar fight and the police put it together."

"And they're coming right for us," Ezra growled. "I really, really didn't want to die with a Collar on me."

"You won't," Zander said. He studied the approaching boats. "We're getting out of here."

Good kisser or not, he never made any sense. "How?" Rae demanded. "You know a few whales who owe you favors?"

Ezra and Piotr watched Zander with as much skepticism, but Zander's face split into a grin.

"As a matter of fact, I do, but they don't always come when I call. But no, that's not what I had in mind." He swung away toward the pilot house. "Piotr, I'll need you for this. You know these waters like the back of your hand."

Rae remained in place, balled fists on her hips. "What do you want *us* to do?" She gestured to Ezra.

Zander glanced at them. "Hold on tight and don't get shot. Oh, and find the life vests."

"Great," Ezra muttered. "Sounds promising."

Zander's boat spluttered to life as Piotr followed him inside. The engine caught, gurgled, then took up its steady, strong roar.

The boat leapt forward, throwing Rae and Ezra off balance and nearly sending them sliding over the stern rail. Both dropped like the animals they were as the boat jumped over the waves, faster, faster.

Rae half climbed the rising deck to the cabin door and let herself below. She expected Ezra to follow but she saw him through the cabin's small windows pull himself along toward the bow, as though he wanted to see where they were going.

"Life vests." Rae went through the bench's storage and cupboards, finding boxes filled with everything from card games to a crowbar but no life vests. "Oh, come on, Zander."

She looked everywhere. The boat listed and danced, and at one point she was plastered against the starboard wall as it turned sharply. When she could stand upright again, Rae opened every locker, drawer, and cupboard but found no life vests. She tried under the benches and in the storage under the bed, but there was nothing.

"Well, that's reassuring," she said out loud.

She did find Jake the Snake in the middle of the bed, curled up and looking unhappy. If a snake could be seasick, he was.

Last night Rae had strongly objected to sharing her bed with a snake. Today, she felt sorry for it.

She leaned down and scooped him up, putting him carefully in the pocket of the jacket. Jake snuggled down, liking her warmth.

Rae climbed back out of the teetering cabin to the deck. The other boats were alarmingly close, their sirens blaring. A man's voice came over a bullhorn: "Cut your engine and stand down."

Zander paid no attention. Rae pulled herself into the pilot house and shut its door behind her.

Zander and Piotr stood together at the wheel, both studying a chart pulled up on a laptop. Outside the window, Ezra was hunkered in the bow, clinging to the rail as they climbed the waves.

"I couldn't find any life vests," Rae announced. "I hope you aren't planning on us swimming for it."

"That's okay," Zander said without looking around. "They're over there, under the benches."

Rae huffed out a breath. "Then why did you tell me to—"

"To take your mind off things," Zander said. "Did you find Jake?"

"Yes," Rae ground out. "He's fine."

"Good. I'll need him." Zander held out a broad arm in her direction.

Rae glared at his muscular forearm but Zander still didn't look at her. She dipped her hand into her pocket and pulled out the snake, who gazed around with interest.

Rae laid the snake onto Zander's outstretched arm and Jake coiled himself around it. Zander held Jake up to the front window. "Which way, my friend?"

Piotr gave Zander a look of concern from his light blue eyes. "You are leaving our safe passage up to a reptile?"

"Sure. Snakes have senses of smell that are beyond even that of Shifters. He knows what I'm looking for."

"Maybe he can find your whale friends," Rae said. She thumped to a bench as the boat gave an erratic leap.

Zander shot her a look. "Funny. Most of my marine mammal acquaintances, as a matter of fact, are seals. They like me because I'm a polar bear who doesn't eat them."

Rae clung to the bench. "Zander, has anyone ever told you you're crazy?"

"All the time. Anyone ever tell you you're beautiful?"

Rae's retort died on her lips. "No, actually," she said, so softly the words were drowned by the boat's straining engine.

Zander heard her. "Then they're idiots." He bent to Jake and moved his hand over the controls. "A few degrees left," he said to Piotr. "Then cut speed."

"Cut?" Piotr asked in alarm. "Those are not only police out there but Coast Guard. They have very big, powerful guns. I know this—they have picked me up before, thinking I am Russian spy or a smuggler. If we can't outrun, it is better to surrender."

"Not an option," Zander said. "Ezra and I are un-Collared Shifters, and Rae's illegally out of her Shiftertown. They'll cage us and do Goddess knows what to us. Rae's dad might be arrested for not keeping her home. We run."

"How do we run if we slow down?" Piotr demanded.

"We won't evade them with speed," Zander said. "We can't outrun boats made to chase smugglers. We'll evade them by stealth. We hide."

Rae pulled herself up as the engine ceased its roar and the boat slapped the waves. The craft wallowed, the seas high.

"Hide where?" Rae asked, staring out the windows. They'd come a long way from shore and there was nothing but open sea, with a smudge on the horizon that was Alaska. "There's nothing out here."

"You'd be amazed," Zander said.

He wouldn't say anything more as they crept along and the menacing boats zoomed closer.

Piotr gave a little moan as he looked behind them. "Oh, my wife is very much going to kill me."

Zander continued consulting with his snake. The man behind them blared over a bullhorn again. "We're coming alongside. Come outside and line up on the deck."

Zander's hand hovered over the controls as he peered straight ahead. Rae went to stand next to him. "You can't."

"Can't what?" Zander asked absently.

"Do what they say. Surrender to them."

Zander spared her a surprised glance. "Do you think I'm going to let them take you?" He returned his attention to the front windows, where Ezra hung on in the bow. "I'd never abandon you, Little Wolf. We're getting out of this."

Though Zander's words warmed her, Rae didn't see how they'd escape. The sea was empty before them and full of boats behind. Those boats were coming up fast and soon Zander's would be surrounded.

Zander whispered to his pet snake. "There? Yeah, I think you're right. You're very smart, you know that?"

Piotr exchanged a worried glance with Rae.

"Out on deck," the man boomed, his voice hard and authoritarian through the bullhorn. *"Now."*

"Or not," Zander said. He brought his hand down on a lever. The fishing boat roared to life and sprang forward.

At the same time there was a *boom* behind them and something very large charged past them to fall into the sea.

Rae, Piotr, and Ezra jerked around but Zander kept his eyes to the front. "They're shooting," Rae pointed out.

"Yep." Zander had one hand on the throttle, the other on the wheel. "Warning shots. They'll do a few of those before they shoot to kill."

"Well, that makes me feel better," Rae said shakily.

"It should. Means we have time to get there."

"Get where?"

"There." Zander nodded ahead of them.

At first Rae saw nothing, then she blinked. On the northern horizon, blending with the dusk that would soon be sunrise, was a patch of fog.

Small at first, it grew larger as their boat rushed at it. Rae had no idea what the fog hid or whether it was a stroke of luck that it happened to form at that moment. But no, Zander had been searching for it, so it must be a constant phenomenon. Rae wasn't familiar enough with oceans to know what it was a phenomenon of.

Piotr was staring at Zander, stricken. "Oh no, my friend. Not there."

"Oh, yes." Zander grinned at him. "There. Hold on—here we go."

He increased the speed to breakneck, the boat lifting and slamming into waves toward the fog. The hull groaned with the effort and Rae imagined that any second the boat would break apart and they'd plunge to their deaths.

Another *boom* came from behind them. A bullet like a miniature missile whistled past the cabin. Piotr went pale. "That is close."

"No longer matters," Zander said.

He cut the engine at the precise moment they hit the fog, plunging them into a world of opaque whiteness and silence.

CHAPTER THIRTEEN

Zander checked the instruments, including the sophisticated depth and proximity indicators he'd installed, and steered with confidence into the ghostly world.

"Where are we?" Rae whispered.

Ezra released his hold on the rail outside and sat up, looking around with a scowl. Beside Zander, Piotr said, "The Graveyard."

"That does not sound good." Rae's voice was subdued as she stood beside Zander.

Her hair smelled like flowers. Zander wanted to lean down and kiss it. He suppressed the wish and kept his eyes on the instruments, but it wasn't easy. Maybe he should send Rae below for a while so his frenzy wouldn't distract him. Not that he thought she'd obey and scuttle away because he asked.

Rae gazed bravely out the window, watching as Zander carefully piloted them around obstacles that couldn't be seen by eye in the fog.

"I've been in and out of here many times," Zander said, trying to sound reassuring. "And I'm still here."

Piotr's round face was pink. "But why do you come *back*

here? It is notorious, this place," he said to Rae. "Full of ship-wrecks, too-thick fogs . . . and fire."

"Don't worry," Zander said. "I haven't seen any volcanic activity in months."

"Months?" Rae repeated. "You really know how to make us feel better."

"I'm not trying to make you feel better—I'm trying to keep you from getting captured." Zander nudged the controls to go around a black rock that emerged rapidly from the fog.

The good thing about these waters was that they were deep. The bad thing was that pieces of islands jutted out unexpect-edly, and because of constant new lava and old erosion, pieces appeared where they hadn't been before.

Rae said, "You mean our choice is to float around here and hope we don't wreck or go back out into the clear water and to cages."

"You got it," Zander said.

Rae's chest rose sharply. Her gaze went to Jake, who'd uncoiled from Zander's arm and now rested on the windowsill. Rae reached over and lifted him, warming him in her hands. Jake already liked her.

Rae let out her breath. "Then I vote stay here."

"Piotr, you can get out here if you want," Zander said. Piotr was terrified, and with good reason. "I'll give you a radio and have you climb out onto the rocks. The Coast Guard will pick you up."

Piotr sent him a look of indignation. "Abandon my friends? Never. Besides, they'd wreck trying to get to me. I'd only be another skeleton left behind . . ."

"Cut the drama," Zander growled. "I've never seen any skeletons in this place. Not human ones anyway."

"That is because they all fall into the sea," Piotr said with a shudder. "Plenty of boat skeletons though."

Zander didn't answer because Piotr had a point. The first time he'd floated in here without meaning to it had scared the shit out of him. Only his Shifter senses of scent and hearing had saved him from becoming another wreck in the Graveyard. The sulfur odor here was strong but the subtle differences in it from place to place had let him find his way back out to daylight.

After that, he'd explored and researched, learning as much about the Graveyard as he possibly could. He'd started venturing in here deliberately, making the place his own.

"It's an island," he explained to Rae. "A very small one, right on the subduction zone. It's a remnant of what formed the Aleutian chain. Most people don't believe the Graveyard exists because it's remote, fogged over in the summer, and locked in ice in the winter. It was once a volcano, with a crater, hot vents, *and* a small glacier. People who try to explore it either can't find it or don't come back. It's become a legend. Fishermen have been telling scary stories about the ghost island for centuries."

"For good reason," Piotr said. "You have heard of the Bermuda Triangle in the Caribbean?" he asked Rae. "It is like that, only much worse."

"The Bermuda Triangle is a bunch of made-up stories about ships that wreck in bad weather," Zander said calmly. "The Graveyard is real."

Rae stood close enough that her body heat touched him. "And you think it's a good place to hide?"

"It is a *great* place to hide. The Coast Guard has decent instruments but even the best sailor will think twice about bringing millions of dollars' worth of boats into the Graveyard. We aren't worth catching."

"You hope, my friend," Piotr said darkly.

Rae said nothing, only peered into the fog.

Ezra rose to his feet and made his way quietly to the stern. He moved slowly and cautiously, making no noise. At the back deck, he stopped and peered behind them. Nothing moved but the waves; no breeze stirred the thick air.

"What do we do?" Rae asked.

"We wait," Zander said. "And I'll try not to run into anything."

The man in the patrol boat, which was surrounded by a sixty-five-foot cutter from the Coast Guard and another smaller boat of the harbor police, watched as the fishing vessel he pursued vanished before his eyes.

Carson McCade lowered his binoculars and retreated into the pilot house. "Where the hell did he go? Why are you stopping?"

Carson owned the boat, and the pilot, Miles Keegan, was an African American former Marine in his fifties. The man had reversed engines, effectively halting them.

"It's suicide to chase him in *there*," Miles said. "I didn't even know the place existed."

"In there where?" Carson fixed his steel blue gaze on the man. He'd learned in his fifteen years of first being a DEA agent and then a freelance bounty hunter that his stare could make people do things more effectively than shouting at them did. "Get this boat going."

Usually Miles would say "Sure thing" under Carson's glare but today he shook his head. "That's what they call the Graveyard. If he went in there, he's dead already."

Miles Keegan, his tattooed arms roped with muscle, his close-cropped beard going gray, wasn't afraid of anyone or anything. As Miles studied the smudge of fog before him, however, his face became stiff with fear.

"Have you sailed in there before?" Carson asked. He and Miles had been moving up and down the Alaskan coast for several years now, flushing out smugglers and traffickers of all kinds, and splitting the bounties. Carson had never seen nor heard of the Graveyard.

"Once," Miles admitted. "I kissed the ground when I got back to port."

"Why? What happened?"

"It's a spooky hellhole," Miles said, sweat on his brow. "And seriously risky. Rocks stick out of nowhere and the fog is too dense for visual navigation. Plus, there are fumaroles that burst out of nowhere and sometimes lava flows. That's why it's so steamy and stinky, even when the wind blows."

Carson peered ahead of them. "What are the chances they come out without running into anything?"

Miles shrugged. "Depends on the experience of the pilot. He headed straight in, so my guess is he thinks he can come out again."

Carson waited only thirty seconds before he made his

decision. In that time he weighed the pros and cons in the lightning fast way he always did.

"We go in," he said.

Miles gaped at him. "You've got to be kidding me."

"Those are Shifters," Carson said. "Dangerous and illegally running around. They've got one of those God-fearing refugee Russians with them, who probably knows these waters better than he knows English. We go after them."

"How about we sit here and wait for them to come out?" Miles said, making no move to obey.

"Is this the only way out?" Carson asked, studying the patch of fog. Not a bad idea to wait until they came blundering back into the light and catch them then.

Miles deflated. "No. You can navigate all the way through— it's more like a series of inlets instead of one harbor. I came out the other side. How, I don't know."

"Then we can't risk it. In we go. Radio the others; tell them to follow."

The radio crackled even as he spoke.

"What the hell are you doing?" came the Coast Guard captain's hard but high-pitched voice. She'd been happy to come chase Shifters with Carson but had gotten pissed off when he'd insisted on taking the lead.

Miles lifted the transmitter and held it out to Carson. "It's for you," he said.

Carson grabbed the mouthpiece. "We're going in there, ma'am. Tell Shifter Bureau to expect a delivery."

"Stand down, McCade. You're not going anywhere."

Carson respected the captain who was just doing her job, but he didn't work for her. He also didn't like to be told he couldn't go someplace he wanted to. "You can follow or not, ma'am. Your choice."

The captain made a noise of irritation and said several un-ladylike things about his appendages. "Wild goose chase, Carson. Good night."

Carson and Miles watched as the cutter veered away, making a quick turn to head back toward open water. The harbor police didn't even bother to radio. They simply followed the cutter, since they'd come out here at the Coast Guard's request to assist anyway.

"Might be easier prey down the coast," Miles suggested. "There's the rumor of heroin smugglers on the Canadian border. Easy pickings, probably."

Bounties on some smugglers were fairly high, plus Carson got a lot of satisfaction from taking down traffickers. The bastards deserved to be fish food.

Shifters, though. While they didn't sell drugs to rock stars, who really should do better things with their money, or hook kids on stuff for life, Shifters were dangerous. Carson knew exactly what happened when Shifters went into a fighting frenzy—the destruction, the death of innocents. The blood. Pain stabbed through him and fired up his anger.

Rounding them up and putting Collars on them was too tame for Carson but Carson obeyed the law. He'd take these animals to Shifter Bureau and collect the bounty. At least more of them would be kept under some control. Shifters needed to be found, Collared, stopped—whatever the cost.

The report tonight of two Shifters in the bar in Homer, one half changing into a nightmare beast, the other shifting fully into a polar bear, had caught Carson's attention. The cops in Homer and the county sheriff had ceased chasing them as soon as they'd leapt onto their boat and torn out of the harbor, but Carson, nearby and listening on his scanner, gave chase, his blood hot.

He'd alerted the Coast Guard that un-Collared Shifters were trying to escape and they'd agreed to send backup. Shifters were a recognized menace, a classified danger.

The Coast Guard captain, however, had been annoyed that they were after only a small fishing boat with a couple of Shifters on board, not an entire pack of them. She'd let Carson know how she felt about being dragged out of bed to pursue them with little hope of reward.

She might not get any reward except a pat on the back but Shifter bounties were high. If Carson took at least two Shifters, valued at fifty grand a piece, to Shifter Bureau, he'd have the money he needed to keep going. Not that he did this for the money alone or that a bounty could ever make up for what Shifters had done.

"Move over," Carson said. "I'll drive."

"Not my boat you don't." Miles, a large and fearsome Marine, looked shaken, but he eased the boat forward. Carson knew Miles hated the thought of anyone but himself piloting the vessel.

Carson felt no fear at all as Miles steered them to follow the Shifters into the fog.

A tense hour passed. Rae finally convinced herself to leave the pilot house and go down into the cabin to get some rest. She had to trust that Zander and Piotr would navigate through.

In the cabin, however, she only sat and worried. Ezra came in after a time, taking a seat at the table.

"All healers," he declared, "are out of their minds."

Rae's interest stirred. "How many have you met?"

"Just him." Ezra pointed overhead.

"He's trying to help," Rae said. "He felt terrible that he couldn't save your dad."

Ezra looked faintly surprised. "Dad was gone—I knew that. I just . . ." He scrubbed his face. "You get used to living with someone for a couple hundred years."

"I never knew my parents," Rae said. "I don't know who my dad was and my mother died . . . I've been told of bringing me in, but I'm not sure. I was alone in the woods when I was found. I don't really remember much about it."

Ezra's eyes narrowed. "You're a black wolf, right? They smell different from gray."

Rae nodded. "As far as I know. I mean, I don't know if I'm pure black wolf or my dad was gray or what."

"Black wolves are rare. Have you tried asking around in other Shiftertowns where they have black wolves?"

Rae widened her eyes in mock amazement. "Now, why didn't I think of that?" She eased back. "Sorry. I get touchy about my past. My dad is the Shiftertown leader and he asked around for years. But he couldn't find any other Lupines who knew me or knew about me."

Ezra gave her a look of sympathy. "That's tough. Being without a clan."

"What about you?" Rae asked. "Where are your clan?"

Ezra shook his head. "Most of them took the Collar. Dad and I held out. So did a few scattered around the state but we don't get together often. If we get out of this, I guess I'll go find one of them."

"Zander's not wrong about you looking for a mate," Rae said. "I have some unmated friends who might be interested . . ."

She let it hang. Ezra looked intrigued for a second then hid it. "Not Collared Shifters. I'm not giving up my freedom to satisfy my hormones. What clan are they?"

"They're not Lupine—they're Feline."

Ezra's sudden outrage was comical. "*Feline?* You'd have me mate-claim a *cat?*"

"Hey, my dad's a Feline and he's wonderful. My brothers too. Living in Shiftertown has taught me to appreciate that all Shifters are special in their own way, no matter what their species." Rae gave Ezra a teasing look. "Even though we know Lupines are the best."

"No," Zander rumbled from the doorway. "Bears are."

His words were bantering, his stance casual as he leaned on the doorframe, but Zander's rigid body shouted alertness, a Shifter in hunting mode.

Ezra came to his feet. "What's going on?"

Zander tapped the doorframe with broad fingers, dark eyes on Rae. "Depends. Do you want the good news or the bad news?"

CHAPTER FOURTEEN

Rae gazed at him with her wolf's eyes and Zander almost forgot what he was going to say. He'd love to see her smile at him as she'd done when they'd sparred with the swords, the smile lighting her eyes. Her eyes had been sweet half closed when he'd kissed her. He wanted to see that again too.

"What?" Ezra growled. "Just say it, bear."

"Good news—we haven't hit anything and we might make it through in one piece." Zander straightened up. "Bad news—one of the boats is following."

Rae rose, bringing the lapels of the jacket together to hide her Collar. She must do that a lot in her life, Zander thought, when she was outside Shiftertown.

"It's as dangerous for them to be in here as it is for us, right?" she asked tightly.

"If the pilot is as good a pilot as me, no. Or, yes. It's dangerous, period. But now Piotr and I have to both make it through and lose them."

"Then we'll surrender." Ezra stepped in front of Rae. "You and me, bear, we give ourselves up, and while they're preoccupied with us, the human can sail Rae to safety. She is Guardian and far more important than either of us."

Rae's small hands went to Ezra's arm to push him out of her way. "You can't do that. They'll execute you."

"Zander and I can attempt escape later," Ezra said. "But you must be free and safe."

Zander's respect for Ezra rose a notch. "That's noble of you, Lupine. But I have a better idea—we'll all take Rae to safety without surrendering. Much more fun."

"Not only her," Ezra said stubbornly. "But the sword. Humans can't get their hands on it."

"And they won't," Zander said. "It's up to you, Little Wolf. Do you want to run with Piotr while Ezra and I battle it out with the humans or stay and fight?"

"Stay and fight," Rae said at once. "We all go or we all stay."

Zander warmed. "Good for you, sweetheart. Not that Piotr would know how to take you out of here, anyway. You should probably stick with me."

"Or I could push you overboard," Rae said, straight-faced.

"I already did the overboard thing, remember?" Zander grinned. "Didn't slow me down much." He kept his voice light, hiding his concern. The boat following wasn't blundering about but coming on at a steady pace. Determined. The pilot just might be as good as Zander.

"Here's what we'll do," he went on. "I'm going to try to elude him in the fog. I know a place to hide. The lifeboat is ready though, in case. If we have to split up, you'll go with Piotr, Rae, who's a better sailor than he realizes. You didn't show your Shifter self at the bar and no one's seen you around before, so they probably think you're human. If it comes to it, Piotr and you can leave in the lifeboat, be picked up in open water. From there Piotr will see you safely home to Montana."

Zander expected Rae to nod, to say his plan was best, that she'd willingly go home to safety.

Rae only met his gaze with a steady one. "I *am* Shifter and I'm not running out on you. The three of us can take whoever's on the boat behind us—it must be small to come in after us, which means not many crew. We overpower them if we have to."

Zander tried to stare her into submission, but she folded her arms and looked stubborn. Rae had courage, that was true, and she'd already proved she could fight. But if she kept her head down, hid her Collar, and acted human, she had a much better chance of coming out of this alive.

Eoin would hunt Zander down and disembowel him if Zander brought any harm to his foster daughter. He'd seen that in the man's eyes.

"We'll play it by ear, Little Wolf," Zander said. "Now, we have to go silent, so pick a place to sit and don't move."

Both Rae and Ezra, instead of staying meekly in the cabin, followed Zander back up to the pilot house, Rae snatching up the sword in its sheath on the way.

Silent running meant no engine, no lights, sitting still, and making no noise at all. Sound carried across water, especially in fog. Submarines went quiet to escape sonar, to appear to be simply another rock on the ocean floor.

Zander didn't know what kind of navigation instruments the other boat had—no matter what, they needed to blend into the darkness, become a part of the island and the wreckage Zander would steer them to. At the same time, he had to keep the drifting boat on course, or they would *be* wreckage.

Rae took a seat on the bench near Zander's chair, and Ezra took the other bench, near the door. Piotr stood at Zander's side, his usually ruddy face pale.

Zander guided the boat into the hiding place he'd chosen. This particular spot had been, he supposed, what had given the island its name of "Graveyard." They glided past the upturned stern of a ship rusted with water and time. Another hull rose on their right, the bottom of the ship sticking out among the rocks. Bright green weed, the kind that liked volcanic rock and ash, had enjoyed itself on the ship's metal.

A sharp crease of rock reared in front of them. Zander steered around it and nestled himself in beside another sunken boat, its bow up, the rest of it underwater.

At Zander's signal, Piotr cut the engine and the rest of the power. Now they were a piece of driftwood, floating among a craggy pile of rock and dead ships.

The boat creaked and water softly lapped at the hull. Zander kept his hand on the wheel, ready to adjust their position as needed.

His Shifter senses heightened as he peered into the blank fog. He could hear everything in sharp clarity, from the noise of the boat searching for them to Rae's soft breathing beside him. He smelled the brimstone scent of the fog, the crisp bite of the volcanic rock, the soft scent of Rae.

He also, with the unnerving ability his healing gift brought him, sensed the dead.

His healing power, as far as Zander had figured out, was part empathic. Far more to it than that, he knew—he'd met a Shifter empath called Seamus, but that Shifter had no healing abilities like Zander did. He'd also met a half-Fae half-Shifter—Andrea, mate of the Austin Shiftertown's Guardian—who had pretty good healing ability but still not what Zander could do. Andrea's magic came from her Fae ancestry, while Zander was pure Shifter. His gift came from Goddess magic alone.

All that boiled inside him and made him keenly aware of exactly how many people had perished in these boats, running blind and far from help. The fact that they were all human made no difference. Zander saw in his mind the position of every single one of them, lying forgotten and lost.

The knowledge clenched around him like a fist, squeezing until he couldn't breathe. The fear, pain, and the bravery with which these people had faced their last moments cried into his brain and wouldn't leave him. Zander's eyes clouded and his hand slipped on the wheel.

A soft touch broke through the whirling mess. Rae had risen silently and now stood against him where he sat in the captain's chair. Her thigh pressed his, and she closed her fingers around his hand.

Rae didn't speak, she only looked into Zander's eyes, but her touch and gaze sent her message to him clearly.

It's all right. I'm with you.

Or maybe that was what Zander wanted her to say. He understood that she, a Guardian, felt the death too.

Ghosts didn't exist, no matter what all those people on

television who tracked them believed. Auras lingered, it was true, grief and violence leaving its mark.

No matter, Rae's touch eased the clamor in Zander's head, and he readjusted the boat against their drift.

Now to wait. They had only to sit here until those on the other craft grew tired of looking for them. Zander was pretty sure their fears would win over their need to capture a couple of Shifters, and they'd turn around, getting out while they could. Not long now . . .

Bright light blazed abruptly into the ship boneyard, lighting up the fog. Water droplets glittered around the boat and on the black rocks that jutted into the sea. The dead in the ships seemed to whisper and stir.

A man's voice, calm and detached, spoke through a loudspeaker. "Surrender to me or I will blow everything in my path out of the water."

Ezra got to his feet, silence moot. "Who *is* this guy?"

Good question. Zander squeezed Rae's hand and rose. "I'll talk to him. Piotr." He gave his friend a nod. Piotr understood— Rae's safety was his priority.

Piotr and Ezra were peering into the light, trying to see, both of them unnerved. Zander rummaged in a cupboard, brought out a bullhorn, hoped it worked, and stepped out on deck.

He clicked it on. "What do you want?" he asked, contriving to make his voice shaky and elderly sounding. "We were only trying to bring in a catch."

Silence. The boat's floodlight was so strong Zander could see nothing behind it. The comforting thought was that the fog was so thick that, in spite of the light, the other guy probably couldn't see him either.

Zander heard another click. Not a bullhorn, he realized too late.

A small missile came out of the fog, right at him. Zander tried to duck but it hit him and sank deep into his side.

Not a bullet, a tranq dart. The man had shot, probably using a rifle with a heat scope. No visual necessary.

"You bastard," Zander managed to say before the deck rushed up at him and he fell like a sack of wet cement.

* * *

Ezra tried to push Rae toward the lifeboats. "Piotr, take her."
     "No way in hell!" Rae yelled.

She twisted from him and ran to where Zander lay face down on the deck, a tranquilizer dart in his side. Rae yanked out the dart and quickly tossed it overboard.

"Is he mad?" Piotr peered into the fog as the second boat loomed. "He will ram us and both boats will go down."

"Help me." Rae tugged at Zander's weight. "We'll go in the life raft. Hurry."

Another shot, this one from a gun with bullets. Rae squealed and dropped flat, Ezra and Piotr slamming themselves down as well.

Piotr crawled on his belly over to Rae. "Yes, we will go in the raft. We will be more maneuverable and can escape."

"Escape to what?" Ezra snapped in an irritated whisper. "Straight into the arms of the Coast Guard?"

"You have better idea?" Piotr asked.

"No," Ezra grumbled. "Let's get him over there."

The boat rocked sharply, bumped by the other craft. The other boat was so well guided that the two vessels only lightly touched, the second boat gliding a few feet back after the tap.

A man stood in the bow with a large rifle with a scope, which he pointed at Ezra. "You're under arrest, Shifter," he said, his voice cold and clear.

"Leave them alone," Rae shouted at him. "They're not hurting anyone."

"They're rogue Shifters," the man replied. "Illegal and dangerous. Step away from them and you won't get hurt."

He made a curt signal behind him. Two other men came forward on the foggy deck, also carrying weapons.

There had to be someone manning the tiller—so much for outnumbering the crew. With Zander out and the men having guns, Rae and Ezra going Shifter and fighting might only get them all, including Piotr, killed.

"What do you want to do?" Piotr whispered to Rae.

Rae thought rapidly. If they could get over to the other boat, see how many they were up against, and maybe disable whoever they were, they might be able to take over that boat and sail it out. Once Zander woke up, their odds would be even better of surviving. Then they'd have to figure out what to do with whoever they captured and get away somewhere in the world where they wouldn't be found and arrested.

Sure. Easy. Rae wasn't a military strategist. She was a Shifter Lupine, whose most difficult decision up until the Choosing was whether she'd go to a Shifter bar with her girl-friends or out camping with her brothers.

Now she was a Guardian, being chased by Shifter hunters in the middle of a weird island, in a part of the world she didn't know. Both Ezra and Piotr were looking at *her*, waiting for her decision.

Ezra wasn't dominant, the realization hit Rae with a bang. Rae was Guardian—no longer bottom of the pack. She was now in that ambiguous place just below leader, like Daragh had been.

What would Daragh do?

Rae had no idea. She had the feeling Daragh wouldn't have put himself into this situation in the first place. Rae had no idea what her father would do either . . .

Not true. Eoin would sacrifice himself so the others could get away and then work to escape on his own. But that didn't seem to be an option here.

What would Zander do?

That answer came a bit more readily.

Rae screamed like a frightened cub and flung her hands in the air. "Please don't shoot me!" she cried. "I had to do what they said."

She sank to her knees, her back to the other boat, bowing her head and trying to look as submissive as possible. She felt Ezra's glare and hoped like hell he'd catch on.

While her body shielded what she did, Rae quickly removed the top half of the sword and tucked it inside her jacket, then folded the leather sheath over the bottom half and tucked it into the other side of the jacket. She'd borrowed the jacket from Zander, so it was huge and easily accommodated the pieces. Or maybe the pieces wanted her to hide them.

She zipped up and looked behind her, still acting fearful, which wasn't entirely an act.

The leader on the boat made another signal to his men. "Take them. Put the girl inside, the Russian below."

His two men moved to the rail. The two boats drifted closer together but the pilot must be talented, because the hulls didn't touch.

The men leapt easily from their deck to Zander's. One man pointed his gun at Ezra's head, the other gestured Piotr and Rae to move ahead of him to the other boat.

Rae deliberately didn't look back at Zander as she went, but fear gnawed her. If they dropped him overboard in his tranqued state, he'd drown.

The leader held out a hand to help Rae over the gunwale. His fingers were strong and callused, stronger than she thought a human's would be. He had buzzed black hair and blue eyes with no warmth in them whatsoever.

Rae's jacket was zipped all the way up, her Collar hidden, but she ducked her head, still playing submissive, in case a gleam of Collar betrayed her.

The man didn't help Piotr, but Piotr, at home on boats, stepped onto the other vessel without losing his balance.

The leader wrapped steely fingers around Rae's arm and marched her toward the pilot house, whose door opened onto the side deck. This boat was a little bigger than Zander's, though Rae didn't know enough about boats to guess how large it was. It was longer and wider, was all she could tell, and had no stands for fishing poles.

She did see that this boat didn't belong to the police or the Coast Guard. There were no official logos or symbols anywhere, which meant this man wasn't connected to any law enforcement agency. He was a vigilante, she guessed, or a bounty hunter, which made him potentially more dangerous than the police or even Shifter Bureau.

The men and women who hunted Shifters for bounty, or just for the hell of it, didn't follow any rules but their own. If the hunted died before they could be brought in . . . oh well.

The leader pushed Rae through the door to the pilot house. The dank coolness of the fog was cut off as he closed the door behind her, leaving her in a small stuffy room, poorly lit, smelling strongly of diesel and sulfur, which messed up her scenting ability.

The large man at the boat's wheel didn't even glance her way, so intent was he on holding the boat steady. Rae noted immediately that he had a gun in a holster at his right hip.

The pilot was large but not portly—muscles filled out his body, his bare arms tight and sporting tattoos of interlocked spirals. He had black skin, close-cropped black hair tinged with gray, and more gray in the whiskers trimmed against his face. His face itself was square-jawed, his dark eyes shrewd but not cruel. This man's hardness was different from that of the leader—the pilot was honed from fighting, but he probably relaxed with friends after the fighting was over. Rae didn't think the man outside ever relaxed.

"Did those Shifters kidnap you?" the pilot asked.

Rae nodded meekly. It was warm enough in here that she wished she could unzip the coat but she couldn't with the sword and her Collar hidden inside. She folded her arms and lived with it.

"Well, you're safe now," the pilot said. "Sit down over there." He pointed to a bench built into the wall. "We'll get you home."

He returned to peering nervously out at the fog and the wrecked boats too near them, his hands never leaving the wheel.

"Who are you?" Rae asked, curiosity working through her fear.

He didn't look at her. "Name's Miles. You all right?"

"Yes. Thanks."

Rae craned to look past him. Ezra and Piotr were nowhere in sight—they must have been taken belowdecks already. The two flunkies were again on Zander's boat, lifting Zander's limp body between them. Zander hung lifelessly, big and heavy, but the two men managed to carry him across to this craft without dropping him.

"Put them in the cages," she heard the leader outside say. "Lock the doors tight and make sure the shock chains are secured around them."

CHAPTER FIFTEEN

Rae swallowed. "Does he have a cage strong enough for Shifters?" she asked the pilot in a timid voice.

"Yeah. Don't you worry, ma'am." Miles sounded as though he wasn't used to reassuring people. He didn't know what to say, and he was more concerned with keeping the vessel afloat.

"Who is he?" Rae asked.

"Who is who?" Miles adjusted the wheel the slightest bit. "Oh, you mean Carson. Carson McCade. This is his boat."

"You work for him?"

The big man shrugged. "I work *with* him. I get my cut. But don't worry about the Shifters anymore. They'll be taken where they won't hurt anyone ever again."

Rae thought about tranquilizers. The ones for Shifters were powerful and lasted a long time—Eoin occasionally had to use them to stop fights from getting out of hand. But there were Shifters, and then there were Shifters. Zander was bigger than most, being a bear, and a polar bear at that.

Rae had heard of a Shifter in Texas, a tiger, who had to be shot with several rounds of tranqs before he'd even get sleepy.

That Shifter was a little different from the others—he'd apparently been born in a lab, the result of experiments. Even so, Zander had gone down a bit too quickly.

Rae also thought about cages. Ones for Shifters had to be specially reinforced because Shifters could kick their way out of anything. Shifter Bureau had cages laced with the same kind of chains as the Collars, to shock if the Shifter tried to break out. Carson's words to his men told Rae he had cages on board specifically designed for Shifters and that Zander was being locked into one.

With all that in mind, Rae calculated how long it would take Zander to get out of his cage and up on deck.

Possibly not long. He'd need help though.

Exactly how she'd overpower Miles, who was large, strong, and armed, and take over the wheelhouse, Rae had no idea. Before she could start thinking about what to do the man called Carson yanked open the door and strode inside.

"Let's get this thing turned around," he snapped at Miles.

"Easy for you to say." Miles moved controls. The boat jumped a little then began to move smoothly backward.

Carson opened a cabinet, removed the scope from his rifle, and carefully tucked the rifle and scope inside. He locked the cabinet with a key and slid the key into his pocket.

He studied Rae a moment or two with his unnerving eyes, then moved to her. He, like Miles, wore a pistol in a holster.

"What's your name?" Carson asked her.

"Rae." Easier not to lie.

"What were you doing to get yourself nabbed by Shifters, Rae? You from Homer?"

"No." Again, she had the feeling he'd easily spot a lie. "I was there visiting. I went to the bar." Rae shrugged. "There was a fight and I got taken off with them." Plausible and very close to what had happened.

Carson's eyes narrowed. They were lake blue, but that lake never had any sun on it.

Carson suddenly reached out, grabbed the zipper of her jacket, and yanked it down. Rae squeaked and ducked her head, praying her shirt still hid the Collar.

Carson was after something else. "You've got a weapon in there. What is that?" His hand went unerringly to the sword's hilt and he yanked out the top half of the sword.

Rae had the presence of mind to shake her head. "I don't know. It's broken but it looked interesting."

Carson studied the sword, bringing it close to his eyes to examine the silver, the runes. Rae was surprised he could hold it, but maybe it was different for humans, who seemed immune to Fae magic.

"You stole this from them?" Carson demanded.

A more difficult question. Rae wet her lips. "No one seemed to want it. It's broken—it can't be worth much."

"It's silver." Carson examined it again. "But the edge is sharp like steel. Weird."

He backed away with it, opened another cabinet, and tucked it inside. "It'll stay safe in there," he said, locking the cabinet with a key.

"You'll give it back to me, won't you?" Rae asked, her worry not feigned. "I mean, I should get something for my trouble."

Carson only gave her a look of faint disgust. "Yeah, you'll get it back."

He'd concluded she was a Shifter groupie, Rae saw. He thought she was a groupie hanging out with Zander and Ezra, who'd gotten more than she'd bargained for when they'd gone wild in the bar fight, and who'd stolen from them when they'd been caught.

Fine with Rae. The man could despise her all he wanted, as long as her plan worked out. She didn't really care what her captors thought of her.

Carson studied her a few moments more, his gaze full of distrust, before he turned back to Miles.

"Head for Anchorage. We'll transfer them there."

Transfer them to what?

Miles didn't answer. He was too busy playing with controls and looking nervously around him. Carson eyed him as sharply as he'd eyed Rae, then he turned and left the wheelhouse.

"I do not like this," Miles said.

The fog outside had thickened. As the boat backed, a

fumarole, or whatever it was called, in the rocks beside them vented a sudden shaft of steam.

Miles jerked the vessel away, but Rae yelled, "Look out!" as a black cliff loomed up on their other side.

"Shit, shit, shit." Miles cranked the wheel and pulled levers. The rock drifted past the bow, inches from the hull.

Rae left her seat and went to the wheel. Miles was sweating, droplets welling on his forehead and trickling down his temples, but he held the boat steady.

As Rae peered out the windows, alert for more obstacles, she noticed what the thick smell of diesel and sulfur had masked. She sucked in a startled breath and looked up at Miles.

Miles snapped his attention from the instruments to her, his eyes widening. If his scent had come to her, so hers had gone to him.

"Aw, damn it." Miles moved one hand from the wheel and grabbed at the neckline of her shirt.

Rae tried to twist away, but too late. Miles yanked her shirt open at the neck, revealing the glint of her Collar.

"You're one of them," Miles said, hand still on her shirt. "Man, oh man, oh man."

Rae jerked from his grasp. "You should talk. You're one of them too."

"What?" Sweat trickled faster as Miles returned to steering the boat. "What are you talking about?"

Did he really think Rae wouldn't know? "You're Shifter." Rae stepped closer and inhaled. "Maybe not full blood. But you're definitely Shifter."

Miles leaned to her, a sudden growl in his throat. "You keep that to yourself. Promise me, or I'll tranq you myself, I swear."

Rae growled right back at him. "What are you doing hunting Shifters and letting them be put in cages? How can you justify that?"

Miles's mouth tightened. "I justify it when I see Shifters tearing up a town and leaving people dead. I justify it when they nearly kill the wife of a good man, turning him half crazy."

Rae's lips parted. "Shifters don't do that."

Miles snorted a laugh. "You don't know what you're talking about, sugar. Shifters *do* do that. I've watched them. You get the rogue ones who escaped the rounding up and they let their frenzy or whatever they call it take over. I've seen it with my own eyes."

"Are you sure they were Shifter?" Rae asked, though with less confidence.

Miles's eyes became as hard as Carson's. "Yeah, I'm sure. I saw them shift, become wolves, and go after people. Very, very sure."

Rae fell silent. Some Shifters claimed that Shifters who didn't take the Collar, with nothing to restrain them, slowly went feral. Maybe it was genetics, the argument went, maybe Shifters were simply changing, finding it difficult to adjust to the modern world. In theory, those who hadn't taken the Collar would succumb to the gradual deterioration of their sanity.

But the Collared Shifter leaders, like Eoin, had begun concluding that the feral tendencies were rarer than they'd thought. Collars were being removed from Shifters gradually, in secret, and the Shifters who'd had their Collars off were fine so far.

Now Miles, a part Shifter, was telling her there were violent, un-Collared Shifters still out there.

"My friends aren't the Shifters you saw," Rae said. "Zander and Ezra are not feral or violent. Nothing wrong with them."

Miles's lips thinned. "They're un-Collared. They have the potential to go feral." He steered them around another rock, the fog brushing the windows. "What about you? Why are you with them?"

Rae wasn't about to tell him. "Long story. What about you? What kind of Shifter are you?"

He looked sideways at her. "Fox."

Rae blinked. "No, you're not. There's no such thing as a fox Shifter."

"Beg to differ," Miles said. "Gray fox. My mother was Shifter, my father human. My father, who was a Marine, died a couple years ago. My mom left after that. Kind of disappeared. She gets in touch once in a while."

Now Rae stared in shock. "She abandoned her cub?"

"Cub?" Miles shot a surprised glance at her. "You mean me? I'm fifty-two. I think I can take care of myself by now."

"That's no age for a Shifter," Rae said. "Shifters shouldn't leave each other. We're close. Family is everything."

Not that Rae had ever known hers. Rage shook her at the

thought of a mother deliberately abandoning her cub. Her own mother had tried to stay with Rae until her dying breath, so Eoin had told her. A mother walking away from her family made her seriously angry.

"Can you get us out of this place?" she asked Miles impatiently.

Miles twitched his fingers on the wheel. The boat was moving dead slow, the white fog pressing around them. Rae could no longer see the outline of Zander's fishing boat.

"Probably not," Miles said. "I told Carson that when we came in here. The gasses are messing with my sense of smell."

"Mine too. Bring Zander up here. He'll know how to navigate through."

Miles shook his head. "Don't think so. Too dangerous. The big man stays in a cage until we get to Shifter Bureau in Anchorage."

"We won't make it anywhere near Shifter Bureau if we are stuck in here," Rae pointed out.

Miles hesitated. Rae read that he knew the truth of her words but he was afraid of Zander. Or maybe he was afraid of Carson, his cold-eyed partner.

"Damn it," Miles whispered. He picked up a handheld radio and let it crackle to life. Rae almost dove for it, worried he was about to betray her, when he said, "Carson, get that Russian up here. He needs to help me."

A few seconds of silence, then a crackle in return. "Copy that."

Miles went back to trying to pilot the boat. Looking at him now, Rae saw the Shifter in him—his movements were almost graceful as he danced his fingers over the controls, his balance perfect.

A fox? Rae had never heard of such a thing. How such a large man morphed into something as small and delicate as a fox . . . She was going to have to see it to believe it.

The door swung open, letting in chill air, fog, smell, and the rumble of engines. Carson, his pistol out, marched Piotr inside, his hand full of the back of Piotr's flannel jacket.

"By the way," Piotr was saying. "I'm an American citizen."

"You're harboring Shifters," Carson said with curt derision. "Which makes you a criminal."

So, *he* was in as sweet a mood as ever.

Piotr shot Rae a glance. She gave him a nod to show she was all right.

Carson shoved Piotr toward Miles. Rae stepped out of the way, trying to fade into the background. She'd learned to be good at that in a houseful of alpha males. Not that Rae had been exactly submissive to them—she'd simply stood back and watched them bluster, then slid around them to do exactly what she wanted.

Carson seemed to have the failing of many human men in believing that females were weaker and less intelligent than males. Shifters rarely shared that idiocy . . . well, except when it came to who could be Guardians.

Carson paid little attention to Rae. As she stood back, she studied the controls and the readouts on Miles's computer. She didn't know what all the lines and squiggles meant but she was sure the solid clumps of red were bad.

"You think *I* can navigate out of the Graveyard?" Piotr was saying, spluttering. "I cannot work miracles."

"Do it," Carson said. "If we go down, you go down with us."

"Oh, hey, no pressure on me," Piotr said.

He bent over the controls with Miles. Miles gave a nervous sideways look at Rae, as though fearing she'd blurt to Carson that he was part Shifter. But Rae would keep his secret. To paraphrase what Carson had just said—if Miles went down, she went down too.

"What is *that*?" Miles asked sharply.

He pointed to something that blipped on the computer screen. At the same time, Rae heard a curious popping sound even over the rumble of engines.

Piotr jerked his head up. "Hard about! Hard about! *Now!*"

Miles, understanding Piotr's alarm, cranked the wheel. The boat listed hard to port as he turned away from the wall of ice that had been running parallel to them. As they rushed into denser, yellower fog, an immense chunk of white and black mountain descended vertically into the sea.

The impact sent a huge wave across the water, shoving the boat sideways. Rae watched black water rise through the fog and blot out all view from the port windows. They were going to turn over—she knew it.

She rushed at Carson. "Get Zander and Ezra. Let them out. They'll die!"

The lurching boat had Rae ramming straight into him. Carson grabbed Rae's shoulders to right her, but not before Rae's hand landed on the man's large bunch of keys. She yanked them free and was heading out the door before Carson's shout left his mouth.

"Stop her!"

Wherever Carson's men were, there was no sight of them on deck. The deck was almost perpendicular anyway, but the gunwale was still above water, if barely. The men were probably staying put below or maybe already in the lifeboat.

Rae clung to railings and ropes on the cabin's outside walls, there for just this reason, and hauled herself to the stern door. It opened easily, letting her into a narrow hallway that stank of diesel and brine.

The doors along the pitching corridor weren't locked, showing her an office, and a couple of bedrooms, one painfully neat, the other a bit more cluttered. No Shifters, not even a sign of them.

They must be on a deck below this one, though Rae wasn't sure how to get there. She refused to listen to the anguish in her heart that maybe they'd simply thrown Ezra and Zander over the side.

A door with ventilation slats at the end of the hall was locked. Rae took up the keys she'd stolen, trying to still her shaking hands as she chose a likely one and slid it into the lock.

The key fit but wouldn't turn. She jerked it out, marked its place on the ring with her thumb, and went to the next one. This one wouldn't even go in. Next one again fit but wouldn't turn.

"Come on," she breathed. She'd have to change to her in-between beast and rip the door out of the wall. No time for anything else.

The next key fit. Rae turned it and opened the door.

Two men came rushing up the stairs beyond the door, weapons drawn. At the same time Carson burst into the hallway behind her. Rae was caught—no way around them. Carson drew his pistol and aimed it at Rae, right between her eyes.

CHAPTER SIXTEEN

Rae felt her wolf come. No way it couldn't. Her Collar sparked once under her jacket, the tearing pain making her yelp.

Carson looked past Rae to his men. "Bring the big Shifter to the wheelhouse. We need him."

The two guards looked momentarily surprised but pasted on hard expressions and disappeared back down the stairs. The distraction gave Rae the chance to clamp down on her shift and remain human, quieting her Collar.

"You," Carson said, still eyeing Rae over his pistol. "Come away from there and give me back my keys."

Rae clenched her hands and didn't move. "I will when I see Zander safe."

"Your loyalty is admirable. But they're *Shifters*. They'll use you and abandon you."

"Because you know so much about Shifters," Rae returned.

Carson's voice was like ice. "They're born wild beasts and that's how they stay, no matter that they can show us a human form. They trick you with honeyed words, and then kill."

Rae raised her brows. "Had a bad experience, did you?"

"You could say that," Carson said. "Shifters killed my

family. Brutally slaughtered them before my eyes. Now tell me how they're furry little animals we all should understand. And while you're doing it, *get over here*."

Rae's mouth hung open. Carson's bone-cold eyes told her he wasn't lying about the killing. Rae wished she could hotly deny that a Shifter would do such a thing, but she knew that Un-Collared Shifters and feral Shifters—any Shifter with enough anger, really—were capable of savagery. She only hoped that someone had caught the Shifters that had done such a terrible thing.

Zander's grumbling voice came up the stairs behind her and she swung around. Zander had chains around his hands and was led by one guard and followed by the second. He had to brace himself on the wall as the stairwell listed.

"What the hell did you do to this boat?" he growled at Carson. "I was enjoying my nap. Couldn't you keep it upright for at least another hour?"

Zander reached the top of the stairs. Rae's face was stark white as she stood in the middle of the hallway and Carson's glittered eyes above his pistol behind her.

"Excuse us, sweetheart," Zander said to Rae. "We need to get by."

The steel chains that bound his wrists had a bite of Fae magic in them—this Carson guy knew what he was doing. The cage Zander had just been let out of had been woven with Fae spells as well, which ensured Zander couldn't break out of it with strength alone.

The first guard wanted Rae to go out ahead of them but Zander kept moving along, forcing the guard to push past Rae. This put the guard between Rae and Carson's gun, which was what Zander wanted.

As Zander brushed against her, his tense body relaxed. Her touch, even this brief one, soothed his hurts.

He'd gotten Rae into this adventure, the kind Zander ran into all the time in his interesting life, and he'd get her out again. If he'd been alone, he wouldn't worry—he'd simply wait to see what happened. But the need to protect Rae rose up and defeated all other concerns.

He sent her a wink as he passed, to let her know that all was well. Zander's reward was a quick scowl. He wanted to laugh.

The lead guard quickened his pace and the one behind Zander prodded him to move. The guy behind him was hefty and had a gun but Zander knew that even chained he could easily break the guy's neck. He decided to let him live and followed the first guard to the open door to the deck.

"Come on, Rae," Zander said over his shoulder. "Let's see what fun we can have."

He stepped into a world of strangeness. The fog had become tinted yellow, both from the fumaroles jetting out from the black cliffs and from the rising sun. Fog swallowed the bow and stern of the boat, ensuring that Zander couldn't see past the gunwale a few feet next to him. But he could hear.

He'd heard the glacier calving into the water and knew that Piotr had gotten them turned aside in time. Another roar from the same direction told him more ice had fallen from cliffs into the sea. Those chunks of ice would sink and then pop up again, possibly right under their boat.

Zander also heard a rumble he didn't like. The beautiful scenery of the Alaska Peninsula had been formed by volcanoes that were far from dead—eruptions happened, and so did plenty of earthquakes. He'd read a statistic that Alaska had more earthquakes per year than the rest of North America combined. He believed it.

They were sailing blind. The boat had righted somewhat, as Piotr or Carson's pilot steadied it, but they were pivoting in a circle, going nowhere.

Carson opened the door to the wheelhouse and stood back so the two guards could crowd Zander inside. Where they thought Zander was going to run to, he didn't know.

Carson pointed his pistol at Zander. "Right the boat and show them how to steer us out of here."

Zander glanced at the gun. "Because threatening to shoot me is going to reassure me. Maybe I'll tell you I won't help until you put all the firearms away."

Carson wasn't impressed with that. "I will shoot the Russian and then the other Shifter," he said, "until you cooperate."

Nothing about Rae. Hmm. Zander rolled his eyes. "Whatever. Piotr, what have you gotten us into? Nice save on the glacier, by the way."

Piotr gave him a shaky look. "It is no problem."

Zander motioned with his bound hands for Piotr to move so he could get close to the controls. He turned his head and looked into the eyes of the tall black man who kept one hand on the wheel. The man stared back at him steadily but his dark eyes flickered with unease.

Zander held his gaze a moment. "Seriously?" he asked, then shook his head. He'd talk with him about being part Shifter later. "Where are we?"

The pilot, *Miles* he'd heard the guards refer to him as, pointed a blunt finger at the chart on the computer. "There. I think."

"Oh good," Zander said. "We sort of know where we are. Rae, sweetie. Make someone bring me a cup of coffee. Waking up from a tranq always gives me parchment mouth."

"You wake up from tranqs often?" Rae asked, her voice calm.

She was wonderful. No crying or yelling or breaking down in panic. "More than I'd care to," Zander said. "I take it straight up, no milk or sugar, or cinnamon, whipped cream, chocolate, or all the other crap people put in coffee these days. Though a shot of vodka wouldn't go amiss."

Zander studied the readouts as Rae said quietly to one of the guards, "Will you please get him some coffee?"

He heard Carson grant assent and a guard walk out, closing the door behind him.

Zander had never piloted a boat like this. It was bigger than he was used to, longer and broader at the same time. The controls were different, but thank the Goddess he was a quick study. Piotr was better at this than Zander—the man could drive almost anything—but Zander's instincts were Shifter, and he had the feeling he would need every single instinct he possessed to take them out of here. He'd love it if Rae could lift Jake out of her pocket to help, but it was probably safer for the poor guy if she didn't.

"Starboard, five degrees," Zander said to the pilot. "Where is that crag—the one that looks like a diving cat? There it is.

What are we doing all the way over here? You two were going to run us aground in about five minutes."

Piotr took this admonishment without a qualm. "Then we have five minutes to spare." He looked into Zander's face as though to ask, *You okay?*

Zander gave him a nod. The tranq hadn't been that strong.

Miles kept his hands on the controls. What the hell was *he* doing working with a guy like Carson? There was a story there that Zander wanted to know.

"Dead straight," Zander told him. "No, *don't turn.*"

A wall had risen in front of them but Zander had encountered this before—in this particular area sunlight glittering on the droplets in the fog made it look solid.

Miles had already jerked the boat. Not good. Zander shot his bound hands out and grabbed the wheel.

"Everyone hang on to something!" he yelled.

Zander cranked them hard to starboard. The remaining guard lost his balance, stumbling, and landed on the floor. Carson kept to his feet, scowling. Rae, sensibly, sat down.

"I could do this better with my hands free," Zander said. The boat leapt under him, the large thing too ponderous for this tight space. Why the hell had they risked bringing it into the Graveyard?

"No," Carson said in a hard voice. He alone remained steady, his pistol unwavering.

"You want me to get us out of here or not?" Zander lifted his chained wrists toward Miles. "Can you open these?"

Miles instantly backpedaled and Zander grinned at him. Miles would feel the bite of Fae magic in the chains but it would never do for Carson to find that out.

"I don't have the key," Miles said breathlessly.

Zander offered his wrists to the rest of the room. "Anyone?"

"Zander!" Rae said in alarm.

The boat had shot through the curtain of glittering, icy fog, but now they headed straight for a black protrusion of land. Zander glanced at it, calculating how much time before they rammed it.

"Take these off and I'll get us out of here safely," he said to

Carson. "If not . . ." He glanced at the swiftly approaching rock and shrugged.

Carson didn't move, pistol held in a professional grip. "Do your best, Shifter."

At that moment a brilliant light flashed outside, followed by a clap of thunder. Zander laughed.

"Oh, good. A rainstorm. Might clear up the fog." Zander shrugged again. "Or it might make it worse."

Another flash lit up the cabin, with another burst of thunder almost on top of it. The lights in the wheelhouse sputtered and then all the controls suddenly went dead.

Piotr cried out in alarm. Both he and Miles grabbed the wheel, which, if they were lucky, mechanically controlled the tiller and didn't need power to steer it. The boat listed to the right and Zander staggered.

"Hurry up," he growled at Carson. "You either trust me or we're all dead."

"After you've sabotaged my ship?" Carson said, his blue eyes like pieces of ice.

"*Sabotage?* When did I have the time? I've been chained up and locked in a cage. I can't control the weather. That's up to the Goddess and her friends."

Carson's eyes narrowed but there was some intelligence behind his obsession. He had to concede that Zander couldn't possibly have organized a thunderstorm or for the controls to go down.

Carson dropped his hand to his belt, then rage flushed his face as he realized he'd never retrieved his keys from Rae.

His brief distraction gave Zander his chance. Zander shoved his wrists at Miles, touching the chains to the man's face. Miles let out a scream and scrambled away from him.

Carson reacted swiftly. He had his pistol up again and pulled the trigger.

Rae had left her seat and now bowled into him, a wolf snarl in her throat. She hit him hard, sending him to the floor.

Zander glimpsed Carson's utter shock and then fury as it dawned on him that Rae was Shifter. *Idiot.* That's what the man got for underestimating females.

The bullet that had left his gun went wide, embedding itself in the wheelhouse's ceiling. Piotr had grabbed the wheel and was spinning it this way and that without much effect.

Carson was fighting Rae, who'd managed to knock the pistol out of his hand. Zander paused to admire her technique—she might have been awkward while training with the sword but with straight wrestling, she was scrappy.

The guard, a big, bulky man, was too busy battling his own inertia in the spinning boat, and the guard who'd gone for coffee was flat on his stomach on the deck outside. Miles, with Shifter ease, regained his feet and was back at the controls, flipping levers.

Zander had to get out of these chains. Only one way to do it.

He closed his eyes, drew on every meditation technique he knew, discarded most of them, and finally simply said a prayer to the Goddess.

Don't let this hurt too much.

He let his bear mind overtake his human one. The polar bear woke up, shaking off the last of tranq, found his paws wrapped with thin, Fae-spelled chains, and became very, very *angry.*

Zander rose, and rose, and rose, his human limbs becoming bear's, thick white fur bursting onto his body. His clothes split and fell away. Long black, razor-sharp claws grew as his hands became giant paws. In only a few seconds, Zander's great head touched the ceiling, and the wheelhouse suddenly filled with a gigantic, seriously pissed-off bear.

He roared as he brought his paws apart to break the chains.

These weren't ordinary chains though. They were specially wrought silver, made by Fae to contain Shifters. Some of the half-Fae shits lived in this world among humans—humans didn't know they were half Fae—and specialized in Shifter restraints. They'd made the cage Zander had been locked into below, a tiny room set aside for the purpose. Ezra had been shoved into a room down the corridor.

The chains weren't very thick but they didn't have to be. The Fae spells bit pain and electric shock deep into the Shifter's nervous system until every nerve ending, every cell was on fire.

Zander's roar of rage turned to anguish. He fought to break the slender but super-strong bonds, every outward push of his arms sending greater agony into him. So much for the Goddess answering his prayer.

Zander tried to get his breath and found none. He wanted to stop, sink down, surrender, anything to take away this white-hot pain, the knife of it peeling at every muscle.

A dim part of Zander's mind told him that the Fae chains were designed to make him do just that—give up. The only solution was to keep fighting.

He was a polar bear, touched by the Goddess, could heal wounds in the blink of an eye. Special, set apart, gifted . . .

What a load of bullshit. Zander was a Shifter like every other and this fucking *hurt*.

He gathered his strength and pulled at the chains again, his roars shaking the wheelhouse. More agony. Shit, these were strong. He'd never break free. Carson would recover and shoot him through his stupid bear brain . . .

Sudden coolness cut through the fevered pain. Zander opened his eyes, his vision blurring, and looked down. Rae was next to him, her jacket open, her Collar peeping from under her shirt.

She had her hands on his side, reaching up as far as she could as he stood on his hind legs. Rae's hands sank into his fur, right over his aching rib cage and banging heart.

The touch of a mate, a tiny voice in Zander's subconscious whispered. The most magical touch of all. It healed, soothed, freed.

The Fae magic was strong, Zander's pain horrific, and Rae's touch could only do so much against it. But it made all the difference.

Zander's breath poured back into his lungs. He let out another ferocious growl and jerked his paws apart.

The chains broke with a bang that rivaled the next thunder-clap. The energy in them was so vast that the chains flew across the room and crashed through the window, shards of glass everywhere. The chains landed with a clank on the deck out-side, skittering down it as the boat rocked.

Zander brought his paws together, his fur bloody. Rae moved her touch to just above the bleeding creases. He felt her anguish for him, her compassion.

To think, he'd almost refused point-blank to let her come onto his boat.

Zander shook himself. He lowered to all four paws and Rae's hold slid away. But she was at his side again, resting her hands on his back.

"You all right?" she asked in trepidation.

Zander gave a bear *mmph* then he let himself shift back to human. That was going to be a bitch, too, but he did it.

Soon his protective fur was gone and he was on hands and knees, his wrists running with blood, his breath labored.

The cabin was dark but for what little light came in through the fogbound and rain-streaked windows and the occasional blinding streak of lightning. Miles must have gotten some emergency generator going, because the boat beneath Zander was vibrating.

In the next lightning strike, Zander saw the guard who'd gone for coffee in the cabin again, his gun aimed at Zander. *Aw, for crap's sake.*

Zander snarled and ran at him, twisting the pistol from the man's hand. Zander trained the gun on the guard, whose eyes lost the hardness of a paid killer and took on fear as he saw his intended victim about to kill him.

"You know what I like about being Shifter?" Zander asked him. He turned the pistol sideways in this hands. "It lets me do things like *this*."

Zander bent the metal in half. The gun popped and broke, and bullets rained to the floor.

Zander tossed the useless pieces aside and punched the guard in the temple. The man quietly slid down the wall, his legs splaying.

Zander turned and punched the other guard, who was trying to sneak up on him, and took his gun away from him. Another break, another pistol rendered useless, another guard knocked out.

"I *hate* guns," Zander said with a growl.

"Zander!" Rae called in warning.

Zander turned to see Carson, who'd faded into the shadows, emerge again. He had a tranq rifle in his hands, the cabinet behind him broken open, and no fear in his eyes.

Before Zander could duck, Carson shot. The tranq dart flew rapidly and surely across the room to bury itself in Zander's bare shoulder.

CHAPTER SEVENTEEN

Rae watched, her heart pounding, as Zander studied the dart sticking out of the solid muscle between his arm and shoulder.

He said, "You son of a bitch," took hold of the dart, and yanked it out.

Rae expected Zander to fold up and collapse but he only took a deep breath and steadied himself on the nearest wall. As Carson stared at him over the scope, Zander dragged in another breath and lurched toward him.

Carson threw aside the tranq gun and went for his pistol. Rae started for them but she knew she'd never reach Carson in time.

Zander did. He snarled and half shifted, his bear paw knocking the pistol from Carson's hand before the man could raise it. Zander lifted the dart still in his fist and jammed it into Carson's arm.

The man blinked, then wobbled as the fast-acting tranq took effect. His legs shook; he swung a fist at Zander and missed. Zander caught Carson as he went down and gently lowered him to a bench. Piotr caught up the tranq rifle, loaded it with another dart from the cabinet, and used it to cover Miles and the limp guards.

Zander turned around and pinned Miles with a dark gaze. "Any more?"

Zander was stark naked, his clothes all over the floor. Miles was dressed and facing Zander with military bearing, but Zander dominated here. Shifters didn't equate nudity with vulnerability—they equated it with being able to defend themselves. A Shifter's greatest weapon was his or her animal, and clothes only got in the way.

It was cold, though, in this early Alaska morning, and Zander's human body would soon begin to shiver. His wrists ran with blood where the chains had torn his flesh. He didn't notice at the moment, his adrenaline high, but after a while, he'd have to wrap up, hunker down, and heal.

"How did you do that?" Rae asked him.

Fire flickered in Zander's eyes and ignited the ones inside her. "Which part?" he asked.

"All of it. Those chains were spelled—I smelled it. And the dart. Why didn't it knock you out?"

Zander shrugged. Blood trickled from his wounds and spattered to the floor. "He miscalculated the dose. I'm a polar bear, bigger than most Shifters. Takes more to bring me down."

"But it knocked you out on your boat."

Amusement entered his dark eyes. "Not so much. It was the only way to get over to *this* ship and commandeer it."

"You faked it?" Rae's anger surged to mix with her relief. "Why didn't you tell me? Here I was all worried about you."

"Were you?" Zander shot her a grin. "Aw, that's sweet. See, we need to get to the mainland and my boat doesn't have enough fuel or stamina to make it." He patted a beam above him. "But this one does."

"Hey, I can't just let you take over the boat," Miles said.

Zander studied him. "True. You could fight me. You'd lose, but you can try. Then I can either lock you into one of the cages below or let you stay up here and help me sail this tank."

Miles sized him up, calculating his odds. "Where are you heading?"

"The lower forty-eight, though we can dock in Canada if we have to. I know people in Vancouver."

"Of course you do," Rae muttered.

Zander heard her, and his lips twitched. "How about it . . . whatever you are. Follow me? Or hunker in a cage trying to keep yourself from screaming every time you touch Fae metal? You're only part Shifter so it might not affect you as much, but I bet it will sting."

"Who are you off to kill?" Miles asked, his eyes hard.

Zander looked surprised. "No one. I'm a healer, not a killer. Right now, I need to heal a sword."

Miles's suspicion deepened. "What the hell does that mean?"

"Sword of the Guardian. Haven't you heard of them? Rae, show him."

Rae wasn't certain she should drag out the broken sword and display it to a Shifter who hunted other Shifters but she went to the locker where Carson had put it. A sift through his keys let her find the right one after a few false tries, and she opened the cupboard. She removed the broken top piece of the sword and held it up.

The blade flashed in the dim light but Rae heard no hum, saw no impish glitter of the runes. Dead.

Miles's gaze went to it, his face screwing up as though he tried to remember something.

"My mom used to tell me stories when I was little," he said. "Something about a magic sword that healed Shifters."

"Doesn't heal us," Rae answered. She thought about Ezra's father, drifting down into dust. "The sword frees our souls. I suppose that's healing, in a way. Sends us out of pain into the afterlife."

"I thought they were just stories," Miles said. "My mom also talked about mists and passages to other worlds. I figured she had a wild imagination."

"Didn't she tell you about the Fae?" Rae asked him.

"Not really. I didn't grow up Shifter. My dad was human. He was a good guy. I tried to be like him. My mom didn't expect me to be like other Shifters, so we didn't talk about it much. I don't even know what *Fae* means."

"Must be nice," Zander said. "Lesson one: Fae are evil shits. Lesson two . . ." He stopped. "Nope. That's about it, really."

Rae slid the blade into the sheath inside her coat, where the bottom half already rested. "I need to have it fixed. That means we don't have time to let someone like this Carson guy capture us."

"Come with us?" Zander asked Miles again.

Miles's dark eyes held anger and uncertainty. "Go with you to what—find a bunch of Shifters? They're killers."

"Not all of them," Zander said. "Some are annoying as hell, but they're not deadly. Well . . . not usually."

Rae sent him a glare. "Not helping."

Zander ignored her. "The thing is, Miles—you gotta take Shifters as they are. Humans are just as deadly to each other, more so, in my opinion. Shifters fight for territory or their cubs and mates, maybe even for revenge, but not so much now-adays."

"I've seen them battle," Miles said, scowling. "I've seen them slaughter. So don't be telling me Shifters are touchy-feely, warm-fuzzy do-gooders."

Miles had obviously had a bad experience, but he couldn't have from any Shifters Rae had known. Shifters did get into fighting frenzy, needing to work off steam, but that's why they had the fight clubs.

Zander turned his head and sent Rae a meaningful look. "So what do you think, Rae? Someone needs a hug?"

Rae did. She was aching for Zander's touch to soothe her and stop the shivering inside her. If he put his arms around her and pulled her against his strong body, she knew everything would be all right.

He wasn't talking about her though. "Yeah, I agree," she said. "But I don't think Miles is going to let you near him."

"Why not?" Zander's eyes widened. "What's wrong with me? Okay, I probably smell a little right now but that's his fault for letting Carson lock me up in a cage."

Miles looked back and forth between them. "What are you guys talking about? Why are you looking at me like that?"

"Come on." Zander opened his arms wide. "You'll feel bet-ter and you know it."

"Zander," Rae said as Miles backed away. "He might be more friendly if you weren't standing there with your junk out."

"Yeah?" Zander kept his eyes on Miles. "I don't think that's the problem. You really are afraid of Shifters, aren't you?"

"After what I've seen them do? You bet." Miles backed away faster, nearly tripping over Carson's inert body.

Zander drove Miles backward, heading him directly for Rae. Rae understood what Zander wanted her to do. She caught Miles when he found himself pinned and wrapped her arms around him from behind. Miles reached for his pistol but Rae was in the way.

Zander gathered Miles into a crushing bear hug. His arms took in Rae as well, squashing all three of them together.

Miles did fight. Rae sensed the terrible fear in him, which went beyond reason. Zander didn't overpower him; he simply stood in place, the bulk of him impossible to move.

Rae felt the tingle of Goddess magic in Zander, the incredible power that let him heal. He was healing Miles, she realized. Digging into whatever horror Miles had witnessed, easing his memory of it, helping him release it.

Miles was stiff, struggling. Rae sensed the darkness inside him, inky fingers of it paralyzing him with fear. She also sensed Zander's magic and his compassion that blazed as large as he was.

Rae knew in that moment, as the compassion entered her through his touch, that Zander didn't heal simply because the magic compelled him to, because he did a grudging duty. He truly wanted to help people, to make them whole again.

It cost him. Rae remembered how he'd lain in the yard at Ezra's house, cramped with the pain he'd absorbed from Ezra's father, Robert. He'd done that so Robert could die in peace.

Why then, why, was this generous and largehearted man all alone?

Same reason she now was, Rae supposed. Shifters were a superstitious bunch. They liked the idea of Guardians and healers but didn't want their weird magic anywhere near them on a good day.

Miles kept shaking, growling as Zander pulled him closer. Rae kept her arms tight around Miles as well, her forearms crushed between both men's firm abdomens. Zander laid his head on Miles's shoulder, looked down at Rae, and winked at her.

At the same time, Rae felt Miles give a great shiver, then start to shrink.

Rae released him in alarm, sliding her arms out from under

Zander to back away. Zander kept hold of Miles until the man shrank rapidly out of his grip.

Zander stumbled forward and fell against Rae, who steadied him. He nuzzled her cheek. "Hmm. Not a bad place to land."

Miles squirmed out from between them, leaving his clothes and his pistol in its holster behind. What popped out from the mound of jeans, T-shirt, and jacket was a gray-furred, long-tailed fox.

"Whoa," Piotr said, moving the tranq gun to it. "Where did that come from?"

"Miles," Zander said. "He's a Shifter." He gazed down at the fox, who glared back up at him. "And he's kinda cute."

"He's *adorable*," Rae said, dropping to one knee.

Miles's fur was a dark gray all over, except for a pattern of lighter gray across his head and around his pointed muzzle. His graying hair as a human, she realized, didn't come from age, but the markings of his fox. He had a little red fur in him too, around his chest and down into his front legs.

Miles turned dark eyes to her, looking almost embarrassed that he'd shifted in front of her. Rae knew that not all Shifters liked to be petted but she took the chance and stroked the top of Miles's head. His fur was wiry but soft and very warm.

"I didn't know there could be fox Shifters," she said.

"Yep," Zander answered. "The Fae shits experimented on a lot of creatures. Not all of them survived, and of those that did, not all were viable. But a couple rare ones got through. Like polar bears and, I guess, foxes."

Zander had his hands on his hips, comfortable standing there without any clothes. He had the body for it, every muscle tight, a dusting of black curls across his chest and another line on his lower abdomen, a glory trail that led to . . . glory. A couple times now, Rae had seen how seriously large he was, and every time, her face and body had gone hot as he'd noticed her noticing.

Zander turned away and caught the wheel, deftly turning the boat before they rammed to their death against a sheer wall.

"Piotr, go down and release Ezra," he said. "I'm going to take us back to my boat and you'll pilot it out of here. All right with you?"

Piotr studied him, his round face troubled. Then he nodded.

"I think you're crazy, my friend, but I will try. What about . . . ?" He gestured to the fox who was sitting next to Rae.

"He'll be fine," Zander said. "We'll take care of him. You just take care of my boat."

"Wait, we're going *back* to it?" Rae blurted. "What happened to getting out of here?"

Zander didn't look at her as he moved controls. "I'm not leaving my boat to rot in the Graveyard. Piotr can follow me out."

Piotr was obviously terrified but the look in his eyes showed perfect trust in Zander. Was everyone around Zander as insane as he was? They were, Rae decided. But they weren't wrong. Zander seemed to engender trust, as though everything he did, no matter how dangerous, would come out right in the end.

Rae must be as insane as his other friends were, because she was starting to trust him too. If he said he could steer them out of this scary place and find a guy to fix the sword of the Guardian, he probably could.

Piotr gave Zander a nod, laid the tranq gun next to Rae, and left the wheelhouse. He lurched on the deck as the boat tipped but caught handholds with the ease of long experience and disappeared below.

Rae kept petting Miles, carefully not reaching for the tranq rifle. She didn't want to spook him. "What are you going to do about these other guys when they wake up?" she asked.

Zander wasn't looking at her. He studied the swirling mists with a frown. "I'll think of something," he said.

"Great."

"Yeah, isn't it?" Zander sent her a grin over his shoulder. "Fishing all day gets boring. This is much more fun."

Rae and Miles shared a look. "Sorry," Rae said to the fox. "He's not my fault. He was foisted on me."

Miles's forehead wrinkled in an expression so like his human one Rae wanted to laugh. Instead, she smoothed it out and kept petting him, while Zander guided the boat through the roiling water.

Zander didn't much want Rae out of his sight, but he asked her to help Piotr lock up Carson and his men. Zander couldn't leave the wheel, Miles was still a fox, and Ezra, when

Piotr helped him into the cabin, was half asleep from tranqs. He leaned back on a bench and closed his eyes.

Zander gave Carson's men small doses of the tranq to make them continue to sleep—tricky, because humans couldn't take the large amounts Shifters could. Too much and he'd kill them, and Zander wasn't a killer.

While Rae and Piotr were busy lugging bodies, Miles hunkered in a corner Zander pointed him to. "Stay," he said. "Good fox."

Miles growled but settled in, watching Zander's every move as Zander piloted his boat.

Once Rae and Piotr were dragging Carson off, Zander exhaled, and in that moment, the fears and horrors that he'd healed from Miles washed over him.

Damn, he hated this. Zander didn't have time to deal with a healing hangover right now, but Miles's emotions poured over him.

Zander felt Miles's remembered terror when he realized his body could change without his control, the world spinning as his vision shifted, his heartbeat rocketing, his skin growing fur. Fear that he was some kind of freak, that his parents would abandon him. The need to hide what he was, work hard to be like his human father.

That worry had never left Miles but that hadn't been what knocked the fear of Shifters into him. That had come later. Zander didn't understand the whole story; he only had flashes of horror. Men who were half beasts ripping someone apart—man or woman, human or Shifter, Zander couldn't see. Blood, the smell of death.

Panic—the Shifters had seen him. Run, run, hide, hide. Shut it out . . . but never forget.

"Shit," Zander said, his skin clammy and cold. He looked at Miles, and Miles looked back with his fox's dark eyes. "I get why you were scared of Shifters. They're not all like that. How old were you?"

Miles didn't answer and Zander didn't speak fox. Not very old, Zander guessed from the emotions. Still a cub, probably.

"Tell you what," Zander said. "I'll find out which Shifters did that and have a chat with them. I'd like to know why they were on a killing spree."

Miles regarded him in surprise and Zander turned back to the wheel. "I can't read your mind. I understand what you went through because I healed your paranoia. You'll get used to me."

Now if Zander could get used to himself. One of these days he was going to heal someone, and be so struck with his or her pain and emotions he wouldn't recover. *That* was the fear that woke Zander in the night, the one that made him so crazy.

Okay, *one* of the things that made him so crazy. Not knowing if the next person he healed would kill him, having to choose every time whether to give them compassion or run away. Compassion, so far, had won, but would there come a time Zander wouldn't be able to convince himself to make the sacrifice? How would he live with himself after that?

"That's my problem," Zander said. "I'm just too darned nice."

Miles snorted what Zander took to be a laugh. Rae chose that moment to walk in.

"Too darned nice?" she demanded. "What the hell are you talking about?"

Her aura was calming, her voice like cool water on the parched places of his mind. A spike of heat shot through Zander's heart, warming his cold limbs and easing the last of Miles's gut-wrenching panic from him.

Zander took his eyes off the scary panorama of the Graveyard to meet Rae's eyes, gray like the mists outside, calm, beautiful. The heat in his heart blossomed into something like pain. *Holy fucking shit.*

CHAPTER EIGHTEEN

Mate bonds didn't always happen. Two Shifters could mate, live together, have cubs, and never form the mate bond. Rare, but possible.

Mate bonds could also form long before a Shifter took a mate in the ceremonies performed by the clan leader under the sun and under the full moon. A beautiful she-wolf like Rae could glare at Zander with her lovely eyes and heat his body to broiling. That warmth would twine his heart, a tendril that would bond itself to her and she to him.

In the middle of the Graveyard, with death coming at them every second, Zander couldn't stop and decide whether this feeling that had smacked him in the face was the mate bond with Rae. Her touch soothed, her look calmed him down, the kiss they'd shared had been smoking hot and had set his imagination spinning.

The moment he had time, Zander was going to take Rae off somewhere private and explore whether they were forming the mate bond or just craving each other's bodies in their loneliness. Either way, they'd have a great time.

Rae was watching him with a puzzled expression, probably

wondering why in the hell he was absently moving the wheel back and forth, as though the heavy fog, looming rocks, and the fresh storm weren't all that important. *And they weren't,* Zander realized. Taking a mate was. Holing up, going into frenzy, having cubs—that was why Shifters were alive. The instinct to mate had been bred strongly into them by the Fae, and Shifters had been happily shagging ever since.

But first, Zander had to get them out of the tricky place he'd taken them into.

Rae found sweatpants and a windbreaker for him, a bit too small for Zander but Rae insisted he put them on. True it was getting chilly in here. *Anything for you, Little Wolf.*

The clothes must belong to Miles—too large for Carson or the guards. Strange how Miles, such a big man, could reshape himself into a small fox. Where did the extra mass go? Zander had ceased worrying about little things like that long ago—magic explained a lot—but he was intrigued.

Zander was a little surprised, actually, when he maneuvered into the narrow channel where he'd left his own boat. Following his instincts, the charts on Miles's battery-powered laptop, the proximity readouts, and the little hisses of Jake the Snake, whom Rae had placed on his shoulder, Zander found his boat. There she was, rocking too close to the walls, waiting for rescue.

Zander guided the larger boat as close as he dared. When Miles had been piloting this craft, he'd brought it within a few inches of Zander's without ramming it. Miles remained fox right now, though, taking refuge from his confusion in that form.

Zander sensed Rae behind him as he held the boat steady a foot or so from his own—felt her warmth, knew her scent, his entire body aware of her. She peered out the window, watching Piotr help a groggy Ezra over the gunwale and make the leap to Zander's boat.

Piotr lifted his hand to Zander, then he and Ezra went into the pilot house.

Zander backed the larger vessel away, turning it slowly, slowly, and then pointed it past his boat, sliding alongside it to go deeper into the fog.

He felt Rae start. "Aren't we going back the way we came?"

"Nope," Zander said. "There are two ways out of the Grave-yard. The first way might have the Coast Guard or Shifter Bureau hanging out in front of it. The second way . . . well, no one knows where it actually comes out."

He sensed Rae's stare and turned to look at her. Her dark hair hung in wisps around her face, curling in the humidity, and her gray wolf's eyes pinned him. "Do *you* know where it comes out?"

"More or less."

He loved the way her eyes flashed when she was exasper-ated. *"Zander."*

"We'll find it. The Goddess looks out for her own."

"You sound very sure about that."

"Listen, sweetheart, if I didn't trust the Goddess every single day of my life, I'd be dead. Or too terrified to leave my house. I'd be living in a tiny cottage in the Shetlands, afraid to touch anyone, figuring the world would be better off if I just stay put. Walking around with the Goddess messing with me every day makes guiding a boat through the Graveyard a walk in the park."

He hadn't meant for his voice to grow so harsh, but Zander didn't exaggerate. When he'd been younger, some days it had been all he could do to get out of bed. He'd known he'd have to heal some Shifter—because in the old, wild days, they could get into many violent situations—and he'd end up in deep, terrible pain, maybe dying for it. He'd spent a long time furious with the Goddess for doing this to him. Why did *he* have to draw the unlucky straw?

Rae had drawn one too. She was young, far too vulnerable for the bad shit that she'd get pulled into. Sailing around the Graveyard was the least of her worries.

To distract himself, Zander touched Jake's cool head. "What do you think, my friend?"

Jake's tongue flicked in and out, in and out, then he gave Zander a look from his steady black eyes.

"I agree," Zander said. "Adjust the heading a little to the north, northwest."

Rae was giving him her long-suffering look. "Snakes can't talk."

"Yes, they can. You just have to learn how to understand what they say. He didn't really say *go north, northwest,* he just wants me to go *that* direction." Zander pointed. "The smell is right."

"We're Shifter," Rae said patiently. "And I can't smell anything but stink. I can't tell the difference."

"But Jake can," Zander said with perfect confidence. "He can also see in the infrared, did you know that? He's got little organs that detect heat signatures so he can find a rat to eat on the darkest night. He can tell warmer water from cooler, or warmer air. And he says it's that way." Zander pointed again into the murk.

Rae gave a fed-up sigh and plopped down to the nearest seat. "If you can get us out of here, Zander, I'll . . ."

She trailed off. Zander sent her an amused glance. "You'll what? Kiss me?"

"Kick your ass." Rae jammed her arms across her chest. "My dad brought me to you to train me and keep me safe from Shifters who aren't happy with me being Guardian. So what do you do? Get me into a bar fight, have us run from the Coast Guard and then be captured by a bounty hunter, and lose us in a dangerous waterway in the densest fog I've ever seen. And now you say you don't know the way out."

"Most interesting night *you've* ever had," Zander said, keeping his gaze forward.

He felt Rae's glare for a while longer and then she dissolved into laughter that warmed the air. "Yeah, you could say that."

Zander risked another glance at her. Her laughter changed her, softened her face, made her eyes dance. Her smile was wide, lips red, reminding Zander how warm they'd been when he'd kissed them.

He wanted nothing more than to take her into his arms, lay her on the bench, and slide his hands down her body. He'd lift her to him, kissing her like crazy, yanking away clothing until they could be skin-to-skin.

His blood was fiery hot, his cock, uncaring about danger, growing hard. He'd sail them out of here and then celebrate the best way he knew how.

Zander took his hand from the wheel long enough to brush back a lock of Rae's dark hair. Rae's laughter died and an answering spark lit her eyes.

No matter what, when they reached safety he and Rae were going to celebrate being alive the way Shifters did, with an all-night frenzy. It would be loud, rough, and if Zander read Rae correctly, amazingly loving. This woman had much to give, if only someone would let her give it.

Zander said to Jake, "All right, my friend. Which way now?"

The boat inched through the rain, which did nothing to slacken the fog. Rae slid into the copilot's chair after a time, while Miles remained on the floor as his fox.

Rae watched Zander peering ahead to the ice walls, rock, fog, waves, and who knew what else, tension in every line of him. He was confident they'd get out, but not one hundred percent positive. Rae wanted to yell at him again for dragging her in here but she didn't want to risk distracting him.

The view out the front window didn't change. That is, it altered from moment to moment, but it didn't clear and show them open water.

Lights on the stern of this boat directed Piotr, who was following close behind in Zander's. If Zander ran into anything, Piotr would slam directly into them and they'd all go down. Comforting thought.

To take her mind off such things, Rae brought out the Sword of the Guardian and took both pieces out of the sheath. She laid them on the front windowsill, careful to keep them from sliding onto the controls.

Two pieces of dull silver, etched with runes, lay inert before them. Daragh had known what the runes meant but Rae hadn't had time to look them up or even read any of his logs about it, which were on his computer back home. The computer was in the small house Daragh had used as his personal retreat but Rae hadn't been let in there.

Rae studied the crack in the silver, which lined up perfectly when she slid the two pieces together. She half hoped to see a magic spark fuse the two together, but nothing happened.

"Sorry, Daragh," she whispered.

Did Rae imagine the slight ripple that ran through the silver? She leaned forward eagerly but the sword simply lay there, flat and unwinking. Yes, she'd imagined it. Damn it.

"Still talking to a dead guy?" Zander asked her.

"Still talking to a *friend* who's gone to the Summerland," Rae said right back to him. "Friends . . . You know, those people who have your back?"

"Peace, Little Wolf, I was teasing you."

"I know." Rae did know it. Zander was easy to grow angry with, but it was hard to stay mad at him for long. He knew just the right thing to say to put Rae's back up and then how to make her laugh.

"When did you know you had healing power?" Rae asked him, curious. "Did you have a Choosing, like for the Guardian?"

"Nah." Zander made a minor adjustment to their course— Jake probably told him to. "I was a cub, minding my own business, when *wham*. Suddenly I'm thrown to the ground by nothing. When I get up, I'm putridly sick. I went back home to find out my dad had been shot. Not fatally," he added quickly, "but a hunter mistook him for a real bear and shot him. Not that hunters were supposed to be targeting polar bears at all, but some people will open fire on any animal, just for the hell of it.

"Anyway, I went to help my mom bandage up my dad . . . and I healed him. Just like that. Bullet popped out under my hands, the wound closed up, and then I was doubling over in serious pain, like I'd been shot myself. My mom and dad freaked out a little bit, and when I felt better, I ran away. I was too young to make it on my own though, so I went back home and sucked it up. But people treated me weird from then on. I learned I could only find peace when I was alone."

"Was this when you were in the Shetlands?"

Zander gave her a nod. "Our neighbors knew we were Shifter—or at least not human—and they didn't care, but they were powerfully superstitious, especially a hundred and more years ago. They thought I was either touched by the devil or by an angel, depending on the mood of the day. Once I was past my Transition, I lit out to see the world. Which was why

I wasn't around when the rest of my clan was rounded up by the humans."

Rae heard the bitterness in his voice. "I'm sorry."

"You and me both." Zander shrugged. "I got over it."

"No you didn't."

Zander shot her a glance, an unreadable look in his dark eyes. "Sure, I did. Don't make me out to be a wuss. I'm fine."

No, he wasn't fine, but his black stare dared her to say so.

Rain lashed at the window and Zander refocused his attention on where they were going. Waves beat at the boat, trying to drive them into the rock walls that seemed to be narrowing.

"Hold on to something," Zander said. "This is going to be tight."

Cliffs closed in on them, surging out of the fog as though determined to squeeze them in half. Rae grabbed the sword and slid it back into the sheath, worried it would fall and get even more damaged.

A rock wall materialized out of the fog and smashed into their side. The impact sent Rae to the floor, the sword flying. Rae lunged for the sword as it skittered and slid across the cabin, *almost gleefully,* she thought. She scrambled after it. The sword ended up nearly running into the fox that was Miles, until he put out a slim paw and stopped it.

Rae stilled, afraid it would burn him, but Miles only lifted his paw without a sound. Maybe the sword chose who it hurt or didn't.

The Graveyard wasn't finished. The boat rocked and pitched, struggling to wrench itself free of cliffs that closed in on either side. Rae remained on the floor, her hand on the sword's hilt, figuring it was useless to try to get up.

Rocks screeched along the hull with the sound of nails on metal. Rae held her breath, expecting at any second for the sides to crack open and water to come rushing in. The boat would upend and sink like the other wrecks, and they'd be forgotten and stranded, slowly becoming ghosts.

The men locked below would die first. They were Shifter bounty hunters, happy to drag Shifters to their doom, but Rae wasn't hardhearted enough to wish death on them. At the moment, though, she couldn't move to get up and help them.

The horrible shrieking sound went on and on, then abruptly ceased. The boat shot out from between the rocks and sped forward, swaying heavily. Rae lifted her head to see Zander fighting the tiller, his muscles working.

"Son of a bitch," Zander said under his breath.

"What's wrong?" Rae pried herself from the floor, the sword in her hand, and pulled herself across the rocking wheelhouse to him. She clung to the chair she'd vacated but remained on her feet. "What happened?"

"The tiller won't respond." Zander turned the wheel back and forth, flipped switches, then smacked the dashboard. "Either that or . . ."

He trailed off, but this time Rae saw what he saw. The fog was clearing. As it burned off, sunlight shone strongly on the sea, turning it deep blue.

The narrow, jagged-rock passage had given way to a wider spread of water enclosed by more rocks on the other side. Mountains soared in the distance beyond that. The beautiful blue water churned around the edges of the cliffs, becoming luminous white foam. In the middle of the open stretch a whirl-pool sucked water down, down, down into nothing.

"So," Zander said, his lips pale but his eyes wide and spar-kling. "This is new."

CHAPTER NINETEEN

"You mean you haven't been this way before?"

Rae's voice rose with her fear. Zander wanted to turn and comfort her but didn't dare take his hands from the wheel. There was nothing wrong with the tiller, he realized, as he looked into the whirling water. The undertow was simply dragging them forward, nothing he could do about it.

"I *have* been this way," he said, answering Rae. "But *this* wasn't here. Must be tidal, or seasonal, or something."

"Great," Rae said. "What do we do? Go back?"

Not an option. Zander hadn't admitted it but getting this far had been a feat of precise navigation that he wasn't sure he could do again. The fact that they hadn't broken open like an egg in that narrow passage had somewhat surprised him.

"No," he said decidedly. "We go through."

Rae's eyes widened. "Go through? How can we? You are seriously out of your mind."

"I know that." Zander laced his arm around her, pulling her against his side. "Sweetheart, I promised I'd take care of you and get you home all right. I will do that. Do you trust me?" He had to raise his voice over the rush of the chaotic, crashing waves.

"No," Rae yelled back.

"Hey, I *will* get you out of here whether you trust me or not. But it would be more fun if you did." He grinned. "Would make me feel all warm and fuzzy."

"I'll give you warm and fuzzy all right," Rae said darkly.

"Looking forward to it." Zander scooped her up his body, pressed swift kiss to her lips, and let her go to hang on to the wheel again. "I'm gonna need your help to take us through this. You up to it?"

"Do I have a choice?" Rae demanded.

Zander seized her and kissed her again—it was just so much fun. "No, you don't. First, I need you to convince Miles to get up off his ass and go over and pilot my boat. I need his senses to steer it through. Piotr's good, but I need Shifter instincts."

Zander directed a glance at Miles, who glared back at him. Rae gave Zander another skeptical look but she laid the sword on the windowsill again then turned and went to Miles, crouching down in front of him.

Zander had no idea what she said to him. He heard Rae's voice murmuring like clear water, Miles's growl in return. She might be telling Miles that Zander was a complete asshole but they needed to humor him.

Didn't matter. Zander needed Miles and Rae needed something to keep her from being afraid. Sitting around in terror helped no one, Zander had learned a long time ago. If he was going down, he'd go down fighting—and laughing—all the way.

Zander had Piotr on the radio. "Hold it steady," Zander said into the receiver. "I'm sending the pilot back to you."

He got a string of Russian in return, which he figured was swearing. "You know, you really are a crazy mo fo," Piotr finished.

"Yeah, I hear that all the time. I'm going to get you out of this, my friend."

"And when you do, my wife will kill *you*."

Zander only laughed and clicked off the mike. He *would* take them out of here, and he knew it. The Goddess had chosen Rae for a reason, hadn't she? And Zander as well. She had something in mind for Rae, and Zander would guess it wasn't being sucked into a whirlpool in the Graveyard.

Or was Zander as nuts as everyone said he was? Easy to

play the idiot to keep himself from pain—maybe he justified everything he did by the fact that the Goddess had gifted him against his will. Maybe the Goddess would think that sending Zander to a watery grave was a fit end.

Whatever. Zander would see that Rae was safe, no matter what. Whether Zander perished along the way was irrelevant.

He heard a rustling and crackling sound behind him and a few moments later, Miles loomed next to Zander. He'd resumed his jeans and sweatshirt and he scowled at Zander in the reflection of the window.

"Where the hell have you brought my boat?" he demanded.

"To our ticket out of here," Zander said calmly. "Piotr's bringing my boat as close as he dares but you might have to jump to its deck. Can you make it?"

More scowling. Now that Zander studied the man's face and hard eyes, he did glimpse the fox in him—a nose that was a little pointed, eyes full of intelligence, a quick way of moving despite his size. His Shifter qualities were slightly dampened by his human blood but Miles was definitely Shifter.

He fixed his dark eyes on Zander, thoughts moving behind them, then finally gave him a nod.

"You wreck my boat, bear," Miles said, pointing a stern forefinger at Zander, "and I'll kick your ass."

"I'll say the same right back to you, fox."

Miles gazed at Zander one more moment, then he quietly put on his boots, took up a coat, and banged out of the cabin.

"Piotr?" Zander said into the radio. "Miles is coming over. Let me know when he's safe."

"He will be when he's sitting at my fireside tossing back a vodka," came Piotr's response. "You're not invited."

"Aw, now," Zander said into the radio. "Don't be like that."

"Rae's invited, though," Piotr said. "Send her over here too."

"Can't. I need her."

The stark truth. He didn't want to let her out of his sight—Zander knew he was the better pilot than Piotr or Miles and he wasn't about to send Rae to anyone who might not be able to get her to safety as well as he could.

We're not going to die. We're going to live through this so we can celebrate in the best way Shifters know how.

Piotr snarled something else but Zander heard underneath the man's bluster and worry a note of excitement. Piotr, in his own way, was as much of a daredevil as Zander.

"He's on," Piotr said, then the radio snapped off into rigid silence.

Zander let out a breath of relief. "Rae, sweetie, we need to let out Carson and his guys. If this doesn't work, they should be able to save themselves."

"You don't mean *we* need to let Carson out," Rae said. "You mean me. You can't leave the wheel."

"I know. Don't worry—they'll be groggy and more interested in surviving than arresting us. We'll deal with that on the other side."

"Why didn't you have Miles release them before he went?" Rae asked, coming up behind him. "They'd be less likely to attack him."

Zander shook his head, liking how her warmth touched him. "Because Carson might have been able to convince Miles to help him take me down, and then we wouldn't have a chance of making it through. Carson won't hurt you—he'll go for me but he's not the kind of man who will hurt an innocent, especially a woman. I saw that in his eyes. He thinks he's the good guy."

Rae opened her mouth to argue then let out a sigh. "Yeah, I thought that too."

"I'm confident we'll get through, but just in case . . ."

"Not making me feel better." Rae hesitated, then she wrapped her arms around Zander, making sure she didn't break his contact with the wheel. She rose on tiptoe and kissed his cheek. "Piotr's wife isn't the only woman who's going to kill you when we get out of this, you know."

"Looking forward to it," Zander said, his blood warming. "Go, Little Wolf. Then get your ass right back here to me." He caressed the ass in question as he gave her a little push.

Rae sent him one of her looks but ducked out of the cabin into the rain.

"If you can hear me, Goddess," Zander said to the water rushing at them. "Make sure Rae is safe. Doesn't matter what happens to me. Just make sure Rae is all right. She's a special lady."

The water crashed and roared as the boat surged forward.

Rae found Carson already awake and almost finished picking open the lock of the cage Ezra and Piotr had put him into. He snarled at Rae. "What the *hell* is he doing up there?"

"Being Zander." Rae unlocked the cage with the key, quickly stepping back as she swung open the door.

Carson crawled out and rose from the crouch he'd been forced to assume. He swayed, still under the effects of the tranq. Rae kept out of his reach as she left the room and went to let out the other guards. They'd been put into separate, narrow cabins but these rooms had regular bunks, no cages. The guards were just waking, sleepy, annoyed, and scared shitless.

"Why are you releasing us?" Carson asked her. He blocked Rae's way out of the last guard's room.

"Because Zander wants to give you a fighting chance." Rae clenched the keys, determined not to let Carson take them. "I wish he *didn't* want you to be out because then I'd know he had perfect confidence that we'll make it."

Carson turned abruptly from her and headed for the stairs. "Shit. What has he done to my boat?"

Again, as Zander guessed, Carson gave no orders for Rae to be held, and neither of the guards, one of them rushing to the head to be sick, looked interested in capturing her.

Rae hurried after Carson, clinging tightly to the handholds as she made her way upstairs and out onto the deck. Carson was already in the wheelhouse when Rae reached it, looming right behind Zander.

"This would be easier without you breathing down my neck," Zander was saying. "Sit down." He gave the command in a hard voice, an alpha Shifter expecting to be obeyed.

Carson cast his gaze over the controls, looked again at the whirlpool beyond where Zander held the boat, and stamped over to a bench.

"Stay down," Carson snapped to his men as they came in

behind Rae, the one who'd rushed to the bathroom finally catching up. The second man looked a little green, but he nodded and sat on the floor with his fellow, well out of Zander's way.

Rae took a seat on another bench but she couldn't stay there. As Zander eased the boat forward, she moved quickly to him and settled in the copilot's chair. Instead of admonishing Rae to take cover behind him, Zander reached for her hand and closed it in his.

Strength came to her, warming Rae and bolstering her courage. Zander was right—why hide from the world and wait to be captured or die during that wait? Why not face life head on and go out fighting, like Shifters were meant to?

Rae tightened her grip on Zander's hand, and he shot her a hot smile. Heat twined her heart, wrapping it in tendrils that didn't let go.

Zander had to release her to pick up the radio and give Miles and Piotr coordinates and directions. When he clicked off Piotr's protests and secured the mike in its slot, Zander took Rae's hand again, kissing it briefly.

"Ready, Little Wolf?"

Rae couldn't stop the grin that spread across her face. "Sure am—Big-Ass Bear."

Zander laughed out loud. "You're paying for that when we're out of this. Here we *go*."

He throttled the boat forward, the engines throbbing as the vessel moved faster. And faster.

Zander's fingers bit down but Rae was holding on to him just as tightly. Zander lifted their twined hands high as the boat charged into the clear water and headed straight for the whirlpool.

"Here comes the tricky part," Zander yelled over the roar of the engines.

He cranked the wheel opposite the spin of the vortex and gave the throttle still more speed. He steadied everything then dragged Rae off the seat and positioned her in front of him. "Hold on to that," he said, closing her hand around the throttle. "It will try to fight you, but hold it steady."

Rae nodded, gripping it tightly. Zander had the wheel in

both hands now, his body against hers, as they raced toward the whirlpool.

Just as Rae thought they'd plunge straight into it, the boat caught on the whirlpool's edge. The water shoved them sideways, slingshotting them past the dark hole in the center.

Zander whooped. Rae yelled with him as the boat climbed the waves, their speed rushing them past the cliffs on the other side of the whirlpool, beyond which was open sea.

Rae's heart beat in exhilaration and the mad joy of it. They'd make it. Zander, the crazy idiot, was doing it. He'd be even more impossible to live with now.

Just as Rae started to join in Zander's laughter of celebration, the boat swung around and listed sharply into the whirlpool's maw.

"Shit," Zander said, exuberance gone. "That should have worked."

"What do I do?" Rae shouted up at him, her hands locked around the throttle. "Ease back?"

"No." Zander's command was harsh. "More power. We need to break free."

"No kidding." A flash caught Rae's eye. "Oh, hey, there goes Piotr."

Her heart squeezed in relief as Zander's fishing boat soared away from the whirlpool and into the sunshine, leaving the deadly waters behind. Piotr, Miles, and Ezra were free, heading out to open sea.

Zander spared a glance for it. "Thank the Goddess. Wait, what is he doing?" His eyes widened in rage. "Trying to come *back* for us?"

"Zander!"

Zander jerked his head around at Rae's shout to see the mouth of the vortex yawn wider before them. "Give it some more!" he yelled to her. "I'm trying to turn. More, *more*."

Rae dragged on the throttle, which was trying to rip itself free of her hands, but the boat was giving all it had. Behind them, Carson snarled and swore but he didn't move to stop them.

On the windowsill, where it for some reason had stayed put, the Sword of the Guardian jumped. Not with the boat's movement, but with impetus of its own. It leapt and clattered, then rang, its music shrilling even over the thunder of engines and the sea.

"It's anxious to stick itself inside us," Zander said with grim humor. "Wants to dust us and get it over with."

Rae didn't think so. She didn't know how she knew what to do but she peeled one hand from the throttle and closed it over the sword's hilt.

The ringing soared, pounding at her eardrums with the intensity of a thousand bells. Zander winced, his shoulders jerking.

"Make it shut up," he yelled. "I want to die quietly."

They weren't going to die that day—Rae suddenly knew that. She shook the top part of the sword free of the sheath.

The blade flashed in the sunlight, jerking Rae so hard she lost hold of the throttle. The next moment, the sword slammed itself to the control board. Sparks leapt from the silver blade into the panel then arcs curved down into the vessel itself.

The boat hurtled forward. It flew once around the whirlpool, then at the exact place were they had spun out of control, the boat broke free and sailed hard and fast into the flat water beyond. The momentum sent them past the cliffs and through the passage Piotr had taken.

They shot from shadows into water bathed in sunlight. The Graveyard dropped abruptly to stern, the fog closed around its cliffs, and the sea calmed.

Zander quickly shut down all the engines. The vessel slowed, then drifted toward the fishing boat that waited for them, white against the blue sea.

The larger boat rocked calmly, floating on gentle seas in the summer sun, and the world was quiet.

Zander wanted nothing more than to take Rae belowdecks and made fast and furious love to her in one of the empty cabins. Hell, he'd even do it on the deck itself, in the sunshine, no matter how many people were on this damned boat.

But they weren't quite free yet. Carson tried to arrest Zander on the spot but his flunkies had gone on strike. The one who'd been sick gave Carson a hollow-eyed stare and said bluntly, "I quit." His fellow guard nodded in fervent agreement.

"Piotr!" Zander, up on deck in the stern, bellowed through his cupped hands at his friend on the other vessel. "Take these guys back to shore with you." He pointed at the guards, who'd come outside to hang on the deck's rail, breathing heavily. "And look after my boat, will you? Don't let anyone abscond with it."

Piotr gave him a salute. "I will if I don't get arrested, you crazy s.o.b."

Zander waved this away. "You know everyone in Homer. You'll talk them out of it."

Piotr shrugged. "Probably. What about Rae? I'll take her home with me too, nice and safe."

Rae, who'd come out beside Zander, shook her head. "I'll stay here," she called.

She looked regretful, as though she'd rather sit in a warm house and eat Russian pastries than follow Zander on whatever loony thing he decided to do next. But they had a sword to fix, training to resume.

Miles came back on board as Piotr drew the fishing boat close. Ezra came too, carrying the packs that Zander had asked him to bring. Miles charged past Zander and Rae as soon as he made it to the deck, heading into the pilot house to see whether Zander had left his boat in one piece.

Ezra said to Zander as he handed him the packs and Zander's samurai swords, "You were right. There's nothing for me at home now. Piotr said he'd look after the house for me. I'm going to go find some other Shifters and figure out my life."

Zander only gave him a nod. "There are plenty of bunks below." Ezra said nothing, only gave him a grateful look and disappeared to the cabins.

Piotr was waving both arms and yelling a parting good-bye at the top of his voice. He gave a final wave then turned away, already talking good-naturedly with Carson's guards. Zander suspected that by the time they reached port, the two men and Piotr would be best friends. Piotr would no doubt take them for a drink before heading home to his wife and kids.

Zander felt a pang of regret as he watched the boat recede. Piotr was a good guy and Zander always hated saying good-bye to him. But when this was all over, he'd take Rae to Nikolaevsk for a visit. Piotr and his wife were gracious hosts.

That left Miles and Carson to deal with. "Miles," Zander said, leaning in the door of the pilot house. "Head for the mainland. Anywhere is fine."

Miles nodded in acknowledgment as he continued checking over readouts and switches, like a hen fussing over his chicks. Zander left him to it and went below, down to the storage rooms where Carson had first locked up Zander.

Zander had put Carson into a room there, which could be locked from the outside. The door had a small round window through which Zander could see that Carson was sitting on the cot they'd dragged in for him.

Carter frowned at Zander when he noticed him looking in. "If you take over my boat," Carson called to him, "the charge will be piracy."

"Don't worry," Zander said. "I'll give it back." Carson snarled something under his breath but Zander, after making sure the door was securely locked, left him to go look for Rae.

He found her in one of the larger cabins on the main deck, sitting cross-legged on the bunk and gazing morosely at her broken sword. The sun coming through the cabin's window glistened in her dark hair and on the sword's silver blade. She'd shucked her jacket, which lay on the floor, and wore a sweater beneath that hugged her breasts.

Zander sat on the edge of the bed. "Hell of a day," he said.

Rae looked up at him, her eyes widening. "Shouldn't you be watching Miles?"

"He's fine. More worried about the boat than us." Zander rested his fingers, which were cracked from the sun and wind, on his thighs. "He won't call the Coast Guard or Shifter Bureau—he doesn't want us blabbing that he's really a Shifter."

"*Would* you turn in Miles to Shifter Bureau?" Rae asked in worry.

Zander looked at her in surprise. "You think I'd do something like that? His secret is safe with me, Little Wolf. He just doesn't need to know that yet."

"I don't know *what* you'd do, Zander." Rae's gray eyes were full of anger, confusion, and fear. "Just when I think I have you figured out, you go and do something even more lunatic than before." She gave him a fierce glare, though Zander sensed that behind it, all she wanted to do was scream at him or laugh. Laughter was better, so he'd try to coax it from her.

Zander put his fist on his chest. "What can I say? I'm a madman."

"No, you're not. You pretend to be, but you're not."

Rae's gaze was too perceptive. "Hey, don't go giving away my secrets," Zander said. "And I really am crazy. It's the only way to keep myself sane."

Rae shook her head but the corner of her lip twitched. "See what I mean? When we're someplace safe and I stop being scared, I am seriously going to yell at you."

"We're never going to be safe, you and me." The words weren't the ones Zander meant to say but they came out anyway. "Trouble will always find Shifters like us. It's how we deal with it that makes us strong."

Rae rested her chin on her balled fist. "If you're trying to make me feel better, you know you really suck at it."

"No, what I want is . . ."

Zander broke off. To hell with this. He rose, reached down, and dragged Rae off the bed and into his arms.

CHAPTER TWENTY

Zander didn't hold back with the kiss. Rae came off her feet, Zander's arms hard around her while he opened her mouth with his.

Rae clung to Zander as his kiss turned fierce. Carson was below them, Miles and Ezra somewhere on the boat, and the cabin door was unlocked, but Rae couldn't seem to care.

Zander kissed her as though he'd never have another chance. His mouth was commanding and at the same time tender. Rae stroked her hands down his back then wormed her fingers under the giving sweatpants to cup his very firm ass.

Zander jumped but Rae didn't withdraw. His backside was tight and nice and she pressed her fingers into it as she kissed him back.

Zander made an *mmph* sound in his throat. He lowered Rae to the mattress and shoved the sword out of the way. The sword fell from the bed, rang once as it hit the floor, then went silent.

Rae couldn't be bothered to see whether it was all right. Zander rose, taking his wonderful heat with him, but not for long. He stripped off his shirt and came down on the bed on top of her, his warmth driving all the bad things away.

Zander slid Rae's sweater and tank top up her torso, fingers finding the back hooks of her bra. He pressed a hot kiss to her abdomen, pushed the garments up to her shoulders, then took her breast in his mouth.

Rae groaned with the joy of it. She arched to meet him, hands cupping his head. His tongue played on her nipple, his mouth hot and wet, a place of fire.

Rae was lonely and scared, had been terrified by the Graveyard, and was mad as hell at Zander for . . . everything. But, oh Goddess, he knew how to hold her, touch her, make her feel wanted, protected, treasured. He caressed with his hands and mouth, his hunger coming to her. Shifters loved sex—for mating, for comfort, for fun. Never any shame in it.

Zander had no shame at all licking Rae's breast, thoroughly pleasuring it before he moved to its twin. He closed his teeth over the nipple, tugging, and the tiny dart of pain seared her with liquid heat.

Rae felt pliable and open. She wanted this man inside her with a mindlessness that would be alarming if she cared about such things right now.

Rae closed her legs around Zander's hips, urging him down. His sweatpants weren't thick enough to hide how rigid his cock was, the beautiful length of it pressing hard on her between her legs. He wanted to be inside her as much as she needed him there.

Zander lifted his mouth from her nipple, taking away the lovely warmth, but he cupped her breasts in his big hands as he dipped his head to kiss her lips.

Yes . . . Rae planted her feet on his thighs, pulling him onto her. His full cock slid along her opening under her jeans, the friction hot and exciting.

Zander planted his hands on either side of her head and dragged his mouth from hers. "No," he said hoarsely.

"Yes," Rae answered. The sound that came out of her throat sounded like a purr but she was a wolf. Must be a growl. She wrapped her entire body around his, rubbing against his cock, unable to stop herself.

"No." The word was firmer this time, though heavy with regret.

"Yes," Rae repeated. She pulled Zander closer, kissing him hard before he could speak again.

He groaned in his throat as he came down to her, the silken ropes of his braids touching her skin. His mouth was hot as he kissed her in need and desperation, and Rae just as desperately kissed him back.

Zander tore his mouth from hers again, his breath coming fast. "Goddess, Little Wolf, you're gonna kill me."

"Then we'll die happy," Rae said, smiling.

Zander growled, the note in it ferocious. "If I start with you, sweetheart, I won't be able to stop myself. I'll keep going no matter what. If the ship goes down, I'll be too busy to care."

"Me too." Rae's chest felt heavy, her nerves buzzing. "We almost died, Zander. We should celebrate."

"No kidding. We will." Zander's eyes were alight with the same fire running through her. "We will, but later. Hell, I'd be in here with you until the boat ran aground and I still wouldn't want to leave. Carson will get free, come in here, and shoot us both."

Rae tried to tell herself Zander was right. They had to remain vigilant—they weren't safe yet. Carson wasn't stupid. He'd find a way to take over again if they didn't watch out.

Rae's body, heart, and desire had other ideas. If they were in so much danger, if Shifter Bureau might be waiting for them wherever they docked, then Rae needed to be with Zander as much as she could right *now*. This might be their only chance.

She reached for him, but Zander pinned her arms above her head. Not bad. Rae wriggled against him.

"Mating frenzy," Zander said, his voice harsh. "It's crushing us."

"You think?" Rae tried to free her hands but Zander was too strong. Only made her position more enticing.

Zander went on, his dark eyes full of heat. "We escaped certain death, the damned sword is flaring all kinds of magic at us, and our mating instincts are running amok. True frenzy. We want to lock our bodies together and not come up for weeks."

"I know." Rae arched, using his weight on her wrists to send her hips up to his. "I'm not hating it."

Zander growled a laugh. "Neither am I, Little Wolf." He removed his powerful grip to touch her lower lip. Rae smiled and bit his finger.

Zander's face darkened. "Oh Goddess. We're so screwed."

"Just hold me," Rae said. "I need that at least."

Zander shook his head, his eyes closing in pain. "No, I'm fighting this. I have to."

Rae desperately cupped his face with her free hand but Zander jerked away.

"No," he said firmly. He opened his eyes, a light in them that broadcast his strength, his drive, and his bear-strong stubbornness. "Only one way we're going to fix this. Even if it's temporary."

He dragged Rae up and off the bed. Rae came readily, hoping he meant they'd find somewhere more private to work off their longing.

Zander shoved Rae's tank top and sweater down to cover her breasts and pulled her into the hall. The boat rocked in the heavy sea, the passageway listing back and forth. Zander carefully towed Rae down the hallway and opened a door.

Inside was a bathroom, one obviously designed for men. Two urinals decorated the wall on one side and the other held two showerheads and a drain. There was a short tile partition between the showers but no curtains or any other screen in front of them. Sailors had to get used to little privacy, she supposed.

Before Rae understood what was happening, Zander had her sweater, tank top, and bra off her, exposing her to the empty bathroom. He unbuttoned and yanked down her jeans then her underwear. Rae was already kicking off her boots. Mating frenzy in the shower could be great. Hot water, soap, maybe some shower gel if the guys on this boat weren't too macho to have it.

Zander looked Rae over once she was naked, a wild light in his eyes. Then he clenched his jaw and pushed her against the far wall of one of the showers.

Rae landed against the tile, which was cold, and bounced right back off . . . in time for Zander to yank the water on and then get the hell out of the way.

A stream of ice-cold liquid poured over Rae's bare body. Zander spun away and was out the door so fast an equally icy draft slammed through the room as the door banged shut.

Rae screamed. And screamed. The water was *damn* cold.

But Zander had known what he was doing. Frenzy left Rae's body as survival instincts took over, along with rage. Rae slapped off the water with a blue-fingered hand.

"I hate you, Alexander Fucking Moncrieff!" Her words echoed in the bare tiled room.

"Yeah, I know." His voice came from down the hall, then there was another slam as Zander left the cabins for the outer deck.

Rae turned to the wall and beat on it a few times with her fists. It hurt—blood stung as it flowed back into her hands.

"Hate you," Rae whispered to the wall, then groaned. "And I want you so much, you stupid, crazy, big-ass *bear*."

Zander dealt with his frenzy by stripping off in the cabin he'd chosen for himself, walking out to the stern of the boat, and diving into the freezing waters. If he'd remained in the bathroom with Rae, cold water or no, he'd have taken her up against the wall.

His frenzy was so high he could taste it, like blood burning his mouth. *Shit.*

The waters of the Pacific woke him out of the haze of need, but only so much. He loved the way Rae tasted—saltiness laced with cinnamon and desire. Before today, Zander would never have been so poetic to say someone tasted like cinnamon and desire, but Rae did.

Zander shifted to bear almost immediately, the only way he could survive a dunk in the icy water. His libido calmed slightly as he started to swim, diving under the boat and making schools of fish explode away from him.

He noticed abstractedly that the boat was a good one. The tight hull had been worked on and painted recently, almost pristine except where rocks in the Graveyard had scraped it. The engines were powerful, strong enough to get them through heavy seas. Zander preferred his fishing boat, but this one would do for a longer journey.

Zander swam for a while longer then finally heaved himself back on deck and shook himself from head to tail.

Rae had come out of the cabins in time to be sprayed all over. She shrieked. "Damn you, Zander. I just got dry!"

Zander huffed a laugh, which came out a growl. He shook again, more lightly this time, as Rae wiped the water from her skin in irritation.

Zander knew that if he shifted to human right now the frenzy would return with blasting fury, so he sauntered past her to the closed door to the cabins. Rae made no move to help him open the door, only watched him, her arms folded across her water-spattered sweater.

Zander hid another laugh, reached out with his paw, and opened the door—just to show her that bears had figured out doorknobs.

Zander heard Rae stomping away as he entered the cabins . . . or attempted to enter. The doorway was narrow—a polar bear was a tight fit, and Zander got stuck. He tried to force himself through but only succeeded in wedging himself more firmly.

Zander heaved a sigh and shifted to human form. The doorframe released him but he fell to his hands and knees before he could catch himself.

Please, Goddess, don't let Rae be seeing this. She'd lose her anger at him and laugh her ass off.

But he heard nothing. Rae had gone, leaving Zander to pick himself up, rub diesel grit from his knees, and saunter to his cabin, his need for Rae not soothed one bit.

Z ander redressed in his cabin then took up his samurai swords, including a bamboo one his friend had also left him, and returned to the deck.

"Rae," he said to her where she sat in the wheelhouse with Miles and Ezra. "Come on. Let's keep training." He signaled to Rae to follow him and disappeared back into the sunshine.

He heard Rae emerge behind him. "How am I supposed to fight?" she asked after she closed the door. "My sword is, you know, broken."

"With mine." Zander held the sheathed samurai sword out to Rae.

At that moment, Miles accelerated. He did it gradually, smoothly, no jerking, but Rae stumbled. Zander reached to catch her, but she lithely regained her balance, grabbed the sword, and spun away from him.

"Nice footwork," Zander said.

Sunshine glistened in the water droplets in Rae's hair and burnished her skin where she'd rolled up her sleeves. "What footwork?" she asked. "I almost fell."

"But you caught yourself right away. You're learning.

Rae held the sheathed sword at her side. "I thought we'd fix the Sword of the Guardian before we did more training."

"You thought wrong." Zander swung the bamboo training sword at his side, making the air hum. "Sword craft isn't something you learn overnight. It takes years. We might as well get started. Besides, it will take our mind off our other problem."

Rae flushed scarlet. Her reaction to him had been unashamed but now she looked everywhere but at him.

Zander found her sudden shyness cute. She'd been beautiful rising to his touch, gray eyes half closed as she wrapped herself around him.

Zander's frenzy immediately flared, his cock going stiff. He was never going to make it. The Graveyard had been a good diversion but now the sun was high, the seas calm, the boat rumbling along at a nice pace. He figured the only way he'd cool down was by letting Rae try to kick his ass.

"Just a warning," Zander said as Rae unsheathed the bright curved blade and he raised the bamboo one. "If you drop *that* sword overboard, I'm throwing you in to get it."

For two days, Miles steered them through the waters along the coast, treating Rae to sights seen only by tourists on cruise ships or the fishermen who plied these waters.

The tall majesty of Glacier Bay curved down to become green and brown mountains and coastal inlets. This long stretch was still Alaska, Miles told Rae, a thin finger of land between the Yukon and the Pacific.

Miles wanted to put in at a town near Juneau for fuel and supplies, which started a long argument between him and Zander.

"I don't want Carson anywhere near land," Zander growled. "Not until we're well out of his reach."

They stood in the pilot house where Miles had glued himself—he rarely came out except to use the head, and then he asked Rae to keep an eye on Zander while he did so. Miles slept in the wheelhouse, as the benches could be turned into bunks. He'd even made friends with Jake the Snake, whose favorite place was curled up on the front windowsill.

"If you run my boat dry, I'll go back over to Carson's side," Miles rumbled in return. "You want us to run out of gas in a stretch of nothing? How hidden will you be if we have to be rescued?"

"I don't trust him," Zander said, scowling. "Carson would find a way to contact someone—he'd yell out the window if he had to."

"Tranq him while we're in the harbor," Miles suggested. "We need oil and to fix a couple things. You banged things up out there."

Zander shot Rae a glance where she stood looking out at the grandeur of the scenery. "What do you think, Rae? You have the most to lose. I'm good at keeping myself away from Shifter Bureau but I'm much more worried about you. They'll go after your whole Shiftertown if you're caught out here."

Zander's dark eyes held plenty of rage, and not a little worry, but Rae knew they couldn't simply sail the boat until it wouldn't go any farther.

"We could try talking to him," Rae said.

Both men made derisive noises. Miles shook his head and said, "He can be a wall."

"And I don't want you anywhere near him," Zander finished.

Zander had become extremely protective of Rae in these past few days. He would deliberately step away from her when they drew too near each other, as though having a certain amount of air between them would keep the mating frenzy at bay.

Didn't work. Rae felt crackling sparks of need whether they were in the same room or not. That need urged her to find Zander and continue what they'd started. She'd had casual encounters with Shifters before, especially right after her Transition, but this was different. The gripping hunger wouldn't release her—she knew it was only a matter of time before they gave up and went for it.

If she and Zander did relieve their itch, would the frenzy then cease? Letting them get on with their lives?

Rae didn't know because she couldn't think beyond that. Even now, when Zander included her in the conversation, she could only drop her gaze to his big hand, wanting its warmth on her skin.

"Miles," she said, dragging her attention back to the discussion. "Let me have the key to Carson's cabin." Miles had taken charge of the keys once they'd been under way.

Zander's voice took on a sharper note. "I said, you're not going anywhere near him."

"Not where you've locked him in. I mean his *cabin*," Rae explained patiently. "Where he slept before you came along. Where he keeps his stuff."

Miles seemed to understand and handed over the key ring. Rae closed her fist around it, thanked him, and started below.

"What are you up to?" Zander was a step behind her as Rae started around the deck for the door to the cabins. His warmth cut the chill and flared her need for him to life.

"Figuring out what Carson's deal is," Rae said as she ducked inside and headed for Carson's cabin. "We can't keep him tranqued or locked up forever."

From Zander's growls, he obviously could, but he went quiet as Rae unlocked the large room that belonged to Carson and went inside.

CHAPTER TWENTY-ONE

Rae wasn't certain what she was looking for but she wanted to know more about Carson. He didn't strike her as the same kind of hunter as the shotgun-toting men and women who roamed the world, wanting to "bag" an un-Collared Shifter. Carson was a bounty hunter, turning in Shifters breaking the rules to Shifter Bureau for reward. Some people—like Carson—were fanatic about keeping Shifters Collared and controlled.

Rae found the cabin painfully neat, lacking any personal touches. Carson's bunk against the wall was little bigger than the cot he slept on in the storage room, the blankets and sheets tucked tightly in, the pillow stored in a cabinet above the bed.

Nothing that could possibly be moved by the ship's motion was loose. Everything was stowed, clamped, or fastened down. Not a book or a photo was in sight, every horizontal surface bare.

The room was nothing like the messy jumble of Zander's cabin on his smaller boat. Rae thought about the junk Zander had strewn everywhere, including the little talismans to enhance spells. She still didn't know what he used those for.

Carson was the exact opposite. Spartan, austere, cold.

"No one is this neat," Rae said decidedly. "No one human, anyway."

Zander leaned one shoulder on the doorframe and watched her. "What do you mean, no one human? If you think he's not, you're wrong. Scent doesn't lie."

Rae shook her head. "I meant *human* in the sense of having any feelings whatsoever. I can't imagine Piotr living like this."

"That's true," Zander rumbled. "Piotr has a warm, comfy house with a wife who loves him. Lucky bastard."

Rae sat down on the bed and began going through the cabinets nearest it. They were all locked but the keys she'd taken from Carson opened them.

Two of the cabinets held books and maps, one a laptop. All these were about the business of running a ship. Rae opened the next cabinet and said, "Aha."

"Aha?" Zander sat down next to her, taking up all the space between them. "What aha?"

Rae drew out a photograph in a frame. It was of a woman, fairly pretty, with dark hair and eyes and a smile that held more warmth than anything in this room. If she smiled at Carson, the man had something inside him he kept buried deep.

Under the photo, which Rae handed to Zander, she found a small metal box with a lock and an electronic picture frame. The box was only a few inches on a side, the padlock tiny. None of the keys on the ring fit it.

Zander lifted the box from Rae's hands. "What are you hiding, Mr. McCade?" he asked and broke the lock with his thick fingers.

Rae felt Zander's breath on her cheek as they both bent over the open box. Inside lay a ring—an unadorned gold wedding band. Rae lifted the wedding ring, examining it, but it was plain all the way around. No inscriptions.

"Look at this, Little Wolf." Zander had clicked on the picture frame. He swiped through a series of photos, most containing the same young woman in the printed photograph. One had Carson and the woman together, Carson smiling, his gray eyes full of warmth. Zander slid his arm around Rae's waist as they studied the pictures together. "Is this human enough for you?"

"Who is she?" Rae touched the photo of the man and woman pressed together and looking happy about it.

Zander brushed a kiss to Rae's hair. "I say we go ask him."

C arson looked up wearily as a key scraped into the lock of his prison cell. If it was the bear coming to give him more food, he'd throw it in the big man's face.

Only Zander had been coming down here—obviously he didn't trust Carson not to overpower the other male Shifter or to talk Miles into letting him out. Carson knew he couldn't fight a man who could shift into a polar bear—but he could annoy Zander as much as he could, biding his time until he got out of here and hauled the lot of them to Shifter Bureau.

Carson hid a start of surprise when he saw the young woman, Rae, in the doorway behind Zander. Neither held a tray of food. The big sword was strapped to Rae's back, the hilt rising above her right ear. The sword was broken, Carson had seen, but even a broken blade could kill.

His heartbeat sped, his battle-ready nerves coming alert. Had they come to kill him?

Rae seemed a bit tenderhearted for a Shifter—or maybe she was just squeamish—so his death might not be a violent one. Carson wouldn't put it past Zander to give him an overdose of tranquilizer. Problem solved. Carson would slide into sleep and total oblivion. Just like Viv.

He was up and off the bunk as soon as Rae turned around the photograph of Vivian and held it out to him.

"Don't touch that." Carson snatched the photo from Rae but stopped himself in time from hugging it to his chest. "It's none of your damned business."

"Who is she?" Rae asked.

Her gray eyes held concern. Carson hardened his heart, remembering that Rae had tricked him at first, pretending to be human.

Looking at her now, Carson wondered how he'd not seen she was Shifter. While not containing the thinness that people considered beautiful these days, Rae's body was lithe and strong. He'd watched her through the high window practicing with the samurai sword on deck, seeing how she quickly learned her balance and how to use momentum as well as strength.

The Collar that winked on her throat brought home the fact that she was Shifter and illegally out of her Shiftertown. She'd not trick him again.

"I said," Carson answered Rae, "none of your business."

"Better tell her." Zander's voice was deep and big, like the rest of him. The bear sometimes behaved like a crazy idiot but Carson clearly saw that this was an act. Zander was careful, watchful, knowing everything that went on around him. He turned his assessing black eyes on Carson now. "She'll pry it out of you if you don't. Rae can't leave anything alone."

"Is she your wife?" Rae asked. She held up the gold ring Carson kept locked away when he was on missions so he wouldn't lose it.

Carson's vision filmed with red. They had broken into his personal belongings and touched the things he held most dear. He lunged at Rae and found himself stopped by Zander's strong arm.

"Give that to me," Carson snarled at Rae.

Rae, to his surprise, handed over the ring. "I didn't realize you were married. What happened to her?"

"See what I mean?" Zander asked. He'd trimmed the goatee on his hard face, which brought out the firm lines of his jaw. No Collar was around his neck but anyone who didn't realize this man was Shifter was a fool. "She'll keep on until she gets what she wants."

Carson had no intention of talking about Vivian with these outlaws but he heard himself saying in a harsh voice, "Yes, she's my wife. She's in a coma."

The concern on Rae's face turned to sympathy. Surprise flickered in Zander's eyes. "Seriously?" he asked. "Aw, man, I'm sorry. That sucks."

"Don't pretend you care," Carson returned. "Shifter filth like you put her there."

"Shifters did?" Rae asked him, her eyes widening. "Are you sure?"

"Of course I'm sure. I witnessed it." Carson's jaw was so tight it ached. "I couldn't stop it."

He needed Zander to let go of him. The bear-man's hand held a lot of heat and that heat seemed to be leeching through Carson's body, weakening him. The last words came out trembling and broken.

"Easy," Zander said, his voice quieting to something almost gentle. Carson found himself guided back to the bunk though he didn't remember wanting to go there.

Carson sank to the cot, holding the ring tightly between his first finger and thumb. He remembered when Viv had started to slide it onto his finger in the church, then laughed at him because he'd fumbled and made her drop it. Carson even now heard the *clink* of gold on the church's slate floor and Viv's laughter.

He wrapped one arm around the photo and then realized Rae was sitting on the bunk beside him, the sword's hilt near him. The crosspiece was old, soft silver, Carson saw, covered with some sort of writing.

Zander remained standing, not about to give Carson the chance to run. Rae said in her gentle contralto, "You're hunting Shifters to try to find the ones who hurt her?"

"I think he's taking it out on *any* Shifter," Zander said to her. "Odds are he'll get to the right ones eventually."

"Stop telling me my motives," Carson snapped. "Shifters are dangerous and need to be confined. Or killed. For what they did to her, I will gladly wipe them off the face of the earth."

"Would your wife want you to do that?" Rae asked.

Carson looked at her, stricken. *This woman is a* wolf, *for fuck's sake,* he told himself. He'd seen Rae become a leggy black wolf, running around and around the deck like the hounds of hell were after her. It had been almost amusing, watching her run and jump, working off whatever was making her itch, before he'd reminded himself she was a wild and dangerous creature.

"Don't pretend to understand Viv," Carson said rapidly, before he could answer, *No, she wouldn't.* Viv had more compassion than anyone he'd ever known. She'd seen good in Carson when no one else in the world had.

"I promise you," Zander said, "not all Shifters are like that. If you tell me about them, I'll help you track them down. Could have been ferals."

"You'd turn on your own kind?" Carson had to blink to bring Zander into focus. His eyes were wet for some reason.

"My *kind* doesn't put innocent women into comas," Zander said with a growl

"If Shifters did this, then they need to be stopped," Rae put in. Her eyes held the same determination as Zander's. She might be Collared but it hadn't killed her spirit.

"What can you possibly do?" Carson asked in disbelief. "You're breaking the law just by being here. You took over my boat, you've flouted every Shifter regulation . . ." He broke off and swallowed. "You can't do what I can."

"Oh, you'd be surprised what we can do," Zander said. "We'll hit land soon. You sit here and think about whether you want us to help you, or run off and summon Shifter Bureau. Depends on how bad you want these guys that hurt your mate."

His *mate*. Carson supposed that in Shifter terms, Viv was his mate. Carson wanted to find the Shifters that hurt her, would do *anything* to give them back every pain they'd made her suffer.

Carson said nothing, only clutched Viv's picture to his chest and shoved the ring back onto his finger, where it belonged.

"Rae," Zander said. The man held out his big hand, half turning to the door. When he looked back at her, Zander's eyes sparkled with something besides brute strength and wildness.

He was in love with Rae, Carson realized suddenly. Whether Zander acknowledged it or not, Carson knew exactly what the look meant, having seen it in his own eyes often enough.

Before Rae went to Zander, she laid down the electronic picture frame that held Carson's many photos of Viv. She stood up, gave Carson another look of sympathy, and walked across the small room past Zander. She didn't take his hand but her swift glance at him as she slid out the door confirmed it. Her feelings for Zander were just as strong.

Zander let her go, fixing Carson with his long stare. "More than pictures in that, isn't there?"

There was. The small drive inside the photo frame held files of all Carson's research into Shifters and notes on his search. He couldn't read the files until he could transfer them to a computer or his phone, but they were there.

"How long have you been looking?" Zander asked him.

Carson saw no reason to lie. "Nearly two years."

Zander's brows went up. "I admire your tenacity. With any luck, your hunt will end soon. But your mate might not be any better, even so."

As that truth smacked Carson between the eyes, he wanted to rise up and beat the hell out of Zander. But Zander wasn't saying anything Carson didn't already know. He made himself sit rigidly, wishing Zander would go the hell away.

Zander studied Carson a moment longer then walked out and closed the door. The lock clicked into place.

Carson didn't care. He touched Viv's face with his blunt fingertips, lay down on the bed, and cradled the photo to his chest.

R ae heard Zander come up behind her as she leaned on the railing on deck, watching the beautiful mountains slide by their port side.

Zander's broad arms landed next to hers, the T-shirt he wore pulled and tugged by the wind. "You okay?" he asked her.

Rae hid a shiver. "The poor guy. This must be horrible for him."

"And yet, he's going to take it out on Shifters," Zander said. "I saw that in him. It's what I would do if something happened to . . ." He trailed off, turning to focus on the rolling green and black mountains of the coast. "I'm going to make sure he targets the right Shifters and leaves the rest of us the hell alone."

"How are you going to find them?" Rae asked. "If un-Collared feral Shifters did this, they might be anywhere. Or dead. Ferals don't last long, from what I hear."

"They can be resilient," Zander said. "Remind me to tell you about a feral I once cured." He gave a shudder. "That was brutal."

Zander wasn't joking—his face was drawn with memory, a haunted look in his eyes. If Zander's healing ability made him experience the same pain as the Shifter he cured, then he must have taken on the uncontrolled, raw insanity that made a Shifter feral. Rae wasn't certain exactly what happened inside when a Shifter went feral, but it couldn't be good.

She laid a comforting hand on Zander's arm. "You all right?"

Zander's shaking eased and he took a long breath. He looked down at Rae's fingers on his sun-bronzed skin. "Probably you shouldn't do that."

Rae started to withdraw then stubbornly kept her fingers in place. They could fight their frenzy . . . couldn't they?

Zander's fists clenched on the rail. "Let's focus on getting your sword fixed and finding the Shifters that hurt Carson and his wife. We can't let Shifters out there go on rampages. Miles also saw Shifters brutalizing others, so there's something wrong, and it's been going on for a while."

"Fine by me," Rae said, but she couldn't make herself let go of Zander's arm. "How are we supposed to find them? Stand in the woods and call out for any feral Shifters to come on by?"

"Ha. Leave the comedy to me, sweetheart. No, we're going to find them with technology. What do you know about the Guardian Network?"

CHAPTER TWENTY-TWO

"I don't know anything about it," Rae said, bewildered. "I know it exists but no one gave me the password or anything. I don't think the other Guardians want me near it."

"We'll ask them," Zander said, a resolute light in his eyes. "You're a Guardian, Little Wolf, whether the other Shifters on the planet like it or not. Take the power and run with it. Guardians have access to knowledge the rest of us grunt Shifters never see—and to be honest, most of us don't care. You're of the lineage of the first crop of Guardians gathered in Ireland back in the fourteenth century. Your sword has been handed down to you from the first Guardian who swung it." He gestured to the hilt on Rae's back.

"But I broke it," Rae reminded him. "I used the sword wrong and I broke it. Maybe that means the Goddess takes back her choice."

"Nah," Zander said. "With the Goddess there's no backsies. You're Guardian, and the rest of the world has to get used to it. Tell the Guardians to suck it up and let you into the database."

Rae's heart beat faster. He was always so sure. "Just like that?"

"Why not? Guardians are weird and full of themselves."

A laugh left Rae's mouth. "Thanks a lot. Anyway, so are you."

"Everyone Goddess-touched is," Zander said, unoffended. "Didn't Daragh ever look you up in the database? Figure out your lineage?"

"If he did, he never found anything." Daragh had never come to her and given her any kind of revelation.

"Or, he just didn't tell you. Maybe he saw you had come from a Guardian line and kept that to himself."

"Daragh wouldn't . . ." Rae stopped herself saying, *lie to me.* Daragh had sometimes been an enigma. He might have been troubled by what he discovered and said nothing in order to protect her. Or, more likely, he hadn't found anything at all.

"Want to go back to your Shiftertown?" Zander asked.

Rae jerked her attention to him. "What are you talking about? I'm supposed to be learning how to be Guardian. That will take the rest of my life, right?"

Zander turned his back to the railing, resting his elbows on it. "There's more going on here than the Goddess Choosing the first female Guardian, Little Wolf. You drew the short straw for a reason and I'd like to know why. We'll go to your Shiftertown, grill your dad, and then call a gathering of the Guardians."

He looked so casual saying that—*Let's question the authority of a Shiftertown leader and then tell the Guardians we want to talk to them. All of them.*

"You're crazy," Rae said.

"It's your right, Little Wolf. Guardians get to call a moot. Which is a very old word for meeting. Any time they want, about anything they want. Doesn't happen often, because a true Summoning forces Shifters to come whether they wish to or not. It's painful. So you might ask them to volunteer before you invoke a Summoning."

"Seriously, seriously crazy." The Summoning was rarely used these days. Only clan leaders and Guardians could invoke it, and they did so sparingly. Once the compulsion to obey wore off those who'd been Summoned, the clan leader would have to deal with some very pissed-off Shifters.

"I know I'm crazy," Zander answered calmly. "It lets me get away with a lot of shit. So does being a healer. We live outside the rules."

"Yeah, you're a badass," Rae said. He was telling her how much power she had now, power she'd never dreamed of as a clan-less young Lupine. It shook her.

Zander's eyes held promise. "Someday I'll show you just how bad I am, sweetheart."

"Sure," Rae said, deadpan. "Can't wait." She frowned. "I don't know much about you at all, actually. You came from the Shetlands, you love Alaska, being a healer is hard on you, and you like to fish. That's it."

Zander's look turned guarded. "What else is there to know?"

Everything. Rae wanted to learn what made him laugh or grow sad, whether he liked action movies or sappy ones, what he liked to eat—besides fish and sandwiches—how he'd met Piotr, who his other friends were, and had he ever fallen in love? Zander was old enough that he might have had a mate, though he didn't hold the profound sorrow of one with a severed mate bond, so maybe not. But he must have had a girlfriend or a lover before this—maybe that was why he preferred being alone, to nurse his sorrow.

All that information might be in the Guardian database.

"All right," Rae said abruptly. "The Guardians do need to let me into the database. I'm one of them now, whether they like it or not."

Zander's grin returned. "That's my girl."

Rae warmed under his smile—which was large like everything else about him. "I'm not your girl, you big lug."

She'd meant it to be teasing but Zander lost his amusement. He swung around and had his hands on either side of her on the railing before she could draw another breath.

"Yes, you are my girl," he said in a rapid voice. "Don't you forget it." His eyes held ferocity as he gazed straight into hers.

Zander curved over Rae, trapping her in place, but she had no desire to duck under him and run. The sword, still on her back, pressed into her shoulder blades.

Rae reached up and touched his face.

Zander's growl turned savage. He bent to her, his hands never leaving the rail, and he kissed her.

His body was warm, cutting the chill from the wind and water. The boat swayed but Zander held Rae firmly, his mouth opening hers. The sword's sheath against her back kept her stiffly upright.

Rae's blood fired, the mating frenzy never far. It wasn't going to go away, that frenzy. Not before it was sated.

Rae moved her hands to his hard shoulders, then his chest, then his abdomen. Zander's kiss turned fierce, robbing her of breath. Rae slid her hands to his waistband, everything he had in easy reach under the thin sweats.

Zander broke the kiss and jerked his head up, his teeth scraping her lips. His was breathing hard, his cheekbones flushed.

"No, no, no, we won't go down that road again, Little Wolf. We'll burn up."

"I don't care," Rae said softly. She cupped his cock through the sweatpants, heart racing as she found him hard, big, and wanting.

Zander pushed himself from her and slammed against the wall of the cabins. "*I* care," he said, the words coming out stiffly. "If I don't back off, I'll be going for a swim in icy waters again. Unless you want another cold shower?"

His eyes glinted with so much heat and mischief that Rae wanted to laugh. He'd do it. Zander took a step toward her as though ready to haul her off to the showers right now.

Rae drew the top half of the broken sword and held it in a defensive stance. "Back off, bear."

Zander snarled. The rumble tore out of him, full of anger and mating frenzy, and Rae held the sword more firmly.

"Put it away," Zander said. "Get your ass back to the stern for some more training. You need it. I'll be there in a minute."

Rae watched him in suspicion, not trusting that he wouldn't drag her to the showers the moment her back was turned. Zander didn't move, one hand on the wall, as he waited for her to go.

Rae backed away slowly, putting a few yards between them

before she slid the sword into its sheath and turned toward the stern deck.

When she looked around again, Zander had vanished. In his place was a pile of clothing and, a moment later, Rae heard a loud splash from somewhere in the bow. Water fountained up and Zander was gone.

Zander had been correct that Miles would know places to drop them off on the coast where they wouldn't have to worry about port authorities, customs, police, or anything else that would slow them down. He needed a quiet place with an airstrip—or at least a place to land—so the cargo plane pilot he'd called could pick them up.

Miles had been able to put in near Juneau, as he'd wanted, to resupply. Zander, Ezra, and Rae had stayed out of sight and Carson had not made a noise. Carson had been subdued since Rae had found out about his wife. He didn't speak much when Zander brought his food but at least Carson was eating the food now without fuss.

Zander made many phone calls and arrangements while they'd waited for Miles to finish restocking. Zander was anxious to take Rae home and get her into the Guardian's database. The Guardian Network held the secrets of the ages—it might tell them how to put the sword back together, where Rae came from, and how to find the out-of-control Shifters who'd hurt Carson's wife.

Might, Zander reminded himself. Or the database might hold nothing but menus for all-Guardian parties. Who the hell knew?

The human pilot Zander had contacted landed in a seaplane in a little harbor Miles sailed into that housed a fishing and hunting resort. Miles moored as close as he could to the plane and Marlo, the pilot, cut his engines and waited for them.

Rae was ready, the backpack of her things Ezra had transferred from Zander's boat in her hand. The sword gleamed on her back as she waited for Miles to lower the small speedboat that would take them to the seaplane.

Zander had resumed his usual jeans, sweatshirt, and duster,

ready to quit the high seas. Ezra waited next to him to board the speedboat, the Lupine also looking as though he'd had enough of the ocean.

"Miles," Zander said as Miles finished cranking the boat into the water. "Come with us. I'll introduce you to some Shifters who'll show you it's not so bad being one of us." He tried a grin. "As soon as I figure out who they are."

Miles shook his head, dark eyes haunted. "I gotta look after this boat. Carson and I own it together and I'm the only one who knows how to run it."

Zander shrugged, pretending he understood, but Miles's loneliness and worry reached out to him. Jake the Snake was staying with Miles, the reptile preferring the freedom of shipboard life to stifling in Zander's pocket. But Miles, in the long run, would need more company than a snake.

Zander wouldn't force the man into an embrace this time. They were out on open deck and Miles looked as though he feared Zander hugging him more than he feared being caught as a Shifter.

Rae had no such compunction. She threw her arms around Miles's waist and held him hard. "Thank you," she said. "Thank you for helping us."

Miles might not have wanted to hug a loud, annoying bear, but Rae was hard to resist. Miles put his big arms around her in return. "That's all right, honey. You gonna be okay with him?"

Rae nodded. "I think so. What about you?"

"I'll survive," Miles said, resolute. "I always do. Hey, you ever need anything from me, you call me, all right?"

Rae nodded, gave him another squeeze, then released him. "I'll do that."

Zander moved to Rae to help her into the boat, where Ezra had already jumped. Ezra had softened way down too. Rae had that effect on people.

Carson's bag landed in the speedboat and Carson followed. He was tightlipped but had announced last night that he'd take up Zander's offer to help him find the Shifters responsible for putting his wife into a coma. Rae had gotten to him too.

Zander said a final good-bye to Miles, handed his swords

to Rae, then swarmed down into the boat and took them back from her. She didn't smile but her eyes were warm. She was heading in the direction of home, and she was happy.

Miles waved as Zander revved the speedboat and steered them carefully away from the larger craft. Rae sat down and waved back at Miles, her smile beaming.

The seaplane was small but the four of them fit themselves into the cramped passenger seats without fuss. There were single chairs with an aisle between, so Zander couldn't sit right next to Rae. He sat directly behind her instead, where he could keep an eye on her as well as on Carson.

Marlo talked to whoever regulated the airspace around here and soon had them up and away.

An hour or so later, Marlo touched down on a lake somewhere in Canada, returned the seaplane to the friend from whom he'd borrowed it, and loaded them onto his cargo plane. This one was a replacement for the one that had gone down a few years ago but it was as old and clanging as the last one, not a comforting thought. Marlo had survived, the thin man as wiry and energetic as ever, so maybe *that* was comforting. Marlo seemed indestructible.

This plane was larger but didn't have seats other than the copilot's chair. Zander sat on the floor in the back next to Rae, she leaning against him as the trip grew long.

It was just past sunset when Marlo landed at an airstrip far from any town. He'd radioed ahead, and a Shifter Zander didn't know picked them up outside the tiny hangar.

Rae knew him though. She'd been snuggled into Zander's side, her scent and warmth delightful, but as she walked sleepily off the plane and saw the Shifter, she came instantly alert. Dropping everything, she ran at the stranger and leapt into his arms.

The Shifter was Feline, Zander saw as he scooped up Rae's backpack and sword and followed. He smelled Rae's scent on the Feline as well.

Rae wrapped herself around the Shifter, jammed a kiss to his face, and laughed out loud. "Goddess, Colin, it is so good to see you!"

CHAPTER TWENTY-THREE

"You've only been gone a week," the Feline said, a hint of an Irish accent coming forth. He embraced Rae warmly and returned the kiss.

"Is that all? Feels like forever." Rae reluctantly climbed down and turned to Zander. "This is Zander Moncrieff. Zander, this is my brother Colin."

Brother. Ah. Zander relaxed but only slightly. Rae and Colin might have been raised as brother and sister, but they weren't related by blood. Weren't even the same species.

Colin was holding on to Rae pretty tightly—but that didn't necessarily mean anything more than family affection. Shifters liked embracing for comfort and support.

Colin stretched out a hand in greeting to Zander without letting go of Rae. "I thought bears didn't have last names."

"Everyone says that." Zander grasped Colin's wrist and Colin's fingers bit down on Zander's forearm with strength. The usual Shifter greeting was an embrace, even a wary one, but the arm squeeze was accepted when the Shifter's hands were full.

"So my dad dumped Rae on you, did he?" Colin asked as he released Zander. He had a wide smile and dark eyes, his light brown hair the same shade as his father's. Mountain lions who'd raised a wolf cub. Shiftertowns made weird combinations happen. "I feel for you, man," Colin was saying. "She's wild, is our Rae. No wonder you're rushing her back home."

"Shut it, Colin." Rae gave him a light punch but she had so much happiness in her eyes Zander felt like he was the one who'd been smacked in the gut.

Zander broke in. "I'm rushing her home because there's shit going on your dad needs to know about."

"Like how the Coast Guard was chasing you around?" Colin's smile left him and his eyes narrowed. "We heard about that." His protectiveness closed around Rae like a fist.

Zander didn't ask how he'd known. Reports of Shifters being pursued in Alaskan waters would have reached Eoin somehow. Shifter leaders had a lot of resources.

"We need to go," Zander said impatiently. "I hope you didn't broadcast that Rae was coming back. I don't want hostile Shifters waiting for us in your Shiftertown."

"I think Dad knows how to take care of Rae," Colin said. "Oh, and that Lupine you wanted from Austin is on his way. He thought it was a good idea to tell Dad he was coming."

Rae finally stepped away from her brother and reached for her backpack and sword. "What Lupine?" she asked Zander.

Her eyes held annoyance that Zander hadn't told her about all the arrangements he'd made before they'd left the boat. However, Zander didn't want to discuss it out here in front of Colin, Marlo, and whatever Shifters could be listening. Eoin and her brothers might have kept it quiet Rae was returning, but Shifters were good at knowing what was going on.

"This is Carson," Zander said instead of answering. "He's a bounty hunter but I'm vouching for him. Ezra's a Lupine who needs somewhere to chill for a while. And he needs a mate. Introduce him around, all right?"

He started walking to the only vehicle on the edge of the field, a black pickup with a four-door cab.

"What Lupine?" Rae asked as she hurried to catch up with Zander.

Zander kept walking. "Guy I know who can look at the sword. I was trying not to say it too loud."

Rae sent him her gray glare. "In that case, you could have told me before we got here."

"I didn't have a chance. Besides, you're cute when you yell at me."

Rae gave him a snarl, pushed past him, and ran to the truck. Watching her hips sway as she went wasn't a bad thing at all.

C oming home for Rae was a mixture of joy and trepidation. Joy as Colin drove around familiar corners where she'd spent the last twenty years of her life among her loving family. Trepidation because she knew many of the Shifters here wouldn't welcome her back. They'd watched her drive out with relieved eyes, glad the embarrassment to Shiftertown was departing.

Zander had been completely right to keep it quiet about the broken sword. He'd been on his cell phone almost constantly before Miles had put in near the seaplane, talking to the Goddess only knew who. He really did have connections all over the place, Rae realized. She was starting to think that if he decided to fly to Mars, he'd know people with rockets that would take him here.

It made Rae wonder what Zander would do once he finished training her. Go back to Alaska to fish? Find a new place to hide out? Trek around the world, healing Shifters hither and yon? And who would help him recover when he took the Shifters' pain into himself?

Rae's heart began to burn. Zander was compelling, not to mention hot-bodied, and he'd no doubt find plenty of female companionship along the way.

The thought made growls roll around Rae's throat. Female Shifters, especially Lupines, were possessive of the males they chose. Nothing was more ferocious than a she-wolf protecting her mate.

Is that how I think of him? Rae wondered with a jolt. Her potential mate? *I need more cold showers,* she decided.

Zander sat behind her in the pickup's cab during the ride to Shiftertown but his nearness made her shiver. She tried to push away remembered sensations of Zander on the bunk with her in her cabin and kissing her on the deck, but it wasn't easy. Even pulling up in front of the two-story house she shared with her dad and brothers couldn't quite clear her mind.

But she was home. Rae leapt from the pickup before Colin had completely stopped the truck, and ran to the man waiting on the porch.

"Daughter." Eoin's love for Rae surrounded her as he lifted her into his arms. "I missed you, sweetheart."

"Missed you too, Dad." Rae clung to him, her eyes stinging.

It didn't matter that Eoin wasn't her biological father or that she was Lupine and he Feline. Love transcended boundaries like that. Eoin was her true dad and this was Rae's home.

She hoped her other brother, Logan, would come to greet her too, but she didn't see him. Eoin answered her question before Rae could ask. "Logan's out looking into something for me. He'll be back soon."

"What?" Rae asked, worry trickling through her happiness. Running a Shiftertown was never easy. "Is anything the matter?"

Eoin shrugged, but Rae saw the concern in his eyes. "Some of the Shifters want to hold another Choosing."

Rae's heart constricted. The clan leaders in this Shiftertown were arrogant and ruthless—traits that made for a good clan leader. But if they opposed the Shiftertown leader, things could get sticky. If she confessed she'd broken the sword, the shit would truly hit the fan.

"Let them," Zander, who'd come up onto the porch behind Rae, said, not sounding alarmed. "The Goddess doesn't like to be second-guessed. Are they willing to risk pissing her off?"

"It might be better to let them go through with the Choosing," Eoin said. "When Rae is Chosen again, there can be no doubt."

Zander didn't look reassured, and Rae privately agreed with him. If Rae was touched at another Choosing, it might only convince the more hostile Shifters that Eoin had rigged it. Unrest in Shiftertowns could lead to violence, no matter what the rules, no matter that the Shifters wore Collars. "Shiftertown leader" was an artificial position, created by humans, and the other clan leaders were always vying for it.

Eoin released Rae and went to greet his guests. Ezra looked exhausted—he was breaking down from grieving—but he took Eoin's welcoming embrace with equanimity, grateful for a place to stop.

Carson looked around with wary gray eyes, hand whitening as he gripped his pack. Zander had convinced him to leave his pistol on the boat with Miles—or Shifters might make him eat it, he'd said. More than once, Carson started to rest his hand on the absent weapon, then flinched when he didn't find it.

"Your hurt is deep," Eoin said as Zander led Carson up to the porch. Eoin didn't try to touch the man—he knew when to take his time. "You are welcome to rest here and heal."

Carson obviously didn't know what to say. He gave Eoin an acknowledging nod, but his suspicions were going to die hard.

"He's all right," Zander said. He closed his hands over Carson's shoulders. "We're going to help him find his enemies, figure out what's up with them, and kick ass if we have to. Carson's actually not a bad guy, just a little confused."

Carson stepped out from under Zander's touch. "I'm not a Shifter," he said. "And the fact that you can help me doesn't negate that you tranqued me, imprisoned me, stole my boat . . ."

"I could say the same about you," Zander said in a light voice. "But here I am, forgiving and forgetting. You do the same, while you're here."

Carson raised his hand. "I'm willing to call a truce. But you walk a thin line, Shifter."

Rae gave Carson a sympathetic look. "Zander has that effect on everyone. But I don't care right now—I just want some burgers. Colin's cooking."

With that, Rae walked past her dad and brother into the house, which seemed to reach out and embrace her.

Rae's exuberance at being home again lasted until after supper. Colin did set up a grill in the backyard and started turning out perfect hamburgers, topped with gooey melted cheese. Logan returned from wherever Eoin had sent him and ate three burgers in one sitting. They all lounged on the porch after eating and sipped beer as they did many a summer night, as the stars came out and frogs and crickets began their nightly songs.

There was no sign of the Lupine Zander had asked to come to their Shiftertown. Rae didn't want to mention him again, not before talking to Zander about it first. She hadn't yet confessed to Eoin that the sword was broken—if Zander's friend could fix it, she might not have to.

Zander related Carson's tale about Shifters going on a killing spree to Eoin and Rae's brothers. Carson filled in details—he and his wife had been staying in a cabin along the border between Idaho and Canada. Shifters had attacked the cabin, and when Carson had shot one, they'd turned savage. They'd beaten both Carson and his wife senseless, stolen or destroyed everything in the cabin, and finally departed. Carson had recovered, but Viv had not. She lay in a hospital in Seattle, on life support.

Carson had reported the attack, of course, but investigations by Shifter Bureau, their military detachment, and local law enforcement, no matter how vigilant, had turned up nothing. Carson, angry and frustrated at their lack of progress, had taken it upon himself to hunt down un-Collared Shifters and bring them in, hoping one day he'd find the specific ones who'd hurt his wife.

"I heard about that when it happened," Eoin said. The night was soft, a breeze keeping things cool. "Indirectly—Shifter Bureau questioned the Coeur d'Alene Shiftertown closely but none of their Shifters had gone missing."

"Rogues," Zander said. He swallowed a sip of beer. "Shifters who never took Collars," he said to Carson. "Some of them go feral."

Rae looked pointedly at Zander's bare neck, but he only winked at her and toasted her with his beer bottle.

"There might be some information about them in the Guardian Network," Zander said. "Speaking of that, Rae needs access to it."

Eoin started. "Why?" he asked, his voice hard.

Zander became watchful, but Rae realized that those who didn't know him might think he didn't care one way or the other. "She's a Guardian. She should already be in."

"Shifters here are not going to be happy if Rae messes with Daragh's laptop," Eoin said sternly. "In fact, his entire house has become a shrine to his memory."

"Since when?" Rae asked indignantly. True, the small house Daragh had occupied apart from his clan—his right as a Guardian, though not all Guardians exercised the right—had not been taken over since Daragh's death. Rae had never imagined living there herself. It was *Daragh's*.

"Since you've been gone." Eoin gentled his tone. "The clan leaders who claim there is no Guardian are keeping Daragh's house intact for the next one."

Rae clutched her empty bottle and kept herself from throwing it. She wondered how long it would be before these Shifters openly defied Eoin and tried to challenge his leadership. They might kill him if he didn't submit, and make sure the reports of his death to Shifter Bureau said "accidental."

"You're Shiftertown leader," Zander rumbled. "Overrule them."

Eoin turned dark eyes to him. "You've obviously never lived in a Shiftertown, lad. Keeping the balance is never that simple."

Ezra, who'd been withdrawn and silent since they'd arrived, spoke up. "The whole discussion is ridiculous. Rae *is* a Guardian. She sent my father to dust. I witnessed it."

"So did I," Zander said. "But I have the feeling the testimony of rogue Shifters like us won't convince anyone. We're not from around here."

Ezra growled. "Shiftertowns. I always said they were a bad idea."

No one contradicted him.

Rae was exhausted. She rose, said good night, and went to bed in her own room, the small one at the top of the stairs.

She'd so longed to be back here when she'd been confined to Zander's boat, but an hour later she was still awake, staring at the ceiling, unable to relax. The space that had been so comforting to her only weeks ago pressed at her now.

Shifters were turning against her, people she'd known for years. The clans had lauded and respected her father for the two decades he'd been Shiftertown leader. Now, Eoin had made one decision they didn't like, and they were challenging his authority.

If Rae couldn't convince this Shiftertown she was truly the Guardian, or if she didn't quit and relinquish the sword, things could go bad for Eoin.

But the sword couldn't be relinquished, could it? No one quit being a Guardian. You either were one or you weren't.

Rae closed her eyes but sleep eluded her. The only way the unbelievers would be convinced was if someone died and Rae had to send them to dust. She certainly didn't want something that tragic to happen simply to prove the Choosing had been true. But that was likely the only thing that would convince them. Even then, she'd guess Shifters opposing her father would try to claim that the dusting had been a trick. It made her stomach hurt.

She must have drifted to sleep despite her worries, because she came alert a short time later, her Shifter senses telling her someone was in the room with her. Rae hadn't heard the door open but she knew good and well that a Shifter stood a few feet beyond her bed.

She reached for the sword in swift silence and only to have it taken away from her. Rae struggled for it but a large hand pushed her back to the bed. Her sleepy confusion cleared, and she recognized the scent.

"Hush, Little Wolf."

Rae abruptly ceased her struggle. The room was almost completely black but she saw the outline of Zander's bulk, a braid swinging over his shoulder.

"Damn it, Zander," she said in a fierce whisper. "What are you doing?"

"Waking you up." His voice was carefully quiet. "Get dressed. We need to have a look at Daragh's computer."

CHAPTER TWENTY-FOUR

Rae led the way along the edges of Shiftertown to Daragh's small house. She'd run around this town plenty as a cub, and she felt herself reverting to the tricks of her teenage years as they moved through woods and down a slope to the cabin that had been Daragh's retreat.

Rae knew how to avoid the busybodies who liked to keep note of everything that went on in Shiftertown, as well as Shifters who were simply out for a run or having quick sex in the woods.

They shouldn't be so predictable, Rae thought as she signaled Zander into the shadows. An older Shifter Lupine strode past, the man looking sharply around him, probably trying to see who was stealing a shag so he could be disapproving about it tomorrow.

Once he was gone, Rae moved silently down the little path that led to Daragh's cabin. Before she could dart to its front door, Zander's hand came down on her shoulder.

"Careful. If it's a shrine now, they'll probably have a sentry."

Good point. Rae faded back under the trees with him and

they watched. The night was cool but not cold, though Rae liked Zander at her back, warming her.

There *was* a sentry. A young Feline just past his Transition walked up to the house, checked the doors and windows, and strolled away. He called to someone in the woods beyond.

"It's fine," he said, sounding annoyed. "Dad just likes to fuss. Let's go."

Rae heard female laughter as the Feline disappeared under the trees. She recognized the voices—those two would no doubt be mated soon. They'd also be distracted for a while, giving Rae and Zander opportunity to enter the house.

She crept forward, keeping to the darkness under the eaves in case there were more watchers. The Feline had demonstrated that the door was locked, but Rae knew where Daragh had kept his spare key. Everyone in Shiftertown did, in fact, and Rae quickly found that it was no longer in its hiding place. However, Rae knew where Daragh had kept his *backup* spare key.

She reached behind a low beam near the back door and smiled in satisfaction when she felt the cool metal of the key. Rae prayed to the Goddess that no one had changed the lock, then let out a sigh of relief when the key turned, letting them into the house.

Zander came in quickly behind her, shutting the door. He closed the shades on the back windows but didn't try to turn on a light. Rae understood—Shifters would see even the tiniest glow leaking through the cracks around the window shades.

Rae relied on Shifter sight and her memory of the place to move unhindered to Daragh's desk. Daragh had kept the cabin sparsely furnished, which made things easier, and as Rae's eyes adjusted, she could see that nothing had been moved.

This house truly had been made a shrine. Every single object was in place, from Daragh's laptop, still plugged in to power, and the empty cup he'd set on the table the night he'd left for a walk in the woods. On that walk he'd been shot by humans out to steal his sword.

Rae's heart burned. The evil of that act enraged her. Daragh had been her friend, had taken care of her. Losing him felt the same as losing one of her brothers.

Zander slid his hands to her shoulders, his warmth cutting

through her grief and anger. "I know, Little Wolf. It was a criminal thing. At least his soul was rescued and his body sent to dust."

His voice was low, soothing. Zander had once asked Rae if she'd been in love with Daragh but now he seemed to understand. Daragh had been a special person in Rae's life, a different kind of love.

"You're his successor," Zander went on. "I think he'd be proud of you and want you to be here."

Rae sighed. "I just wish he was around to tell everyone that."

Zander's voice held a hint of laughter. "You'll have to tell them yourself."

"You have so much confidence." Rae seated herself at the desk, on the chair she'd seen Daragh in so many times, and opened the laptop.

"Helps to have confidence when you're crazy." Zander leaned in to study the laptop's screen, which was blank and black. "Never liked computers."

Rae refrained from pointing out he used one to navigate his boat, and pressed the power button. "Turning it on makes a big difference."

The laptop hummed and beeped, various lights glowing orange then green. The computer quieted into a gentle hum, but the screen remained black, not even a cursor to break the emptiness.

Zander knocked on it. "You sure this thing's on?"

"Yes, I'm sure." Rae peered at the screen, tapped keys, and then deflated. "Maybe it's broken."

Zander touched the keyboard, brushing her fingers. "Maybe you have to know the ultra-secret, secret password."

"Which I don't." Rae looked around the desk, which was as blank as the laptop. "I don't think Daragh wrote it on a sticky note."

Zander didn't move his fingers from Rae's. He said quietly, "From what I heard, when Daragh was killed and the sword stolen, it was so some hacker chick could get herself into the Guardian Network. So, what does the sword have to do with it?"

Rae had no clue. She slid her hands out from under Zander's, picked up the sword, and withdrew the top part of the blade from the sheath. Runes crossed the hilt and ran down into the blade, curving around the crosspiece. Even in the darkness, the silver shone, the runes etched into it like black threads. The top of the hilt held a medallion that resembled the ones on their Collars, the Celtic knot.

Daragh had known what the runes said but he'd never talked about them. Rae ran her fingers along the broken blade, tracing the strange letters she couldn't read.

Zander lifted the sheath and turned it upside down so the bottom half of the sword fell out. He caught the blade without cutting himself and laid it in front of the laptop.

"Put the top part here." He tapped the table.

Rae carefully laid the top half of the sword in line with the bottom, then she and Zander pushed the pieces together. As had happened on Miles's boat, the jagged cut fit like two pieces of a puzzle but the sword remained broken.

Two runes, one above the other, reached across the cut, the break having sliced them exactly in half. Rae had no idea what that meant, if anything.

Zander leaned to study the sword, his head close to Rae's breasts. His warmth and scent soothed her but she resisted reaching to stroke his hair.

"Press the *A* key then the *R*," he rumbled. He pointed at the two broken runes before she could ask why.

"You can read that?" Rae asked in surprise.

"Vikings were all over the Shetlands back in the day, and they left stuff. Archeologists are always deciphering runes—I hung around the digs when I was a cub and learned what they did. My Shifter ancestors were Vikings if you didn't guess."

With his white hair and giant build, Zander did look very Norse. "All right." Rae moved her fingers to the keyboard and typed *AR*.

They appeared on the screen as runes, identical to those on the sword. Rae pressed the return key.

When nothing happened, Zander said, "Try the other way around."

RA. Still nothing happened. "A password isn't going to be only two letters," Rae pointed out. "Not for something so protected."

Her words were drowned out by an intense humming

coming from the sword. The thing had been silent since it had helped them out of the whirlpool, but now it vibrated and sang. The humming should have rattled the blade on the desk but the sword was a magical thing, not emitting true sound, so the desk was oblivious to its vibrations.

The runes Rae typed grew and spread across the screen until white pixels swallowed everything black. The white grew fuzzy, like a static snowfield, and then the static parted to reveal the image of a man.

He was a Shifter, a Feline by the look of him. He had a Collar around his neck, very dark hair, and intense blue eyes. Rae stared at the screen, wondering if she'd somehow messaged someone, then when the man didn't move, she realized this must be a recording.

"Greetings," the man said, his voice rich with an Irish accent. "You have entered as a new user. Please type in your 11-digit password."

"What?" Rae said back. "What password?"

Rae frantically opened the drawers of the desk, looking for any scrap of paper, and finding them empty. Zander was watching the screen with narrowed eyes. "No one gave her a password," he growled. "They barely acknowledge she's Guardian."

The man only blinked and waited. "He can't hear you," Rae said. "I bet it's a failsafe."

The man blinked again, then he said, "In that case, enter a new password. Anything you want. Probably should make it a *little* cryptic."

He waited. Rae peered at him, but he still seemed to be a recording, programmed to make certain responses.

What the heck? She keyed in 483Zander&2.

The man on the other side studied the screen, slid his gaze sideways to Zander, then said, "Sure, that will work. Welcome, Guardian, to the Guardian Network. What do you want to know?"

"Sean," Zander said clearly. "Cut the crap. What are you doing?"

The corners of Sean's eyes crinkled but he didn't smile. "Waiting for Rae to finally log onto the database. I got bored."

Rae started, then her face heated. "You should have said

you weren't a recording." How embarrassing. "What do you mean waiting for me to finally log on? How long have you been sitting there?"

Sean shrugged. "Oh, off and on since you were Chosen." His attention moved to something else in the room. "There's my lad." He opened his arms and a small boy trotted to him. Sean scooped him up. "Kenny, this is Rae and Zander. You met Zander before, remember?"

Kenny raised a hand in childlike greeting but didn't smile. He had gray eyes, wolf's eyes, assessing and watchful.

Rae leaned forward, her voice softening. "Hi, Kenny. You sure are cute."

Kenny gazed at her a moment then his small face blossomed into a smile. He reached out and touched the screen. Sean let him then pulled Kenny back into his lap. "He's a handful, I don't mind saying. What took you so long to get here?"

"We've been a little busy," Zander said. "And no one has let her near the Guardian Network."

Sean gave one shake of his head. "I'm sorry, Rae. The Guardians themselves are divided about you. I, for one, believe the Goddess truly Chose you. *You* know she did."

Rae had no doubt, since she'd been vibrating with the Goddess's choice since that fateful day.

"Be careful, lass," Sean said, becoming serious. "A few of the Guardians have said they'll try to block your way to the Network and to make note of the information you try to find. I set up a gateway through my computer so any login attempt you make will come to me first. Your searches would be watched, but what *I* look up is none of anyone's business. I know how to hide my trail. So . . . What do you want to know?"

Rae gave Zander a questioning look. She had never met Sean Morrissey, Guardian of the Austin Shiftertown, but she'd heard about him. Her father liked the Morrisseys and considered them allies. Zander had obviously met Sean before, and Zander was turning out to be a surprisingly good judge of character.

Zander gave her a nod. "Sean's a good guy. I'd trust him."

"Aw," Sean said. "I never knew you felt that way about me."

"Don't push it." Zander glowered. He looked at Kenny, pushed his fist toward the screen, and Kenny on the other side touched his fist to it. "Keep it cool, little guy. Say hi to Olaf for me."

Kenny nodded and sat back in his father's lap, a too-serious expression on his face. He was going to be an alpha, Rae suspected. Was one already.

Rae gathered her courage. "One thing I need to find out is how to fix this." She lifted the sword by the hilt to show Sean the broken piece. The light from the computer glittered on the jagged cut.

Sean's blue eyes widened. "Shite. What the hell happened?"

"It wasn't her fault," Zander said quickly. "She was defending me in a fight. I didn't think the things *could* break. Must have been some cheap, crappy silver."

"Don't be daft," Sean growled. "All the swords were forged by Niall O'Connell, the master swordsmith, meant t' be passed through the generations. He used Fae silver—very rare. The swords are twined with spells. They don't break."

"Well, this one did," Zander said. "Tell us how to put it back together."

"I don't have any bloody idea. The issue has never come up."

"This sword was broken before," Zander pointed out. "When it was stolen, the medallion came off, according to Broderick." He tapped the silver piece on the end of the hilt. "But now it's back on like it never happened."

Sean shook his head. "Swords have minds of their own. Seems like it anyway. If that one broke, it was for a reason. Maybe it's symbolic—it won't go together again until the Guardians accept Rae. Or maybe she has to figure out how to fix it herself. I've lived with a Sword of the Guardian most of my life and I still don't understand it."

Rae lowered the sword to the table in disappointment. She'd half hoped she'd get into the Guardian's database and find a file entitled *How to Fix your Broken Sword,* or something equally as useful.

Zander looked just as discouraged. "So, know any swordsmiths?" he asked Sean.

Sean shrugged. "Not really. They're out there, but it will take special skill, not to mention Fae magic, to work on a Guardian's sword."

A growl filled Zander's throat. "No Fae is getting near Rae."

"I wasn't suggesting they do," Sean said. "There are some Shifters who have a way with metal though."

"Yeah, Broderick and his family," Zander said. "I've already asked him to come up here. I don't know if he can help though."

"Meanwhile . . ." Sean said. "You could try deciphering the writing on the sword."

Rae leaned forward in sudden interest. "How? I don't know anything about Fae runes. Is there a book? A translation program?"

Sean's laughter came back. "Now, why would the Guardians of old have made it easy for us? There's a bit about the Fae language in the database, but each sword is unique, made for its original Guardian. Every Guardian has to figure out the runes for himself."

Zander sat back with a grunt. "Thanks, Sean, you've been a lot of help."

Sean looked wise. "Rae accessed the database because you found the runes that let her in. Obviously, you can read them."

Zander scowled. "I know the Norse letters. Not Fae—it's a completely different language."

"It's a beginning," Sean said. "Now, I have to sign off. My mate wants to go for her run. You know how wolves are." His eyes twinkled as he grinned at Rae. "Sean Morrissey, over and out." He reached forward and touched a key on his laptop. His picture and Kenny's winked out, Rae's screen going black again.

Rae sat back glumly. "Well, that wasn't helpful."

"No, maybe it was."

To Rae's surprise, Zander had lost his annoyed look and was thoughtfully studying the blank screen. "How?" Rae asked in irritation.

"I would guess Sean couldn't say all he wanted to, no matter how good a firewall he has. He had to be vague. But he's right—the runes on the sword are the key. I can *transliterate* the runes, but I don't know enough Fae to trust myself to *translate* them. But that doesn't matter. I know a—"

"Don't say you know a guy!" Rae cut him off. "You can't know everyone in the world."

"Sure I can." Zander's amused look returned. "I know a guy who can read Fae—because he *is* Fae—not his fault. I just need to make a phone call."

Zander led Rae out of the cabin, the sword on her back again, after she'd closed down the laptop. Zander watched Rae lock the door, start to return the key to its hiding place, her body curving as she reached up, then decide to drop the key into her pocket. Good for her.

She joined him, walking close by his side as they slipped into the woods.

Zander had wanted to bring the laptop with them but Rae argued that if those watching the house noticed it gone, they'd immediately suspect her and Eoin and come after it. In Zander's opinion, Eoin should guard the computer himself and tell the other Shifters to suck on it, but Eoin had been right when he'd said that being Shiftertown leader was complicated. A job Zander thanked the Goddess he was never likely to have.

Zander took Rae's hand as they moved silently through the woods, her fingers warm in his. The Feline who was supposed to be standing guard was enjoying himself with his mate under the trees beyond the house. Anyone walking by would sense that—and hear them too. They weren't trying to be quiet. The sounds of their lovemaking faded as Zander and Rae moved swiftly up the path.

When they reached the darkest part of the woods, about half a mile from the main Shiftertown, Zander pulled Rae to a halt, his hand on her shoulder. "Hold up."

Rae instantly came alert. "What?" She scanned the shadows under the trees. "What's wrong?"

"Nothing." Zander turned Rae to him and cupped her face. "I just need to kiss you." He leaned to her and let himself stop holding back.

CHAPTER TWENTY-FIVE

Kissing Rae made everything bad go away. Zander tasted the warmth of her mouth while he wrapped his hands around her hips to draw her closer. Her kiss in return was welcoming, growing more intense as it went on. They were alone, no one knew where they were, and Zander let the frenzy come.

He slid the sword from Rae's back, dropping it gently onto the pine needles that surrounded them. Then he lifted her, holding her in strong arms.

Rae fit against him as though she'd been made for him. Her breasts were soft against his chest, her eyes half closed as she wrapped her legs around him, fingertips finding purchase in his back.

The night was warm, Rae against him hotter still. Mating frenzy had hold of her but Zander loved that she wanted *him*. This town was full of sex-crazed Shifters—every Shiftertown was—but Rae had wrapped herself around *Zander*, her dark braid like a rope of silk in his hands.

He needed to touch her, to be inside her. Here in the woods? Too crude.

He wanted to do it somewhere quiet, beautiful, soft, so Rae

would gaze up at him in contentment. Zander knew a guy who could fix that up.

In the meantime, Rae roved her hands down his back and under his waistband, sliding her fingers to the bare flesh of his backside. She wanted him as much as he wanted her, making no coy pretense of shyness.

Zander tugged up her shirt and tank top, finding the warm silk of her skin. She'd taken off her bra to sleep and hadn't resumed it, and he cupped her breast, the weight of it sweet. Zander slid his thumb over the nipple, smiling into her kiss when the nipple grew firm for him.

Rae moved her fingers to the front of his jeans. Before Zander could stop her, she'd unbuttoned and unzipped, and then her cool hand closed around his cock.

Zander dragged his mouth from hers and barely stifled a snarl. "*Damn*, Little Wolf."

Rae only gripped his cock harder and ran her fist all the way to his balls.

"Ah, son of a . . ." Zander's head dropped back as hot sensations flooded him, but he held Rae firmly, not letting her fall.

It was a tight fit, her hand between them, until Zander's jeans chose to go slack and fall to his knees. Rae pushed his underwear out of the way, and then his ass was exposed to the night air, the most beautiful woman in the world with her hands on him.

Zander could tell she didn't have much experience stroking a man and he felt raw joy about that. Rae was willing to learn though. She cupped him then slid her hand to his tip, fingers exploring.

Every touch, every stroke sent erotic fires through Zander's blood, which only made his cock stiffer and Rae's touch even more electric. Zander clenched his jaw, trying to keep himself still. It was a hell of a choice whether to lay her down, yank open her clothes, and thrust inside her, or just let her play.

Either would kill him. Rae's eyes glistened in the faint light under the trees, and her lips parted, red and moist. Zander licked across her mouth, tasting heat.

Rae's fingers worked magic. Zander's hips moved, wanting her strokes, wanting *her*.

"You're beautiful, Little Wolf. I've never seen anything so beautiful as you, never felt . . . You make me whole again."

The words came out an incoherent mumble but Zander meant every one of them.

Rae said nothing at all. The little noise in her throat when he kissed her once more made him want to come.

If he did that, his scent would be all over her—everyone in Shiftertown, including her father and protective brothers, would know what they'd been doing out here in the woods. Zander didn't mind so much but Rae might, and it could be dangerous for her. Not from her father and brothers, but the other Shifters. Zander wanted to keep her safe, would to his dying day.

Rae sped her caresses and Zander deepened the kiss. *Want her. Need to fill her, hold her, make her my own.*

Zander nipped her lips and dropped open-mouthed kisses along her throat, the silver of her Collar warm against his lips. She made him wild, crazier than ever.

Zander cupped her face in one big hand, keeping himself from kissing her again. "Rae, damn you woman, *stop.*"

"Why?" She gave him a hot smile. "You had your hands all over *me*—why can't I touch you? *Feel* you." She stroked him as she said it and Zander groaned.

"You're killing me, Little Wolf."

"Good." It was a whisper, full of promise.

Zander let out another groan, then he snarled and jerked himself away from her. Hardest thing he'd ever had to make himself do.

He nearly fell as his jeans and underwear tripped him but he kicked them all the way off. Rae's gaze raked down Zander's body as he yanked off his T-shirt and dropped it to the pile of his clothes.

Rae hugged her arms to her chest, her shirt covering her again, eyes dark in the shadows. Her mating frenzy called out to him, and Zander wanted to respond to it.

Not until she was safe. He wasn't going to let any Shifters stumble over them while they went at it in the pine needles. Maybe one of the hostile Shifters would "accidentally" injure Rae while trying to keep her away from the un-Collared mate-frenzied bear. If Rae were to die, that would be the end of the female Guardian problem.

Rae let out a soft cry as Zander forced his body into that of his bear. The only way he could stop himself from taking Rae down to the damp ground or bending her over the nearest fallen log was to go bear and get himself away from her.

The thought of her bending forward, reaching down to open herself to him, made Zander tear away from her, baring his teeth when she took a step toward him.

"Fine," Rae snapped. She tugged her shirt over her head and tossed it aside, then her tank top. She slid out of her jeans then bent to take off her underwear, her breasts swaying.

"If you can do it, so can I." She shook her hair back, growled, and changed with amazing quickness into a wolf.

Her coat was the same glossy black as her hair, her eyes light gray, her ears pricked and alert. Rae growled at him again, a cute snarl, and then she dashed away, straight into the woods.

Zander tamped down a roar of frustration. He scooped the sheathed Sword of the Guardian up in his teeth and ran after her.

Rae heard him coming. She'd hoped he would chase her, though she'd assumed he would simply pick up the sword and walk home, shaking his head at her antics.

But no, Zander was behind her, his snarls muffled as though he had something in his mouth.

Rae wanted to laugh. What came out was a wolf howl. Zander made her mating frenzy come alive, until she wanted nothing but to touch him, stroke him, push him onto his back and straddle him. Rae was never this shameless, but Zander did something to her.

Not surprising, a small part of her mind told her. She and Zander had been thrown together, survived adventures, and found refuge in each other. Of course she'd started to feel the mating desires. It was biological.

Rae's human mind told her this, but the wolf in her snarled that her human form was making her stupid. The wolf understood the madness Rae felt and what it really meant. *Mate.*

Zander was coming fast. Rae knew these woods, had known them forever. She ducked around fallen trees and around boulders, then ran down a long hill and across the stream that was chilly even in summer.

Zander simply barreled around or through all the obstacles and gained on her. He was right on her heels as she came out of the stream, and in the next two strides, he took her down with one swipe of his paw.

Rae landed on her belly in dirt and pine needles, her legs every which way, but he hadn't hurt her. He'd tackled her *gently*. She rolled and struggled up, spinning to face him. Zander tipped the Sword of the Guardian onto the ground and growled.

He was a beautiful bear. Rae admired Zander while she pretended not to—his soulful black eyes, fur that was so white it shone faintly in the darkness, his expressive face, his giant black paws tipped with huge claws. Rae darted around him and caught the tip of his flat tail in her wolf teeth.

Zander snarled and spun in place faster than a giant bear should be able to. But Rae was faster, a wolf in her element, leaping out of the way before Zander could catch her.

Zander made a bear *hmph*, picked up the sword, and started to stroll away. Rae trotted after him, staying just far enough behind him so he couldn't grab her.

Zander *hmphed* again . . . and then took off. Rae's wolf bit back a howl—*Hey! What the hell?*—before she charged after him.

She dashed around a stand of trees, right into Zander. The laughter in his eyes pissed her off only a moment before she found herself taken down by a couple thousand pounds of polar bear.

Rae fought in panic before she realized he wasn't hurting her. Zander pinned her, yes, but he didn't crush, wasn't trying to vanquish her. He'd dropped the sword a few feet away from them, and it began to hum.

Zander closed his mouth briefly over Rae's neck then licked the top of her head and grumbled low in his belly. *Peace, Little Wolf. Lie here and enjoy the night with me.*

Rae wasn't certain how she understood him—maybe it had to do with the sword happily ringing next to them. She slowly dragged herself out from under him, but once she was free she very gently nipped his ear then lay down close to him.

Zander moved his large front paws until they encircled Rae, bringing her snugly against his chest. Rae curled up, feeling incredibly safe and warm. Nothing could hurt her while Zander was near.

Would he always be near? Her wolf, as contented as she was at the moment, realized that Zander could leave anytime he wanted. He could disappear into the world and never return. He wasn't Collared or restricted to a Shiftertown—he could go anywhere he wanted, take any mate he wanted.

Rae's dart of jealousy eased off at once, because her wolf knew exactly how to prevent every female Shifter in the world from chasing after him. She might not be able to keep Zander from leaving Montana, but she could stake her claim.

Her wolf licked the underside of Zander's jaw then breathed her scent onto him. *Marked.*

Zander blinked dark eyes in surprise. Then he gave a growl that was almost a purr and breathed *his* scent onto *her.*

His next growl was one of great triumph. *Marked. Mine!*

Zander walked in through the front door of Eoin's house the next morning more refreshed than he'd been in a long time.

He'd slept great after he and Rae had found their clothes, dressed, and walked home, even if he'd spent the rest of the night alone in the room over the garage instead of with Rae. His choice—if he'd taken the bedroom in the house Eoin had offered, he'd have found a way to cross the hall and get into Rae's bed.

She'd scent-marked him. Zander rubbed his hair, still damp from his shower, as he made for the kitchen and the smell of breakfast. His heart was light and he rejoiced.

He'd been trying to keep his scent from her to protect her, but she didn't seem to have any worries about it. Once she'd broached the issue, he'd figured to hell with it.

A scent mark meant that Rae wanted more from Zander than simply sating her mating frenzy. Female Shifters didn't usually scent mark—there were many more Shifter males than females, so the ladies didn't worry as much about competition—but that didn't mean they couldn't.

Zander had already known *his* interest in Rae went beyond the mating frenzy. But she'd indicated with the scent mark that she wanted all other females to back off him, meaning Zander was no longer fair game.

And it wasn't a cute *Hands off, ladies. He's mine.* It was more *Stay the fuck away from him, bitches, or I'll kill you.*

Did not at all help Zander's mating hunger that Rae was saying she considered him hers, that he was more than a night in the sack to sate herself. He wanted to shout it to the world— *She's mine, all mine.*

Of course, as soon as he walked into the kitchen, every Shifter in the room snapped his head around and fixed him with a sudden glare. The scent mark was easily discerned, didn't matter how long Zander showered or how much soap he used.

Rae wasn't there, thank the Goddess. If Zander had to fight her dad and brothers to the death, he didn't want Rae around to be hurt.

Logan, the oldest of Eoin's sons, rose from the table, and planted himself in front of Zander. "That better have been her choice, bear."

Zander carefully walked past him and reached for an empty cup on the counter. He made no moves that could be considered a threat, though he also made it clear he was no submissive. He'd respect Eoin's territory but wouldn't obey him blindly.

"Ask her," Zander said, pouring coffee into his cup. "I was as surprised as you are."

Logan only watched him, though Colin relaxed a little and remained seated.

Zander went on calmly. "She has my scent mark in return— entirely accepted by her. This way, if anyone wants to give her crap, they have to go through me."

Eoin, whose eyes had flicked to that of an alpha lion, gave Zander a nod. He hadn't stood up, but he hadn't needed to. He could intimidate standing or sitting. "I agree. It was a good thought."

The two brothers finally gave Zander grudging nods, taking their father's decision as their own. Zander let out a silent breath of relief. If he'd had to fight them, he'd have hurt them, which would have grieved Rae.

Ezra, who had been sitting at the table, well away from the

unspoken battle, said, "Zander will make her a good mate. Rae needs a clan."

"What does that mean?" Carson asked. He too was at the table, looking a bit surprised he was taking a meal with Shifters and not hating it.

"No one knows Rae's pack or her extended clan," Ezra explained. "It's taboo to mate within a clan, so when a Shifter's isn't known, it's harder for them to find a mate. Zander is pure bear, unlikely to be related to her, so it's perfect. When are the sun and moon ceremonies?"

Rae chose that moment to walk in. She took in her brothers, father, Zander, Ezra, and Carson all turning to look at her, and her cheeks went flame red.

As usual when Rae got flustered she covered embarrassment with anger. She stalked past Zander to the coffeepot, dumped coffee into the remaining empty cup, and slammed the pot back on the stove.

"Do you all have nothing better to do than watch a woman get herself coffee?" She fixed the room with her gray stare. "That's pretty sad."

Ezra flushed and returned to his breakfast. Her brothers looked abashed and wouldn't meet her eyes. Only her dad and Carson kept their gazes on her.

Zander chuckled and saluted Rae with his coffee cup. Little Wolf had just showed everyone in the room exactly where they stood in her hierarchy.

Eoin rose and went to Rae, his expression softening. "I'm happy for you, child. I truly am." He reached for her and enfolded her in an embrace.

"It's only a scent mark," Rae said, trying to sound offhand. She leaned into her father as he hugged her, closing her eyes to hold him tightly in return. When they eased apart, Rae wiped her eyes. "My wolf thought it was a good idea, that's all. I can always take the mark away."

Zander gave her a level look. "You have to catch me first. And by the way"—he thunked his cup to the table and went to the stove to fill up his plate—"I'm not taking mine back."

Rae shot him a startled glance but Zander only moved past her without looking at her. The fact that she was his now surged through his blood. The males in this town had had their chance. Tough shit for them.

Rae headed for the stove once Zander was seated at the table, as though she didn't trust herself near him. She heaped scrambled eggs from the big frying pan onto her plate and laid a couple of pancakes from the griddle on top of them. She'd worked up as much of an appetite last night as Zander had.

Rae turned away, a full plate in her hand. "We'll talk about it lat—"

There was a loud popping sound and a man sprang into existence in the kitchen. He was tall and lean, with a runner's strength, and had eyes like dark holes into nothing. He also carried the strong, unmistakable scent of the realms of Faerie.

Every Shifter but Zander snarled, hackles rising. Rae gasped out loud, but instead of dropping her plate or anything else dramatic, she set down her breakfast, shifted into her half-wolf, and went for him.

CHAPTER TWENTY-SIX

Rae had almost completed her leap when Zander caught her around the waist and hauled her back. She was a volatile armful as she snarled, fought, and tried to bite, but Zander held her fast.

"Don't be inhospitable," Zander said in her ear. "This is Stuart Reid. He's a friend. I called him to come up here and talk to me."

Rae turned her wolf-human face up to him. Her muzzle was full of black whiskers over which her gray eyes fixed on him. Even as her ferocious beast, she was cute.

Rae let her muzzle recede as she became fully human once more. "*He's* the guy you know?"

"Yep. He's Fae but not the same kind of Fae." While Reid had the long, lean Fae features, his hair was midnight black, his skin darker than that of the Fae most Shifters knew about. "He lives in the Las Vegas Shiftertown now. Your dad's met him a couple of times at Shifter leaders' meetings."

"Which you've never attended," Eoin said sternly. "How do you know what goes on at Shifter leaders' secret meetings?"

Zander kept his eyes on Rae. "I know a lot of things. Don't

worry—Reid isn't regular Fae. He's dark Fae, or whatever he calls it."

"*Dokk alfar,*" Reid said in his deep voice. "Not *hoch alfar*—the High Fae. Different species." Sounded like he explained this often.

"He can teleport," Zander said. "But only to places he's seen before, so I made a little movie with my phone last night and sent it to him. Hope you don't mind."

"I deleted it," Reid said quickly to Eoin. "I promise I will not violate your territory or your privacy."

Reid had obviously lived with Shifters a while—he knew just what to say to soothe Eoin down.

Eoin's irritation was only for Zander. "Maybe discuss it with me next time, Moncrieff?"

"I didn't want to disturb you," Zander said. "And didn't have time to warn you this morning. Anyway, Reid's a good Fae and I need to consult with him. Want eggs?" he asked Reid, gesturing to the stove.

"No thanks," Reid said. "I had breakfast. Wouldn't mind coffee though."

Eoin had already opened a cupboard to take down an extra cup and pour the brew. He was not about to let anyone else in his house serve a stranger—especially a Fae. If the stranger attacked, the strongest Shifter of the household would be right in front of him with a steaming hot beverage in his hands.

Reid only thanked Eoin politely and sipped the coffee.

"How everything in Vegas?" Zander asked conversationally. If he got the man talking about ordinary things maybe everyone in the room would relax.

Reid understood. "The Lupines are settling into their new homes well. Eric and Graham have learned to work together without tearing into each other, though they still argue. Graham's mate is heavy with her first cub, and Graham acts as though no one else in the world has sired a child before."

Zander grunted a laugh. Graham McNeil, leader of the Lupines in the Vegas Shiftertown was a blustering pain in the ass, but his bluster hid great caring and canny leadership skills. No one but his mate would dare say that to his face, however.

"Otherwise, all is quiet," Reid finished.

"Good." Zander set his empty plate on the counter. "Let's take a walk. Rae—join us."

Rae set her half-eaten meal on the counter without bothering to argue. She quietly lifted the sword she'd leaned against the kitchen cabinets and walked out behind them.

The morning was crisp and clear, a beautiful summer day. Rae would have preferred to spend it on a run or grabbing fishing poles and heading with her brothers to the lake. A lazy day fishing and napping in the sun would be perfect. But she had things to worry about and she wasn't about to let Zander walk off alone with a Fae—no matter how trustworthy Zander said he was.

Zander kept a swift pace, leading Reid into the woods along the same route he and Rae had taken last night. He didn't go all the way to Daragh's place—that would still be watched.

Zander stopped them in a small clearing in the trees, a quiet space warm in the sunlight, the breeze that sighed through it cooling and soft. A flat-topped black boulder rested on the dark earth, deposited here by a glacier eons ago.

"Rae?" Zander said, signaling her forward. "Want to show him our problem?"

Rae didn't. The sword was sacred to Shifters and this man was Fae, no matter how much Zander reassured her about him. Reid didn't seem intrinsically evil, but Rae had never met a Fae before, so what did she know?

"It's all right," Zander said. "I wouldn't have brought him here if I didn't trust him. And I can always break his neck if I turn out to be wrong."

Reid didn't look worried. "I don't betray Shifter secrets," he told Rae. "I know a bear Shifter who would kill me, and I don't mean Zander."

Rae didn't know what to make of that statement but she did believe that Zander could flatten this Fae in a heartbeat. Zander had easily held her back from attacking Reid, even though Rae had been in half-beast state, which should have matched or even surpassed Zander's strength in his human form. Rae hadn't even come close—Zander had held her as easily as he would pick up a paperclip.

Reid watched with interest as Rae unsheathed both halves of the sword and laid it on the rocks. The silver glinted in the sun, the runes sharp outlines. The sword made no noise at the moment. No humming, nothing.

Reid stared at it. "It's broken."

"No shit," Zander said without heat. "We want to know if the runes on it tell us how to put it back together."

Reid leaned closer to study the blade but Rae noticed he didn't try to touch it.

She looked Reid over while he examined the sword. Fae had always been portrayed to her as having white-blond hair, like Zander's, with pale skin and intense black eyes. Reid had the eyes, but his hair was soot black, and he had a deep tan from living under the desert sun. Rae wondered what *dokk alfar* were, why Reid lived in a Shiftertown, and how he survived outside of Faerie. The Fae didn't like iron, this world was full of it, and so the Fae had long ago decided not to venture too far into the human world.

"Hmm," Reid said.

Zander moved in impatience. "Can you read it or not?"

"I can." Reid straightened up, in no hurry. "But it doesn't make any sense."

"It's Fae—I don't expect sense. I just want to know how to stick it back together."

"It's not so much instructions as a story." Reid let his finger hover above the runes. "It's a tale of two lovers who were forced apart, endured madness and torture, and then found each other again. They became one and then went to the Summerland, hand-in-hand." He pointed to the swirl of runes on the hilt then lifted his hand away.

Zander frowned. "Well, that's uplifting."

"I don't know if it's a Fae legend or a Shifter one," Reid said. "I've never heard it. The Fae woman whose magic is in the swords might have used a tale that was popular at the time, or the Shifter swordsmith told it to her. I can only guess."

"Great," Zander said. "How does this help us?"

Reid studied the sword a moment longer then lifted his shoulders. "I haven't the faintest bloody idea."

Zander growled. "You've been hanging around with Shifters too long. You sound just like them."

Reid shot him a dark look. "I'm in exile. Don't rub it in."

"The trick with exile is to learn to enjoy the hell out of it. What do you think, Rae?" Zander slid his arm around her waist. "Have you ever heard a story like that?"

"Other than *Romeo and Juliet*? No." Rae shook her head, trying not to like the warmth of him against her so much. "It isn't quite the same, though, is it? These lovers reunited—does it say for how long before they went to the Summerland?"

Reid examined the runes on the hilt again. "It's cryptic. It might mean they lived together for three hundred years or it might mean they found each other and were wiped out in five minutes."

"Zander's right," Rae said. "Seriously uplifting."

Reid pointed to where the runes had split with the break. "That's exactly where the lovers were reunited and battled to stay together."

"Thought so," Zander said. He pressed a kiss to the top of Rae's head and released her. "Thanks, Reid. Appreciate it."

"It's an interesting problem," Reid said. "If I uncover anything else that might help, I'll let you know." He took a step back, as though clearing space around himself.

"Wait!" Rae reached out to him. "Are you just going to go? At least stay for lunch."

Reid shook his head. "I don't like to stay away for too long." He shot them a wry smile, which lit up his face and made it darkly handsome. "The cubs I help take care of get unruly. Besides"—he grew somber again—"I'm Fae. They're used to me in the Las Vegas Shiftertown but I wouldn't last long here."

"My dad wouldn't let anything happen to you," Rae said quickly.

"That's as may be," Reid said. "But I make Shifters uncomfortable and that makes *me* uncomfortable. Even you attacked me first, asked questions later."

Rae's face heated. "Yeah, well, you scared me. And *someone* didn't warn me you were coming."

Zander ignored that jab. "I thank you, my friend." He held out a hand to Reid, and Reid clasped it. No hugging, but not because Zander was wary of him, Rae sensed. "If you ever need a favor, you call me."

Reid's teeth flashed in a brief smile. "I'm guessing you'll need my help before I need yours. Take care, Rae."

He drew a breath, focused somewhere to his right, and vanished. Air displaced with a slight *pop*, and wind stirred Rae's hair.

She jumped. "Oh, that is *weird*."

"He says it weirds him out too," Zander said. "He's sacrificed a lot, that guy. The Fae were as cruel to him as they are to Shifters."

Rae lifted the lower half of the sword, looking at the runes that told the story—whether a sad or happy tale was left up to the reader, she supposed. "Where did he come from? How did he end up in a Shiftertown?"

Zander leaned against the boulder, sun dancing on his hair. "It's a strange story and he's never told me directly. But what I've heard from others is that his clan was on the losing side of a war inside Faerie. Reid is what's known as an Iron Master, meaning he can make iron do anything he wants—at least he could inside Faerie. The high Fae feared him because of that, so they captured him, killed most of his clan, and dumped Reid in the human world, doing spells so he couldn't get back.

He huffed a laugh. "The High Fae shits believe that exile from the perfect world of Faerie is a fate worse than death. Reid tried for years to get back in to take his revenge but he's not as interested anymore. Not after he rescued a bear Shifter woman called Peigi from a bunch of rogue Shifters. Now he dedicates his time to taking care of the orphaned cubs from that raid. Shifters aren't so bad, he's decided. I'm thinking Peigi had a lot to do with his change of heart."

Rae listened with interest. "Are they mated?"

"Not yet. They both have issues they're working through. Maybe someday."

Rae found herself leaning on the boulder next to Zander. The warm rock and the sun on her face felt good. "If he can teleport, why doesn't he just teleport back to Faerie?"

"He said it doesn't work that way." Zander rested his arm

behind her. "He never could teleport until he came to the human world, and he can only manipulate iron—magically—inside Faerie. He doesn't know why. But he's a decent guy and a good resource for information about the Fae or anything Fae made."

"Like a Sword of the Guardian," Rae finished. "How did you meet him?"

"I spent some time in the Austin Shiftertown this spring. Reid popped in for a visit with the Las Vegas Shiftertown's leader. Well—he flew in. Eric can't teleport and Reid was polite and took regular transportation."

"I was wrong," Rae said as she rose from the boulder and returned the broken sword to its sheath. "You do know everyone."

"And now you know me." Zander closed his hand over her wrist and kissed the inside of her forearm. Fires tingled under her skin. "Stick with me, kid. Won't be long before you know everyone in the world too."

Z ander said nothing to the others about their meeting with Reid or the sword when they returned home. Eoin didn't ask—but he wouldn't, Rae knew. Her father figured every Shifter's business was his own, unless it endangered those in his jurisdiction.

Rae knew she'd have to confess about the sword sometime. If they couldn't fix it or find someone to, she'd have to tell Eoin and face the consequences, whatever they were. As far as she knew, no one in the history of the Guardians had broken a sword.

Carson knew—he'd seen the sword in pieces but he hadn't said a word. Rae was grateful, though she wasn't certain why he kept his mouth shut. He'd been subdued since he'd come here, though watchful.

Zander disappeared after they returned to do who knew what—make another round of phone calls? Meet with more of his mysterious friends? Solve the problems of the world? Rae wasn't certain she wanted to know.

Zander did reappear in time that afternoon for the send-off

for Ezra's father. They hadn't had time or ability to do the ceremony on the boat, but every Shifter needed a send-off, so those they left behind could say good-bye.

Eoin set up the fire pit they used for ceremonies, building the fire high, the tongues of flame pale in the strong sunlight. Other Shifters gathered, many of them Lupines, to help Ezra say farewell. Death was never easy for Shifters and grief lasted a long time. Helping others remember a loved one always drew Shifters closer together.

Zander stood beside Ezra as Ezra fed a picture of his father into the fire then bowed his head in prayer. Rae thought of the feisty, outspoken Robert, pretending strength until the end to spare his son worry. Rae said her own prayers for him, wishing him well in the Summerland.

She knew why Zander stood so near Ezra, nearly touching him. Zander was readying himself in case Ezra gave into grief, as he'd done on the boat, sinking into that deep place that Shifters went when the world hurt them too much. Zander was prepared to take that pain from Ezra if necessary, healing his psyche.

Zander always would do these things for others, Rae realized, no matter how much he blustered about wanting to be alone and undisturbed. Since Rae had met him, Zander had done nothing but give.

After the ceremony, Eoin announced he had set up a meeting with the Idaho Shifter leader to try to find out more about the Shifters who'd attacked Carson. The man would be arriving soon but not coming to the house. Eoin had arranged to meet him at a roadhouse—neutral territory. Eoin had also invited a few of the clan leaders to accompany him so there would be no talk about Eoin having secret meetings with other Shifter leaders.

"Take backup," Rae said in alarm.

Eoin gave her a reassuring look. "My trackers, your brothers, Ezra, Carson. This is an informal meet. We'll have beer, we'll talk."

In the distant past, clan wars had started under even more innocuous circumstances, but those were the bad old days, Rae tried to tell herself.

She knew why Eoin didn't suggest she accompany them. The other clan leaders might be hostile to her and he wanted to keep the meeting focused on finding feral Shifters. Eoin would never, ever take Rae into a place where she might be in danger.

"Zander, your opinion would be welcome," Eoin said.

Zander shook his head. "Can't. Have things to take care of. Tell me what you find out." Without further explanation, he headed off into the woods, disappearing quickly from sight.

Rae watched him go with foreboding. It wasn't like Zander to promise to help someone and then have others take over. He was up to something.

Eoin scowled in Zander's wake but let him go. "Are you going to be all right here, sweetheart?" he asked Rae.

He didn't mean physically. No matter how much the other Shifters in this Shiftertown blustered, they would never enter Eoin's territory and touch the leader's daughter. They'd want to keep their limbs intact.

Rae nodded. "I'll meditate a little until the fire goes out. I'll be fine."

Eoin put his arms around her and kissed her cheek. "Thank you, Rae. Goddess be with you, daughter."

Rae hugged him back, the familiar feel of his embrace dissolving her tensions. She loved this man with all her heart.

"You too, Dad." She put her hands on his shoulders. "Be careful."

Colin turned from the path that led around the house and said, "Don't worry, little sis. If anything goes wrong, we'll kick ass."

"This is a mission for information *only*," Eoin growled as he released Rae. "Keep your claws in your paws. I mean that."

Colin laughed, and the ring of it warmed Rae's heart. "He's so easy," her brother said, winking at Rae. "He always thinks I'm going to dive right into trouble."

"Because you usually do." Eoin cuffed his son gently across the top of the head, then they went around the house together. A moment later, Rae heard the truck starting up.

That left Rae alone and in peace for the first time in many days. She breathed a sigh of contentment, seated herself cross-legged in front of the fire pit, and whispered a prayer to the Goddess.

"Tell me what to do," she finished. "If you Chose me—why? What do you want from me?"

The flames flickered and crackled, giving away nothing.

"Hey." Zander's booted feet landed right next to her. "So, are they gone, Little Wolf?"

CHAPTER TWENTY-SEVEN

Rae let out a yelp. She was up, the sword in its sheath held in front of her like a club before she'd realized who she faced. Her heart pounded, every nerve alert.

"Shit, Zander," she said, lowering the sword. "What the hell? You don't sneak up on a Shifter like that."

"How should I sneak up on a Shifter?" Zander gave her a blank stare with his very dark eyes. "On my tippy-toes going *shh, shh, shh*?" He carried a backpack in one hand and had his swords slung over his shoulder with the other. "I wasn't trying for stealth, sweetheart. You were out of it."

Rae knew she hadn't been *that* out of it. Zander could move incredibly softly and quickly, and giant polar bears shouldn't be able to do that.

"What do you want, Big-Ass Bear?" she asked in irritation. "I thought you were off calling your friends all over the world."

"Only a couple of them. Making arrangements." He turned away. "Time to keep up your training, Little Wolf. Come on."

He headed toward the trees at the edge of Eoin's territory, expecting she'd follow. Rae, after letting out an aggrieved sigh, did.

Zander strode along the path they'd taken with Reid, but he veered off before it led to the clearing, and struck out south along the lake.

On the far side of this lake, which was about a mile across, was a small human town and a lake resort, where wealthy city dwellers came to get away from it all. The way to the resort was blocked off by a high fence and gate, so that the resort goers didn't have to worry about Shifters running up to their cabins—or any wild animal for that matter.

Rae eyed the fence as they neared it—why humans thought Shifters couldn't climb it or tear through it whenever they wanted to, she didn't understand. Zander, for instance, calmly pulled out the links of the fence from the dirt, rolled it back out of the way, ducked under, and held the fence open for her.

"What are you doing?" Rae asked him. "This way is off limits to Shifters. If you want to go into town, we can drive. They're used to seeing Shifters there—it's where we shop."

"Not interested in the town," Zander said without changing expression. "I hear there's a great resort over here, with private cabins right on the lake. *A fishing and birding paradise, or just a place to relax.* According to their website anyway. I booked us a cabin."

Zander continued to hold the fence open as though wondering why Rae didn't come through.

"Shifters aren't allowed." She took a step back. "Didn't you hear me?"

"I wasn't planning on telling them we were Shifters," Zander said patiently. "I already checked in, so we don't need to go through the lobby."

"You already . . ." Rae shook herself. "*Why* did you book a cabin?" She eyed him in suspicion.

"Little Wolf, your dad's great for taking us all in, very hospitable, but there's too many people in your house. Nowhere to train in private, nowhere to talk without at least three people listening in. Daragh's house is watched, so I needed an alternative."

Rae blew out her breath. Zander was right that training would be easier if they had privacy, especially when she didn't want to brandish the broken sword. But taking her to the humans-only lake resort was audacious—something only Zander would do.

"If we get caught, my dad will be held responsible," she said. "Humans are touchy about the no-Shifters rule."

"We won't get caught," Zander returned without worry. "The manager is a friend of Piotr's, who vouched for me. What lady I bring in is my business."

Rae gave a growl. "You know, you really are crazy." She ended her trepidation by scrambling under the fence, coming to her feet as Zander arranged the chain links the way they had been. He knew what he was doing—anyone looking at the fence would never know it had been opened.

Zander led the way along the path, which was shielded by tall trees. The lake was quiet today, no one fishing in the open, no one in the shadows on the far side.

The resort's cabins were as private as advertised. The one Zander took her to was nestled in a fold of the lake's bank. Trees rose behind it but none obscured the view of the water. A small gate led to a well-kept flower garden in front, the cabin itself more of a cottage than a rustic dwelling. A Dutch door let in air and light, and the windows all faced the lake. No other cabins were in sight.

Zander opened the door with a key and went inside, looking around first before he signaled Rae to follow. The cabin was good-sized, with a wide living room, a kitchenette, and a bedroom and bath behind another door. Rae could move in here with no problem at all.

The resort had left a basket of fruit, cheese, and chocolate truffles, along with two bottles of wine, one red, one white. A bouquet of red roses stood in a vase next to the basket.

"They must have given you the romance package," Rae said, running her hand along the sinuous bottle of chardonnay. "They think we're a couple celebrating an anniversary or something. Lucky mistake. I could go for some wine, cheese, and chocolate."

"It wasn't a mistake," Zander said. He dropped his bag and swords on the sofa and closed and locked the door.

Rae's heart began to thump. "It's a tight space for swords in here."

Zander turned from the door and moved in that quick way of his so that he was in front of her, his eyes black like a starless night. "Right now, I don't give a fuck about swords."

"No?" Rae asked, her voice soft, though her heart banged and warmth rode low in her belly. "What do you care about?"

"Being with you." Zander slid his hand behind her neck and closed his fingers around her braid. "You looking at me with those gray eyes makes me want to throw the rest of the world to hell so I can kiss you."

Rae tried to think of something poetic in response as she rested her hands on his chest. All that came out was "Uhn."

Zander's eyes glinted. "You say the sweetest things."

"You're a shit," Rae whispered.

"I know," Zander said, and kissed her mouth.

This kiss was different somehow, even from their encounter last night or anything that had happened on the boat. Zander no longer held back, no longer kept himself in check. He was her protector, but now he would be her lover.

As was meant to be, something inside Rae whispered.

Zander's hard mouth opened her, his hand on her braid not letting her go. He'd been tender before, no matter how much they'd played but now he stripped that tenderness away, until Rae knew only his strength, his fire.

Rae gripped his shoulders, holding herself up, her fingers not making a dent in his hard flesh.

He shoved one hand under her shirt and tank top, lifting both up and away. Rae hadn't bothered with a bra this morning—she often left it off for ease of shifting—and soon she was bare to his touch.

She wanted to see him as well. Rae tugged at his T-shirt, pushing it up until it was tight across his shoulders. She broke the kiss to lick his bare chest.

Zander rumbled with growls. He slid his hands under her backside and lifted her against him. Rae's breasts crushed to his hard chest, and his long braids brushed her skin, the beads cool.

Zander's kisses turned fierce, his mouth moving on hers.

The spread of Rae's thighs fit well against the hard ridge in his jeans, making her want all fabric between them gone.

He turned with her in his arms until Rae's back was against the cabin's painted wall. Zander's body was hard, smooth skin over strength, his muscles tightening as he steadied her. His dark eyes held depth that drew her as he lowered his head to kiss her neck, then bite it.

Rae rocked back as Zander nibbled and suckled, his teeth catching in her Collar.

"I want this off of you," he said, his breath scalding. "I don't care whose turn is next—I'm going to make Eoin jump you ahead of the line. I don't want anything touching you that can hurt you."

He tugged at the chain with his teeth as though he'd rip it from her neck then and there. He then kissed where he'd bitten with gentle lips and feathered kisses to her shoulder.

Rae ran her tongue across Zander's throat, which was bare of any Collar. His pulse beat under her lips, Zander free of all restraints, a wild man who kept himself in check by his own strength. Un-Collared Shifters didn't necessarily have to go feral, he was teaching her by example. For all his seeming craziness, Zander had tight control of himself.

That control was being pushed now. He turned with her again, as though dancing her through the room, until they ended up in the tiny bedroom.

The room dimly reminded her of the forward cabin on his boat, not much in it but bed, she thought as Zander lowered her to it. No tossing her down, only a gentle thump to the mattress. Rae was on her back, hips on the edge of the bed, already arching up to him in need.

Zander slid off her boots then unfastened and unzipped her jeans with steady fingers, tugging them down and off. He pushed Rae back with a strong hand as she reached for her underwear, then hooked his fingers around the waistband and pulled them from her himself.

He stood up as she lay naked and exposed, the quilt warm against her back. Zander's eyes softened, and all the harshness left his face.

"You are so beautiful." For a moment he stood lost in

wonder, self-restraint no longer needed. "I don't think you understand how beautiful you are."

Rae flushed, aware she was lying there in nothing but her socks. Zander's slow gaze on her body made her feel beautiful—no longer the awkward Lupine who never could keep up with her agile and graceful Feline brothers.

Zander's look told Rae he liked what he saw of her curved but compact body, flyaway dark hair, and eyes that were plain gray, without the brilliant colors or soulful darkness of other Shifters'. He ran his fingers across her throat, down between her breasts, and over her belly to the swirl of hair between her legs.

"Beautiful and strong," he said. He slid his hands to the creases of her thighs and nudged her legs apart, coming to stand between them. "Staying away from you has been hell."

Rae swallowed, the feeling of his jeans against the sensitive skin of her inner thighs hot and exciting. "The mating frenzy can be hard to fight," she said in a hoarse whisper.

"It's not the mating frenzy." Zander's thumbs found her opening, caressed it. "It's *you*. You save my life, you ease my pain, and you act like you don't know why that's special. *No one* ever saved my life before, Rae. Only you."

His hands warmed her skin, his touch exciting her and making her thoughts blur. She figured he meant she'd saved him in the bar fight when she'd slammed the sword into the shotgun, keeping Zander from being hit point-blank. He'd still been shot, but only grazed. The scar from that wound had faded, barely discernible now on his tanned flesh.

"I didn't want them to hurt you," she said shakily. "You were my ride."

Zander's smile spread across his face—his real smile, which only showed up when she surprised him. He leaned to her and kissed her deeply, then took his mouth down her body in the path his fingers had traveled.

Rae sucked in a breath when he pressed an openmouthed kiss to her most intimate place, and another when he abruptly rose from her. Rae was suddenly cold without him and lifted herself on her elbows, a protest on her lips.

Before she could speak, Zander stepped out into the front room but was back almost immediately, the Sword of the

Guardian in his hands. He took both pieces from the sheath and laid them across the dresser, the broken pieces fitted together.

"What will we need that for?" Rae asked in surprise.

"An idea of mine. The runes where it's broken say the couple gets reunited." Zander's eyes sparkled as he came back to her. "I bet I know what those two did when they found each other again. Maybe it's what will put the sword back together."

Rae blinked. "And that's why you brought me here?"

"It's *one* reason I brought you here." Zander cupped Rae's face. "I have a lot of other things on my mind."

He leaned to kiss her again, but Rae drew back. "I don't like it . . . watching."

Zander looked puzzled, but just then the sword made a faint *ting*, as though it were laughing. Zander grimaced and swung away into the bathroom. "Yeah, I know what you mean."

He emerged with a towel and dropped it over the sword, which went silent. Without another word, Zander stripped himself of his jeans and underwear and returned to her.

The next kiss wiped away Rae's doubts, fears, and worries. She lay back as he came down to her, the bed embracing them both. Zander kissed her face, her throat, his weight covering her but not oppressing. His body was protective, wanting, not demanding or subduing. Zander was with her, taking care of her.

He moved his mouth to her breast, covering it. Rae groaned as she slid her foot up his leg, wanting to pull his heavy cock inside her but not wanting the warm sensation of his mouth on her to cease.

Zander circled her nipple with his tongue, then licked between her breasts to her throat. He lifted his head and kissed her, his mouth hot from her breast. At the same he drew one finger firmly along her opening. As Rae jerked hard with pleasure, Zander slid himself inside her.

Rae lost the kiss as she gave a strangled cry, the amazing feeling of him robbing her of breath. Zander filled and spread her, a tight fit, but Rae also had the instant and striking sense that he'd been made for her.

Zander growled low in his throat, his eyes half closing. "Goddess, I knew you'd feel good, but I never thought . . ." He groaned as he slid another inch inside her. "I want to stay in you forever . . ."

Rae wanted to quip that it would be impractical but she couldn't, because she wanted that too. Forever in Zander's warmth, hearing his deep voice as he loved her, that rumble of it vibrating her whole body.

The hardness of him found her open spaces, filled her, completed her. Rae lifted her hips and Zander slid all the way in, easy for him because she was so slick. Rae wanted him with her body, her heart, her soul.

Mate, the wolf inside her said joyfully. *The other part of me.*

Zander gazed down at Rae, his eyes dark with raw need. He pressed a long kiss to the corner of her mouth as he began to thrust.

Even if he is a bear, the wolf said with a grin, and then Rae lost all sense of words and thoughts.

Zander surrendered to the incredible sensation of being inside Rae. She opened to him all the way, welcoming him, no holding back. Rae didn't do things by halves—she gave all of herself.

She was giving all of herself to him now. Zander's hips moved as he tried to be inside her as far as he could, greedy for her and her heat.

The loneliness that was Zander's life splintered and fell away. All the pain he'd sucked into himself, all the grief when he'd failed to heal someone, even the joy when he'd helped them, was gone on the breath of the wind. Nothing mattered in his past, or his future. Only this present mattered with Rae beneath him, her gray eyes darkening in passion.

Rae was also sweet, soft, and sexy, and Zander lost himself in the hot joy of her. To hell with the world and all its crap. He was with Rae, who gripped him tight, squeezing his cock inside her. Let the frenzy come. Screw it.

Zander growled as he sank into the bed with her, Rae's eyes the most beautiful sight in the world as she gave in to desire. Zander thrust, and thrust again, every slide in and out an astonishing thing. If any experience in his life had been this good, he didn't remember it. Nope, *nothing* had ever been this good.

He drowned in Rae's scent, her touch, the noises she made as they rocked together. She was beauty itself, and she was sassy and strong, and Zander would never have enough of her.

Rae gave a sharp cry as her climax engulfed her, then she went crazy, kissing him, crying his name, dragging him deeper and deeper inside her.

Zander gave her what she asked for, bracing his fists on the bed as he drove into her, Rae's feet planted on his backside and pulling him in. He grew dizzy as his coming surged up and then smacked him hard.

He heard his voice tearing through the room, Rae's answering cries, and the faint shimmer of the sword on the dresser. Then every sound was swamped by the roaring in Zander's ears, though he heard the snarls in his throat.

I love you, Little Wolf.

Zander had no idea if he shouted the words or his mind only filled with them. The sounds coming out of his mouth were incoherent, and then he no longer cared.

Rae had hold of him, her coming strong, and Zander matched it. They clung to each other, kissing, crying out, kissing again as they fell together, joined and whole.

Rae laughed languidly at him as her head touched the pillows, one finger coming up to brush his face. Zander realized before he crashed down beside her and headed for oblivion, that she was wiping away his tears.

When Zander peeled open his eyes, the sun had moved, his throat was raw, and every part of him was sore. Rae lay beside him, stretched out on her side as she watched him, a half-full glass of wine in her graceful hand.

"Are you back with me?" She smiled down at him then took a sip of the bloodred wine. "I was trying to decide whether to eat all the food or be nice and leave you some."

"Eat it," Zander said, his voice a croak. "I'll live on being with you."

Rae's gray eyes lit with amusement. "That will only last until you get hungry. Here, have a cracker." She shoved a piece of flatbread spread with herbed cheese into his mouth.

Zander's throat closed up but he managed to chew and swallow, then take the wineglass she lifted from the nightstand and held out to him. He gulped wine, refraining from coughing, then set down the glass and wiped his mouth.

"Did it work?" he asked. He gestured to the towel-draped sword. "Did it go back together?"

"I don't know," Rae said. "I've been afraid to look."

Her eyes held trepidation, worry that he wanted to wipe away. Zander heaved himself up, pushing aside the quilt she must have tucked over him.

"All right," he said. "We'll look together."

CHAPTER TWENTY-EIGHT

Zander didn't let himself speculate, hope, or pray. He stepped to the dresser and plucked the towel from the sword.

It sat there, winking in the sunlight, still in two pieces. Rae let out a sigh and thumped down on the bed.

"Damn it," Zander said softly. He had hoped this would work because he had no fucking clue how to fix the bloody thing. A human swordsmith or even a Shifter one might ruin it—it needed Fae magic.

But no way was he going to open a way to Faerie to look for a Fae swordsmith. They had sword makers there, but the chances of coming across a trustworthy one willing to fix a weapon originally forged to thwart the Fae were tiny. None of Zander's stupid ideas were panning out.

Rae sat down on the side of the bed, lifted the wine bottle she'd left on the nightstand, and refilled the two glasses. She held one out to him.

"We could always try again," she said.

A beautiful woman, bare to the sunlight, holding out a glass of ruby-red wine and suggesting, with all sincerity, that they should have sex again was difficult to ignore. Her gray eyes caught and held sunlight and warmth.

What idiot would be fool enough to resist her? Zander plucked both glasses from her hands and set them firmly down on the nightstand. Then he snaked his arms around Rae and took her mouth in a warm, afterglow kiss.

Rae slanted him a sly smile as he eased her down to the bed. At the last minute, Zander rose and twitched the towel over the sword, then returned to Rae and her warmth.

They tried again, and again. And then again. After the fourth time, Rae thought she'd be exhausted, but her body seemed to be giving her an endless supply of energy.

Or maybe it was simply the joy of being with Zander. He'd go from playful and funny to tender and slow, touching her with warm hands while he gazed into her eyes. Then to crazy and rough, grabbing Rae by the hips and flipping her over to enter her from behind. That time had Rae screaming and clawing at the covers, in the most astonishing pleasure she'd ever known.

After crackers and truffles to fortify themselves, Zander loved her again, gently this time, his strokes long and slow. Rae lay back and basked in him, knowing that the heat around her heart might mean the mate bond was forming. She said nothing, knowing it would devastate her if he didn't feel the bond in return.

No matter what they did, though, the sword remained broken. Zander at one time left it uncovered and they put up with its hum, though Rae stopped paying attention once their lovemaking turned fervent.

The blade never fused together. The two of them giving in to mating frenzy obviously didn't have anything to do with the sword.

They stayed in the cabin through the night. Zander ordered out food and then went to the road to fetch it so the delivery person wouldn't come to the cabin itself. Zander said he called Eoin as well, telling him he'd keep Rae with him—to train, of course.

Her father would know exactly what they were doing out here, Rae was certain. Eoin wanted them to mate, but Zander had said not a word about the mate-claim, ceremonies, nothing.

Zander was un-Collared, free to come and go as he pleased—Rae wore a Collar and was bound to a Shiftertown. As Guardian, she was doubly bound. She wouldn't be able to leave for long stretches at a time in case she was needed. Zander mating with her under sun and moon would tie him to a Shiftertown where he didn't want to be. Rae doubted he'd easily give up his freedom.

As they ate warmed-over pizza at the front room's table in the gray light of dawn, Zander told her about his phone conversation with Eoin.

"The leader of the Idaho Shiftertown couldn't tell him much," Zander said. "He'd heard of the incident with Carson and his wife, but by the time his trackers could get north to investigate, the ferals had gone. They followed the trail for a while but lost them and didn't want to go too far into the wilderness. The Idaho Shiftertown leader said he'd put feelers out but he couldn't find any more information. His Guardian looked into it as well."

Rae nodded as she listened and chewed pizza. Tomato sauce, cheese, and pepperoni tasted surprisingly good at five in the morning after a night of sex, especially chased with warm red wine.

"Is that why you didn't want to go with my dad to the meeting?" she asked when she finished. "Because you knew the leader didn't know anything?"

Zander shrugged. He'd resumed underwear and T-shirt while they ate, thin fabric stretching over his hard body. Likewise Rae had put on her tank top and undies, not wanting her bare skin smeared with pizza grease.

"I figured he wouldn't have found out anything about the ferals," Zander said. "If he had, he'd have sent word to other leaders in the area, which includes Eoin. But asking around lets Carson and Ezra have something constructive to do instead of sitting around thinking about their troubles."

Of course. Zander was trying to take care of everyone at

once. "So how are we going to find them?" Rae asked. "We promised Carson."

"I've put a lot of people on alert, both Shifters and human, about the ferals who hurt the Carsons, asking far and wide if anyone has any info. Sean is keeping you out of the Guardian Network to keep you safe from other Guardians but that doesn't mean he can't do searches of his own. He'll find something."

"Miles witnessed something similar, you said." Rae shivered. "It's horrible. Why would Shifters go after other Shifters?"

Zander grunted a laugh. "You're young and cute. Shifters used to tear each other up all the time. Clan wars, mate challenges, hierarchy changes . . . Shifters have a history of violence. We were originally bred as fighters, remember. Battle beasts for the Fae."

"Yes, but that was a couple thousand years and many generations ago." Rae took another swallow of wine. "I hope we got over it."

"Mostly." Zander wiped his fingers on a paper towel and closed the empty pizza box. "But there's a kernel of savagery inside every Shifter, no matter how long we've been around. That's why Shifters go feral. They become the battle beasts and can't snap out of it. I healed a feral not long ago." Zander quieted, his eyes going still. "It was horrific. I healed him, but then I was mindless. I wanted to kill, to rip apart everyone in sight. Since I'm a big-ass bear, like you say, I was unstoppable. A fearless cub—a little boy one-tenth my size—was the only thing that took me down."

He shuddered, his remembered terror touching Rae. She set down her plate and glass and reached for his hand. Zander didn't hide his grateful look when he closed his fingers over hers.

"*You* weren't feral," Rae reminded him. "It was only your healing gift giving you hell."

"I know that." Zander's grip tightened. "But I might not have come back from it. It was easy to slip to the other side, and I don't have a Collar to stop me. Shifters can look human but we're not. We're all one step away from the savage."

"Except for the cubs," Rae reminded him. "We take care of

them—even my dad picked me up and took me home with him, when he had no idea who I was, who my parents were. You stopped yourself for a cub, you said. Tell me about him."

As Rae had hoped, the mention of the cub made Zander's haunted look recede. "Cutest little polar bear you ever saw," he rumbled. "Name of Olaf. I thought about asking to adopt him but he's so happy living with a bunch of bears and humans, all of them smitten with him, that I didn't have the heart to take him away. So I visit him. Maybe when he's older I can teach him about being a polar bear. He's an orphan, like you. Maybe I can be the clan he never had."

Zander would do that, Rae saw. He'd take care of the cub, like he took care of everyone else.

"You're a softy," Rae said. "For a big-ass bear."

Zander's eyes took on their usual glint, his fear and his relief evaporating. "You watch who you're calling soft, Little Wolf." He shoved aside the plates, glasses, and pizza box, reached across the table, and dragged Rae onto it. "You're going to pay for being so nice to me."

He didn't bother with Rae's tank top or his T-shirt. He yanked off their underwear and started loving her on the polished wood of the tabletop. Rae laughed as his thrusts came hard and fast, then again when they rolled off to the floor.

Neither of them worried much about it. Zander slid back inside her and Rae sank into him and let the happiness come.

Z ander dragged himself off the bed a few hours later. They'd retreated to the bedroom for a deep sleep after their frenzy in the living room, and now someone was banging on the front door.

Rae opened sleepy eyes but Zander signaled her to stay put, grabbed his samurai sword, and strode out. The scent on the other side of the door was Shifter but Zander drew the sword before he glanced out the window to see who had approached.

Like polite Shifters, they stood a few yards from the cabin, just inside the flower garden. They'd announced their presence and now waited to be admitted to Zander's territory. The cabin *was* Zander's territory at the moment—renting a place for a few days counted.

Zander lowered his sword and opened the door. "'Bout time you got here."

The younger of the pair took a step back. "Goddess, that is *not* what I needed to see right now."

Zander hadn't bothered to dress, so he stood fully naked in the doorway, his sword at his side. "What's your problem, Mason?" he asked. "Gone all squeamish on me? Goddess help your mate."

"Just cover that up. Bears, I swear, are fucking clueless."

The older Shifter laughed. "Get over it, little bro. He's got a woman in there. I'd say we can come back later, but I'm not waiting another two days for you to finish."

Zander growled. "More like two *weeks*, but I get it. Be right back."

He slammed the door and strode into the bedroom, sheathing the sword and finding his clothes. "Broderick and Mason McNaughton," he told Rae by way of explanation as he pulled on his underwear and jeans. "They're from Austin. I asked them to come up here and look at the sword."

Rae peered at him over the quilt. Goddess help him. Her dark hair had come out of its braid and hung tousled to her shoulders, and her face was flushed with sleep. Zander wanted nothing more than to crawl back into the nest with her and snuggle down into her warmth.

Zander pulled on his T-shirt, realizing that his chest was dotted with love bites. Rae liked to chew on him.

"I can get rid of them if you want," Zander said to her. "Send them to your dad's house. We'll meet them there."

"No." Rae threw back the quilts and dragged a hand through her hair. With her breasts bared, the covers bunching around her hips, she was sexier than ever. "I want to talk to them. Why do you think they can fix the sword?"

"Because they're good with metal. You sure you want them in here?"

Rae nodded. "Give me a sec and I'll come out."

Zander's mating frenzy, not sated at all, buzzed as he watched Rae reaching for the garments strewn around the bedroom. The curve of her back as she leaned to the floor led to her tight backside; the soft round of her breast moved as she snatched up her tank top.

It was all Zander could do to turn away from her, shutting out the seductive sight as he closed the bedroom door and went to admit two Lupines grouchy from traveling. Air and morning light rushed in as he opened the front door, along with Broderick and Mason.

"Nice place," Broderick said, looking around. "No way they let Shifters in here."

Zander didn't answer. He made an expansive gesture to the living room. "Make yourself at home."

Mason plopped to the sofa and put his booted feet on the coffee table. "You don't have a TV in here."

"It's supposed to be romantic," Zander told him. "You don't bring a lady out into the woods and then watch football. Or baseball. Whatever the humans are playing now. You fish all day, make love all night. No need for television."

"Barbaric," Mason said, shaking his head. "At least tell me there's beer."

Broderick took the chair next to the sofa and stretched out his long legs. "There's wine." Broderick waved at the two empty bottles that stood by the nearly gutted basket. "At least, there was. Romance, remember?" He turned aggrieved gray eyes on Zander. "You'd think the idiot didn't have a mate."

"How is Jazz?" Zander asked Mason. He remembered the cute woman who'd found him in his remote Alaskan cabin when he'd sworn he'd covered his trail. She'd looked at Mason as though her world changed when she cast her eyes upon him.

Mason lost his mock sullenness and flushed. "Jasmine's good. Really good."

"He's being modest," Broderick said. "What he's not telling you is he got a cub on her. She's due around the first of next year."

"Awesome news," Zander said in all sincerity. He came up behind Mason and clapped his hands on the younger Shifter's shoulders. "Congratulations, kid."

"The blessing of the Goddess upon you," Rae's voice came to them from the now-open bedroom door. Rae stood poised on the threshold, once more in her jeans and white tank top, the sheathed Sword of the Guardian in her hands. "Cubs are wonderful things." She sounded wistful, as though she didn't quite believe she'd have cubs of her own.

Both Broderick and Mason came to their feet, gazing at Rae in amazement. Rae gave them her gray-eyed stare in return, fearless as always. She wasn't afraid of two blustering, overly arrogant Lupines.

To Zander's surprise Broderick and Mason said nothing. Not *So, is this her?* Or *Yeah, I can see why you didn't answer the door.* They only stared, stunned, and Rae didn't move.

"This is Rae Lyall," Zander said. "Guardian of the Montana Shiftertown. Rae—that's Broderick McNaughton and his youngest brother, Mason. They're luthiers and also do metal-working of amazing intricacy. They're artists."

"He means we make guitars and other stringed instruments," Broderick rumbled. "And music boxes. Real ones, with clockwork gears."

Mason shook himself out of his stupor and silently opened the backpack he'd slung to the couch. He drew out a box of meticulously inlaid and polished wood and held it out to Rae.

Rae's face softened as she set the sword on the table and took the box in curiosity. It was very small, about three inches by two, the lid embedded with a mosaic of crushed semi-precious stones.

Rae opened the box and Zander came to look at it over her shoulder. The innards consisted of a gleaming brass cylinder covered with bumps and the tiniest cogs and wheels he'd ever seen. He knew that every piece had been fabricated by Mason's and Broderick's large, blunt hands in their hidden workshop in a warehouse district in Austin.

"You turn it on here." Mason stepped forward and clicked a switch next to the cylinder.

Music filled the room. The box didn't have the simple tinny tinkle of cheap music boxes sold at gift shops, but a full, rich resonance. Zander didn't know what the piece of music was but it was complex and beautiful.

"Jasmine wrote the tune," Mason said, sounding almost shy. "She thought you'd like it."

"I do." Rae closed the box and held it to her chest. "It's beautiful. Tell her thank you."

Mason kept staring at Rae and so did Broderick. Zander lifted the Sword of the Guardian from the table. "All right, stop ogling my mate. I asked you up here for your professional opinion."

Broderick's gaze moved to Zander, his eyes lighting. "Mate?"

Zander hadn't realized the word had come out of his mouth. But why not? He'd been thinking of *Rae* and *mate* synonymously for a while now.

"You heard me." Zander started to unsheathe the sword and then realized the other three hadn't followed him.

He glanced back to see Mason and Broderick still staring at Rae, as though they'd never seen a female Lupine before. Of course she was sexy and beautiful and also the first female Guardian they'd ever seen, but even so . . .

"Leave her alone," Zander said, his protectiveness surging.

"Sorry," Mason said. "It's just that you look a lot like—I mean a *lot* like . . ."

"Our mom," Broderick finished.

Rae blinked. "Your mom?" Zander looked at them in surprise too.

"Our mom when she was younger," Broderick amended. "She passed a few years back. But we have pictures of her. You're her spitting image."

Rae's face lost color, her eyes becoming a lighter gray. "How can I be?"

Zander came to stand next to her and pinned Broderick with his stare. "What are you trying to say?"

Mason shrugged and answered for him. "I don't think we're saying anything. It's just weird."

Not to a woman who'd never known her family. Rae had no idea who she was or where she'd come from. Now two Lupines were telling her she resembled a matriarch of their pack, which might mean Rae was related to them, or at least was a member of their clan.

Zander tried to calm his speculations. It wasn't all that

mysterious for Shifters to resemble one another. Each Shifter species had been bred from similar genetic stock eons ago. Rae was a black wolf and these guys were gray—though their mother's clan might have been black wolf. Zander didn't want to give Rae false hope but he didn't want to crush the hope either.

"We'll check," Zander promised her. "How about we fix the sword first?"

Rae shook herself. "Sure." She made herself turn away from the two Lupines, take the sword from him, withdraw the broken pieces, and lay them on the table.

Broderick stepped forward and looked down at the blade in dismay. "Oh, come on," he groaned. "I just put this damned thing back together."

CHAPTER TWENTY-NINE

Rae blinked as Broderick balled his fists and glared at Zander. The sword, as though waking from sleep, started to hum. Loudly.

"Zander didn't break it," Rae said over the noise. "*I* did."

"This is Daragh's sword, isn't it?" Broderick asked. "The one that was stolen? Yeah, I recognize its tone."

The sword swelled into a happy crescendo and then thankfully died away into a quiet ring. Rae knew the story of Broderick returning this sword after it had been stolen—he'd been the one to release Daragh from the Fae and finally send him to dust. Rae hadn't witnessed the dusting—only Daragh's immediate family and her father as Shiftertown leader had been there.

"The medallion was broken off when I found it," Broderick told Rae. "But it went back together without much effort. Why won't it do that now?"

Zander said, "If I knew how to fix it, I wouldn't have called you. The sword likes you, Broderick, and you're good at making metal parts for your boxes and instruments. I figured if anyone had a chance at putting it back together, it was you."

Mason put his fists on the table, gazing at the sword with the same interest as Broderick. "Instrument making and sword-smithing are two different things," he said.

"Not really." Zander touched the hilt. "Hot metal, artistry . . . Like the samurai swords. They're weapons and works of art at the same time. I would have taken this to the man who made my samurai swords but he's been dead a couple hundred years."

"The Shifter swordsmith has been gone even longer," Broderick said dryly. "Seems wrong that the skill wasn't handed down."

"I'm guessing no one thought we'd need it," Zander said. "The swords lasted eight hundred years without a problem before."

"Goddess, I hope they *all* don't start breaking," Broderick grumbled.

Mason ran his fingers along the blade. Rae held her breath but he touched it without trouble, no burning.

When Broderick had gazed at her with such intensity and announced she resembled their mother, her heart had leapt and her pulse hadn't calmed since.

It wasn't so farfetched to believe they were related—Shifter clans had been broken up when they were put into Shiftertowns, with clan members scattered all over the world. Rae's mother could have been separated from her clan long before her death. She had no idea.

Also, Broderick had succeeded in driving this very sword through Daragh's heart and sending him to dust. Only a Guardian could dust another Guardian. Broderick wasn't one, but the story went that the sword *chose* him to help out Daragh. Afterward, Eoin had asked Broderick to stay in Montana and see if he'd be their Shiftertown's next Guardian but Broderick had declined.

Six months after that, Rae had been chosen. If Broderick and Rae were related, all this would make sense—they both might be descended from a Guardian, or at least from a clan with Guardian blood.

Zander had given her a warning look when Broderick made his pronouncement. He didn't want her to get too excited in case they proved to be no relation at all.

Rae couldn't help it. For the first time in her life there was a possibility that she'd found her family. She hadn't met Broderick when he'd come here to send Daragh to the Summerland—he'd left the moment he'd finished and Rae had never seen him.

Broderick touched the hilt but he did it in trepidation, as though he expected a spark or flame. Nothing happened—the sword remained a cold hunk of silver.

"We'll need a forge," Broderick said, resigned.

"No problem," Zander said. "I know—"

"Cheese and rice, Zander," Rae cut him off. "You can't know a guy who has a *forge*."

Zander's dark eyes sparkled. "Sure I do. You know him too. You boys up for a trip north?"

Rae found herself once more saying good-bye to her father and brothers and once again boarding Marlo's cargo plane and heading north to Alaska. Carson stayed behind, as did Ezra, both of them wanting to help Eoin in the search for the Shifters who'd hurt Carson's wife.

Eoin didn't question Zander's abrupt announcement that they needed to return to Alaska but by his look, he was going to soon demand the whole story. He was trusting Rae—and Zander—but he'd want the truth. Rae hoped to be able to tell him while showing him the repaired sword.

The guy Zander knew who had a forge was Piotr. The plane landed at an isolated air strip north of Homer in the middle of the night, but Piotr was there, in Zander's own truck, to pick them up.

Piotr hopped out of the cab and came at them with arms outstretched. "My friends!" he boomed. "It is good to see you again!"

He threw his arms around Rae first, lifting her in an exuberant hug, his smile as big as ever.

"You are keeping Zander from trouble, yes?" he asked Rae when he thumped her back to her feet. "You will love my wife, young Rae. She is so looking forward to meeting you."

Rae hoped Piotr didn't exaggerate. Any woman might be

alarmed at her husband bringing home three large and loud Shifter males and a young woman with a broken sword.

Broderick and Mason were a little distrustful of Piotr at first but by the time they were halfway to Piotr's house in Nikolaevsk, the brothers were joking and laughing with the man like old friends.

Piotr lived in a large house on a stretch of land a little outside the town. The night sky was a riot of stars when they arrived, swaths of white unfolding in majesty.

Piotr's house went with him—the interior was filled with bright colors, deep-pile rugs, and soft furniture, everything made for comfort. A corner of the living room contained a cloth-draped niche covered with medieval-looking pictures of a mother and child done up in blacks, golds, and reds. *Icons,* Zander told Rae. They depicted the mother goddess of Piotr's religion.

The entire house had been furnished for practicality yet coziness. Winters here were long and dark but Piotr's house would be cheerful with a fire on the big hearth and the kitchen bubbling with good smells.

Even in summer, with the light lingering, the kitchen held thick, warm scents. Piotr's wife, Irena, came to greet them, a ladle in her hand. When introductions had been made, which included Irena pulling Rae into a firm embrace, she led the way to the kitchen, waving the ladle and telling them she hoped they'd brought appetites.

Irena was not as bulky as her husband, but her face was as pink, her eyes as bright, though hers were hazel. She had a blue scarf over her hair, so Rae could not see its color, but her brows were dark. Irena wore a long skirt and blouse, which she moved around in with ease as she served a meaty stew plump with dumplings.

She had beer for the Shifters, coffee and tea for whoever wanted it, and water for her sons, no matter how much they protested they were old enough to drink beer. One was nine, the other seven.

The kids already loved Zander and didn't seem too worried about Mason and Broderick. The clamored to tell Zander all about the cool things they'd done since they last saw him and wanted to show him Dad's new snowmobile and other things.

Finally Piotr raised his voice. "I cannot hear a word in my own house. Zander is a guest. Let him eat his meal in peace, *volchok*."

Zander rumbled a laugh. He gazed across the table at Rae, his dark eyes holding her. "That's what I call you. It means Little Wolf."

Rae's face went very hot, especially under the interested looks of the entire Ivanov family. "What's Russian for big-ass bear?" she asked, sounding innocent.

"Zander," Piotr said, and then roared with laughter.

The others laughed too, the meal ending jovially.

Rae had never known that humans could be as close and loving as Shifters, though she admitted she'd never had much contact with them. Humans were the people who'd locked away Shifters, but since she'd met Zander, she'd realized that humans had degrees of good and evil, just like Shifters.

Once supper was over, Piotr led them out to his big shed where he stored his snowmobiles and kept his forge.

Rae wasn't certain what she'd expected when Zander had said "forge." She pictured a wide hearth with a roaring fire, a big anvil, and iron everywhere, but she'd never seen a real smithy, only read about old-fashioned ones. Piotr gestured them to a box about two feet square that rested on a stand, with propane bottles nestled on the stand's bottom shelf. The opening to the firebox was on the forge's side, to contain the heat inside, Rae supposed.

Piotr flipped a few switches and got the forge going. "Takes a little bit to warm up," he said. "You think it will be safe for your sword?"

"Sure, if we don't plunge it in and leave it to melt," Zander said. "This is why I asked Broderick and Mason to try. They know how to work soft metals without ruining them, and the sword already likes Broderick."

"Don't remind me," Broderick said, grimacing. "I was glad to see the back of that thing." The sword, which Rae had laid on a workbench near the forge, hummed once then went silent. Broderick glared at it. "And I hate when it does *that*."

Piotr, who'd heard nothing, glanced curiously at them then went back to setting out his supplies on the workbench. He had several anvils of different sizes, hammers, files, and other tools Rae didn't recognize.

"What do you make?" she asked him. "Horseshoes?"

Piotr grinned at her. "I'm not good with horses, so no. Though one of my neighbors down the road has horses and uses my place to make the shoes. No, I make handy things like pump parts and pieces for my boat and also some decorative trinkets."

He moved to a table on the far side of the room, pulled a brightly colored blanket from it, and stood back to let her look.

The table was strewn with wrought-iron art. Some pieces were meant for fences or gates, Rae could see, but others had been made to be hung on walls or porches for the sheer beauty of them. One piece was a frame that looked like an arched Tuscan window, with the spaces between the vertical rods filled with delicate iron leaves and curlicues. Another was a tall, narrow room divider, its patterns intricate, the metal twisted into thin spirals.

Piotr had also made crosses, strong yet lovely symbols of his faith. Rae had seen plenty of church crosses in human towns, but Piotr's had a second, shorter crosspiece near the bottom. The Russian Orthodox cross, Piotr told her. He lifted a smaller piece that looked like a picture frame but its negative space was decorated with iron leaves and flowers, all of them burnished with gold.

"For you," Piotr said. "You hang it on your wall and remember Piotr."

Shifters didn't usually make polite protests when offered a gift, but she put her hand to her chest.

"I can't," she said. "It's too beautiful. It must be very valuable."

Piotr scoffed. He lifted the frame and put it into her hands. "I made it for you. When I came home, I said—I must make something for that nice Rae for putting up with me and my friend Zander. Take it. It is yours."

Rae held it gingerly. The iron piece was heavy and delicate at the same time. "Thank you," she said breathlessly. "I will treasure it."

Zander was watching her. His enigmatic dark eyes told her nothing, and he turned back to Broderick, helping move the tools and anvil he and Mason had chosen.

Rae had never watched anyone do metalwork before. Her brothers fixed up cars and motorcycles, but it wasn't the same thing. As Mason gently took up the bottom half of the sword's blade in a pair of tongs, Rae touched her lips in trepidation. It was like watching her child be approached by a dentist with forceps. She was sure it would be fine, but . . .

As Mason started to ease the blade into the forge's heat, Rae asked abruptly, "Won't melting it erase the runes?"

Mason stopped just shy of the forge and looked back at Broderick. He'd donned goggles and his gray eyes blinked behind them.

"Who knows?" Broderick answered. "It's your call, Rae. Your sword. What do you want to do?"

For once, Zander didn't offer an answer. He only looked at Rae, waiting for her to decide.

Rae wet her lips and hugged Piotr's gift to her chest. "Go ahead," she said. "Get it over with."

Mason drew a breath and plunged the blade into the heat.

Zander went to Rae's side as she took a sharp breath. His warmth helped but she still shivered when Mason stepped back and made no move to take the sword out. "It has to sit there a while," he said. "We're trying to soften it, not melt it."

It was agonizing to wait. Piotr tried to distract Rae by showing her more things he was making but she hastened back to the forge as soon as Mason brought out the blade. He plunged it into water then set it aside, still clamped, while Broderick put in the second part.

They were going to wait for that one too, Rae realized. She did see, as she watched anxiously, that as the first blade cooled, the runes remained intact. In fact, they looked sharper than ever.

"Now what?" she asked.

Broderick answered. "We'll put the pieces together and try to hammer them into one, heating as we need to."

"It's silver," Rae said nervously. "Not steel. Wouldn't it be easier to melt it and remold it?"

"It's Fae silver," Mason answered her. "Which isn't the same thing. It has spells or something in it to make it harder. Plus the original sword maker worked it like steel, folding it instead of pouring and hardening it. We *could* melt the whole thing down and start over, but then it probably wouldn't be a Sword of the Guardian."

Rae sighed. "I wish Daragh would have written some of this stuff down."

Broderick gave her a quick look. "I met Daragh. Before he . . . Before I sent him to dust. He was brave as hell but I know he never meant to die so soon."

Who did? Rae wondered. She tapped her fingers against the iron frame Piotr had given her, her toes curling in her boots.

The next thing she felt was Zander's strong hand on her arm. "Let's you and I go outside," he said. "Let the experts work."

Mason sent him a look of relief. Rae heaved another sigh, knowing she was hovering like a worried mother, and allowed Zander to tow her from the workroom.

The night had darkened finally. Zander watched Rae stride around the open ground near Piotr's house a while before he hauled out a wooden lawn chair and pulled Rae down to sit in it with him.

There were no deep woods here—trees, yes, but not like the forests of Rae's home. Nikolaevsk was on a relatively flat plain that ran up to knifelike mountains, the view beautiful when the sun was up. For now, stars marched across the sky, the path of the heavens.

"You all right?" Zander asked Rae. He liked her warmth in his lap as he cradled her against him. It might be summer, but Alaskan nights were cool.

"I broke the sword," Rae said glumly. "And now it's being melted and hammered. The Guardians are going to kill me, if they get to me before my dad does. He's put his neck on the line for me, defying so many other Shifters."

Zander didn't answer, only held her closer. Rae had broken the sword to save Zander's life. If the Guardians didn't like that, they could eat it.

Zander wished he could tell Rae to throw the sword away and run with him to the other side of the world—to hell with it—but the Goddess didn't work like that. Once she'd touched you, you could never get away from her.

Rae snuggled into Zander's chest without any coaxing, and he closed his eyes as he breathed the scent of her hair. When they finished this experiment—successful or not, Zander would take her someplace remote and beautiful. A tropical island perhaps where they could shut out the world and explore what they'd started to find together.

"Zander," Rae said softly.

"Hmm?" Zander kissed the top of her head. "What is it, baby?"

"If you knew Piotr had a forge, why didn't you just bring Broderick and Mason up here right away? I mean, once we got away from the Graveyard?" She lifted her head to look at him.

Zander knew the answer but he picked his words carefully. "You wanted to go home," he said with a shrug. "Be with your family. I wanted to meet them—and have them meet me. Plus, I didn't know if Broderick or Mason could do anything at all and I didn't want to drag you around Alaska when you could be home and happy."

Zander had moved his gaze to the horizon as he spoke, the lights of the tiny town glittering in the night. He felt Rae's gaze sharp on him and he looked down to gray eyes that reflected the starlight.

"You took me home because you knew I wanted to go home?" she asked.

Zander pretended to think about it. "Yep. I guess so."

Her brows drew down, dark streaks on the pale smudge of her face. "Damn you."

Zander tightened his arms around her. "Hey, don't worry. I'm done being nice."

At least, that's what he started to say. Rae launched herself at him and started kissing him.

Sweet Little Wolf. Rae held him with strong hands as she parted his lips, kissing him deeply. Zander tasted her frenzy, in no way sated, exactly like his own.

Rae turned in the chair to straddle him, cupping his face in her hands. Zander's heart heated to near-pain as he pulled her against him.

The world could go to hell, the sword with it. There was nothing better in Zander's life than kissing Rae out under the stars—except maybe making love to her under those stars. He'd do that too.

The workshop's door banged open, sending warm yellow light into the cool darkness. Mason emerged, still wearing the leather apron he'd donned to work on the sword.

Rae jerked her head up but she didn't scramble to her feet. She kept to Zander's lap but he felt her brace herself for bad news.

"It won't work," Mason said, his words filled with disgust. "It looked like it came together a few times but once it cooled again and we picked it up, the blade just split. I think it wants its Guardian. You come in and try, Rae."

CHAPTER THIRTY

Rae held the hammer the way Broderick had showed her and positioned it on the blade, her mouth dry. The goggles Piotr had given her were worn and scratched, making everything misty, and the leather apron hung heavily on her torso.

Mason and Broderick had heated both pieces of sword in the forge and laid them across the anvil. Now they stood back and waited for Rae to tap the blade together. The runes glowed hot, every letter picked out in fire.

What are you saying? Rae asked it silently. Reid had translated the letters to a story but there had to be more to it than that. *What do you want me to do?*

The sword only hummed, its music undimmed by the heat.

Rae drew a breath, lifted the hammer, and struck.

The blade moved together, the hot metal catching and holding. Encouraged, Rae struck it again, then again. She began to hammer in earnest, not too hard, not too gently, as Broderick had instructed.

Her face warmed from the heat of the metal, perspiration trickling from where the goggles gripped her face. The blade flowed together. It was working.

Rae kept on beating it softly, melding the sword with little taps. They'd cool it then file and polish it, Broderick had said, and no one would ever see the break.

Zander stood on the opposite side of the anvil, his skin gleaming with the same heat. He didn't look as hopeful as Rae, only eyed the sword watchfully.

The hammer's head felt a little loose all of a sudden. Rae tapped it once more onto the sword.

The hammer broke with a pinging sound, the head flying. The Shifters and Piotr ducked out of the way as the hammer's iron head sailed past them, smacked into the wall, and clattered to the cement floor.

Rae stared at the broken hammer, wide-eyed. "Sorry," she said to Piotr.

Piotr took the handle from her. "It is only a hammer. They sell many of them in Homer."

Rae felt bad for breaking it but when she looked at the sword, elation drowned out remorse. The sword lay before her, whole and unblemished. It winked under the work lights and reflected the forge's red glow.

Rae wanted to pick up the sword, but Broderick told her it should sit for a while, cooling down and hardening. Finally, when Broderick said it was ready, Rae reached down and gently closed her hand around the hilt.

The sword came up with ease, its weight and balance back to normal. Rae carefully turned with it, both hands holding it steady.

Mason and Broderick backed away with Shifter instinct. No one wanted to feel the touch of the sword. Zander didn't move, but he kept a careful eye on Rae.

"It seems all right," Rae said. She turned the sword slowly from side to side, letting the blade move through the air. "I suppose I won't know if it's truly fixed until I use it."

Broderick took another step back, raising his hands. "Not ready to be dust yet, thanks."

"I didn't mean that." Rae grinned at him then moved into a fighting stance Zander had taught her. "You didn't bring your bamboo practice sword, did you?"

"Not out here," Zander answered. "You don't need me.

Pretend an evil Fae has just popped out of nowhere and do a lunge at him."

The move was one Rae liked. She shifted the weight of the sword, her lower hand steadying the hilt, thrust her right foot forward, and jammed the point straight at the imaginary Fae. It went through him, slaying the invisible Fae, but the blade stayed whole.

Rae's heart squeezed in relief. "Hot damn. Thank you, Mason. Broderick. Piotr." She swung around to Zander and sent him a teasing look. "You too, I guess."

Zander gave her a little nod, his eyes warm. "Anytime, Little Wolf."

Rae whooped and spun the sword at her side.

The sword's weight changed abruptly. Rae heard a snap like a crack of thunder, then a ring, and a clanging. The bottom part of the blade struck the floor and went spinning away, the top part still in her hand. The jagged crack between the two pieces was back, exactly as it had been before.

Rae screamed. She threw the hilted piece away from her, sending it skittering after its fellow, then she slammed herself to the ground on her backside.

"I give *up*!" she yelled.

Zander and the two brothers said nothing as Rae balled her fists and pounded the floor. Only Piotr ventured, "When metal is weakened, it is for always. Sometimes it can never be put right again."

Rae managed to bite back the next scream, but she couldn't stop her words. "Well, that's just fucking *perfect*!"

"Little Wolf," Zander began, his voice incredibly gentle. "We—"

Whatever he was going to say was drowned by the shrill peal of his cell phone. Zander growled as he grabbed it.

"Go for—" He caught Rae's glare and amended his greeting. "Yeah?"

His expression stilled. Rae's heart thumped, remembering the last time he'd been interrupted by a phone call. Ezra's father had been dying and she'd been needed to perform the duty of a Guardian. She couldn't this time, could she?

Zander shook his head at her, as though telling her this call

was different. "Where?" he asked. "Are they sure?" Another
pause. "I know, I know. If *he's* sure, then it's true." Another pause
while he listened. This time, Zander snorted a laugh. "Right, I'll
tell her not to come, but you know how obedient she is."

Rae heard an answering laugh, one she recognized, then
Zander said his farewells and hung up the phone.

"Where doesn't my dad want me to go?" Rae demanded.
"Even though I'm going anyway."

"The Olympic Peninsula," Zander answered without bothering to argue. "My friends have found the feral Shifters."

Z ander's anger tightened as they made their way south in
Marlo's cargo plane. He was famous for keeping anger in
check when everyone around him was falling apart, but right
now, it was rising to consume him.

Rae sat unhappily next to him, cross-legged on a blanket,
the Sword of the Guardian in front of her. Why the dumb-ass
blade wouldn't go back together, Zander didn't understand. It
was magical, so what the hell?

Why the Shifters of Rae's town were such dickheads that
they couldn't lift a finger to support her, Zander didn't understand either. He had the feeling that the sword was being a pain
the ass to symbolize the divisiveness of the Shifters or something like that. Once they accepted Rae for what she was,
acknowledged the Goddess's choice, maybe *then* the sword
would go together. Had nothing to do with mating—that had
been Zander's wishful thinking.

Feral Shifters who'd hurt a good man and his wife were
running around, wild and free, while the beautiful Rae got shit
on by her own people. It was enough to make Zander want to
go on a polar bear rampage.

A decent rampage might help tamp down his mating frenzy
as well, he reasoned. *Might*. All Zander knew is that he wanted
to hurt everyone who'd hurt Rae then grab her and hole up with
her until they were exhausted, sated, and happy.

Rae was asking him a question, raising her voice over the
plane's engines. "How did the Shifters get found so fast? Carson looked for two years. You had two days."

"Five days," Zander corrected her. The front of his brain answered her while deep down inside his Shifter beast was becoming a roiling ball of fury. "I started making inquiries when we were still on Carson's boat. I know a lot of people who know a lot of people. It's like the Guardian Network, except it's not cryptic in a computer and no one needs a password."

Broderick laughed out loud. "He means he has people like Dylan Morrissey and Kendrick Shaughnessy doing him favors. Plus the secret weapon. Tiger."

Zander shrugged, pretending rage wasn't hot in his chest. "Like I said. I know people who know people."

Broderick sent Rae an understanding look. "What he's not telling you is that Dylan's already been hunting down rogue Shifters, little by little, and he has resources, both human and Shifter. Then there's Tiger."

"I've heard of him," Rae said. "He came to our Shiftertown with you, but I didn't meet him."

"Tiger's not right in the head." Broderick tapped his own skull. "But he's brilliant. He's the result of stupid human experiments—they were trying to create a super-Shifter and abandoned Tiger when they couldn't handle him. He's got shit going on between his ears that no one understands, but when he's sent to track someone, they get tracked. He probably already had a bead on these guys when Zander asked about them."

"Tiger's a good person," Zander broke in. "Better than a lot of so-called 'normal' Shifters I know. Not that any Shifter is normal."

"Thanks a lot," Rae said, but he saw the glint of amusement in her eyes. As upset as she was, she could still banter with Zander. He liked that.

Or would if he wasn't so pissed off. Zander willed the plane to go faster so he could be on the ground and kick some ass.

The Olympic Peninsula, west of Seattle, was a place of rugged mountains, deep forests, and vast beauty. A huge chunk of it was a national park, which would be full of hikers and campers in the summer and, apparently, a bunch of un-Collared, violent Shifters.

The rogue Shifters had chosen to set up camp in an isolated area where no roads led but that would be easily accessible to wolves, wildcats, and bears. Eoin told Zander and his party this when they met up on an empty beach, down the hill from where Marlo had landed. How many were out there, Eoin didn't know for sure yet. Eoin hadn't wanted to risk his trackers—led by his own sons—to spy on feral Shifters without backup.

Dylan Morrissey and the Austin Shifters arrived shortly after Zander's party did, brought in by one of Marlo's pilot friends. Dylan was a Feline Shifter with a lot of black-maned lion in him. In the past, he'd been leader of the Austin Shiftertown, but he'd "retired" in favor of his son, Liam. Humans believed Dylan retired anyway, but Dylan considered himself now free to dominate the entire territory of South Texas. He put other Shiftertown leaders in place and kept his eye on everything that went on in the area. He also was in thick with Shiftertown leaders and Guardians throughout the country, moving like a liaison between them.

While Dylan was loyal to his sons, Liam and Sean, he was an alpha over other alphas, and not many Shifters could oppose him. He had resources that made Zander's network look puny—Zander had become one of *Dylan's* resources, whatever Broderick might think, not the other way around.

Then there was Tiger. He stood on the isolated beach as the others gathered, his back to them while he stared out to sea. Green cliffs rose around the cove, covered with thick tall trees. The wind blowing off the surf was cold, in spite of the rising summer sun.

Tiger was motionless, sunlight glinting on his orange and black hair. Tiger was as big as Zander when they were both in human form, and the Bengal tiger he became was massive.

Zander broke from the group to approach Tiger quietly, though he made sure the man knew he was coming. Sneaking up on Tiger was always a bad idea.

"Hey, big guy," Zander said.

Tiger didn't turn. He continued to gaze at the ocean, the surf pounding and curling to run up on the empty beach. Waves slid along the pale sand then eased back out to meet up with the churning water again.

"What are you looking at?" Zander asked. He shaded his eyes but saw nothing on the waves. No boats, planes in the sky, nothing.

"I have never seen the ocean before," Tiger said.

Zander started to ask, "What, *never*?" But he stopped himself. Tiger had spent the first decades of his life in a cage, never even let out of a basement. From what Zander had heard, he'd taken a long time to adjust to simply being outside. Dylan now kept a close eye on him, though from what Zander had seen, Tiger did pretty much what he wanted. He helped Dylan out of gratitude, not submission.

"It's beautiful," Zander said. "There's nothing like the Pacific."

Tiger gave him a look that said he didn't have any idea what Zander meant by that but was too polite to say so.

"I will bring Carly here," Tiger said, turning back to the water. "And Seth. They will like it."

Carly was Tiger's diminutive Texas-girl mate who could do anything she wanted with him. Seth was Tiger's cub, born not long ago. Tiger's granite hard face and fierce yellow eyes softened a long way when he said Seth's name.

"So how's fatherhood treating you?" Zander asked him. "How is the little guy?"

Some Shifters found it intrusive for another Shifter to ask after a cub, especially one as newborn as Tiger's. The protectiveness that kept cubs alive and away from volatile Shifters was strong.

Tiger, however, only let his mouth twitch into a hint of a smile. "He is robust." Pride rang in his voice. "He keeps us awake all the time, yells louder than anyone in the house. He will be a strong Shifter."

Tiger's eyes were alight. If he'd been human, he'd have brought out a smartphone with a boatload of pictures on it and started showing Zander every one of them. But Tiger and devices didn't go together, and a man with perfect recall didn't need photos.

"Congratulations," Zander said with sincerity. "You deserve this."

Again, Tiger looked slightly nonplussed by his words, but

as usual, he didn't worry too much about it. To Tiger, other Shifters were the crazy ones, not him.

"Cubs are wonderful things," Tiger said "You should have one. Or many." He glanced behind Zander and Zander knew exactly who he was looking at.

Rae tripped across the sand toward them, the sword on her back catching the light. Zander had known she was coming before he turned around—her step, scent, and the lightness in the air when she was near was embedded on his senses.

"I'm working on it," Zander said, giving Tiger a meaningful look. "Please keep your cryptic hints to yourself."

Tiger only kept staring past him at Rae, not acknowledging him. Rae reached Zander's side, gazed at Tiger without fear, and held out her hand.

"Are you Tiger? I've been wanting to meet you."

Tiger frowned in puzzlement at her outstretched palm then put both his hands on her shoulders and looked into her eyes. "You are Guardian," he said.

Rae flushed. "Some people think so."

Tiger's frown deepened. "No, you are *Guardian*. Whether only some think so doesn't matter."

"We're working on that too," Zander told him.

Tiger glanced at Zander, his golden eyes troubled. "You must protect her. She is of the Goddess." Tiger leaned down, put his arms carefully around Rae, and drew her into a Shifter hug.

Rae started, but she lifted her arms to encircle Tiger's big body and hug him back. Tiger relaxed slightly once he had Rae in his embrace, his eyes closing almost in relief.

If he were anyone but Tiger, Zander would be bristling and telling him that was enough touching of his mate. But Tiger was insanely in love with Carly, and flirting with someone else's mate was a concept his brain didn't wrap itself around. Tiger was reacting to Rae as herself, as Guardian, as Goddess-touched.

Tiger loosened his hold but spoke into Rae's ear before he stood up. He might think he was whispering, but Zander heard every word.

"You must take care of Zander as well," Tiger told her, then tried to drop his voice even lower. "He's a little crazy."

* * *

Dylan and Eoin arranged the attack with military precision. Rae couldn't help a dart of pride as her father did what he was best at—organizing and taking care of Shifters.

Tiger and the other trackers had gone scouting and had pinpointed the feral Shifters. They'd set up an encampment deep in the woods and they'd chosen the site well. No approach could be made without the ferals knowing about it and, in fact, they were already well aware that the other Shifters were here and gathering to strike.

"But wait," Zander said to Rae as Eoin turned to discuss a detail of the plan with Dylan. "There's more. Humans have joined them."

Rae blinked. "Really? What humans would join Shifters?"

Zander, who'd gone on the scouting mission with Dylan's trackers, shook his head. "I think humans call them survivalists. People off the grid." He chuckled with grim humor. "You can't get more off the grid than feral Shifters."

Broderick put in, "They've built a sort-of encampment with a fence and booby traps. Like that will keep us out."

"It's weird," Zander said. "The humans seem to be running the show, but that can't be right. Shifters don't take orders from humans. If these Shifters are feral, they'll tear apart any human who tries to out-dominate them. Which tells me the Shifters are using these humans, for whatever reason."

"Hiding," Rae suggested. "If the local police find out about the encampment, they'll think all inside are human survivalists, not Shifters. Any hint of Shifters hiding out here, and Shifter Bureau comes in with the army."

"Could be," Zander said. "These Shifters are canny, but they can't be that canny. I've evaded Shifter Bureau for twenty years without going feral, attacking innocent people, or hiding behind humans with illegal weapons."

"You do hide behind humans," Rae said. "You hide in human towns, in plain sight, making friends so people will look the other way."

Zander's gaze darkened. He was tense, coiled like Jake the Snake ready to strike. Rae sensed his growing need to fight, the violence that lurked inside every Shifter wanting to come out. Zander didn't have a Collar to stop him, and his polar bear was ready to do damage.

Rae couldn't feel worry about that, or blame him. She wanted to lash out too. She sent him an understanding look then turned from him, ready to rejoin the others. "All right. Let's do this."

Zander's hand landed on her shoulder. "Is it any use for me to tell you to stay on the beach and keep out of danger?"

Rae shot him a grin. "What do *you* think? I'm a wolf, sweetie. She-wolves are the most ferocious of all. Haven't you heard?"

The answering glint in Zander's eyes ramped up Rae's excitement. He gave a mock sigh. "You're going to make my life hell, aren't you?"

"You better believe it, Big-Ass Bear," Rae said, and hurried away before he could try to stop her.

Zander made himself feel better about Rae coming with them by having her in his squad. Eoin gave him a look that told him Zander had better make sure she stayed in the rear and didn't come up against any dangerous action. Zander knew that wouldn't be easy, but his giant polar bear could knock her out of harm's way if necessary.

Carson was also in Zander's squad. Eoin had tried to dissuade him from coming along, saying that fighting Shifters who were probably feral was certain death for a human, but Carson didn't care. Zander couldn't join in the argument— Carson was avenging his mate, and Zander would never stop the man from doing that.

"Your mate's still alive and needs you," Zander reminded him. "Just remember that."

Carson looked white about the lips but nodded. He was armed with a pistol and a tranq rifle, the only one of them who carried weapons.

Projectile weapons anyway. Zander had brought his samurai sword and Rae had the Sword of the Guardian, broken though it might be. Zander would make certain the samurai blade was ready for Rae's use if she needed it.

Tiger and the trackers had discovered that there were twenty rogue Shifters in the ferals' encampment and about as many humans. Dylan and Eoin had brought enough Shifters between the two of them to counter that number with some left over.

The encampment was surrounded by trip wires and wireless devices, meant to send small explosives or bullets at the unwary. Humans, no matter how careful, would have been hurt by them but the traps were useless against Shifters. Shifter sight and scent could find the mechanisms quickly. Tiger, with his strange abilities no one really understood, knew where all the booby traps were just by giving the approach a quick scan.

Far more dangerous were the humans inside the lines of the camp. When they saw the Shifters coming, they raised shotguns and rifles and opened fire.

CHAPTER THIRTY-ONE

No Shifter was foolish enough to be caught in the volley. The Shifter trackers who'd rushed to draw the humans' fire dropped and fell back, letting the Shifters who were encircling the encampment attack.

Zander led Rae at a crouching run a long way around to the back of the camp. The camp itself was a loose gathering of tents and metal shacks, some of which looked as though they'd been there a while.

The problem feral Shifters had, Zander reflected as five of them came out of nowhere, was that they could no longer mask their scents. Bathing went out the window as soon as a Shifter started to go feral and any other Shifter could smell them a long way off. The rank odor hit Zander well before the ferals came at them, giving him time to put his plan into action.

The ferals had taken their half-beast forms, the strongest for fighting and best for dexterity. Broderick and Mason were already in their half-wolf states and had skirted the ferals to rush them from behind. Carson, exposing himself in the open, aimed and shot at a human who was covering the ferals.

Carson's first shot knocked the rifle out of the man's hand, the second wounded him, the man falling with a yell of pain.

Carson's job, Zander had told him, was to wing the humans attacking and to protect Rae. Rae didn't know about that last part.

Zander dumped his samurai sword next to Carson and shifted to bear. He roared as he came down on his polar bear feet and launched himself at the nearest Shifter—a large, mottled, half-beast wildcat of uncertain type.

Zander fought against the wildcat's teeth and claws, snarling at the beast's fetid breath. The man's face was half human, his eyes crazed and red. Feral. No doubt about it.

Rae hadn't shifted. She knew she had to guard the Sword of the Guardian, no matter her boast that she-wolves were the best fighters. Zander saw her out of the corner of his eye as she picked up the samurai sword, unsheathed it, and held it ready.

After that, life was a blur. Zander roared as the feral sank ragged claws into him but they couldn't penetrate much past Zander's fur. What concept of *polar bear* didn't this asshole understand?

Zander heard the crunch of bone as the feral went limp under his hands. Zander's rage hit coldness as the healer in him suddenly wanted to repair the damage.

The feral was still alive. Zander laid him down but forced himself to turn away. Icy realization bit him. He'd have to heal these guys when they were done, and it would kill him. Zander had always feared the day when those so far gone would take every spark of energy he had so that he couldn't recover. Today might be the day.

He glanced at Rae, who stood with sword raised, balancing perfectly as he'd taught her. She was protecting Carson, like a shield-maiden with the sun dancing on her hair. He never wanted to leave her.

Another feral struck and Zander had to bury his worries and concentrate on staying alive. Going down while he brooded wouldn't help anyone. Screw it—if Zander had to waste himself today, he would, as long as it meant that Rae was safe.

Broderick and Mason were fighting like the uncontrolled wolves they truly were, but they had Collars, which slowed them down. Zander fought his way over to them, throwing the next feral he was battling into the path of Carson and his tranq gun. Carson shot, and the feral howled and went still.

Two down, three to go. Zander and the McNaughton brothers fought hard and Carson's tranq gun went off again. Four down. Rae shouted as she swung the samurai sword at the feral who broke free. Bright blood appeared on the feral's side and then he collapsed under Broderick's claws. *Five.*

Zander straightened up, breathing hard. They'd need to go help Eoin's team—

And then the woods abruptly filled with more Shifters. The stink of the ferals assaulted Zander's bear nose and made even Carson swear. Zander lifted on his back legs, rising up and up to scan the battlefield.

They were everywhere. *Only twenty,* Tiger had said, and Tiger was never wrong. Eoin's and Dylan's trackers, and Zander, had confirmed that number.

"What the fuck?" Broderick snarled.

Zander got a whiff of what the ferals' collective stink at first masked. A faint bite of sulfur and smoke came to him, along with a cold breeze that was incongruous with the soft month of June, even in the north. The wind was icy, as though someone had opened a window to a place in which winter raged.

Fuck.

Zander shifted rapidly down to human. "Mason, get back to Dylan and find out what the holy shit is going on. Carson, take Rae to the beach. No, back to the plane, and tell Marlo to get the engines running."

Whether Rae would have argued with him or gone obediently, Zander was never to know. Human men surged out of the trees at that moment, flanking the Shifters. Zander's band was surrounded, with no choice but to fight.

Zander had cured a feral a few months ago, as he'd told Rae, and had nearly gone insane in the aftermath. He remembered the loss of control, the red rage in his brain, the strange hunger for *something* he'd never been able to identify. He'd only wanted to savage everyone around him, would have done so if Olaf, the polar bear cub, hadn't stopped him.

As Zander fought against odds that suddenly multiplied, he

felt the feral urge come forward, blotting out anything civilized he'd forced upon himself. For all his claim that he could live un-Collared and outside Shifter hierarchy without it affecting him, Zander knew that the untamed beast lingered inside him. He habitually pushed others away and holed up alone because that gave him time to get the beast under control before he went near anyone he could hurt.

The other Shifters were right about Zander. He really was batshit crazy.

He had to keep these ferals away from Rae. Zander moved back to her even as he fought, noting that Mason and Broderick joined him in forming a circle around Rae and Carson. There was no way for Mason to get away now to bring back intel—he'd never leave his brother to fight alone, in any case. As much as they blustered with each other, the McNaughton family was close.

The fragrance of brimstone bothered Zander most of all. The back part of his brain sifted through confusion—that particular scent and cold combination meant someone had opened a gateway to Faerie, which meant this camp was on a ley line.

But the ferals were *Shifters*. And the humans were human, not half Fae, not half anything. Zander would have smelled that—Tiger would have known it instantly.

Why the hell would Shifters be popping in and out of Faerie? No wonder Carson hadn't been able to track the ferals back when they'd attacked him and his wife. No wonder the Idaho Shiftertown leader and his trackers hadn't found them either. The ferals hadn't gone to ground; they'd gone to another world. Why? And why had they come back to hole up here?

Questions to ponder later. The main issue at hand was how were Zander and friends going to survive?

The ferals attacked, roaring their triumph. Carson took a few down with his tranq gun and also his pistol, but he would run out of ammunition soon. Mason and Broderick turned and fought hard alongside Zander but their Collars were shocking them, which would wear them down sooner or later. Then there was Rae, vulnerable, with the Sword of the Guardian to protect.

Zander, Eoin, and Dylan had been stupid and arrogant to come up here, sure they could take down a small nest of ferals and their new human friends without much effort. They were paying for that arrogance now—this would be a battle to the death, a bloodbath.

As Zander clawed, pummeled, bit, fought, one thought was foremost in his brain. *Get Rae to safety. Protect the mate.*

Rae snarled as two ferals came at her. She took one step back, burst into her half-beast form, and went at them with the samurai sword.

Damn, she was sexy. Her lithe body dodged and moved as she fought with athleticism. She made a fine warrior—Zander's samurai friend would be proud. He noted with interest that Rae's half-wolf form handled the sword better than did her human body, a split second before he barreled into the ferals she fought and tore them away from her.

Rae glared at him with wolf-sharp eyes. "What the hell? I had them!"

She didn't have the Shifter who leapt at her now, a leopard with a too-crazed look in his eyes. Zander sent him flying with one swat of his paw, and Broderick ripped into him, Broderick's Collar sparking.

Zander took the moment of relative calm to shift to human, his skin covered with blood, scratches, and bite marks. One of his braids had come unraveled, the beads in it scattered on the ground. "Get back to the shore!" he shouted at his squad. "Protect the Guardian. They can't get the sword."

"It's broken," Rae yelled. "What does it matter?"

Zander rounded on her, the snarl in his throat holding near-feral fierceness. "Get the hell down to the beach, Little Wolf. I'm not losing you. Carson, take her."

Carson didn't want to. He wanted to kill feral Shifters. Zander saw in his eyes his terrible need for vengeance, to gut those who'd hurt his wife. He couldn't save Vivian, but he could kill those responsible. That was all he'd lived for these past two years.

Zander faced him. "Don't let what happened to Viv happen to Rae. *Please.*"

Carson's fury matched Zander's. His face was dark with anger, his eyes fiery. The savage instinct that lurked inside humans as well as Shifters gripped him hard.

Zander said nothing more, only pinned Carson with a stare. They only had a few seconds before Zander would have to simply pick up Rae and Carson both and run down the hill with them.

Carson hated Zander at that moment, Zander saw in his eyes. Carson didn't want to make a choice. He wanted to fight until all the Shifters were dead and then go back to grieving.

Carson glanced at Rae, who hadn't said a word. She'd shifted to human as well, her clothes torn from the change to her half beast, and waited. She understood exactly what Zander was doing.

Carson's jaw clenched. He threw Zander a look of killing rage but turned away, slung the tranq rifle over his shoulder, and said, "Come on, Rae."

Zander's relief was short-lived. Broderick and Mason were backing toward him, fighting for their lives against at least a dozen ferals. Zander shifted back to bear to help them. He roared at Carson, who grabbed Rae's hand and ran with her toward the path that led down to the shore.

There was nothing to do but retreat. The crazed thing inside Zander wanted to dive into the middle of the ferals and not stop until all were dead at his feet. The tiny spark of sanity he had left told him it would be a last stand. He'd go down swinging, but he'd go down. If he did, he'd be no help to Rae, to Shifters who were hurt in this battle, to anyone.

Zander slashed and ripped, then turned and ran, herding Mason and Broderick before him.

Carson had Rae halfway down the trail. Feral Shifters surged to either side of them, the faster Felines sprinting ahead to cut them off. Carson and Rae were forced to veer straight into the woods along rocky cliffs and keep running.

Too many were coming. Zander waited until Mason and Broderick had caught up to Carson and Rae, then he turned to face the ferals, planted his feet, and roared—the giant, earth-shaking roar of the polar bear.

The front line of Shifters hesitated. They were a motley bunch, wolves and Felines with ragged coats, hatred in their eyes, claws ragged, gums black with disease. Yet they were fighting together, organized, popping in and out of Faerie like they owned the place.

They looked at Zander, Zander looked at them, and then the ferals attacked.

I tried, Rae, was Zander's last coherent thought before a dozen feral Shifters were on him.

Rae heard Zander roaring. She broke from Carson and started back up the hill, roots and rocks clutching at her boots.

Carson was right behind her, hand closing on her arm. "What the hell are you doing?"

Rae shook him off. Broderick and Mason cut in front of her, blocking her way up the hill.

"We'll go back and help him," Broderick said, breathless. "Zander's strong and the Guardian's sword needs to be protected. *Go!*"

"Fuck the sword!" Rae snarled. "The stupid sword is not more important than Zander. Than *any* Shifter." She unslung the Sword of the Guardian from her back and dropped it to the ground. "Take it. I don't want it anymore."

She pushed around them and sprinted up the hill, feeling lighter than she had in weeks. Behind her she heard Broderick growl. "*I'm* not touching that bloody thing."

Zander was fighting hard when Rae reached him, his white fur scarlet, blood dripping from his fangs. He roared and struck, scattering Shifters, but too many sprang up to go at him again.

Rae let herself shift to her half beast between one step and the next. She could do that when she was agitated and this situation counted for some serious agitation. She flourished the samurai sword and swung it hard.

A wildcat screamed as the blade sliced him, then he came at Rae, claws reaching. Zander intercepted him and slammed him to the ground.

Zander growled at Rae, but just then a feral wolf landed on his back, claws and teeth tearing into Zander's flesh. Rae struck him away from Zander then swung around, sword singing as she danced and sliced, moved and thrust.

Broderick, Mason, and Carson reached them and now the two Lupines were fighting furiously, trying to clear a path so

Rae and Zander could escape. Carson, deep anger in his eyes, took down ferals one at a time with the tranq gun.

Rae rolled across Zander's back to come to her feet and swing at another feral. Her Collar was shocking her but she didn't care. She could barely feel it as the crazed wolf inside her fought to defend her true mate.

True mate?

The stunning thought cut through her fighting frenzy. *Well, why not?* Rae couldn't imagine her life beyond this not involving Zander.

Her heart warmed and burned. The wolf in her knew. *Mate bonded. Yes.*

The split second of acknowledgment allowed a Feline Shifter to get under Rae's reach. One moment she was drawing back the samurai sword, the next, a set of claws pierced her stomach and ripped it open.

She swung the sword, but weakly, barely cutting the Feline. He fell in the next moment, neck broken, giant bear paws twisting his head around.

Rae's legs gave out and she found her knees hitting the wet ground, a little sapling scraping the hell out of her arm and side as she went down.

She heard Zander's roars and the ferals' jackal-like cries. Carson was swearing, Broderick and Mason snarling in fury.

Dizziness sent Rae falling forward, the samurai sword sliding out of her hand. *Doesn't matter if I'm hurt,* she thought dimly. *Shifters heal quickly. Right?*

The next thing she knew, Mason was lifting her, and then she found herself on something hard, furry, warm, and moving fast. Rae had been here before, on Zander's back. The last time, he'd run with her out of a bar where they'd all been drunk and working off steam, and Rae had hung on and enjoyed it.

She hung on now, locking her fingers around Zander's fur. He swayed as he ran, but he could *move*.

Rae tried to turn her head and see what was happening behind her. Mason and Broderick were back there, and Carson. She couldn't leave them. Plus she'd lost the samurai sword and thrown away the Sword of the Guardian. Stupid. *All* the Shifters and Guardians would be pissed off at her now.

Sorry, Daragh, she thought muzzily. *Hey, if I come to the Summerland today, don't be mad at me, okay?*

Rae thought she heard Daragh's low chuckle, then his smart-ass voice saying, *If you abandon your mate right now, cub, I will kick your ass.*

"Wrong way!" Carson was yelling behind them.

Zander didn't swerve. He kept charging. A big-ass bear like Zander didn't need a path, Rae decided. Things just got out of his way.

Even so, once she saw sky again instead of trees and more trees, Rae knew they were on the wrong beach. This cove was different, less sandy, with cliffs forming a U-shape out into the sea. A good place to defend, Rae thought critically, but they'd have to fight to the last Shifter standing before her dad, brothers, or the other Shifters could reach them. And they'd probably get wet.

Wolf paws caught Rae's shoulders and lowered her from Zander's back. Mason again, with Broderick right behind him. Zander shifted to his human form and caught Rae, his dark eyes glinting red but with terrible fear behind his anger.

The ferals were coming down through the woods, humans with them, and those humans had rifles with scopes.

One of the humans called out to them, taking aim over his weapon. "You don't have to die, you know. Join us, Battle Beasts, and you can live another day."

Zander jerked his head up, the beads on his intact dreadlock glistening in the sunlight as he slowly turned around. He studied the array of Shifters and humans, at least fifty of them, waiting to rush across the narrow strip of sand and kill them all.

Zander said, in a voice that rolled around the cove and echoed up into the woods, "Not today, Fae slaves."

He raised his arm high and made a pointing signal with his hand.

The *boom* from the sea shook new pain through Rae's bones, and she cried out. An explosion blossomed on the shore, right in front of the ferals. Humans and Shifters scattered, yelling, men shooting wildly, then screaming when yet another explosion tore through the air.

Rae, supported by Mason, tried to shield her face, but debris cut it, stinging her eyes.

Then Zander had her in his arms, lifting Rae against his chest. Out on the water, a heavy rubber raft was speeding toward them, the man at the helm familiar.

"Miles!" Rae tried to shout. "It's Miles." Nothing came from her throat but a feeble whisper.

"Hush, Little Wolf," Zander said. "Almost there."

Miles drove the raft right up onto the sand. He leapt from it, dashing to help Zander and Rae into it, then climbed back to the tiller. Mason, Broderick, and Carson wasted no time shoving the raft around and heaving themselves in.

As Miles gunned the engine and the raft skimmed back across the water, Rae peeled open her eyes. Zander was holding her, his braids, one now minus its beads, brushing her skin. She saw a glint of silver, and turned her head enough to see that Broderick held the sheathed Sword of the Guardian; his brother, Zander's samurai sword. Broderick did not look happy, but he clutched the sword grimly.

Zander caressed Rae's face, moisture on his dark lashes. "Hang on, Little Wolf. I won't let you go." His hand went to her chest and she felt a hot tingle, a brush of his healing magic.

"Where did you get a *rocket launcher*?" she tried to ask.

The corners of Zander's lips twitched and he shrugged. "Wasn't hard. I know a guy."

CHAPTER THIRTY-TWO

Rae was dying. Zander knew it even as he lowered her onto the bunk she'd used when they'd been on Miles's and Carson's ship before. The feral had torn open her abdomen, her blood was pouring out, and the feral's dirty claws had the potential to give her a deep infection.

They'd found Piotr at the helm of the boat, which Miles took back from him as soon as everyone was aboard. Miles steered into the next cove, then he and Carson launched the raft again to go pick up Eoin's and Dylan's Shifters who'd retreated to that beach.

Zander closed the door of Rae's cabin, laid the Sword of the Guardian on the cabinet by the bunk where she lay, and knelt on the floor.

Rae's wound was bad. Healing her was going to hurt like a bitch and knock him out for a long stretch, and Zander didn't give a shit. He'd take the pain of death itself to keep Rae alive.

The boat listed as Miles took them into deep water. Zander's worries about the feral Shifters, and the deep dread that had bitten into him when the human had called him *Battle Beast*— the Fae's name for Shifters—receded and vanished.

Nothing was more important than saving Rae.

Zander peeled away her tattered clothes, carefully lifting them from the wound. She'd shredded much of her shirt and jeans by shifting in them and Zander was able to simply slip the fabric from around her. Rae's eyes remained closed, her face wan, her chest moving with shallow breaths.

Outside, he heard Rae's brothers in the hall, followed by the rumble of her father. "Open the door, Moncrieff," Eoin commanded. The handle rattled.

Carson's voice followed, firm and angry. "No. Let him do what he needs to."

Mason's Lupine voice joined his. "Zander's a healer. He's the only one with a hope of saving her. But you have to leave him *alone*. Trust me."

Mason had seen what happened, knew what Zander had to do. Zander was silently grateful to his friends as the voices in the passage faded and were gone, a *clank* telling him they'd closed the outer door to the cabins.

Zander put his hands on Rae's bare and bloody abdomen. He started to close his eyes but jerked them open again. He wanted to look upon her face. If this didn't work, Zander didn't want Rae slipping away while he wasn't watching.

He knew how to put himself into a deep meditative state without closing his eyes. But when he tried to clear his mind, which was a riot of fear, grief, and loneliness, the quietude didn't come.

I can't lose her, I can't, he thought desperately. He knew that the heat wrapping around his heart was the mate bond, the mystical joining of a Shifter and his mate. The fact that the woman lying before him was his true mate put a different spin on things. If Zander couldn't heal her, he might as well die with her. A broken mate bond was devastating—many times the Shifter never recovered.

I've only just found her! he shouted silently to the Goddess. *I haven't had any time with her. No time . . .*

Zander was supposed to relax and begin his chant to the Goddess, picturing something calm and beautiful, but the only images that came to his mind were of Rae. Rae climbing up into his boat for the first time, resentment in her gray eyes.

Rae's dark head bowed over his finishing line as she untangled it with deft fingers, the scorn in her sideways glance that had made Zander want to laugh.

Rae standing up in her underwear, screaming when Jake the Snake made his presence known in her bed. Her clumsy swings of the sword when Zander had started to train her, then her eyes going soft as he'd kissed her for the first time. Rae's terror when she'd had to drive the sword through Ezra's father's heart, her silent plea for Zander to help her slide it into the right place.

Next, her laughter as she won the drinking game, Rae throwing up her hands and shouting her victory. Then her sudden rage and dismay when the man in the bar tried to shoot Zander, her courage in running to his rescue. Her courage again when they'd floated through the Graveyard, her fearlessness when she'd stood up to Carson and made him let Zander out of the cage.

She'd come to Zander at the resort cabin, uninhibited and unashamed, letting her mating frenzy match his. Rae had loved him wholeheartedly, rising to his thrusts, drowning in her joy and pulling him down to drown with her.

Zander couldn't lose her. He'd die a thousand times in his heart every day if the Goddess took this little wolf away from him.

The chants, the prayers wouldn't come. "I can't," Zander whispered, his hands curling on her belly. "Don't leave me, Little Wolf. I love you too fucking much."

Rae's eyes opened a crack. "Love you too, Zander."

It was a mumble, but her little smile, the warmth in her eyes, suddenly removed all doubt.

"Goddess, mother of us all, lady of the moon," Zander began in a rapid voice, which grew louder as he went on. "I beseech thee to get your *ass* down here and fill me with your holy goodness and all that crap, and Let. Me. Heal. My. *Mate!*"

The words exploded into the room and the Sword of the Guardian *tinged* faintly in response. Zander trailed off to a growl, and all was silence.

Total silence—Zander didn't hear the rumble of engines, the slap of water on the hull, the voices of a dozen alpha

Shifters in a confined space with a problem on their hands. Nothing.

The air in the room took on a sudden freshness, erasing the diesel smell. A breeze brushed Zander's cheek and he thought he heard the faint note of feminine laughter. Then a man's voice, a low vibration of it. *The little wolf cub is all growed up, isn't she? Heal her and then heal my sword, bear. They're both very special to me, but Rae is the most special of all. Take care of her, or you'll hear it from me when you finally cross over.*

Daragh, Zander realized. People from the Summerland were talking to him now. Shit, he really *was* insane.

"Rae," he whispered. "I love you. Before the Goddess and in front of witnesses—okay, one witness who is in the Summerland—I claim you as mate."

Rae's eyelids flickered again, the gleam between them weak before it faded altogether.

Zander bent his head, sent every bit of concentration he possessed to his healing gift, and willed Rae to live.

Fire flared through Rae's body, hotter and with a fury more painful than anything she'd felt in her life. She screamed but nothing came out of her mouth.

Her abdomen was searing, her blood hotter still. Rae jerked and found a weight holding her down. She had to get away, run, escape this agony.

Rae peeled open her eyes to find herself on a bunk in a cabin that was pitching and moving. She clutched the bunk, pain unceasing, and realized that the weight on her was Zander.

His hands, pressed to Rae's abdomen, were red with blood—her blood. Zander's head was bowed, his body sagging, his white hair splattered with scarlet.

Zander was healing her. The fire came from Rae's flesh knitting and melding back together, far faster than would happen naturally, even for a Shifter. Rae wanted to scream and scream, the pain as excruciating as when the feral had gutted her, only it was lasting far longer.

He had to stop. Not only was Rae going to die of the agony, Zander would absorb it and feel every bit of what she was feeling now. Part of the process, he'd told her, no shortcuts, but she was sick at the thought that she could only lose her pain by transferring it to him.

"No," Rae tried to say. She raised her head but dizziness hit her and she fell back to the pillow. "No," she whispered.

Zander raised his head. His eyes were already clouded, his face ashen. "Yes," he said firmly.

"Stop," Rae said, voice rasping. "I'm Shifter. I'll get better."

"Not from this you won't." Zander bent his head again. "For the Goddess's sake, do as you're told for once, Little Wolf, and stay still."

Rae couldn't fight him. She was far too weak to do anything but lie here, whether she liked it or not.

The Sword of the Guardian rested on the cabinet alongside the bunk, where whatever sailor or officer used this room could store his belongings. Rae reached up and touched the hilt.

The sword sparked, sending a jolt of electricity down her arm. The spark was answered by one from her Collar, pain biting into her neck. Rae tried to jerk her hand from the sword—wasn't she being tortured enough without the sword and her Collar punishing her too?

She couldn't let go. Her fingers seemed to be fused to the hilt, and now the sword was humming, singing, filling the room with undulating noise. The waves of it hit Rae and tore a groan from her throat.

Zander raised his head and growled weakly, "Shut *up*, you gods-fucked hunk of metal."

The sword only rang louder, as though it laughed. Rae's pain lessened the tiniest bit—such a small amount, she was afraid to wonder if she imagined it.

But no, second by second, the pain began to fade. Rae swore she felt all her hurts flow up into her Collar then into her right shoulder, down her arm, and straight into the sword.

A moment later, Rae knew it wasn't her imagination. A stream of white-hot fire surged from her body into the sword, the power of it lifting her from the mattress. The sword sparked and gleamed until Rae had to slam her eyes shut against the glare.

She screamed as a final gush of pain cascaded from her to the sword. Rae fell back down onto the bunk so hard it rocked on the bolts that kept it locked to the floor.

"Son of a—" Rae broke off as she raised her head, her strength returning.

Her abdomen was wet with blood, but the wound was closed. Only a few hot pink streaks across Rae's stomach attested to the fact that it had been clawed open.

Zander eased his hands from her, his face completely gray, his eyes empty. But he smiled. Triumphantly.

Then he folded up bonelessly to the floor, hands over his abdomen, his mouth peeling back in a silent scream as all the hurt Rae had endured began to consume him.

Zander swam back from a place of darkness and throbbing agony to the sweet smoothness of Rae's touch.

He lay on his back, but instead of the hard cement floor of the cabin, he felt the give of a mattress and warmth. Softness pressed into his side, but that cushion was Rae.

She was curled up around him, her body as bare as his. The pain ripping through Zander's torso had not long ago been inside her, but now Rae lay next to him in quiet relief. Her cheeks were pink, her skin warm and whole. Healed.

"Come back to me, Zander," she was saying. "I can't lose you."

Zander tried to answer but not even a grunt would come out of his mouth.

He felt the press of Rae's lips on his cheek, her hand smoothing his chest. Where she touched, the pain eased. Zander wanted to encourage her to continue but he couldn't speak.

"I meant it when I said I loved you," she said softly, her breath warm in his ear. "I *do* love you. I thought the Goddess was playing a joke on me when she sent me to you, but I guess she knew what she was doing." Rae leaned closer, her next words so quiet Zander barely heard them. "I accept your mate-claim."

Zander was definitely feeling better. The horrible burning

in his abdomen subsided a notch, even more so when Rae ran her hand over his hip.

"Touch of a mate," Zander murmured.

"What?" Rae leaned down, her dark hair tumbling to his chest. Her hair felt good, silken, loosening the tightness inside him. "Zander?"

"Touch of a mate," Zander repeated. "Makes the healing faster. I knew—when you got through to me back at Ezra's, when I took on Robert's pain, I knew."

Rae blinked, then her eyes warmed. "Yeah, I kind of knew too."

She continued to touch him, the strokes of her hand brushing coolness across his hot skin. Zander turned his head and touched a kiss to her lips.

Rae's fingers stilled, then she deepened the kiss, her lips and tongue moving. She uncurled her body and stretched it out alongside his, her breasts and thighs against him.

Oh, yes, so much better. Zander raised a weak hand and lifted the weight of her hair, conjuring up the energy to kiss her back.

Her mouth was a place of heat, of goodness and strength. Zander regained more equilibrium as the kiss went on, his dizziness floating away.

The cabin lurched, the boat hitting a swell. It rocked the bed, sending Zander onto his side, facing her. Rae smiled as she kissed him again and slid her arms around him.

Zander's pain receded enough for him to start to enjoy her, tasting her mouth, his hands molding her hips, waist, breasts. The whole room dipped and swayed, the Sword of the Guardian sliding dangerously along the cabinet. Zander put out one hand and stopped it, and at the same time rolled Rae under him. She gave him a welcoming smile, her gray eyes warming with passion. The sword gave an answering ring.

The last of Zander's pain dissipated as he slid himself inside Rae. And then nothing mattered but the two of them together, holding, caressing, Zander's thrusts growing stronger as he tried to be as far inside Rae as he could.

Rae entwined him in her arms and loved him back, her eyes like brilliant stars.

* * *

Rae woke a long time later. Zander was spooned against her in the narrow bunk, relaxed in sleep. The lines of pain on his face had gone, and a little snore came from his mouth.

Rae touched her abdomen but the fiery streaks that had creased it were now small pale scars. She was not only healed, but she felt better than she had in a long time. Any soreness she'd acquired from traveling, running and climbing, fighting and fleeing was gone. Rae felt only a pleasant rawness from the lovemaking that had grown intense, but that was all right with her. Zander truly had the healing gift, and Rae marveled.

Or maybe it was the mate bond. Her heart was warm, the joy surging inside her a very close thing to the terrific orgasm she'd had with Zander before they'd collapsed into sleep.

Rae wanted to laugh, dance, shout it to the world.

I love crazy Zander Moncrieff and we share the mate bond!

Rae thought about how the sword had rung and glittered while Zander had healed her, and then again when they'd made love.

She reached for it, hoping against hope. Maybe the healing magic combined with the mate bond was the miracle they needed to put it back together.

Rae touched the sword in trepidation, then she drew a breath and tugged it free of the sheath.

Her heart plummeted as the top half came out easily, the jagged cut still in place.

"Bloody hell!" Rae yelled.

Zander jumped and came awake, alert and tense, every inch a Shifter. "What? What happened?"

"This!" Rae held the broken sword up in front of his face. "Goddess—what does a girl have to *do*?"

An hour later, Rae found Carson leaning on the stern rail, gazing across the water as the sun slipped below the horizon. It was beautiful out here, peaceful, the deck a much better place to be than the confined spaces inside.

Zander, after he'd scowled at the sword and said he gave up, had led Rae to the wheelhouse, where they'd said hello again to Jake the Snake, who'd curled happily around Zander's arm. Zander had put him back in the box Miles had made for him and taken Rae to the ward room down the deck, where the other Shifters had gathered.

All the Shifters from Eoin's group were there, and most from Dylan's. Tiger wasn't with them—he and the remaining Austin Shifters had managed to make it to Marlo's plane and fly out.

Dylan, Eoin, and Zander discussed the fight and what it might mean. A ley line, feral Shifters, humans . . .

It meant they were screwed, Rae knew. Not long ago, Shifters in the Las Vegas Shiftertown had discovered that the Fae had been making swords that would trigger Shifter Collars to render Shifters helpless. Apparently, several Fae clans were working to re-enslave the Shifters—Battle Beasts as they were called.

Had the feral Shifters found a way to cross to and from Faerie—and why? Eoin now asked. Were they working for the Fae or against them? The idea that Shifters would voluntarily work *for* the Fae was farfetched, but what if the Shifters had already been enslaved, body and mind? Ferals didn't always know what was going on inside their own heads. Dylan, Eoin, and the other Shifters had gone on speculating, and that was when Rae decided she wanted some air.

She leaned next to Carson now and gazed at the azure and pink sky, the sun lingering on the wide horizon. "When I see something so beautiful," she said in a quiet voice, "it's hard to believe there's evil in the world. I mean, why can't we all just enjoy the glory of a sunset?"

Carson didn't answer. The two of them simply stood for a time, neither of them speaking as the sun slipped lower. Then Carson said in a hollow voice, "You almost died. I nearly got you killed, and a lot of other people, with my need for revenge."

Rae turned to look at him. Carson's gray eyes were haunted, his face drawn.

"You couldn't know that the attack on you and your wife was part of a nefarious Fae plot to re-enslave Shifters," Rae said, trying to sound reasonable. "Who gets up in the morning thinking that?"

"I blamed all Shifters everywhere," Carson said, the words bitter. "I made their lives hell instead of asking one to help me."

"And when you did find one to help you, you got Zander." Rae let herself laugh. "You drew the short straw that day."

"No, I got *you*," Carson said, and Rae's laughter cut off in surprise. "I finally found someone who cared about Viv and understood what I needed to do."

"Sorry it didn't work out," Rae said softly.

"Maybe it did." Carson returned his gaze to the horizon. "You and Zander pulled me out of a very dark place and returned me to the world." He shook his head. "I need to get back to her soon. I don't like to stay away too long, in case . . ."

He trailed off and Rae didn't know what to say to comfort him. *It will be all right* sounded lame, because she had no idea whether anything would be. She gazed silently with him across the water as the ball of sun sank under the dark blue water.

As the sun disappeared, the very top sliver of its disk seemed to hover above the horizon. The sliver brightened, then glowed a sudden, brilliant green. Rae gasped, and just as her breath left her, the green glow disappeared, and the sky returned to its red-orange hue.

"Hey, did you see that?" Zander's hands landed next to Rae's on the rail, his tight arm brushing hers. "A green flash. Awesome. Haven't seen one in a long time. See, the air has to be just right—"

"*Zander,*" Rae interrupted him. "You're a healer. Can we see if it will work on Vivian?"

CHAPTER THIRTY-THREE

Zander turned sharply to Rae. His expression of wonder faded and his look became guarded. "I'm a *Shifter* healer, Little Wolf. I've tried to heal humans before. It didn't work." The sadness in his eyes attested to that.

"Will you try anyway?" Rae asked. "I've heard that a green flash is a sign from the Goddess. Maybe she wants us to try." Rae didn't truly believe in signs, but what the hell? She wanted to help Carson and didn't know how else to do it.

"Us," Zander repeated slowly, holding her gaze.

"We make a good team," Rae said. "So yeah. *Us.*"

Zander watched her for a long time. He'd replaited his braid, weaving green beads into it this time. He must carry a supply around with him.

Zander's touch was tender as he traced Rae's cheek. He leaned on the rail after a time and gazed out at the western horizon, which was deepening to dark blue. "All right," he said, voice neutral. "We'll give it a shot."

* * *

Vivian McCade was in a private nursing home in Seattle. Eoin drove them there after Miles put in the boat at Port Angeles. Eoin insisted on coming with them, not wanting to let Rae far from his sight. Her injury had hit him hard.

Rae and Eoin hid their Collars under light jackets—the rain that began to fall as they drove into the city was the perfect excuse. There was no disguising the Sword of the Guardian, however, which Rae wouldn't leave behind. Carson, who was recognized as soon as he walked into the nursing home, said it was an antique they didn't want to leave in the truck while they visited, which was technically true.

The receptionist only nodded behind her high desk and went back to her computer.

Vivian's room was large, decorated in pleasant shades of yellow and blue, with a wide window to let in plenty of sunshine, though right now, thin rain was pattering on it. The furniture—soft chairs around a coffee table, a bookcase, and a plant stand—attempted to disguise the fact that this was, in fact, a hospital room. The head of the bed was slightly tilted up so the dark-haired woman resting on it looked comfortable. Machines beeped quietly on the wall behind her and tubes snaked into her body, keeping her alive.

Carson's expression took on one of love, anguish, and resigned despair as he approached her. On the nightstand was a photo of Vivian and Carson, a duplicate of one Rae had seen on his photo device. The couple smiled at the camera, wrapped around each other, happy.

Zander remained skeptical that he could heal Viv but the fact that he'd volunteered to come and try encouraged Rae. She'd seen how terrible Zander's pain was after he healed someone, but he did it again and again instead of running away. He'd told her his healing gift had made him a recluse and yet whenever someone needed him, there he was.

Carson closed work-hardened fingers around Vivian's limp hand as he sat down in a chair beside the bed. "I've brought some friends, sweetheart," he said as though she could hear him—and maybe she could. "This is Rae and Zander, and Rae's father, Eoin. They're good people."

A week or so ago, this man had done his best to capture Rae and Zander and send them to Shifter Bureau. Today he was calling them friends. Funny how things turned out.

Eoin seated himself at the far end of the room. Rae unstrapped the sword and laid it on the table near the bed, out of the way. The thing still was broken and Rae would have to confess that problem very soon.

One thing at a time. Rae stood back as Zander pulled a chair next to the bed, sitting down and taking Vivian's other hand.

"This might seem weird," Zander said to Vivian—like Carson, he behaved as though she heard and understood every word. "But I promised Rae I'd try. I have to tell you, when Rae gets under your skin, she stays there. I've claimed her as mate and she said yes. I'm still reeling about that."

"Get on with it," Rae said softly. Zander had made the claim again, in front of Eoin and the others, before they'd disembarked the boat. None of the Shifters had been very surprised, including Eoin. Shifters always knew when a mating was meant to be.

Zander kept Vivian's hand in his and spread his other arm across the mattress next to her. He bowed his head, drew a breath, and began his chant.

The prayer to the Goddess, in the old Celtic language, droned in Zander's deep baritone, filled the room. Rae drew closer to him, listening, the sound releasing all that was tight inside her.

She glanced at the monitors above Vivian's bed, not knowing what the numbers and lines meant. They beeped softly, unchanging.

Carson watched the monitors too as Zander's chant went on, Zander's voice flowing in its strange, low tone. A droplet of sweat beaded on Zander's face and rolled down the side of his neck.

Carson's frown deepened as the machines kept on with their monotonous blips. Nothing was happening. No change, good or ill.

Zander continued chanting as the clock on the wall moved to the quarter hour, then the half. Eoin moved restlessly, but he didn't get up, only watched.

"It's not working," Carson snapped.

Zander's chant cut off. He lifted his head and let out a breath. "I know," he said, his voice scratchy from use. "I healed a non-Shifter before, but he was full of magic, even more than Shifters. I don't know if I can help a human. I'm sorry."

The pain in his voice was heartbreaking. Zander had so much compassion inside him, it must tear him up when he couldn't heal someone. No wonder he hid out in the middle of nowhere, alone.

"Keep trying," Rae said softly. "Maybe human metabolisms are slower to respond. Shifters heal pretty fast, you know."

Zander caught her gaze, the bleakness in his eyes reminding her she'd been pretty far gone herself. Zander's plea, *Don't leave me, Little Wolf. I love you too fucking much,* had reached Rae through her pain and brought her back.

Love you too, Zander, Rae had said, and she'd meant it with all her heart.

She gave him a smile of encouragement. Zander's mouth turned down, but he bowed his head and began the chant again.

Rae let herself relax under his voice, laying her hand on Zander's shoulder before she realized she did it. The vibration of his chant came up through her palm, suffusing her with warmth.

Carson continued to hold his wife's hand, gazing down at her with love and anguish. Under the thrall of Zander's voice, though, the tightness eased from his face.

Vivian was far gone, Rae sensed. Somehow she knew when Zander touched her hurts, felt it in his body. Under her hand, Zander went rigid and he shivered.

"Dark," he whispered. "So dark. Alone."

Rae leaned closer, rubbing his back. "It's all right, love. I'm here."

"Stay. Don't leave me."

"No." Rae rested her cheek between his strong shoulders. "I'll always be here for you. No matter what."

Zander began whispering again, the words guttural and strange. Rae slid her arms around him, resting her hands on his chest, right over his heart.

Rae felt the magic rushing out of Zander into Vivian's body

and realized after a moment that it was also rushing out of herself. She and Zander were both Goddess-touched, which meant the same magic flowed through each of them, though in different ways.

Their magics twined through their pressed bodies, gathering into a white light to stream from Zander's hand, much like what had streamed from Rae into the sword when Zander had healed her. On impulse, Rae reached out and grasped the hilt of the sword, feeling the silver hot against her palm.

The light swelled, overwhelming the room's fluorescents and the weak daylight coming through the rain-streaked window. Rae realized that the light was also going into *Carson*, flooding him until his skin glowed. Carson started, but he clenched his jaw and held Vivian's hand tighter, as though determined to protect her through this weirdness.

The light surged until Rae had to close her eyes. At the same time, Vivian jerked. The machines began to beep like crazy.

Rae forced her eyes open, the light still filling the room. Carson sprang to his feet, though he didn't let go of Vivian's hand. "You're hurting her. Stop!"

Zander either didn't hear him or he couldn't obey. He closed both hands over Vivian's arm, his chant growing louder, its rumble vibrating the room. At the same time the sword let out a rich note that swirled around Rae and drilled straight into her head, like a high-pitched bell. The sound rolled on and on, growing louder until Rae wanted to scream with it.

Vivian gasped. Her eyes flew open, her pale face flushing as blood rushed into it. The monitors went ballistic and Carson's hand clamped down on Vivian's. Running feet sounded in the hall, the nurses charging in to see what was happening.

"Carson?" Vivian looked at her husband in confusion. Her voice was weak, scratched, dry. "Who the hell are *they*?"

She scowled and motioned with her eyes to Zander, who had sat up, his white braids hanging, green and blue beads glinting. Also to Rae, who stood behind him, dressed in a man's shirt and sweatpants—all Miles could find for her on the boat—clutching an ancient sword.

The nurses burst in and started shouting. Vivian clung to Carson's hand and Eoin got to his feet.

Rae turned from them all and drew the Sword of the Guardian.

It came out shining, whole, and unblemished, weighing heavily in her hand. The runes glowed, the sword rang once, as though with laughter, and then it quieted.

Zander's hand closed over Rae's on the hilt. "Well, look at that." His voice was weak and he had to lean on Rae to remain upright.

The others in the room were completely ignoring them in the chaos around Vivian's bed. Vivian's voice grew stronger as she demanded Carson to tell her if he was all right and what had happened.

"I guess it took both of us together, Little Wolf," Zander said. He nipped her ear . . . and then he passed out.

Tiger had managed to capture one of the ferals. Zander found this out after Eoin's son Colin drove Zander, Rae, and Eoin back to the Montana Shiftertown from the airstrip where they'd landed from Seattle. Zander stumbled out of the pickup at Eoin's house, exhausted and hoping he and Rae could return to the lake resort—alone.

Sean Morrissey greeted them on the porch. "Hello to you," he said, his Irish accent going broad. "Guess what we have in the backyard?"

The feral Lupine trussed up in chains near the fire pit was coherent, made that way by fear. Zander guessed fear of Tiger, who stood stoically near him, his arms folded, watching the feral with his intensely focused golden eyes.

Other Shifters from Eoin's Shiftertown—the clan leaders, the trackers—had gathered to listen, looking grim.

"Tell them what you told us," Sean prompted the feral.

"You're all dead," the feral said. Zander supposed that at one time he'd said this in a defiant tone but his defiance had now been replaced by pure terror. "If you join them, they might be merciful."

Rae stood next to Zander, the sword's hilt poking him in the arm. Ever since the thing had been fixed, it had been humming faintly, just a little beyond hearing, bent on driving Zander crazy. Maybe they could break it again.

He still didn't know exactly how the sword had gone back together. His healing magic had flowed through himself, Rae, Carson, and Vivien, and the sword had joined in. Lots of Goddess magic, pain, suffering, hope, fear, and a shit-ton of love had been swirling around that room. Carson was human, but Shifters had human in them, left over from the faraway days when Fae had messed with genetics and magic to create a man-beast. Maybe the latent humanness in Zander and Rae had touched Carson and Vivien, lending them their Shifter strength.

Or some shit like that. It was hard to tell with Goddess magic. He and Sean should discuss it when they discussed everything else they needed to talk about.

"Join who?" Zander asked the feral sternly.

Sean answered for him. "The Fae. Don't make him say it." He shook his head in disgust. "He starts this paean of praise that's surely sickening, especially coming from the mouth of a Shifter."

"They have saved me," the feral said.

Zander, who'd spent most of his life full of messed-up magic, easily recognized it in someone else. "He's been spelled. Brainwashed. Have you all been?" he asked the feral.

The feral nodded. "They will return, with the Battle Beasts, and destroy all in their path, as they sweep to victory in their most glorious—"

"All right, shut it," Sean growled. He turned to Eoin. "Basically, the Fae have found a way to enslave un-Collared Shifters, either making them go feral or searching for ones who are already feral—I'm not clear on which. Dylan already knows all this. He asked me to bring this guy to you, Eoin, so you'd understand."

"Shit," Zander said. "If they're already working on manipulating Shifters through their Collars, and now they've found a way to ensorcell *un*-Collared Shifters, that's going to mean . . ."

"A second Shifter-Fae war," Eoin speculated glumly. "Well, we knew it was only a matter of time."

Rae looked worried, her hand stealing to Zander's. The Shifters had won their freedom from the Fae a thousand and more years ago after a long and terrible struggle.

The tales of Shifter captivity had been passed down through

the generations—horror stories of Shifters forced to fight other Shifters as well as Fae warriors, to be cut down by the hundreds. Female Shifters had been forced to create cubs to replace them; packs, prides, and clans had been separated; mates killed as soon as the mate bond formed; experiments performed to create different and stronger kinds of Shifters. What the humans had done to Shifters paled in comparison to what the Fae shits had done.

"That can't happen again," Rae said softly.

"We won't let it," Zander assured her. He turned back to the feral. "Tell your Fae masters they can kiss our asses."

The feral stared at him in worry and then for one brief moment, sanity flared in his eyes. The guy was a Lupine, probably had a mate and cubs, a clan, a pack. He'd gotten pulled into all this by sadistic Fae bastards.

"Kill me," the feral begged. *"Please."*

Rae took a step forward. "We'll help you," she said. "We can get you free. My dad and Zander will . . ."

"No," the man almost sobbed. "Kill me. It will come back. I can never be—"

Rae had taken another step toward him. The feral snarled, insanity taking him over again. He shifted to his half beast, and with a sudden burst of strength, broke through the chains. The chains flew apart, making the Shifters dance back, and the feral went for Rae.

Zander was in front of Rae in a heartbeat. Before he could leap forward and wrestle the feral down, Tiger stepped behind the Lupine, grabbed the back of his neck, and broke it.

The feral went limp, life instantly fading from his eyes. Tiger lowered him gently to the ground.

For a moment the Shifters in the clearing gazed down at the dead feral, the Lupine's face relaxing in sudden peace. Whatever spell had gripped him had gone.

But they couldn't leave him there for long. If the Fae had enslaved his body, they'd certainly rush to take his soul.

The other Shifters realized this too. "Sean," one of the clan leaders said. "Your sword. Quickly."

"No," Zander said. "Rae."

The Shifter, a Feline, glared at Zander. He was one of the clan leaders who didn't believe Rae was truly Guardian.

Tiger gave the man his hard-eyed stare and the clan leader closed his mouth over whatever argument he'd been about to launch. "It should be Rae," Tiger said, his voice calm but edged.

Sean nodded, making no move to unsheathe his sword. "It's Rae's Shiftertown. She's Guardian here."

Eoin stepped next to Rae, as though ready to defend her if any other Shifters tried to stop her.

The clan leader looked at all those arrayed against him, sighed, and lifted his hands. "Very well. But hurry. *If* she can even do it."

A nervous swallow moved down Rae's throat, but she drew her sword. The Sword of the Guardian rang, glistening in the sunlight, the runes seeming to move.

Rae glanced at Zander but he took a step back. He couldn't touch the sword or be seen helping Rae in any way, in case the others tried to claim it was Zander's magic that made the sword work, not hers. This was Rae's task, no one else's.

Tiger had arranged the dead Lupine full length on the ground, his arms at his sides. He'd done it gently, respectfully.

Rae approached, the sword held in one shaking hand. She firmed her grip on the hilt then reached down with the other hand and touched the feral's forehead.

"The blessings of the Goddess be upon you," Rae said in her musical, soothing voice, then she straightened up.

Rae put both hands on the sword's hilt, positioned the point over the man's heart, hesitated, then moved it the slightest bit over. She didn't look to Zander for reassurance or guidance. She didn't need to anymore.

Rae drew a sharp breath, wrapped both hands more securely around the sword, and drove the blade straight into the feral's heart.

Zander felt a tingling warmth, heard a whisper of thanks, and then the feral dissolved to dust. Rae bowed her head, the point of the sword resting on the earth.

After a moment, she raised her head and let out a Lupine howl, a sound joined by Sean and Eoin and Rae's brothers and others in the clearing—Shifters mourning the dead. Zander's bear growled as well. Only Tiger remained silent, his golden eyes still.

Once everything quieted, Zander saw that the clan leaders

were staring at Rae, shock in their eyes. They truly believed her Choosing had been a mistake, or a trick. They'd expected her to fail, for Sean to have to come behind her and finish the job.

Well, there could be no doubt now, Zander thought in both sorrow and satisfaction.

Rae Lyall was the true Guardian of the Montana Shifter-town. Zander loved her, and the next ceremony in this Shifter-town would be a happy one.

CHAPTER THIRTY-FOUR

The boat rocked under a moon that was two days past the full. Zander greeted it as he stepped out on the deck of his fishing boat, which floated in dark water south of the Alaskan coast. It was good to be back.

Rae emerged behind him, her hair in a sloppy braid, her face flushed from lovemaking. She'd pulled on a tank top and sweatpants, the top hugging the swell of her breasts.

She spread her hands on the rail, looked up at the moon and the stars, and sighed in happiness. "It's beautiful here."

Even more so with Rae by his side. They'd come to the boat after the sun and moon ceremonies were done in Rae's Shiftertown, Eoin giving them the final blessing under the light of the full moon. The man's eyes had been wet but his voice strong as he declared them mated.

Carson and Vivian had come to the full-moon mating, along with many of the Austin Shifters and all the Shifters in Rae's town—they accepted her as Guardian now. Shifters in other towns might be slower to believe, but at least those in Rae's Shiftertown now supported her.

Carson and Viv had missed the ceremony under the sun,

but Vivian had been resting and recovering, and apparently grilling Carson about everything that had happened since she'd been hurt.

Vivian was full of fire, giving Carson shit every minute she could, even as she held on to him, obvious love in her gaze. Carson looked as though he'd been smacked between the eyes, but the despair had gone from him, his black anger eased. Carson had joined in the discussions before the ceremony about the feral Shifters and the feral Lupine's revelation about the Fae, Carson ready to help kick some ass. Vivian was well, but Carson still itched to make the ferals who'd hurt her pay. Vivian was less adamant, but she understood that Carson needed to vent. They seemed to be good partners for each other.

Zander looked at Rae's moonlit face and knew he'd found as good a partner in her. He was also glad he'd insisted on this honeymoon trip. If he was going to give up his peripatetic life and settle down in a Shiftertown with its new Guardian, he reserved the right to escape with her sometimes. He'd bring her out to his boat or explore the wilds of the world with her, whenever they needed time alone. Rae seconded his request—the Shifters had given Daragh his space, and she could have hers.

"I've been thinking about Vivian's healing," Rae said after a time.

"Yeah?" Zander had given up figuring it out. The sword was whole, Viv was doing well, everyone was happy. End of story.

"It's like everything finally connected." Rae studied the stars, her face serene. "You and I were alone, each looking for someone who understood us. We found each other and finally came together. The sword was broken, and it came together. Viv and Carson were forced apart, and *they* came together. We each needed the other half of our whole, and your call to the Goddess brought magic that found the emptiness in us and filled it. We were connected, and joined."

Rae finished with a satisfied nod, as though pleased she'd worked it all out.

Zander shrugged. "Sounds as good an explanation as any." He supposed the Goddess could have decided that Rae and Zander, stronger together than they were apart, had the power to heal anything—humans, the sword, themselves. Or it was just the Goddess enjoying herself. She'd been messing with Zander his whole life—why should she stop now?

He took a step closer to Rae. "I like the idea of two halves making a whole. How about we go back below and put our halves together again?"

Rae snorted a laugh. "You are so full of shit." She started to turn to him, then said. "Oh, wait. We never opened Sean's gift."

"Been busy." Zander moved behind her, resting his hands on either side of hers on the rail. Rae cuddled into him, her backside caressing him enticingly through her thin sweats. "It's been nice to give in to mating frenzy."

"As long as we eat once in a while," Rae said, her voice full of laughter. "To keep our strength up."

"Piotr stocked the boat well," Zander reminded her. "We'll be good for days."

Miles's mating gift had been to pick them up on the Washington coast and deliver them to Zander's fishing boat, which was nestled into a secluded cove, anchored and waiting for them. Piotr's wedding gift—his and his wife, Irena's—had been to give the boat a good cleaning and fill the refrigerator and cupboards with Irena's good cooking. Piotr had also made sure they were well provided with beer and one special bottle of vodka. Rae had hung the wrought-iron frame Piotr had given her on the wall above the cabin's table and declared that the boat was now perfect.

Rae turned in Zander's arms, rose on tiptoe, and gave him a kiss on the mouth. Zander's frenzy, nowhere near sated, stirred. He began to close her into his embrace but Rae smiled and slipped out, and Zander's arms came together on empty air.

"I want to see what Sean gave us," she said over her shoulder as she headed for the cabin. "While we're regaining our strength."

Zander felt plenty strong but he followed her to the cabin below, which Irena had thoroughly neatened. Zander knew Piotr hadn't organized it—the man liked clutter.

The Sword of the Guardian greeted them with a peal of welcome. The sound was muffled, however, because Zander had shut the sword into a cupboard, after throwing a blanket over it. The thing was obnoxious.

What Sean had given them was a faux-leather tube about three feet long and four inches around with a lid firmly pushed onto both its top and bottom. He'd thrust the tube at Zander before they'd boarded the plane to take them back to the ocean, an amused look in his blue eyes. Zander had lugged the thing the hours it had taken them to reach the boat, then slung it into a corner to concentrate all his attention on Rae.

Now Rae cleared the table of the remains of their dinner, eaten when they'd last come up for air. Zander opened the tube, curious now, and withdrew a long roll of paper. The paper had the same weight and feel as a map but when he and Rae spread it out across the table, they saw that it was covered with lines and writing.

Sean had drawn a family tree—actually two of them. Names in minuscule type covered the page, connected by thin, curlicued lines.

Above one tree was the word *McNaughton*. Above the other, *Dimitru*.

Zander picked out Mason's name, along with Broderick's and their two other brothers' under the McNaughtons. In the Dimitru line, he recognized the name Kenzie, who was the mate of the leader of the North Carolina Shiftertown.

Near the bottom of each tree was a name: Lillias McNaughton under the one on the right and Andrei Dimitru on the left. A double dash connected these two and a small vertical line led down from them to the name Rae Dimitru.

Rae stared at the name, her face draining of color. Slowly she reached out and touched the ornate, old-fashioned handwriting.

"Is this me?" she asked, her voice breathy.

Zander had turned the tube upside down and shook out the second piece of paper he'd heard rattling in there. He snatched it up as it fell, unrolled it, and skimmed the words. "Looks like Sean wrote an explanation." He held out the paper to Rae.

Rae shook her head, raising trembling hands. "Read it to me. I don't think I remember how right now."

Zander leaned back on the table while Rae continued to focus on the names, and began.

To Rae Dimitru:

When Broderick told me he thought you might be a relation and Zander said you've always been curious about your heritage, I took it upon myself to research it, a task made much easier once I knew where to start. Your Guardian had looked into your parentage long ago, when you were found, but no one could discover anything about you at all.

At last, I learned that the McNaughton clan had a scandal a hundred or so years ago, when Lillias defied her pack and ran away with one of the Dimitru pack, a Romanian wolf called Andrei. I couldn't find the exact circumstances of their meeting, but both clans at the time lived in the old world—the Dimitrus in Romania, the McNaughtons in Scotland and France. Somewhere Andrei and Lillias crossed paths, fell in love, and took each other as mates.

From what I can understand, both Dimitrus and McNaughtons opposed the match—I have not been able to find out why—and the pair fled to America with a huge wave of other immigrants. They lived together in the wilds of Canada in bliss, until Andrei was killed by hunters, likely mistaken for a wild wolf.

Lillias was heavy with a cub at the time and she brought it into the world, but she was weak and passed soon after, leaving the cub alone. The cub wandered, looking for someone to take care of it, when it was found by Eoin Lyall and his friend, the Guardian, Daragh O'Sullivan. The little cub knew its name was Rae and nothing more.

I figured out where Rae Dimitru stands in the lines of both clans and printed this out for you so you can see for yourself.

The line of McNaughton contains Guardian blood, the clan having produced four Guardians over the centuries. I also found a curious story—almost a prophecy, if you will—that when the need was greatest, the Goddess would touch one of Guardian blood, female like herself, to help the Shifters against a coming storm.

I don't know whether this story is true or just Shifter

*mystics babbling. Maybe the Goddess simply got fed up
with us asshole male Guardians and decided to get one
right for a change.*

*Whatever is the case, the cub called Rae Dimitru grew
up to be a strong young woman who fell in love with a crazy
bear named Zander Moncrieff. And they lived happily ever
after.*

The End

Rae's eyes were wet when Zander folded up the paper. His
own eyes stung, but he only said, "Sean is so full of himself."

Rae wiped her cheeks with the back of her hand. "He says
he printed it out? This is handwriting."

"The Guardian Network is a weird place," Zander said.
"You'll see that now that you can get into it."

"Not right now," Rae said, flustered. "Let me get used to
this first." Something on the paper caught her attention and she
frowned and leaned down to peer at it. "Look at this."

Zander followed her pointing finger. Next to Rae's name,
though it hadn't been there a moment ago, letters appeared that
spelled out: *Alexander Johansson Moncrieff (Zander).* Below that
was another vertical line that led to the words, *Fill in the blank.*

"He really is a shit," Zander said.

"Sean is wonderful." Rae turned to Zander and rested her
hands on his shoulders. "He just gave me a family. Another
one, I mean."

Zander cupped her waist and pulled her firmly against him.
"I don't know—I've heard those Dimitrus can be crazy. Crazier
than me."

Rae smiled suddenly, warmth bursting through gloom. "I
can go meet them and see for myself."

"And then I'll introduce you to *my* clan, and we can decide
who has the insanest in-laws."

Rae's eyes sparkled like sunlight on the sea. "I can't wait."
She threw her arms all the way around him. "Thank you,
Zander."

Zander smiled into her skin as he lifted her and held her tight.
"Sean did the legwork. I hope you don't thank *him* this way."

Rae pulled back, still in Zander's arms, and touched his face. "I know *you* told Sean everything and had him start looking. Don't say you didn't, because I know better." She kissed Zander's lips, her mouth warm. "Thank you," she repeated.

Zander's heart throbbed with the mate bond. "You're welcome, love." He'd do anything for this woman, including fly up and pluck down a rainbow to wrap herself in if she wanted it.

Rae kissed him again, the mist in her eyes clearing as mating heat returned. "It's nice up on deck," she said casually.

Zander thought about making love to her under the stars, watching the moonlight in her eyes.

If they could reach the deck. Zander turned around with Rae in his arms, his body tightening, his frenzy leaping up and blotting out all other thought.

They made it to the stairs. By that time, Rae was pulling off Zander's clothes and her own. Zander lifted her and pressed her against the wall, thrusting into her in the narrow space. After that, they more or less fell out onto the deck, where they reached for each other again, Rae's hands hot on Zander's skin, her kisses firing his blood.

Zander slid himself inside her once more, under the blazing spread of stars, Rae's smile more beautiful than the sparkling constellations. Her breath was warm, her fingers strong as she pulled Zander down into her.

My mate. My love. My life.

"I love you, Little Wolf," Zander said, his voice hoarse.

"I love you too." Rae's grin blossomed, her look going sly. She curled her fingers on his backside and started to laugh. *"Big-Ass Bear."*

Turn the page for a sneak peek at the
next book in the Shifters Unbound series

RED WOLF

Coming soon from Berkley Sensation

"Come on," the Lupine Shifter drawled. "Show us what you can do, C-c-c-coyote." He exaggerated the stammer, his eyes full of meanness.

Not Coyote, asshole. Red Wolf.

Dimitri knew he'd never say that without mangling it, so he gave the Lupine a universal sign with his third finger.

The crowd around them roared with laughter. The Lupine was naked, and so was Dimitri, as they both stood in the cement-block-lined ring in the open-walled barn that was the fight club. Dimitri had never seen the Lupine before, but that wasn't surprising. Shifters came from all over South Texas and beyond to try their luck in the ring.

The refs for this fight—a jaguar called Spike, a huge bear named Ronan, and a wolf called Corey—backed away, clearing the space around them. "Fight!" Ronan said in his giant Kodiak voice.

The Lupine struck immediately. His Collar, the chain that in theory kept Shifters subdued, sparked like crazy. The Collar that lay around Dimitri's neck was fake and did nothing.

Dimitri opened his arms and caught the Lupine in mid

spring. The Lupine changed to wolf on the way, and Dimitri went down under a writhing, snarling, biting gray wolf.

Dimitri rolled with the impact, digging his fingers into the Lupine's fur. He avoided the claws, teeth, and sparks from the wolf's Collar as he kicked and shoved the Lupine off him.

Dimitri didn't like to shift too early in the fight. When he did that, his wild tendencies tended to take over. He had no Collar to suppress him and fighting frenzy came easily. He wanted like anything to best this asshole, but if Dimitri let the frenzy come, he could kill the Lupine before anyone could stop him.

Dimitri rolled to his feet. The wolf rushed him, but too recklessly. Dimitri had time to sidestep, grab the wolf, and use the Lupine's momentum to send him flying to the other side of the ring.

The Lupine skittered, face down, into the low cement wall. The crowd who'd bet on Dimitri laughed and cheered, loving it.

The Lupine's friends booed. "Man up, fucking coyote!" someone yelled. "Fucking coy— *Oof!*" The Shifter's grunt of pain was lost in the noise, but Dimitri saw him quietly fold up.

He grinned. Jaycee was here.

She appeared just outside the wall in sweatpants and a tank top that hugged her curves. "Kick his *ass*, Dimitri!" she yelled. "Or I'll come in there and do it myself."

The crowd's boos turned to her. "Keep your woman under control, coyote," someone shouted.

Dimitri didn't respond, waiting until the refs made sure the wolf was still in good shape to fight. If the jeering Shifters wanted to take on Jaycee, good luck to them. Their funeral.

Dimitri waited in the middle of the ring, lacing his fingers and stretching them, brushing dirt aside with his bare feet. The wolf's claws had raked his side, but not deeply, the cuts barely stinging.

Ronan said something to the wolf, then he nodded and backed off. "Fight!" Ronan called.

The wolf sprang instantly. Dimitri knew he wouldn't fall for the sidestepping trick again, so he reached out, grabbed the wolf around the neck as he leapt onto Dimitri, and started squeezing.

Claws scrabbled on Dimitri's bare flesh. Dimitri felt his shift come, his beast instinctively protecting itself. The wolf's claws met fur, though Dimitri's hands remained hands as he became his between-beast.

The two went down in a tangle of dust, claws, and teeth. The Lupine's Collar sparked hard, the electric arcs singeing Dimitri's furred flesh.

The Lupine's gaze went to Dimitri's Collar, which lay dormant. Dimitri slammed the wolf to the ground with his between-beast strength, then became fully wolf.

Let the jackass call him coyote *now*. Dimitri savagely bit and clawed, and the wolf bit and clawed in return. They rolled in a ball of fur and teeth, hitting the wall and then rolling away. Dimly Dimitri heard the crowd roaring, and his mate's shout.

"Dimitri, *get him!*"

Dimitri rolled the wolf over, pinning him with his large red wolf paws. His wild state was taking over—it told him to kill the threat and walk away. Only a lifetime of discipline allowed Dimitri to tamp down his instincts and remember this was a fight for enjoyment. Not real.

The wolf snarled his rage. He knew he was losing, knew he'd underestimated the odd-looking red-furred wolf with the stammer.

Dimitri opened his jaw to go for the Lupine's throat. He was aware of the refs' feet—two pairs of motorcycle boots and one pair of running shoes—surrounding them. The refs would call the fight and pull Dimitri off before he could kill the Lupine. Maybe.

Dimitri struck. At the same time, he felt a prick in his belly, like a claw had scratched him, then a strange lassitude filled his brain.

It wasn't quite like a tranq, which could knock out a Shifter in a few seconds. Something like a calm peacefulness stole over him, one that made Dimitri want to back off the wolf, let him go, maybe embrace him when they regained their feet.

He looked down at the wolf, who had half shifted back to human. The man-beast wore a self-satisfied look.

Drugging an opponent was against the rules. Hell, it wasn't even done when fighting in the wild.

"You t-t-total b-b-b-b . . ." Dimitri couldn't get the word out. The refs hadn't yet caught on that there was something wrong. Only a second had gone by, though it was stretching for Dimitri. The refs were giving Dimitri a chance to finish the fight, or for the Lupine to throw him off and continue.

He heard an uproar at the side of the ring, but he couldn't make out what anyone was shouting. Words slurred into one another, and Dimitri's grasp of English deserted him. Russian started going as well. Pretty soon, he'd be only able to growl in wolf.

A streak of fur zoomed into the ring. The refs reached for the leopard who'd sprung in, trying to stop her, but she writhed and twisted away before they could grab her.

She pushed between Dimitri and the Lupine, slamming her strong paw to the Lupine's half-beast face. The Lupine must have had only one dose of the drug, because he shifted back to full wolf and started frantically fighting the leopard.

The leopard sprang straight into the air, as only cats can, and the wolf's teeth snapped on nothing. The leopard landed behind the wolf, grabbed him by the scruff, and shook him. She growled as the sparks from his Collar went into her mouth, but she didn't let go.

The ref, Spike, with jaguar speed, went for her. Before he reached her, the leopard shook the wolf one more time, dropped him to the ground, and smacked him with her paw. The wolf went limp.

Spike as jaguar planted himself in front of the leopard, his ears flat, his fangs bared in a snarl. The leopard regarded him in disdain, sat down on her haunches, and delicately licked one paw.

Dimitri rolled over onto his back, trying to laugh his ass off. It came out a wavering wolf howl.

Some in the crowd laughed, loving it. The rest of them were roaring in fury, even the humans who'd come out to watch Shifters fighting each other.

"The match is a draw," Ronan said in his big voice. He sounded regretful.

"Stupid bitch ruined the fight!" a Shifter yelled.

"'S why women aren't allowed in the ring," another chimed in. He was bolstered by many voices shouting agreement.

"Get her out of there!" another suggested.

The crowd surged forward. Two Lupines hauled themselves over the cement blocks and went for the leopard. Spike was right there, planting himself in front of one, but the second made it through, the other refs too far away to stop him.

Whatever drug had laid Dimitri out faded and died as he saw the threat to his mate. He surged up, heat burning away the last of the sedative, and he rushed in a low wolf run to the Lupine heading for the leopard.

Jaycee had turned around, facing the second Lupine with a leopard snarl. Dimitri bowled her over, sending her, surprised, to the dust, and then launched himself at the Lupine.

The Lupine, still in human form, went down. The crowd cheered or booed, and then they streamed forward to join in the fight.

Dimitri's instincts changed from protective rage to alarm. The Shifters were blowing off the rules and storming the ring, becoming a mob. Humans gleefully joined in.

When Shifters didn't stop themselves, they became destructive killing machines, uncaring who they took down with them. That was what they'd been bred for centuries ago, why the Fae had won so many battles with Shifters in the forefront.

Dimitri whirled for Jaycee, driving her back from the crowd, herding her with snarls and snaps of teeth out of the ring on the other side.

Jaycee had a hot temper and could be reckless, but she was no fool. She ran out ahead of Dimitri then shifted back to human form, rising into a beautiful naked woman.

Dimitri tamped down on his need to admire her full breasts and the curve of her hips, her wheat-colored hair that was always messy, and her tawny leopard eyes. She rubbed Dimitri's fur in a quick stroke, then moved off to make sure the more vulnerable humans and young Shifters got out of the way of the now-crazed crowd.

The Shifters didn't care that their original target had just walked away from them. They started fighting the refs, Dimitri, each other.

Ronan had gone Kodiak bear, the huge creature bellowing as he shoved wolves and wildcats out of his way. Spike was fighting with the honed swiftness of a Feline, taking down Shifters with one strike each. Spike was the number-one fighter of this fight club for good reason.

The third ref, a wolf called Corey McNaughton, was younger than the others, less experienced. Dimitri put himself with Corey, snarling and fighting, protecting as he battled.

The place became chaos. Dimitri fought in silence, anger making him fierce. If the police came, they'd all be screwed—tranqued, rounded up, possibly killed. Dimitri's Collar was fake, as was Jaycee's. Other Shifters from Dimitri's enclave also had false Collars, which they put on when they had to interact with humans. If the humans in authority found out about the fakes, they'd all be up shit creek. This riot had to cease.

Shifters in fighting frenzy, though, were all but impossible to stop. This was what the humans feared—Shifters out of control, going on killing rampages, slaughtering humans and taking over. Stupid, because there were far many more humans in the world than Shifters, and Shifters rarely worked themselves up into this kind of collective frenzy. But right now, he could understand their worry.

Dimitri tripped over the Lupine who'd been his original opponent, the one Jaycee had knocked out. The Lupine was coming around, human now, and Dimitri shifted back to human and hauled him to his feet.

Dimitri shoved the Lupine toward a relatively calm part of the ring. "Get out of here," he snarled at him, speaking with the clarity he achieved when his emotions were at their most intense. "Asshole."

The Lupine gave him a look of sly amusement. What the hell was so funny, Dimitri didn't know. He pushed the man to the side of the ring and over the blocks.

The Lupine turned to study Dimitri from the other side of the low wall. "Yeah," he said, nodding. "You'll be perfect."

"For what?" Dimitri yelled, not sure he'd heard him over the crowd.

The Lupine smirked and walked away, his shoulders back in arrogance, then he disappeared into the darkness beyond the arena's flaring light.

Another Shifter smacked into Dimitri, carrying him sideways. Dimitri gave up on the Lupine and rolled back into the fight.

Jaycee was yelling at a couple of Shifters who were barely

past their Transitions—their fighting blood would be at its hottest. Dimitri waded over to help her.

Behind him, a truck was pulling up, a big thing, unmarked, with a water hose coiled behind it. *Shit, where had a Shifter found . . . ?*

He stopped worrying about it. Dylan, the most powerful Shifter in South Texas; or his son Sean, a Guardian; or Kendrick, Dimitri's leader would have the resources to come up with a water truck on the spur of the moment.

Dimitri reached Jaycee and the overgrown cubs. They were Collared, from the Austin Shiftertown, and eager to fight.

"Time to go," Dimitri said. He swept open his arms, carrying Jaycee and the two younger Shifters out from under the old barn that was their arena and into the night.

Behind him, squeals and howls rose as a hundred Shifters suddenly got very, very wet.

"Jaycee," Dimitri said.

She turned from shoving the younger Shifters into the trees at the edge of the clearing, inquiry on her face.

Dimitri wanted to yell at her, demanding to know what the hell she was thinking rushing into the ring like that, breaking every rule of the fight club. She'd endangered herself not only from the crazy Lupine fighting Dimitri, but every Shifter in the place.

He thought about how she'd fought the wolf, almost casually avoiding his attack and then smacking him down into unconsciousness.

"What?" Jaycee asked when he didn't speak. "You mean, why am I such an idiot?" Sometimes she'd talk for him, so he wouldn't have to struggle with what he wanted to say.

Dimitri shook his head. He reached for Jaycee and dragged her to him, her fine flesh bare against his.

He tucked his hand under her soft hair and turned her startled face up to him, his mouth coming down on hers in a long, hard kiss.

Around them, chaos reigned, Shifters shouting and furious as the water truck cooled down the hot mob. None of that reached Dimitri, in a bubble of calm with Jaycee.

Her mouth was hot, her body the same, her kiss holding her

fire. She wrapped her arms around him and stepped closer, letting him know she could give into mating frenzy if he did.

The chill in the air to either side of Dimitri kicked him out of the warm place into which he'd been sinking.

He lifted his head to find Kendrick, his leader, a white tiger Shifter, on his left, the hilt of the Sword of the Guardian rising above his shoulder. On Dimitri's other side was Dylan Morrissey, a Feline every Shifter around answered to.

Jaycee lifted her head, color flooding her face. She kept close to Dimitri, hiding her body, her sudden shyness making Dimitri's protectiveness surge.

"Dimitri," Kendrick said in his growling voice, which was deceptively soft. "Jaycee. We need to talk."

FROM *NEW YORK TIMES* BESTSELLING AUTHOR
JENNIFER ASHLEY

The Mackenzies Series

THE MADNESS OF LORD IAN MACKENZIE

LADY ISABELLA'S SCANDALOUS MARRIAGE

THE MANY SINS OF LORD CAMERON

THE DUKE'S PERFECT WIFE

A MACKENZIE FAMILY CHRISTMAS

THE SEDUCTION OF ELLIOT MCBRIDE

THE UNTAMED MACKENZIE

THE WICKED DEEDS OF DANIEL MACKENZIE

SCANDAL AND THE DUCHESS

RULES FOR A PROPER GOVERNESS

THE SCANDALOUS MACKENZIES

THE STOLEN MACKENZIE BRIDE

A MACKENZIE CLAN GATHERING

Praise for the Mackenzies series

"The hero we all dream of."
— Sarah MacLean, *New York Times* bestselling author

"I adore this novel: it's heartrending, funny, honest, and true."
— Eloisa James, *New York Times* bestselling author

"A sexy, passion-filled romance that will keep you reading until dawn." — Julianne MacLean, *USA Today* bestselling author

jenniferashley.com
facebook.com/BerkleyRomance
penguin.com

M1318AS0715

LOVE
ROMANCE
NOVELS?

For news on all your favorite romance authors,
sneak peeks into the newest releases, book
giveaways, and much more—

"Like" Berkley Romance on Facebook!

 BerkleyRomance